# THE MINE

This novel is a work of fiction. The characters, names, dialogue, incidents, organizations, and plot are the products of the author's imagination or are used fictitiously. Any resemblance to any persons or events is purely coincidental.

Book and cover design by Daniel R. Cobb.

ISBN: 9781441474353

Copyright © 2009 by Daniel Cobb.

All rights reserved.

Published by Daniel R. Cobb in association with CreateSpace.

Printed in the United States of America.

# Acknowledgements

Many people offered their encouragement and advice during the writing of this book and I am grateful to all of them. Please forgive me if I can't name each of you here.

I am grateful to my good friend, Jack Thornton, who was brave enough to wade through the entire first draft, over 500 pages, offer his good advice, and still remain positive. My only cost was a fifth of Dewar's. My thanks also go to Gyuszi Suto, my warm friend from Romania and another brave reader. I must also thank Heidi Dahlin and Anne Mitchell, my friends at the Sierra Club, who provided great insight and needed energy in the final stages.

Finally, my gratitude goes to the enduring patience and support of a lovely woman from Italia. Mother to our three wonderful sons, she fills my heart, and she keeps me honest—or at least tries.

# THE MINE

# Chapter 1

Gabe Riplinger sat in the dark and watched. Cold drizzle gathered on the windshield and he hit the wipers once. He punched the electric door locks again, and then cracked the window an inch to fight the fog. The acrid smell of burnt steel and diesel blew in. Passing traffic threw rain spray between tall buildings. Dark and monolithic, the structures and steel fences formed a seamless box around the lot, a trap with one entrance. He had parked against a building, facing out, to maintain a view to the street. A police cruiser sailed by with lights flashing. An hour previous, a dark sedan had parked across the street, deep in shadows, and killed its lights.

Gabe watched the car and winced as his heart pulsed painfully. For an old man with angina, arrhythmia, and a dozen other ailments, a dilapidated industrial zone was not where he wanted to be on this cold November night. In the darkness, resting on the seat next to him, was the box.

He glanced at the vague form and rubbed his bristled face with shaking hands. A large cardboard box labeled *Harry and David*, it sat heavy with its contents: Five hundred thousand dollars. Not apples and pears, but five hundred thousand in fifty-dollar bills. Two hundred bundles were each bound by a red rubber band. On a recent night, the cash and a 45 caliber revolver had covered his wife's quilted bedspread, and with his arthritis, he had lost count twice. Now the box crouched next to him like a dangerous animal. The money frightened him. This place frightened him.

It had been the bills, the endless hospital bills. The sickness had come on her quietly, starting in her brain and working down into her spinal column, attacking and destroying. His eyes clouded as he stared at the car's dark outline and remembered her suffering. Cancer wasn't a fluke, one cell gone bad. It was conscious, intentional evil.

Doctors responded en masse with heavy radiation and drugs, toxic concoctions that wracked her feeble body, but the assault never paused. In desperation, they tried experimental treatments, exotic new medicines that he didn't understand. The insurance company refused and happily dropped her. It didn't matter. He would have done anything had there been time, Mexican faith healers, witch doctors. The church ran round-the-clock prayer vigils, but it all came to nothing. Poor Mavis. His wife and best friend of 38 years, Mavis was dead in ten hideous months.

He buried her early that summer. When the insurance bailed, he was left with the bills. He took a new mortgage on the old home and maxed out the credit cards. It wasn't enough. Impossible bills. Impossible. And they knew. They used her death to get to him. They approached him as he sat alone in a church pew.

The money arrived like an answer from God, or perhaps someone else. The box appeared magically on the back porch of his home. Resting inside, on neat stacks of cash, the contract was printed on a single slip of paper. One word: *Justene*.

Across the street, the sedan was barely visible in the drizzle. There had to be another car nearby. Gabe rubbed his hands and shivered. Heat was out of the question; the motor's fumes could reveal him to police. He was exhausted and had been for months, but was wide awake. Fear did that. Fear kept him awake at all hours, fear of her dying, fear of the loneliness, of the future. They had been childless; it had turned out that he was shooting blanks. He could never give her a life and in the end, he couldn't save hers.

He wrapped the steering wheel with his arms. He rested his chin, breathed in the acidic air, and stared at where the car had parked, and the peripheral world melted away. His vision collapsed down to that elusive shadow until it evaporated.

Gabe hit the wipers. He scraped his burning eyes and stared. The dark line re-emerged. They were waiting. Why? What the hell are they waiting for? If he could just get this night over with, just get past this! He had made a mistake! He had taken the bait, the worst decision of his life. Now he was their prize. He was their big fish, a fat June hog.

Gabe released the wheel of the Cherokee and smeared his bifocals on his sweat-soaked shirt. Traffic was gone. Save for a few distant streetlights, the world was hidden. He should go to them, he thought. Go and tell them. It had to be them, who else would be out here in the middle of the night, in the rain? They picked this spot, who else? He clutched the keys that hung in the ignition. Just go tell them.

Twin shafts of silver cut into the night. The dark car surged across the road and gained speed. Gabe grabbed for the keys as the car swept up and stopped, inches away. He fumbled with the locks as the big man threw the door open and bodily yanked Gabe out. Broad hands ripped the jacket and shirt, exposing his white belly to the bright headlights. Another one stood in the dark and watched.

The big man threw Gabe face-first against the Jeep, and then whipped him around again. "He's clean!"

"So how much?!" the voice in the dark demanded. "What'll it take?"

Gabe's white torso trembled. "Wha, what?"

"Greed! How much more, Mr. Riplinger?"

Gabe's heart slammed convulsively. "No, no! I, I want out!"

A moment of sheer incredulity passed in the driving rain.

"What?" the big man almost laughed, his broad face, a contorted mask in the lights. "What?"

"I don't want the money! Please!" Gabe pleaded. "It's here, all of it!"

Gabe slowly turned, reached inside the Jeep, and wrestled the heavy box out. He pushed it at the tall man, who had taken a couple steps back. "It's all here. I just want out."

The two stood. Gabe again shoved the box at the taller man, but he took another step backward.

The one in the dark barked angrily. "It doesn't work like that! We have a deal!"

Gabe knelt carefully down and dropped the heavy box on the wet pavement. He then stood and slowly climbed back into the Jeep, avoiding their eyes. Move fast. The nearest hospital is six miles away. Any second, just keep moving! The door slammed and the engine caught. Gabe threw it into gear, ducked low, and burned a wide, howling arc around the car.

Ten weeks later.

Trees blocked the light from the street, cloaking the house in darkness.

"Hold the light for me," the man whispered.

He handed her the small flashlight while he fished the key from his pocket and tried to slide it into the corroded lock. No luck. He turned the key over and pushed it in. Two clicking turns. He turned the knob and pushed.

A loud creak announced them. The black entry yawned.

The woman's hand found the light switch on the wall and the toggle gave a sharp snap. There were only darkness. "Oh, great!" she whispered.

She panned the flashlight across the black room. Under the small orb, dark wooden floors stretched bare up to the walls. A black woodstove sat on a brick pad against the far wall. She strained to hear any sound, any noise, and her mind spawned images of mice, rats, or maybe a homeless person camped in an upstairs room. The dark house was a tomb. On the front porch, a wind gust pushed them. He nudged her in, picked up a box off the porch, and after stepping inside, closed the door with a thud.

"Ryan!" she whispered.

His voice smiled. "Cool!" he teased. "Let's light the fire."

"Should we be here, now?" she queried.

He stepped toward the woodstove and set the box down on the brick base. She trailed, holding a boxed pizza, a medium Hawaiian with extra pineapple. Under the flashlight, he fished out two short, red candles. He lit both and slowly set them on the mantel. Reluctant flames cast a feeble light. From his box, he crumpled a few pages of newspaper and stuffed them inside the stove. On this, he placed several pieces of dry pine kindling and a few larger pieces. He lit another match and the dancing yellow curl spread slowly. The pine caught and began popping.

He closed the stove door and whispered. "The bags."

They exited the house and hurried down the dark steps to the truck. Wind gusts carried fat raindrops. Inside the truck, he grabbed sleeping bags; she took a plastic bag containing two bed pillows. They returned to the front porch as a loud deluge of rain commenced. Once inside, she locked the door.

He rolled out the sleeping bags in front of the fire; she laid the pillows at the head. He produced an opener and opened a bottle of wine, a brand just expensive enough to warrant a cork. He set two stemmed glasses on the brick and filled them. They glowed ruby in the firelight. She unlaced her black boots and slipped them off and he followed her lead. They peeled off winter coats and sat down on the bags. He took both glasses and handed her one.

She smiled and whispered. "We did it."

Smiling broadly, he lifted his glass. "To us."

They tapped glasses. "To us." She took a sip.

He tipped his back and emptied half of it. They rose on knees and embraced, arms enfolding and hands exploring. But then she pulled away. "It's cold."

He opened the stove and filled it with pine. He rubbed his hands furiously while the storm drummed the windows and the house cracked with the wind.

She turned toward the black windows, and then the deep shadows that cloaked the hallway and stairs. "We're alone?"

"Just us."

Her eyes hesitated in the shadows. "How do you know?"

He filled his glass again and topped hers off. "Meggy, take your clothes off."

She returned to him and took a brave gulp of wine. The growing fire poured heat into the room. She smiled mischievously. "You don't want any pizza?"

He shook his head. "Not pizza."

She arched up and pulled the sweater over her head, disheveling glossy brunette hair that tumbled down over her shoulders. He gazed at her, in snug jeans and a black bra. He emptied a second glass of wine. She reached behind and slowly released the bra, and the firelight danced across her breasts. He fought off his sweatshirt and they entwined again, all at once kissing and struggling to rip off the other's jeans.

## Chapter 2

Ryan Evans set his coffee down on a desk covered in papers. The 27-year-old wildlife biologist entered his computer password and waited, sipping coffee from "Sammy", a ceramic mug shaped like a fat blue salmon. A gag gift from his wife, Meagan, Sammy was ugly defined, with glossy green lips, bulging red eyes, and a fish-tail handle.

Buried deep in the fifth floor of a concrete office building in Portland, Oregon, Ryan's cube was filled to capacity by his desk, a chair, and a cabinet. Papers, binders, and reference books filled the cabinet and book case above the desk. More binders were stuffed under his desk, barely leaving room for his feet and a waste basket. Ryan's cube was a clone; fabric-covered dividers sectioned the floor into a maze of identical pens.

Oregon's Department of Environmental Quality was headquartered here, filling six floors of a monolithic ten-story building. The second floor held Air Quality; floors three and four held Land. Water Quality and DEQ's upper management occupied the fifth floor. Government gray pervaded, but individuality sprouted like lilies on an alpine slope: pictures of summer vacations, a third-grade Christmas program, wind-surfing in the Columbia Gorge.

Friday morning in Water Quality was Sticky Bun Friday. For two quarters, one could start the day with a jumbo pecan cinnamon roll. The task of getting the buns from the bakery on this Friday morning landed on Karina Jordan, a slender young chemist with short red hair. Visibility of the elevator from which Karina and the buns would emerge was a feature of Tommy Swensen's cube; it was positioned just so. Accordingly, it was Tommy's charge to make the anticipated announcement. "Buns!"

Men and women, biologists, geologists, chemists, and analysts, converged on a break area near the center of the maze. Ryan set his coffee aside and pulled a bag of paper plates and plastic ware from a credenza. Karina, still in her raincoat, dropped the four large pastry boxes on the table and stepped back.

A small crowd formed and a rotund, bearded man in his thirties was first. "This almost makes coming in worthwhile," Stu proclaimed. With a straining plastic fork, he shoveled a bun onto a plate, plopped into a chair, and began eating the dripping pastry with his fingers. Chopped nuts fell into his thick red beard, perhaps never to be seen again.

Karina stood back with her hands on her hips, her head shaking.

Tommy, a young man from Maine, turned to Ryan. "Did you get everything unpacked?"

Ryan nodded. "Glad I took the time off. We spent the first few days cleaning and the week going through boxes. We still have odds and ends."

Stu chewed on one side of his mouth and spoke out of the other. "But you made it in for Sticky Bun Friday."

"The work here hasn't gone away," Ryan replied. "Anyway, thanks for the help with the move in."

Stu nodded. "A lot of work. I'll call it in sometime."

Karina shot a scowl at Stu. "He didn't have that much," she retorted. "The fridge. The washer and dryer. A little furniture."

Stu stood and fished his pockets for more change. He dropped the coins into a bowl and loaded another bun. He licked the molasses off his fingers. "Ryan, the first move is a breeze. Settle down and have a few kids. Next time, you'll need a semi and a football team. My house is full of the junk my wife buys. A waste of money."

"Really?" Karina responded. "Whose money, Stu? Your wife is an orthodontist, she makes three times your salary."

Stu's face flushed pink to match his red beard, which Ryan noticed, seemed rather bright this morning.

Karina noticed it too. Her eyes narrowed. "You dyed your hair."

"What?" Stu snorted, still licking his fingers. "Hogwash."

"You did. It's like magic markers. Good Lord, your hair's on fire. And that beard."

Tommy turned away, barely stifling an outburst of laughter from a mouth full of pastry.

Stu's cheeks glowed red, amplified by the brightness of his hair. "What the hell ever!"

Karina persisted. "I can't believe you dyed both your hair and your beard. Even the moustache? What didn't you color?"

Stu's eyebrows furrowed sharply. "I don't use hair color!"

The group stood around the table, smiling, chewing, and looking in awe at Stu's newly red hair. Stu fumed.

Out of sympathy, Ryan changed the subject. "Is everyone ready for tonight?"

Gabe Riplinger, the manager of the Water Quality Division for 14 years, was retiring. The event was planned for seven. They each nodded, still examining Stu's hair.

"Have they announced a replacement yet?" Ryan asked.

Karina replied. "No, they haven't. I don't know how they expect to plan for a transition if they have no one in place before Gabe leaves."

Ryan noticed that Stu had left his cinnamon bun and was eyeing Karina. Stu could never leave an argument with her. It was a compulsion he had, something resembling a high school crush. And she rarely avoided firing back.

"You bringing that nice fella you met in San Francisco to the party?" Stu asked, with a subtle sneer. "What was his name, Julian?"

He pronounced it "Hoolian", and the bomb was tossed. Karina had been gaga about Julian for weeks, a handsome, polite man she had met at a writer's conference in Seattle. She'd even introduced him to the group. And then, nothing. No more news of Julian. Everyone had quietly deduced that the subject was off limits.

Karina paused for only a beat, and then tossed her hair as she walked away. "No! Seattle! And don't ask! You boys don't OD on the pastry, especially you, Stu. That fat ass of yours can't afford it."

Surrounding the maze of cubes on the fifth floor was a perimeter of actual offices. Each of these came with walls, oak doors, and vertical windows that offered sliced views of neighboring buildings. The Director of DEQ and the senior managers occupied this high-rent district. Ryan found Gabe Riplinger leaning in close to his computer screen. Black framed glasses rested low on his nose. Silver hair was groomed back. Gabe wore jeans and a white shirt with pearl snap buttons, attire not typical for someone in his position.

The knock on the door caught Gabe's attention and he turned. "Ryan. You're finally back. How's the house?"

Ryan sat down in the guest chair next to the desk. "We're settled in."

## THE MINE

Gabe pushed the glasses up. "You've been out almost two weeks. I thought maybe you retired."

Ryan smiled. "I requested it and you approved it."

Gabe's weathered face wrinkled with a grin. "I did. Find any leaks from the rain?"

"Maybe a small one in the mud room, but dry inside. The first night, we lit a fire in the wood stove. Pizza for dinner. It was good."

"It's a good place for you kids."

"We'll be doing repairs for years."

"Goes with the territory, Mr. Evans. You're a home owner now. Just don't forget, the springers will be running in March."

"Springers" are the spring run of salmon returning to the rivers to spawn.

Ryan nodded. "Don't bring the dog next time? A wet retriever in a boat is a bad thing."

Gabe's face wrinkled again. "You don't like getting wet? Fine, no duck chasing for Shakespeare." His gaze shifted. "You know, Mavis would fish with me out there when it warmed up. She'd bring a book to read and let the pole sit in her lap. I'd beg for a fish to take my bait, and a big chinook would nail her rig. Nearly steal her pole to boot. Give us both a heart attack."

Gabe was still in mourning, well after a year. When the two men were alone in Gabe's office, he often slipped into recollections of horseback riding or traveling or fishing with his wife. Ryan had played therapist for months.

"Are you ready for tonight?" Ryan asked.

"I hope you all don't over do it."

"It's nothing. We're taking you out to Baskin Robbins for a bowl of ice cream. Just one week left. How are you going to handle all the free time?"

Gabe leaned back and took a deep breath. "You're kidding. I've been ready to retire for a while."

"Why haven't they selected a replacement?"

"Maybe they don't need one," said Gabe

"Hardly. By the way, there's something I've wanted to ask you about. Justene. It's been nearly four months since Nelson and I finished up the analysis. When will it get decided?"

The reaction startled Ryan. Gabe's smile drained away. The words were clipped. "It's not through review yet."

"But they've had it for months and the EIS gives every reason to kill it. I had the impression it would die on the spot."

Gabe's eyes checked the open door and then returned to face the kid. With DEQ for only three years, Ryan was idealistic and full of energy. The kid was fatherless and Gabe had taken to him.

Gabe lowered his voice. "You did a great job with it, Ryan. The applications, the analysis. You might decide that a new commercial project will create an environmental wreck, but this one's big."

"All the more reason for DEQ to kill it. You know it's a time bomb."

"But we're not the ones making the final decision. We're getting a lot of pressure on this."

Ryan leaned in. "What kind of pressure?"

Gabe hesitated. He then stood and quietly closed the office door. When he returned to the chair, he leaned in close and rubbed his thick hands together. Worry lines crossed his face.

"Now Ryan, listen. I'm going to tell you something, but you keep it to yourself. I've looked at this closely. I've recommended rejection of the permits. Your analysis is dead-on, it's a terrible site for a leach mine, especially something that massive. There's no re-engineering they can do that'll make it work. My recommendation carries a lot of weight, but this is big. It has more review to go through, three other departments are looking it over."

"When will we know?"

Gabe shrugged. "A month, six weeks. Listen to me, Ryan. I know how you feel. Your position is well-known. But I want you to drop it."

Ryan studied his boss. "Why?"

"Because it's political. It could get ugly. Your work with Justene is done. You drop it now."

The newly purchased home of Ryan and Meagan Evans was in the southwest side of town. Here, 70-year-old maple trees lined the sidewalks, their heavy branches arched over the streets. Built in '41, the faded Victorian was set back across a deep yard. The agent had described it as a "fixer upper, a real opportunity for the right buyer". Ryan had smirked when he heard this pitch. The "opportunities" were extensive: an old roof, worn floors, leaky faucets, peeling paint, and outdated everything. But the house had character. It was big and set on an acre lot, with trees, a garden, and plenty of green grass. After months of searching, Meagan had fallen in love with it.

The two were now barely three years out of college; he worked for the state, she worked as an associate veterinarian at the West Hills Animal Clinic. She had offered to ask her parents for help with the down payment on the home, but Ryan had refused, even with his college debt. So after three years of dedicated self-denial, the young couple had saved enough money for a down payment. The sale closed the 23rd of December, with the move in just after Christmas.

Friday evening, the light of the woodstove flickered through the living room window. Ryan parked his International truck around the side and entered through the back door, which accessed a mud room. He hung up his jacket and slipped off his shoes. He was still getting used to the smell of the old house. Sophie, Meagan's wheaten terrier, greeted him with a furious tail.

In the kitchen, she approached him with a cup of hot chocolate. Blue jeans and a white sweater hugged her figure. He placed the cup on the kitchen table and they embraced fully, legs and arms. The novelty of being in their first house together somehow made everything new again.

"How was your day?" Meagan asked.

"Too long."

Still embracing, Ryan's hands began to wander. She pulled away slightly. "We need to get ready. You need to shower."

"You can join me."

"I already did my hair. Gabe will be here by 6:30. How was your day?" she repeated.

Ryan exhaled resignation. "Okay. Yours?"

"We had to put down a German shepherd that had been hit by a car. That was tough, a young male. And the Siamese gave birth. Five little fur balls, they're gorgeous."

Ryan rolled his eyes. "We don't need a cat."

"But I didn't get to have pets as a kid. I would house-train them."

"Them? When I was young, my cat, Bootsie, would crap in my shoes."

Meagan pushed the hair from her face and smiled. "Cats are perceptive. She obviously didn't like you."

He didn't smile. She changed the subject. "So how is Gabe taking this? Is he ready to retire?"

"No. He claims he is, and he looks pretty worn out these days. But he lives and breathes that place."

"Have they chosen a replacement?"

"Not yet."

The continuing frown on his face left a question. She rested her arms on his shoulders. "You're going to miss him."

He nodded slowly.

"What else?"

Ryan expelled a sigh. "Justene."

She knew the name well and simply nodded. It was the subject he loved to hate.

He continued inexorably, as a train leaving the station. "The state hasn't rejected the applications yet. When I finished it, the way Gabe spoke then, I thought it would die fast. He's against it as much as I am, but that was months ago. Now, I don't know. He says it's too political."

She sighed. "I wish they'd make a decision. The protestors are a pain. I had to go into downtown at lunch and they had streets blocked off. Traffic was terrible."

"Well if I wasn't working for DEQ, I'd join them. The mine is a cesspool. It's wrecking the watershed and downstream are towns, cities. DEQ should have killed it by now."

Meagan gazed at her husband. He was tall, with curly, coffee hair. Brown eyes. He had a man's jaw line, but a boy's dose of freckles. Rather than taking her to a movie on their first date, he had spirited her deep into an Oregon forest and hoisted her in a safety harness high into the crown of an ancient Sitka Spruce. He was precise, even intimate in how he pulled the harness around her legs and waist and put on her helmet. They spent the night on a research platform, studying a brood of spotted owls. It seemed crazy, but he talked her into it and the experience was unforgettable. He never made a move on her that night. He was busy watching the birds. Ryan was different; her father called him strange. Over different summers, he took her along on university trips, once to Madagascar, then to Denali. He revealed things to her that most people would never witness. And high in the wide bows of a moss-drenched Sitka, she had fallen in love.

She pulled herself back to the moment. "What will you do if they approve the permits?"

A hard sigh. "I don't know. Let's not talk about it."

"Okay. Gabe will be here soon."

"Did we find my suit?"

"I did, yesterday. Had it cleaned. It's in the bedroom closet."

"Thanks. You're a gem. What about my ties?"

She shook her head. "Not since you packed them."

"They have to be somewhere."

"Maybe with your tools? Your tackle box?"

"Funny."

"I bought a tie for you on the way home, it's on the bed. The selection wasn't good, I hope you like polka dots. Oh, and the shower. Something's wrong. It doesn't get hot enough."

"I thought it was my imagination."

Gabe arrived on time, dressed in a charcoal suit and polished black cowboy boots. A large silver and turquoise bolo tie graced his shirt. Meagan gave him a quick once-over, adjusted the tie, and from there he was driven to a destination known to all but him.

Evelyn Gibbs, Gabe's Administrative Assistant, had planned for the event to begin at 7:00 at the Sweet Water Inn, and at 6:30, she was counting place settings and adjusting floral arrangements. In the kitchen, she checked on the prime rib and coho.

At 7:00 sharp, Ryan opened double doors to a large banquet room and 60 coworkers and their spouses, all dressed in suits and gowns, greeted Gabe. Cheers and applause welcomed him as *Hail to the Chief* played from a sound system Tommy had set up.

Evelyn came forward and gave the man of honor a hug and a kiss on the cheek. She was in her late fifties, with red-rimmed glasses, red lips, and dark blond hair, "large hair" as Meagan called it. Evelyn's Texas accent was warm. She wiped her lipstick from Gabe's face with a handkerchief, giggled, and then kissed him again, full-mouthed.

Cheers erupted and Gabe blushed profusely. A flute of champagne landed in one hand while his reports came forward to shake the other.

"You did it!" Ryan shouted above the din.

"I did what?" asked Gabe.

"You survived 29 years of state bureaucracy."

"What happened to ice cream at Baskin and Robbins?"

Ryan laughed. "You didn't think you could get away without a good send-off?" He nodded to Evelyn. "She gets the credit. She and Karina planned everything, right down to the color of the napkins."

Karina appeared and gave Gabe a hug. "We're gonna miss you, cowboy! You can come back to work any time! I'll even share my sticky buns with you!"

Evelyn frowned and Gabe laughed. "Deal," he answered.

After several minutes of back-slapping and hand-shaking, Tommy put on a slow sax tune and several couples found open space on the floor.

Evelyn grabbed Gabe's arm. "Come here, honey!" she commanded.

She had never addressed him as "honey" before, but in one week he would no longer be her boss and the obvious was finally being stated. The younger couples watched as she pulled him to the center of the floor. Evelyn glowed, Gabe blushed, and the crowd cheered.

Ryan tugged Meagan out onto the floor. She wore a long velvet gown, royal blue, that hugged her trim body. Her long brunette hair framed long silver earrings.

She resisted. "I don't dance that well."

"Me neither, but you're too pretty to hide at the table." He pulled her close. "Meggy, you're too beautiful. My coworkers are staring at you."

Meagan shook her head. "Shush."

"So what are you doing after the party?" he asked.

She looked him in the eyes. "Well I'm sorry, but I'm going home with my husband."

"He's a lucky man. What happens after you get home?"

"That depends on whether he behaves."

After an hour of dancing and champagne, dinner was served on round linen-covered tables. Golden linen napkins with matching candles and a floral centerpiece dressed each table. A table near the center held Gabe, Evelyn, Karina, Ryan, Meagan, and others. The crowd dined and laughed. The champagne flowed.

Near the end of the meal, as dessert was arriving, Arland Lochner, the Director of Oregon DEQ and Gabe's manager, stood up next to Gabe's chair. He tapped his glass with a spoon. The music was turned down and the conversation quieted. A slender, balding man, Lochner rested a hand on Gabe's shoulder.

Lochner cleared his throat. "First, we need to thank Evelyn for the work she put into this event. She did an amazing job."

The group applauded energetically. Sitting next to Gabe, Evelyn nodded, and when the chorus went on, she finally raised her napkin and hid behind it.

Lochner continued. "All right. I have not been looking forward to this day. We all want to retire eventually, myself included. But Gabe," Lochner looked down to the seated man. "You've been with this department much longer than I have. In fact, you trained me and you helped to train nearly everyone here. You've been with DEQ for nearly three decades. Your leaving will take some serious adjustment for all of us."

Applause sounded while Gabe smiled and then looked down at his hands.

Lochner resumed. "Gabe, I had Evelyn research your career with DEQ, we snooped through years of your records. There is just too much. I could rattle off a long list of major accomplishments, but that would take all night. You've been a driver or involved in everything, the computerization of our workflows, the standardization of work processes. You've overseen Applications and Permitting, Business and Public Relations, every major initiative. You've helped DEQ grow up. We will miss your knowledge, your wit. And we'll even miss your fishing stories, although I've come to doubt every one of them. The fish keep getting larger!"

Well lubricated, the crowd roared.

Lochner tapped his glass like an impatient high school principal. "But Sticky Bun Fridays will be staying with us. You started the tradition and we have permission to include them in DEQ's next quarterly budget, in honor of you. We'll all need membership at the health club, but so be it. Gabe, you have an open invitation to drop by anytime. The door is always open."

Cheers erupted. The younger men took up with "Speech! Speech!" until Gabe finally stood.

The 63-year-old looked his age. He was reasonably fit, with an erect stance and thick, silver hair. A paunch hid his beltline. But his face revealed the impact of his wife's loss: the eyes of resignation, the accumulated stress lines. He looked out to his reports and their spouses and the room fell to a hush. Many were in tears. He blinked and took a sip of water. The familiar smile, lopsided and disarming, showed itself.

The voice was gravel. "Well..., let me say first, I wasn't expecting all of this. Thank you, Eve, Karina. Thanks everyone. But I still have one more week left. Can we do this again next Friday?"

Warm laughter accepted the invitation.

Gabe pulled a deep breath. "Mavis would have loved this. I've enjoyed working for DEQ. You folks are family, she said it many times. We never had kids, but over the years a lot of people have called DEQ home and I got to watch young people marry and their families grow up." Gabe cleared his throat and Evelyn's arm went up, patting him on the back.

"Let me say that it has truly been an honor to have worked with each of you. I've enjoyed it more than I can tell you. So yes, I'm retiring. But that doesn't mean I won't be busy. With my extra time, I can get more involved in conservation and environmental issues. There is plenty to do, even for an old man. I'm thinking of building another drift boat, and I've got the horses. And I've found a riding partner. I discovered that Evelyn, here, likes to ride horses. I guess it makes sense, being from Texas."

From the back, Stu stood, wobbly, and shouted, "She's a keeper, Gabe!"

Stu's wife yanked him back to his chair.

Gabe nodded. "And don't any of you forget, the Memorial Day barbecues are still at my place! I have plenty of room for the kids to run and you're welcome to drop by." Gabe raised an arm and pointed to the back. "And Stu, I will be in for my sticky buns! You can't have mine!"

More laughter ensued, laughter that was hampered by tears as the dreaded moment approached. Gabe would work another week, tying up loose ends, but this moment marked the end of an era.

Stu stood again, pulling against his wife's arm which jerked on him in vain. With a vibrant red face and hair to match, Stu held his beer bottle high. His voice boomed. "To Gabe!"

The crowd stood with glasses raised. A pause followed while Stu searched his pickled mind for a toast. He held up both hands, hoping this might bring forth a suitable utterance, but nearly fell over.

Meagan filled in. "To the next 29 years."

The rest quickly joined in. "To the next 29 years."

The knock came at 8:30 Sunday morning, insistent and unnerving. Gabe answered the door wearing a mis-buttoned plaid shirt and a silver stubble.

"Is the car still for sale?"

A stranger stood on the porch. He wore a beige jacket and slacks. A white ball cap from Rudy's Fishing Supply was perched on his head, the logo stitched in red.

Gabe squinted painfully through the partially open door. "Yes?"

"I saw it last week, out under that tree." The man turned and pointed through the rain to a massive old elm out front. "With a *For Sale* sign. It's a Buick isn't it? What year?"

"96"

"Do you mind if I take a look at it?"

Gabe eyed the man. He was average height, fit, with sandy hair. A little rude to be here on a Sunday morning, before church.

"It's around back, in the garage," Gabe replied. "Come on."

Gabe closed the door behind the visitor and led him through the house and into the kitchen. "You want coffee? It's fresh."

"Sure."

The host tucked in his uneven shirt, took a cup from the cupboard, filled it, and set it on the table. "There's milk and sugar." He nodded to the table. "Have a seat, I gotta find my eyes."

Gabe headed down the hall in search of his glasses.

The stranger sat and surveyed the kitchen. A single plate rested in the drying rack. One coat hung on the wall, next to the back door. An old dog, a golden retriever, lay asleep on a rug in the corner.

Gabe returned with his eyes enlarged by the lenses.

The man smiled. "My daughter, she's in her second year of college. I promised her that if she did well in school, I'd buy her a car."

"Where is she going?"

"Oregon State."

Gabe extended his hand. "Gabe Riplinger."

"Rickman Mellard." His hazel eyes smiled.

They shook across the table.

"My alma mater. How many kids?" asked Gabe.

"Just the girl."

Gabe nodded as he slowly eased into the chair. "Car belonged to my wife, Mavis. The cancer got her a year ago." Gabe stirred milk and sugar into his own cup.

"I'm sorry," Rickman offered.

Gabe sipped the coffee and nodded, accepting the condolences. "You live around here?"

"Beaverton."

"What do you do?"

"I'm a software engineer for a small firm. My wife and I were driving through last Sunday. Saw the car, but didn't have time to stop."

Gabe nodded again. "You can lay your jacket on the chair."

"I'm fine."

Gabe took another sip. "Well it's a shame about the Beavs," he said.

An awkward pause passed. "I'm sorry?"

"The Beavers?"

Rickman nodded, faintly tentative.

Gabe frowned. "Football? You have a kid at OSU and you don't follow the Beavers?"

Almost invisibly, the man's right cheek twitched. Sports, for chrissake. He grew irritated with himself for being caught on something so insanely stupid, but recovered quickly.

"When I have the time, your honor, which isn't very often. Work and all."

"Well they lost their star quarterback, for godsake. Kid ripped up his right knee. Tough break." Gabe nodded, proud of this valuable nugget of football knowledge he could share.

"That is tough." Rickman nodded in total agreement. He took a few quick sips of coffee. "Actually, I'm in a little hurry."

Gabe filled half of his cup with two percent and stirred in another helping of sugar. "The whole world's in a hurry. You got that cap. You do any fishing?"

"Not enough."

"I've got a drift boat. I fish the fall and spring runs for coho, chinook." Gabe's eyes indicated he could use the company.

"Sounds like fun." Rickman nodded, with his jaw shoved out, impressed with this talk of football and fish. Only his name wasn't Rickman and he had no children that he cared to know of. He wasn't here for the car.

"Rickman" emptied his coffee and pushed it to the table center. He smiled. "You want to sell that Buick?"

A sigh fell out of Gabe. He gazed at his coffee cup, the Eiffel Tower cup, white and cobalt blue. It was the one left of a matching pair purchased years ago during their single trip to Europe. Mavis had dropped its mate. She was dead, gone every day, but her belongings remained as though waiting for her to return. Dresses and shoes, books on self-help. *The Closer Walk with Christ*. An unfinished oil painting of Mount Hood hung proudly in the living room. Even her make-up waited. He would slowly fill a box of clothing for the Goodwill or the church but never quite deliver it. Now it was her Buick. She had done no driving the year before passing, and now it sat. He had considered giving it to their church, but seeing it around town would have been hard. And he needed the money.

Gabe took another sip, sat for a minute, and then slowly stood. He grabbed his coat off the brass hook and led the way out the back door, across the wet grass and into the garage.

In the car, Gabe rolled down the driver's window. "I'll back it out."

Gabe reached up for the electric opener on the visor. Just then, Rickman thrust a small handgun through the window. In the garage, the one shot popped like a hammer.

## Chapter 3

The noise was relentless. In the office of the Chief Geologist of Summit Resources, Inc., the sound was a repeating, angry drum. Jensen Greer pitched his pen on the desk and it bounced and sailed. He pushed away and strolled to the windows that covered the wall to the carpet. He avoided looking down at first, as if he only intended to gaze out at white Mount Hood, or the storm clouds rolling in from the south. His eyes soon surrendered to the street far below, to the protestors. Well over a thousand were there. They overflowed the sidewalk, onto the streets and into Washington Park.

Greer scowled at the sight. With their signs pumping the air, they swarmed like winged insects. Another thousand marched the block that circled the Wells Fargo Building. From the bed of a pickup truck, a man bellowed through twin bullhorns. The crowd roared and their demands echoed up between the office buildings. Summit Resources, Inc. was seeking to expand the Justene open-pit gold mine in eastern Oregon, from 1800 to 6600 acres. Oregon's Department of Environmental Quality had approval authority over permits to expand the mine. And at this moment, it seemed to Greer that every environmentalist in North America was trying to shut the mine down. Every group known had marched the block over the previous six weeks: half-brained liberals and homeless idiots with nothing better to do, drop-outs and Generation X-ers with pink hair and metallic crap hanging from every body protrusion. Green Peace had been joined by Green War, a tiny, violent group local to the Northwest. Lately, the crowd was growing larger and the tone was turning harder. Even the winter storms hadn't throttled them.

At first, the police had tried to shut the demonstrators down, but news cameras had captured violent confrontations and the resulting public outrage had stung the mayor. With cameras always ready and elections coming, the mayor's new directives were explicit. Let them demonstrate. Let them march and chant, wave signs and sing "Kumbaya", but as long as they didn't completely choke traffic or destroy property, stand down. Quiet little Portland had become host to CNN.

Jensen Greer wanted to vomit. The mob had plastered the downtown with posters of him and the five corporate officers of Summit Resources, with names and home addresses! Jesus Christ, the "Gang of Six" they were called! They had roughed up Greer, had smashed the windshield of his new Porsche. He and the others were reduced to coming and going at varying hours, using rental cars and taxis. Limos were out.

Next to Greer's desk stood a heavy brass heron with a long, pointed neck and beak, and he fantasized now of heaving it out the window and impaling one of the bastards. He imagined the headlines. "Environmentalist Killed by Endangered Bird!"

But the window didn't open, dammit.

Below him, a mounted cop was using his horse to push the crowd away from the main building entrance. A young woman in a white jacket—Greer had seen her before—raised a sign that said "Protect the Earth" and began wailing on the officer. He reached for the sign, but the horse suddenly reared up and the crowd pulled him off the animal to the ground. Officers in riot gear rushed in. They shoved the woman against a police van, handcuffed her and a man, and attempted to push them into the van.

This was all that the crowd needed. Fifty of them surged, swinging their signs at officers. Some threw rocks and bottles. Tear gas canisters were lobbed. Horses reared and the horse without its rider went down. After struggling to its feet, the animal bolted through the crowd and galloped down the street.

The mob retreated from the tear gas, revealing the woman in the white jacket. She was squashed to the ground unnaturally, with an arm twisted up behind her. A red pool formed around her head. Greer leaned into the window, fighting the vertigo. An officer draped his jacket over her as sirens wailed. From down the street, paramedics arrived and loaded her into the van.

Enraged, protestors swarmed again. A few began swinging baseball bats they had concealed under trench coats, bashing car windshields and glass storefronts. A fire truck unloaded a torrent of water and more tear gas was thrown. A hundred officers in riot gear charged and beat those bent on confrontation. More police vans appeared and SWAT officers shackled and bodily loaded 20 frontline protestors. Officers took positions around the entrance to the building, joining security guards. The hardliners were hauled off, but they would be back, probably that afternoon.

"Saturday!" Greer barked to no one. It was Saturday, for chrissake, and the bastards were still at it! For the next six weeks, the CEO had demanded that Saturday be just another damned work day, so here he was. The entire company was pissed off.

Greer turned from the glass and hissed a mouthful of expletives. His office was sumptuous: Brazilian mahogany paneled the walls; thick Persian carpet covered Italian marble floors. He loved the view, but needed to move to an interior space. The siege was killing him.

He checked his Rolex and screamed at the intercom. "Miranda!"

Without waiting, he stepped to the door and flung it wide. Miranda's desk was 20 feet away in a low-walled pen with four other women, all secretaries for the company's executive staff.

"Where is Sarinov?!" Greer demanded.

Miranda was a single mother of two young boys and she was often on the phone with the school or day care, as she was now. She crouched involuntarily and covered the mouthpiece with her hand. "I believe he's spending the day offsite."

Greer was not half-bad looking: charcoal black hair, brown eyes, straight teeth, and a dimple when he smiled. Sort of a tall Tom Cruise, the secretaries had agreed. But smiles were banished. Greer was an all-consumed company man, an egotist and a temperamental pain in the ass.

The other women ducked behind computer monitors as Greer approached Miranda and shouted. "That's not what I asked! We're flying to Justene at nine! Has he come in yet? Or did he get rolled by those animals?"

Miranda bit her quivering lip. "I'm sorry, Mr. Greer, I don't know where he is."

Greer threw a handful of papers onto her desk. "Run this report on the Cold Springs site through spell check. It's full of typos! Fix it and print it out! I need it without typos! And get me another coffee!" He turned, but stopped and stabbed the air with a finger. "The helicopter is due on the pad in 20. I need that report now! And call me the second you see Sarinov!"

Miranda nodded rapidly as she dropped the phone, grabbed the papers, dropped them on the desk, and then jumped up and ran for the coffee maker.

Greer stormed back into his office and slammed the door. He knew he was losing it. He could tell he was getting close when his finger tips tingled. The goddamned protestors. And the thought of flying in that damned tin box, into the mountains, with another storm rolling in! Greer rubbed his face and paced the office.

A knock sounded and Miranda entered timidly. She tip-toed across the carpet, deposited the cup and saucer on his desk, and fled. Greer grabbed a whiskey bottle from a credenza and topped off the coffee. He took a hot gulp as the beating of helicopter blades bounced off the windows.

Twenty minutes passed and Greer's office door flew open. In a black ski parka, CEO Jacob Sarinov stood in the opening with his arms stretched wide. "Let's go! This bird bills 500 an hour."

Of Russian descent, Jacob Sarinov was tall, with short, black hair and a face always in need of a shave. He wasn't heavy, but his face and hands were big, and with his intense gray eyes and sharp nose, the expression was usually grave.

Greer grabbed his parka from a chair and followed his CEO. Attire was usually Armani; today it was jeans, boots, and parkas. Greer snapped the printed report, now packaged in a binder, from Miranda's outstretched hands. His wide eyes met hers to ask, *is it finished?*

She nodded vigorously.

Atop the building, the co-pilot led them across a rain-soaked walkway to a sleek, gray helicopter. He slid the door open while the cold wind buffeted his jacket. Sarinov climbed in and pointed Greer to the adjacent seat. The aircraft seated five passengers; today there would be two, plus the pilot and a copilot. The door slid shut and they fastened seat belts.

In gloved hands, Greer handed the binder to Sarinov and spoke above the gathering whine of engines. "The Cold Spring report. It's a little rough, but I have to tell you, it's not worth it. There isn't enough gold in the ground to justify continuing work there."

Sarinov looked at the binder in his hands. "We've put a million into the site just opening it up! What about the earlier survey?"

"It's several years old and it disagrees with all our data. We've drilled eight samples and based on those, I don't believe we can make money at Cold Spring."

The jets peaked and the helicopter leaped into the air. Greer's stomach cringed.

"How many more mine sites do we have scheduled for a survey this quarter?" Sarinov asked.

"Two. The first is in Idaho, Miner's Creek. The other is here in Oregon, White Cloud. It's south of Mount Bachelor."

"What's the nearest town to Miner's Creek?"

"A crossroad called Oxbow, 70 miles from the site. It's nowhere."

Sarinov's head jerked around as he bellowed above the whine. "I want producers, Greer! I had high hopes for Cold Spring!"

Greer looked at his boss, at the arched eyebrows, the gaping mouth of incredulity. "Jacob, I'm telling you what I know. You're looking at less than half a gram of recoverable gold per ton."

Sarinov scowled as Greer turned to peer out at the receding city below, any fixed point. The jet exhaust was worsening his nausea. Bulbous, black clouds were racing in from the south. The Columbia River appeared, vast and swollen with winter rains. The dark water churned and roiled below them.

Greer wiped sweat from his forehead while his CEO continued yelling. "Find me more sites, Greer! High yield! I want a new producer every twelve months."

Greer knew the mantra; it had been hammered in. "I'll do my best, but I won't open a barren mine just to blast a hole in the ground."

"What about Sugarloaf? Haystack?"

Greer scowled visibly. Sarinov obviously never read Greer's weekly reports, the same reports his boss demanded.

"Sugarloaf is up," Greer replied. "Gold yield is at 5.3 grams per ton, thank you. Utah has approved permits for Haystack, contingent on limited revisions. We expect to finalize engineering over the next month. Requests for construction bids are out and we're getting replies. We should have Haystack on line in Q4, nine months. Haystack will be a major producer. Schedules are tight, but they both look good."

Sarinov's silence was his only acknowledgement. With contempt, the CEO tossed the Cold Spring report into the seat in front, reclined his seat, and closed his eyes.

Greer had been with Summit Resources coming up on three years, and Sugarloaf was his first mine, his pick, high in the Colorado Rockies. He had conducted the surveys, revised the engineering for Colorado DEQ compliance, and submitted the applications, all 600 pages. Gold yield per-ton was ramping fast and over its life, the mine would yield nearly a billion in profits. Haystack was next and Miner's Creek would follow. Greer was new to the company, but in a short time, he had become their type-A golden child—literally.

Below, the Columbia River Gorge cut deep into the Cascades. Bullet-rain streaked the window. Greer sneered to himself. Only fools flew in this weather.

Oregon's exposure to the Pacific Ocean and its multiple mountain ranges can create weather conditions ranging simultaneously from heavenly to fierce. The Cascade Range bisects the state north-south and acts as a giant dam, raking out the deluge from Pacific storms. On the south coast, Gold Beach residents can enjoy unseasonable warmth, while 12 hours later, a spring snow storm kills climbers on Mount Hood.

Marking the border between Washington and Oregon, the Columbia River cuts through the Cascade Range like a jagged knife. At places, the Gorge is over three-quarters of a mile deep.

The chopper flew over the chasm and on past The Dalles. Here, past the Cascades, the terrain shallows out and the climate is more arid. The dominant vegetation is white rabbit bush and juniper. An old farmhouse, solitary and likely deserted, passed beneath. The pilot continued due east at 220 miles per hour.

In Oregon's northeastern corner, elevations in the Wallowa Mountains take off again, catching the rain and snow to feed forests of Ponderosa pine and Douglas fir. At this point, Sarinov unbuckled his seatbelt, moved forward, and spoke to the co-pilot. The man got up without hesitation. Sarinov took his seat and slipped on a headset and sunglasses while the co-pilot retreated to the seat in front of Greer. At the controls, Sarinov descended the helicopter into a deep, V-shaped valley. Serrated, snow-covered ridges raced by at eye-level. Greer resented the violation of law and common sense. Sarinov had boasted of taking a couple helicopter lessons, but he wasn't yet licensed to fly. But no one said "no" to Sarinov.

A deep-blue lake opened up, perhaps five miles long and a mile wide. Greer had forgotten the name. In the broken clouds, a full white moon looked down while its reflected twin looked up from the cold water, like escorts. There was no sign of man, not a car or a cabin. The few roads were lost in the forests.

Sarinov dropped the helicopter in 50 feet above the water and a flock of white tundra swans leaped from the lake to flee the howling machine. Fast-approaching trees forced him to pull up sharply. They continued deep into the mountains and the headwaters of a river, around a sweeping turn where abruptly, the forest ended. Here, in the side of a majestic mountain, a mammoth gash had been carved. In a glistening white and emerald wilderness, an 1800-acre open-pit strip mine lay like a crater on the moon: Justene.

On the mountain's northeast side, the deep, terraced hole was three quarters of a mile wide and over a mile long. Inside, four dark ponds were arranged in a semi-circle. Dark brown and burnt orange in color, each covered 12 acres and contained a deadly soup of mercury, lead, iron, arsenic, cyanide, and sulfuric acid. An occasional flock of geese or swan would mistake a reflective pond for fresh water, land, and die within seconds. Their bloated carcasses littered the ponds.

In the center of the pit were three rectangular mounds of crushed rock that had been excavated from the mountain. Called heap leach mounds, these ore piles rose like terraced pyramids, over 1200 feet square and 160 feet high. A grid of black tubing covered each pyramid and rained a mixture of sodium cyanide and water. The resulting chemical reaction liberated the gold, silver, and other heavy metals from the ore. Buried beneath the millions of tons of crushed rock, a vinyl liner one-quarter inch thick channeled the gold-rich fluid into pipes. The pipes carried it to the gold building for extraction. The used solution was then pumped back into the four cyanide ponds where more cyanide was added so that the mixture could be reused. The toxic remains of the crushed mountain filled four dumps located to the northeast.

Greer pressed close to the window. The size of the operation was difficult to grasp. Nothing whatsoever lived here. In a region teaming with wildlife, this place was barren—except for the humans who worked it.

Sarinov set the chopper down. It bounced hard as sleet vacated the pad in all directions. The jet engines slowly unwound to a stop and Greer, Sarinov, and the pilots emerged from the chopper. From half a mile away, the low rumble of crushers and loaders reverberated across the pit. The exhaust of jet fuel and diesel hung in the cold air.

Nine gray industrial trailers were sited just off the pad. Another five trailers and a few small buildings were scattered behind the first group. Together, these provided office space, a cafeteria, and housing for the 60 people who worked on-site, including 12 guards. The crew was a collection of former loggers, road crew workers, and a few oil platform workers up from the Gulf. Employees were required to stay on site for five weeks straight and got the sixth week as paid time off. Weekend shifts were rotated. Most escaped to Fort Myers or Walla Walla.

A short, squat man stood a few feet off the helipad. He had broad shoulders and a large head of thick black hair, chopped military-style. Westfall was the site foreman and head of security. Ten years earlier in Key West, a street fight had left him with a long scar that split his earlobe and bisected his right cheek.

Westfall thrust out a hand. "Boss." The voice crackled from cigars and six years as a Marine drill instructor, which had ended dishonorably after he beat a recruit unconscious.

Sarinov ignored the outstretched hand and turned to the pilots. "We leave at 1:00. There's food and coffee in the cafeteria trailer. Lunch is at noon."

Justene was a dangerous place, especially for the uninitiated. The pilots would spend the morning sequestered in the cafeteria. They headed toward it now through a channel cut in the snow.

The three climbed the metal steps and entered Westfall's office trailer. Inside, the gritty air reeked of cigars. Two ancient Steelcase desks were positioned in the center. Matching filing cabinets lined the left wall. On the right, a brown vinyl couch and an equally uncomfortable-looking chair discouraged sitting.

Westfall removed his jacket and laid it over the chair. Wrapped around his barrel chest, a sagging leather holster held a heavy gray pistol. He pointed with his bearded chin. "There's coffee."

A coffee pot, dingy yellow, sat on a waist-high fridge. Next to it sat a bag of plastic cups.

At the window, Sarinov smeared the grit with a finger and peered out between the plastic blinds. A quarter mile distant and through falling sleet, a heap leach pad was visible.

"What's yield?" Sarinov asked.

This question was the reason they were here. The Justene mine site was Sarinov's choice, made before Greer joined the company. Although no one spoke it, the site had been a bad pick. Even after nearly four years, it had still not turned a profit, but CEO Jacob Sarinov had selected it, and with the hundreds of millions of dollars poured in, he wouldn't let it go.

Westfall unwrapped a Swisher Sweets cigar and stuffed it into his mouth. Pride filled his screechy voice. "We broke 2.8 grams per ton of ore. That's up from 2.6 last month. We should break 3.0 in another quarter." Westfall patted his shirt pocket for his matches.

Sarinov growled against the window. "Don't light that. This place is bad enough without your cheap cigars. I need 3.8 grams of gold, per ton."

Westfall knew the number, 3.8. The magic number. He grunted acknowledgement and then hacked a wheezing cough several times, turning a bright red.

"How full are the cyanide ponds?" asked Greer.

Westfall shrugged. "Eighty percent, give or take."

Greer's eyebrows jumped. "They can't be over 60 percent right now, to take up the spring rains and snowmelt."

Westfall spoke to his unlit cigar. "You expecting a flood, Jenny?"

Jensen Greer could barely contain his contempt for Westfall. He had quickly concluded that the man knew nothing about mining, had no formal education. His only quality, if it could be called that, was that he was Sarinov's consummate kiss-ass. And "Jenny" was the name Westfall had given to him over a year ago. He despised it, but saying anything would only give Westfall more pleasure.

Greer responded. "The ponds were at 40 percent in November. The state sets our uptake capacity."

"Yeah, and the state don't send its office ladies up here," Westfall sneered.

Greer spoke slowly. "It's in the monthly report I just filed with Salem, the numbers you faxed me last week. We're claiming the ponds are at 50 percent."

Westfall looked to Sarinov, as if to question Greer's authority.

Greer continued. "How much cyanide?"

Westfall chewed his cigar. "Jenny, this isn't your show."

"I'm here to try and improve your yield. How much cyanide are you running?"

"Point one, there abouts."

Sarinov spoke to the glass. He sounded bored. "Go to 0.15. No, make it 0.2. I like even numbers."

Greer couldn't believe what he was hearing. He moved closer to his boss. "Jacob, .05 percent cyanide is the maximum our permits allow."

Another chain of hacking coughs erupted from the foreman. Westfall dragged his sleeve across his mouth and sneered at Sarinov. "Why did you bring him up here?"

The CEO turned from the window to face them. "Are we getting all of the gold?" Sarinov asked. "If we crushed finer, could we pull another gram out? If we increased irrigation, ran more solution?"

Greer persisted. "We don't have capacity to run more solution. The holding ponds need uptake capacity."

Sarinov's head shook back and forth. "Dammit, Greer, maybe you missed this. I need 3.8 grams of gold to break even here, and the longer it takes, the more I need. Do you have an answer for me? I bring you up here to help, and you quote me the goddamned permits? Screw the permits! Westfall, give me finer ore. Increase irrigation. And up the cyanide to 0.2."

Greer blinked. He had agonized for months over what he was about to say. He moved next to his boss and whispered it. "Jacob, we're getting all the gold there is."

Jacob Sarinov's lips compressed tightly together. "Bullshit!"

Greer continued. "We're breaking laws here. My name is all over the state reports."

Sarinov eyed Greer directly. "So, that's what you're worried about? Your own ass? The numbers are faxed to you, you file those with the state, and everything is clean."

Greer blinked again. Did he hear it right? "But our deliveries show how much cyanide we use."

"No, they don't," replied Sarinov. "Our suppliers know how to keep records."

At this, Greer was speechless. The meeting had been a revelation. He formed the next words carefully. "We're breaking significant laws. The rainfall—"

Westfall's fist slapped his desk with a bang and the cigar flew from his hand in fragments. His screeching laugh filled the trailer. "What the hell, Jenny! You think we're gonna get a hurricane through here? This isn't the damned tropics!"

Greer glared at the Neanderthal with the gun at his side.

Sarinov's head shook back and forth in exaggerated motion. "Greer, get on the team. State permits are written for the freak winters, the hundred-year flood. We'll do whatever it takes to make a profit here, and you'll do whatever it takes to keep the state off our ass. You're big boys, handle it. I don't care how. We're a million miles from nowhere, no one comes out here. If they do, Westfall and his security team will escort them out."

# Chapter 4

The day after Gabe's retirement party, Ryan was outside sweeping dead leaves off the covered front porch. Earlier, he had vacuumed most of the house while Meagan dusted and finished making up a guest bed. She had argued that the house wasn't ready for guests so soon after the move, but Ryan had persisted, and now he was pushing the broom around under the covered porch, sweeping dead leaves into the rain-soaked wind. He checked his watch again just as a beige BMW paused in front of the mailbox. He lifted the broom and gave a wave. The car entered the driveway. A tall, blond-haired man emerged in the drizzle. Then a woman got out, umbrella first, and they ran up the uneven brick walkway.

"Over the river and through the woods!" Alex Palmer boomed as they stepped onto the porch.

Ryan extended his hand, but his friend ignored it and gave him a bear hug. "Been a while, doc."

"It has." Ryan opened the front door and the guests followed him in.

Alex and Ryan had been friends since childhood. The two had shared classes, had fished and hiked together, had double-dated girls and gotten drunk on tequila lifted from Palmer

Senior's liquor cabinet. They had toilet-papered the house of the high school football coach when his cheerleading daughter refused to go out with Alex. Ryan sometimes felt ashamed about all the stunts they had pulled as kids.

Ryan hung their coats on a rack behind the door and stood the umbrella open in the corner. "How was the drive down?" he asked.

Alex answered. "The rain followed us all the way. The Evergreen Bridge was closed, we took the 405. I always forget how far Portland is from Seattle."

Ryan nodded. "Especially in the rain."

Anne leaned forward and hugged Ryan. "How are you? Where's Meggy?"

"We're good. You two take a seat. I'll tell her you're here."

The large room swallowed up the sparse furniture. The couch was faded red-and-green plaid, with plastic wood-tone trim and recent arm covers. In front of the couch sat an old coffee table with unmatching end tables. These things were "gifts" from Ryan's Aunt Sirrey in Seattle. On his father's side, Aunt Sirrey was 60, divorced, and slightly wacky, with bright yellow hair. She lived in a houseboat on Lake Union with six cats, about a hundred potted plants, most of them dead, and wind chimes that never quit ringing. Across from the couch, an old green corduroy recliner completed the ensemble.

The two visitors sat slowly on the couch. Anne's eyes panned the downstairs. "The house is huge. Are you two going to fill this up with kids?"

Ryan paused at the landing to the stairs. He gestured with his thumb and whispered. "Don't get her started on that. It never ends."

Meagan had descended the stairs and now brushed against her husband. "What never ends?"

Ryan grinned. "The rain, sweetie."

"I heard you." Meagan continued, smiling. "We haven't seen you two since summer."

"Since the trip to Victoria," replied Anne. The guests stood and Meagan crossed the room and hugged them both.

Ryan took his seat on the recliner. "We've got dinner scheduled for 7:00, so we have some time to talk and show you both the house. Meagan made hot chocolate. It's hot chocolate or beer."

"I'll have a beer," Alex replied.

"Let me help," Anne offered. The women walked into the kitchen.

Alex sat back, and his body sank so deep into the couch that his knees blocked his view. He leaned forward again and tried to look comfortable. "So how's work, Doctor Ryan?"

Ryan wasn't a doctor; the two men had made a game of overstating each other's credentials. Ryan grimaced. "Busy. The Willamette River is a chemical sewer and all I do is write permits so that companies can keep polluting. Portland Harbor has been a Federal Superfund Site for 10 years, it's filled with metals, PCBs, dioxin, and still no progress has been made toward cleanup."

Alex smiled wryly. "Sounds like a disaster, doc."

"Did you know that every time it rains, Portland's sewers dump straight into the river? This is Oregon and we don't have capacity to handle rainfall? For chrissake, you can't swim the river in the summer without getting sick. They call it "river nose." Yet people ski, swim. Only when deformed kids are lurching around Sunday brunch at the Marriott will anyone notice."

"Deformed kids?"

"We catch fish with deformities."

"Ryan, you never change."

"Where's the idealism? Back before you got your MBA and that JD of law rag, you were all about cleaning up the planet.

In high school, you were going to get rid of all the gas hogs and convert the world to solar."

Alex shrugged. "Replaced by reality."

Ryan frowned. "Do you remember when we got arrested?"

A smile grew on Alex's face. As a senior high-school stunt, Ryan had talked a group of students into donning colorful women's bathrobes (over street clothing), pulling on face masks, and mobbing the main entrance to a newly opened mall that specialized in women's boutiques. Their intention was to protest the mall's construction over an old gravel pit that had been used for years for illegally dumping spent chemicals, old tires, and broken appliances. According to environmentalists, inadequate cleanup had been done before the site was filled in and the mall was built. Ryan, Alex, and 20 others were charged with disturbing the peace, protesting without a permit, and other infractions. The charges were later dropped.

Alex was still shaking his head. "We were crazy then. Money makes the rules, Ryan. It's a cliché, but money makes the world go round."

Ryan sneered. "Spoken like a good capitalist. You've sold your soul. Speaking of your soul, how do you like the new beemer?"

Alex played with his blond moustache. "It's nice. We'll take it to dinner, you can drive."

The women returned with hot chocolate, no beer. Anne sat next to Alex while Meagan took a spot on the arm of the squeaky recliner that Ryan was seated in.

Ryan took the cup of chocolate from his wife. "So Anne, how goes the internship?"

Anne Hartstene rolled her eyes. She was slender, with a pretty face, but obviously tired eyes. A graduate of the medical school at the University of Washington, she had just begun an internship at the Seattle Pacific Medical Center, a three-year program.

She pulled the dark hair back from her face. "I work six days a week, twelve hours a day. Three weeks of night shifts, every quarter. Don't ask me what day of the week it is. I reported in on my one day off a few weeks back, if you can believe that. They run my life. I just show up."

"Tough schedule," Meagan offered. "You're technically a doctor now. Can I ask, do they pay you well for this?"

"Well I have the education, but no experience, right? This way I get the experience and the center gets cheap doctors. It's how it's done everywhere. As far as pay, it's $45,000 a year. But with almost 80 hours a week, it works out to about 10 dollars an hour. No overtime."

"That takes dedication," observed Ryan.

Anne put a hand on her fiancé's leg. "Alex says I should have followed Meagan and become a veterinarian."

Meagan laughed. "It's not the same, the gratification. You get feedback, your patients can talk. The best I get is a lick in the face and a wagging tail. Ryan says I come home smelling like wet fur."

"At least you get to come home," Anne replied. "But enough about all of that. You bought this big house. Let's see it."

Meagan's voice became tentative. "Well, it's a mess. Not everything is unpacked. We're going to replace this furniture soon. The house needs a lot of TLC, the previous owners lived here for over 40 years, raised a fam—"

Ryan interrupted. "Quit apologizing, Meggy. Come on."

With mugs in hand, they toured the home, noting the wainscotted walls and antique chandeliers. The previous owner had left two brass and Capiz shell lamps that brightened the living room. The upstairs hosted four children's rooms, a master bedroom, and a bath. Dark hardwood floors produced an echo, and the house had a distinctly musty odor. The hall carried a draft, but the guests ignored the defects. Points of interest became a hallway chute that deposited laundry in the basement and, in the master bathroom, a free-standing iron bathtub with ball and claw legs.

Anne spoke as she cupped the hot chocolate in her hands. "That tub is a collectable."

"I suggested that we replace it, but Meagan said no," replied Ryan.

Meagan spoke. "It's at least 50 years old. I think we can get it resurfaced. I'll tell you what though," she continued as she moved to a window partially covered in bed sheets. "On a clear day, you can see the top of Mount Hood from this window. And when we get new curtains installed, I'll be able to stand here and not feel like someone is out there, between those trees, watching me."

Meagan did a curtsy in front of the window.

Ryan frowned. "Soon, Meg." He continued as they made their way to the stairs. "We need a new roof, new paint, new kitchen and bathroom floors. New curtains. We might refinish this flooring or go carpeting. And eventually, new kitchen cabinets."

Anne offered encouragement. "You'll be happy with it when you're done."

"We might be dead by then," Ryan replied. "Oh, and Meg. We have mice. I saw one running into the mudroom this morning."

❖

Outside, the rain had tapered off and stars shone between the clouds. Alex handed the BMW keys to Ryan. "Tell me what you think."

Ryan drove the car out of southwest Portland and onto Front Avenue. The women talked about window coverings while the men talked about turbo chargers and heated seats.

Downtown along Front Avenue, the river is bordered by Tom McCall Waterfront Park. The center of the park hosts a large fountain and a few acres of grass that slope down to the water. To the south is a collection of four-star hotels, boutiques, and restaurants. They parked the BMW in a garage and walked a short distance to the Harborside, a restaurant overlooking the Riverplace Marina.

The Harborside is built like a giant staircase, with each wide step affording a row of tables. The Saturday night crowd packed the place, but after a 15-minute wait, the hostess led them to a booth on the third deck. The table offered a view of the marina and the lights across the river. Silver-blue salmon fish decorated the walls. Oil candles flickered in small red bowls. As soon as they were seated, a man with a long, blond pony tail rushed over and took an order for drinks. The women ordered Chablis and the men ordered a pitcher of dark ale.

Ryan opened the menu. He hadn't taken Meagan to such a nice place in a year. Finding the scampi he was looking for, he looked to his wife. "What do you like, Meg?"

"I'll try the black cod."

The waiter reappeared and huffed impatiently.

Ryan continued. "You two see what you like?"

Alex closed the menu. "I'll try the ahi tuna."

Anne nodded. "Same for me."

The waiter nodded with serious eyes and protruding lips. "Excellent choices." He finished taking orders and left.

Ryan looked at Alex and nodded toward the window at the dark river. "There it is. Portland's own Superfund Site."

Alex looked out at the water. Meagan rolled her eyes as she rose from the table. "Well while you two are talking pollution and fish, Anne and I will visit the ladies room."

After the women left, Alex motioned a stray waiter over and ordered a bourbon on ice. He then leaned forward with a grin on his face. "How do you like the car?"

"The BMW? Nice. Reminds me that I drive a garbage can."

"Your International was born before you were. Why do you keep it?"

"Because my job doesn't pay as well as yours. And I need it for the house repairs."

"So you're what now, an ecological engineering environmentalist?"

"Environmental Engineer Two. I got a raise. Another dollar-fifty an hour."

Alex's eyebrows jumped in mock surprise. "Wow, no kidding?"

"At this rate, I'll be making eighty thou' in 20 years. Proof of the high value we place on a clean environment."

"Do you wear the white lab coat with the pocket protector now?"

Ryan smirked. "Screw you."

Alex leaned back and grinned. "Talk to me, Ryan. I'm your therapist. I'm your best friend in all the world."

"No, you're not. You've become a damned capitalist. You're the enemy now. Traitor."

Alex laughed out loud. "That's it. Get it out."

Ryan nodded toward the windows. "Last year I discovered that DEQ allows these toxic mixing zones, where a company runs a line of pipes along the river bottom and discharges untreated waste fluid directly into the river. These zones are the size of football fields. They sample the water, say a half mile downstream after this poison has diluted, and if it's below limits, they can claim they've met DEQ requirements. It's a farce. And they don't post signs to warn anyone, so no one knows."

Alex's smile sagged. "Hasn't it always been this way?"

Ryan threw a hand in the air. "Exactly! The water is toxic and no one cares! But here's my personal favorite. We have this cesspool east of the mountains, the Justene Gold Mine? The site spews mercury, lead, arsenic, all kinds of acids. It's in some of the most sensitive ecology in Oregon, and the company has applied to expand the mine by four times, 6600 acres! Ten square miles! I wrote up most of the analysis, took me eight months. I documented every reason to close it down. We've been sitting on it for months and DEQ still hasn't rejected the permits. I don't understand."

"You've mentioned this before, once or twice. You need to relax, doctor. Drink down this pitcher of beer. Then we can go take a piss in your river."

Ryan raised his glass. "Fuck you and thanks for listening."

Alex grinned. "I do what I can."

"So, Wall Street. How about you? I guess you're rolling in the dough now."

Alex leaned back with his beer. He always projected the look of confidence, something he picked up from his father. Alex wasn't one to brag, but the cocky facial expression was always there.

"Things are good. Microsoft is always evaluating new products and businesses, either to understand them for competitive reasons or to purchase them outright. It's all about growth. The company grosses six million dollars every hour of every day. It started in a college dorm room and they currently have 50 billion in cash and assets. The place is a money machine."

"You work for a monster."

"It's a benevolent monster."

"Right. Nothing that big is benevolent."

Alex gulped his ale and winked. "They've been awfully benevolent to me."

Ryan leaned forward. "But can economies continue to grow forever? Honestly, Alex. Our capitalist model is for endless growth in profits and markets, in consumption and pollution. So now, we have China and India coming on line. What happens when the planet overheats and the ice caps melt? What happens when the big coastal cities flood out and the oceans die? The world needs to tax big oil and convert to green energy. Otherwise, we're screwed."

Alex's expression showed true puzzlement. "Jesus, you've gone wacko on me, Ryan. Markets drive change and the problems self-correct. Change is driven by need. It's not always smooth, but it works."

"Oh, really? Maybe in some little microcosm, but global warming and environmental collapse, these problems are planet-wide! There's no market triggers to address global warming. People don't connect their lifestyles to melting glaciers and hurricanes."

"And you, Ryan Evans, are to change it all? You're going to save the planet?"

"I'm not alone. Besides, it has to start somewhere."

Alex smiled. "Well, good luck with that. You're gonna schedule this in between remodeling the house and the job? Listen, doc, I hear you. But only markets can drive change. Government is too incompetent."

Ryan's hands opened up. "So what you're saying is that we humans are just too fucking stupid to govern ourselves?"

Alex thought for a moment and then shrugged. "Yeah. Money is the catalyst. Free markets and greed." Alex's bourbon came; he tipped back the glass and ordered another.

"You're getting shit-faced."

Alex grimaced and chased the bourbon with the ale. "Yes, I am. But you can't. I almost forgot, you're driving my beemer."

"What's the celebration?"

The question went unanswered as the women returned. After they got settled, Alex leaned forward with his arms on the table. "Actually I do have something to celebrate." He lifted the pitcher and topped off Ryan's glass, and then his own. "I've joined a newly formed group at the company, to explore emerging opportunities."

The women sat quietly.

"Is that good?" Ryan asked.

"I think so. It's called the Internet Media Group. The group's mission is to grow new opportunities in Internet-based entertainment. We report directly to the senior staff."

Ryan smiled tentatively as he lifted his glass. "The senior staff at Microsoft? Congratulations."

Anne smiled modestly. "He's been dying to tell you."

Meagan raised her glass of wine. "Congratulations! It sounds complicated."

"It's a great opportunity." Alex lowered his head and whispered. "I got a pile of stock options and a fat raise."

Ryan nodded again, grudgingly. "Congratulations, Palmer."

Alex grinned, emptied half the pint, and set the glass down. "That and they're moving part of the group to Hong Kong. I may be moving there in a year. I start lessons in Cantonese next month."

Ryan's mouth dropped. "Hong Kong?"

Alex nodded.

"That's big," Ryan conceded.

Meagan spoke. "That's huge! What about Anne's internship?"

Anne pressed her lips with the napkin and placed it in her lap. "Well, I'll have another two years to go when he leaves, if he does. After that I might join him in China for a while."

"What about the wedding?" asked Meagan.

"It's up in the air," replied Anne. "We might do it next summer, and make it rather simple. We don't have the time for anything big."

Ryan and Meagan nodded slowly, taking it all in.

"When you two pick careers, you don't screw around," Meagan said.

The couples sat across from each other and smiled. Alex hailed a waiter and ordered his third whiskey. The conversation rotated lightly between jobs.

After the food arrived, Anne changed the topic. "What are your plans for this summer?"

Ryan shrugged. His future suddenly seemed almost bleak. "We're prisoners of the house, will be for the next couple years."

Meagan eyed Ryan. "We'll get some time this summer. Maybe you two can join us in Victoria."

With the alcohol, Alex's red face bobbed. The words began piling together. "We'll do that. We'll go sailin' over ta BC. Rent a boat outta Anacortes?"

"Do we know how to sail?" Anne asked.

"Ryan knows. Right, Ry? We sailed with your dad on the Columbia, years back, 'fore he died. 'Member?"

Ryan nodded. "Yes."

At 9:30, Alex insisted on dessert for everyone. He attempted to order another bourbon, but Anne signaled the waiter and vetoed it. By 10:30, Alex was on his last legs.

Ryan flagged down the waiter, who came to the table with their coats. "We need the check," Ryan said.

"It's been taken care of," the man replied.

"What do you mean?"

"Mr. Palmer gave me his card before you sat down."

Ryan turned to Alex, whose face was buried in his arms. "Alex."

No response. Anne stood from the table, her coat in hand. "He's wanted to do this, especially the part where you ask about the check. Too bad he missed it."

They pulled Alex to his feet and stumbled down the steps to the lobby. Ryan left the three to wait while he retrieved the car.

# Chapter 5

His head was splitting. He could hear the laughter downstairs. In the hall bathroom, Alex found his aspirin in the vanity bag and swallowed three dry. Blood shot eyes greeted him in the mirror. He chased the pills with cold tap water and then plunged his face in it.

The three were seated at the kitchen table when Alex entered. Anne spoke. "It's alive."

Alex dropped into the chair next to her and squinted in the kitchen light. Dark blue china, silverware, and white napkins were laid out on a white table cloth. Meagan poured a cup of coffee and placed it in front of him.

Alex rubbed his temples. "What time is it?"

Ryan answered. "9:30, old man. We were about to head upstairs with a defibrillator."

"Was I a jerk last night?"

"No more than usual. But thanks for dinner."

Anne poured glasses of orange juice while Meagan pulled plates from the oven and set them on the table. They served up the ham, eggs, waffles, and yogurt. They ate and talked about Anne's internship and Meagan's work as a veterinarian. Ryan avoided discussing Superfund sites; he had promised Meagan the night before. The talk soon returned to Alex's career and the possible move to China, but here the conversation became forced. A pact was being broken, a future they had talked about many times over pizza and beer, over summer campfires. They had planned to raise families together, to drive the kids to T-ball and soccer. Different plans were being made now. The women talked in short sentences. They invented topics, exotic vacations they could take together when schedules allowed. Certainly, they would find the time.

When the second pot of coffee was empty, Alex pushed back from the table and smiled.

Meagan eyed him. "What?"

"Anne and I have a little something we wanted to give you two."

As Meagan and Ryan protested, Anne took her purse from the counter. She produced a white envelope and gave it to Meagan. "It's a house-warming gift," she said.

Meagan took the envelope. "You didn't need to do this, after paying for dinner?"

She opened the card. It was white, simple, and offered wishes for a strong family and home. Inside was a gift certificate for $5,000 to Silvia's Designs, a home interiors place well known in the area.

"Oh my God." Meagan's eyes welled.

Alex grinned broadly. "You don't like the card?"

"This is too much."

"Use it for the curtains," said Anne. "No more nude shows in front of the bedroom window."

Ryan reached for the card and the certificate slipped onto the table cloth. His mouth opened. "$5,000?"

Meagan agreed. "We can't take this."

Alex and Anne both laughed. Anne spoke. "You have to. It's our money, we can do with it what we want."

Later, outside, they talked next to the car, under the bare maple tree and the darkening clouds. The women held back tears and promised to get together soon. The beige BMW pulled out of the driveway at noon.

Out the front window, Ryan watched the wind sweep the long bows of cedar trees. He looked at the spot where Alex's car had been parked minutes earlier. Alex Palmer had always been a friend. They had met in Little League. Alex's father had been the coach and Alex was the star pitcher. To Ryan, their friendship had often seemed unlikely, given their differences. His childhood home was a tiny faded blue rambler on the poor side of Meridian, "the Ave." That home had been demolished a few years back, along with the entire decrepit neighborhood, to make room for yet another shopping mall.

The Palmer house, a mile distant, was in the wealthy Rainier Crest development. The spacious home had a three-car garage and a patio large enough for a barbecue pit and a swimming pool. In high school, Alex drove a red Prelude. He never worked and played varsity basketball. Good-looking, he dated cheerleaders, drank too much, rarely studied, and still pulled As and Bs. And he had grown up with a father. They were like brothers, perhaps because neither had one.

Meagan slipped up behind Ryan and interrupted his thoughts. "That was awfully generous."

"No kidding."

"They're going to be busy. China, for Pete's sake."

Ryan didn't answer. He stood with his hands in his pockets and watched the wind blow through the trees.

She slipped an arm around his shoulder. "You all right?"

His voice sounded tired. "They don't pay state biologists anything. There's no money in pond scum."

"Not yet, but pond scum will be big some day. Bankers will be screaming for pond scum."

Ryan's voice was muted. "I grew up poor. Poor sucks."

She turned from the window to face him. "We're not poor, Ryan. And you do important work."

"I should have become a geneticist. I could create super tomatoes that could survive a nuke blast. I could work for the beast and make real money. We could visit Tuvalu before Greenland melts and the Pacific islands all drown."

She draped her arms around his neck. "Our combined incomes are nothing to laugh at."

Ryan grimaced. The fact that she made more money than he did often grated on him.

"I didn't choose a geneticist, or an engineer. I chose you. You do incredibly important work. No one questions that their water and air are clean."

Ryan snorted. "But they aren't. The rivers and oceans are dying. West coast rain is polluted from Chinese power plants, the mercury is carried all the way across the Pacific. I wonder about raising a family in such a toxic world. Jesus, we're poisoning ourselves."

Quietly, she gave up. She had heard countless variations of this theme before, and he was in a mood.

"Is he right?" Ryan asked.

"Who?"

"Alex. He says it's pointless. He says we're too stupid to govern ourselves. We're just hostage to the whims of global markets."

"You two like to provoke each other."

"I should open a dry cleaning chain. Make tons of money and flush the used fluid down the toilet."

"Are you jealous?"

Ryan sighed. "Of Alex? No. Maybe."

"Don't be," she whispered.

She stepped in between his legs, pulled him close, and kissed him. She searched his eyes, his face, the thick line of wavy brown hair. She whispered in his ear. "Three kisses."

The three kisses rule was his creation. If he could give her three full-mouthed kisses that passed the wetness test, she would relent. She was the judge. Over time, they had become lengthy, body-convulsing kisses that went on and needed a flat surface.

# Chapter 6

Jensen Greer would have been satisfied with less. After graduating from the Colorado School of Mines, he might have settled near his home town of Boulder and worked for a local mining company as one of many geologists, perhaps eventually rising to foreman of a mine site. He might have stayed with one firm, retiring with a gold watch and a 401K.

But his wife, Barbara, had other plans. They were a team, she said. He was the brains and she was the ambition. A full year before he graduated, she was scouring the help wanted sections of the major papers across the U.S. and Canada, checking the industry's trade publications, running Internet searches, and talking with headhunters. She landed his first job, with Newmont Mining, but the stay was short before she had him moving on to the next. Four job changes in ten years, each earning a reasonable raise. He needed a break. Prospective employers were starting to question his loyalty. And like a race horse after a hard season, he was exhausted.

Then came Summit Resources. Located in Portland, Summit was looking for a Chief Geologist and the starting salary was far into six figures. Assuming successful placement, the position would mature to VP of North American Operations.

To Barbara's shock, Greer rebelled. He was sick of the moves. So for five weeks, she cried and yelled and withheld sex until he finally caved. This was the one she had been looking for. She coached and harangued him right up to the interview, which lasted three full days. Barbara spent her hours pacing the Marriott in Portland and obsessing over all of the what-ifs, ricocheting between euphoria and fear.

Greer commenced work for Summit six weeks later as Chief Geologist. If all went well, the VP spot would be his three years after that. And on this day (nearly three years later) with salary, bonuses, and the explosion in his stock options, Greer's income was up more than ten-fold from his pre-Summit earnings. Barbara's Bet had paid off.

Barbara's Bet awoke early Monday morning, showered, and shaved. Over a tailored white shirt, Greer put on a teal tie speckled with small silver diamonds. He slipped into a dark, gray-green, pen-striped suit before pausing at the bedroom doors. The peach comforter fell into the vague outline of her body. Bleached blond hair flowed between the pillows. Barbara wouldn't be up before ten.

He padded down a sweeping stairway, across a marble landing, down the hall, and into the kitchen. It was a professional kitchen, with deep counters and double-everything: two stainless steel ovens, matching fridges, twin sets of red porcelain sinks. Ornate cabinets of exotic hardwoods ringed the walls. At the island, under rows of copper pots and pans, a 24-year-old nanny named Bridgette was busy preparing breakfast.

An eating area much too large to be a nook grew from the kitchen. It was faced on three sides by windows and French doors that opened to a vast deck. The glass offered a full view of the valley, the cities of Beaverton and Hillsboro, and the Coast Range. Flush with the windfall of Summit stock options, Greer had purchased the property more than a year previous. The 5,000 square-foot home sprawled over two levels and, with too much alcohol, he could become lost while searching for his wife. Or Bridgette.

# THE MINE

Past the eating area was an oversized family room where a small child sat on the carpet, cross-legged, in front of a yellow talking bird. Greer smiled at his daughter. "Hey Patty girl, how about a hug?"

"Daddy!" The six-year old girl in fuzzy pink pajamas turned from the wide screen and ran the distance to him. She didn't have her mother's blond hair, but his darker look. She slid across the hardwood and nearly collided with him.

He swooped her up in both hands and laughed. "Whoa! How's my chitterbug?"

A dimpled smile and plump red cheeks answered him. "Fyeene. Bridgette's making French toast!"

He parked her in the oak high chair next to his as she looked up with wide, brown eyes. "Are you having some?" she asked.

"Don't I always?"

Bridgette had set the breakfast table with milk for the girl, his coffee, and her own glass of orange juice. A student at Lewis and Clark Law School, she was attractive, with light brown hair pinned loosely back and a figure she dressed for. She smiled as she set down three plates. It was the morning ritual.

The previous fall, Greer had returned home from work on a Wednesday to find Barbara and the beige Lexus out shopping and a young, unknown female in the downstairs entertainment room, relaxing in his leather recliner and watching reruns of 90210 on his 60-inch, HD wide-screen. After a few minutes of confused intercourse, he retreated to the den with Patricia and called Barbara on the cell. "Who is this girl in the house?"

Barbara's answer was short. "She's our nanny."

Shortly afterward, Barbara informed him they also needed to hire a cook. Barbara never claimed to be a cook—it was not her thing (Greer concurred)—and Bridgette was okay with French toast and Lucky Charms, but was busy with college classes in the afternoon. The maids were not cooks. The two muscular, stern-faced sisters from Estonia visited three times a week to vacuum, make beds, and do the laundry, but they refused to cook. A professional cook, Barbara had explained, could help manage dinner parties.

So a thick, short, middle-aged woman named Izabel, from Guatemala, arrived at 5:00 p.m. each weekday afternoon with groceries. She usually had dinner ready by 7:00.

Patricia sat now on her knees in the chair and began to giggle. Greer cut and fed a bite from his plate to his daughter. With her chubby hands around the fork, she jabbed a square of French toast from her plate and pushed it up at Greer. He tried to catch it in his mouth, but instead she poked him squarely in the chin. It was a game Patricia never tired of.

Greer's face became mock serious. "Oww!"

The child let out a squeal.

The drive began just fine. Descending out of the West Hills in a light rain, Greer took Highway 26 into the city. But by the time he exited the Vista Ridge Tunnel and got within four blocks of the building, they were visible. A few had recently picketed the security gates around his community, but they favored the glass-and-stone Wells Fargo high-rise. To them, it symbolized the greed they so despised. Plus, the CNN cameras were downtown. Traffic, police, and protestors clogged the streets. Greer inched his way along and watched the Accords and Camrys creep through, unchallenged. Young men and women were looking for the "Gang of Six." They were looking for a red Humvee, or a yellow Porsche, or today's black Suburban with its tinted windows and oversized tires, and the second Greer turned onto Adams Street, they spotted him. Five of them converged on the vehicle menacingly and tried to see inside. Greer crouched down as traffic ground to a grueling halt. Smoked glass hid his face, but they knew his license plates. "GLDIGR." It had been a moment of gross egotistical stupidity at the DMV, or perhaps he had been thinking of Barbara. He soon regretted it.

The SUV inched forward and they began banging on the hood with their signs and fists and swearing profanities. Like flies to a corpse, others noticed and swarmed on the truck. The chanting erupted. "Ban the poison! Kill Justene!" The swarm grew. The screams melted into chaos and the pummeling of fists on the truck became deafening. Faces crammed against the glass. Young men in black trench coats, a teenage girl with cropped yellow hair, they screamed and spit profanities. "You sonofabitch!! You goddamned pig! Kill Justene! Kill Justene!"

The torrent pushed Greer down into his seat. Tight hands gripped the wheel. He fought to keep his wits and not punch the gas pedal or throw it into reverse. Either choice would pin protestors between cars, break legs, maybe kill! It had never been this bad! Just a slip of the foot! A simple accident! They were lucky he was rational!

Police with batons finally arrived and dragged them off. Mercifully, the garage entrance appeared on the right and officers directed him in. One protestor ducked to follow, but was pulled back. Greer parked into a reserved spot on the second level. He opened his collar and loosened the tie. His body shook. His head fell into his hands. He wanted to scream in the hollowness of the garage, but nothing came. He finally pulled himself from the Suburban, pressed the remote alarm, and headed for the elevator.

The lobby at Summit Resources occupied two levels. A white marble floor glistened in the light from the two-story windows. Cherry-paneled walls extended up to an ornate ceiling of deep white soffits. On the left, the hostess sat behind a long onyx counter. Clarie was 28 and of Asian decent, seen in her dark brown eyes, brilliant red lips, and jet black hair. The wall behind Clarie glistened in black marble. High on it, six characters made of clear lead crystal were mounted. Each was three-inches thick and two-feet tall. Gold leaf had been applied to the back side of each piece and the shimmering gold characters together read SUMMIT.

At the far wall in front of a row of windows, men and women were lined up at the coffee bar. From Summit's Legal Department, they chatted and gazed out at the city. The commotion of protestors below was audible, but they didn't seem to notice.

Greer exited the elevator, passed through the main doors, and shuffled across the lobby. He usually nodded and lingered on Clarie, but not today. He began heading for the coffee bar, but a man stepped forward and grabbed his arm. His whisper was urgent. "Greer, where have you been?!"

"Battling the animals!"

"Come with me." The heavy, sweating man grabbed Greer's elbow and steered him through more glass doors, down a hall, and into an office.

Greer's voice rasped. "Where's the fire?"

Rodney Warren, the company's Chief Financial Officer, closed the door behind them and walked across the room to his massive executive chair. It squeaked in protest as he landed. "Sarinov's in a conference call with analysts. He wants you in on today's dog and pony."

Greer was surprised. "What?"

"The analysts, the brokerage houses. He wants you to give them an appraisal on the Justene mine. The expansion, expected yield in 12 months."

"Why me?"

"You're our Chief Geologist. It'll sound real coming from you." Warren shoved the papers into Greer's face while checking his watch. "You've got 20 minutes. I'm picking up at 9:15, then at 9:30 it'll be your turn. Just give a quick overview of Justene, use these numbers. Then a short Q-and-A."

Greer was suspicious. "What kind of questions?"

"Mostly bullshit. They don't know anything."

"Why the hell does he want me talking to analysts?"

"Because of your position, Jenny. You're our fair-haired boy making a miracle of Justene."

Greer scowled. 'Jenny?' The hated name was spreading. He grabbed the papers and thumbed through the five pages. They listed the current and projected gold yields from Justene. More tables listed dates of completion of the expansion in phases over the next 18 months and the increasing total output as new leach mounds were brought online. Final numbers showed the expected, total output over the mine's 20-year life.

Greer shook his head. "Whose numbers are these?"

"Sarinov's."

"But these numbers are off, they're high by at least 50 percent. He wants me telling analysts this, this…" Greer didn't use the word he wanted.

Warren's eyes rolled upward. "These aren't financial statements, you're not under oath! It's just the damned yield out of one mine! For chrissake—"

"I could see five or ten percent, but this?"

Warren glared. His forehead was perpetually bathed in sweat and the sparse hair was assiduously plastered to his head in charcoal-black lines. "Greer, by the time the expansion goes through, yield will be up! Between now and then, we can't have Justene killing our stock."

Greer held the script up between them. "Is this legal?"

Warren's puffy face glowed. His eyes darted to the phone. "I've got eight accountants and another five corporate attorneys keeping us legal! These aren't binding statements. This is simple PR!"

The phone rang.

Warren snarled. "Dammit!" Another ring. He shook his finger and arm so violently that the jowls of his face shook. "Drop this boy scout crap! Get ready to pick up!"

Warren grabbed the phone.

Greer kicked open his office door. It was only 9:00 and he needed a scotch.

"Miranda!" he yelled over his shoulder.

"Yes, Mr. Greer?"

"Get me a double Americano from the lobby bar!"

Greer dropped his briefcase. He tossed the "script" on the desk and sat. He massaged his temples. Construction diagrams for the Haystack mine buried his desk and an adjoining table. He had meetings with Reynolds and Strout Engineering to prepare for, and meetings with his own engineers to finalize plans for Haystack. There was the Miner's Creek survey to complete. But right now, his CEO wanted him lying to analysts, who would promptly repeat everything he said to the market!

But there had been other moments like this. Like the company-paid trip to Whistler. The lodge was overrun with company execs, fund managers, state people, even a senator. They acted like frat boys, choking down lobster and Corona, and disappearing into the lodge with their paid "escorts". And someone had actually taken pictures! Christ, they were so drunk and preoccupied with nude lap dancers, no one noticed the camera. And then there was the Christmas trip to Aruba, with the wives and the people from Kennedy and Sorensen, the house that handled Summit's IPO. Plus a small throng of DC congressmen. Constituents in Utah and Colorado would have been proud. On the flight home from Aruba, he had decided to pass on any more trips. They didn't need him and common sense screamed liability. Barbara differed, of course. She called it "making connections."

But this conference call, this time it would be his words. He would be the source on record.

# THE MINE

Greer's thumbs gouged his temples. The phone's ring jolted him. He stared at it. A second ring. Miranda opened the door, coffee in hand. She quickly left the cup on his desk and vanished. On the forth relentless ring, he picked up.

"Jensen, are you ready?" Sarinov's voice was serene. He could have been on the beach in Cozumel.

"Why am I talking to these people?" asked Greer.

"They're looking forward to hearing from our future VP of North American Operations. The position has some public exposure, we've talked about this. You've got the numbers?"

"Jacob, these numbers are quite a stretch. And the expansion permits haven't been approved yet. How can I do this?"

The phone was quiet.

"Jacob?"

Sarinov exhaled a sigh. "Jensen, have a little faith here. First, the expansion is about to be approved. I know because we have friends that keep us up to date on these things. But more than anything, you need to learn how this game is played. These aren't government filings, this is simply an insider's look at our firm. Look. The market is a finicky bitch. If we released actuals on Justene now, we'd take a hit that would suck half a billion out of our valuation. For you personally, you would loose what? three, four million? Do you really want that?"

The numbers. Always the numbers. Greer scratched his forehead.

"Do you remember the day I hired you?" Sarinov asked.

Greer remembered. It was in Sarinov's previous office in Lake Oswego, in a brick building overlooking the river. A late summer day. Sarinov's red Ferrari was parked outside. A large framed photograph hung on Sarinov's ego wall of a man hanging in space from under a tiny granite cornice. He was wearing Speedos and sunglasses. The picture was taken half a mile up, on the face of Half Dome in Yosemite. An unbelievable shot. Unbelievable. And the damned tagline at the bottom?

*Success Takes All of You!* Encouragement? Or a warning? And the man in the picture was, of course, Sarinov.

Greer's voice was resigned. "Yes. I remember."

"The market is everything to us, Greer. Everything. Are you ready?"

"Yeah."

"Atta' boy. Five minutes."

# Chapter 7

A river is an illusion: a wide, glittering path that winds peacefully between cottonwood trees and concrete, flowing by homes, farms, and factories. Sunlight dances and the river's rich hues shift over the day, gradually dimming until city lights shimmer. The human body is 60 percent water. We are inevitably drawn to the river; it tugs at us subliminally. It pulls at us like an ancient umbilical. We seek solace on its banks. We dream and make love there; we marry there. The river's tranquil surface suggests that an idyllic truce lives between us and it, and that all is well. But the mirror hides much and we give little thought to what lies beneath.

Like most major American rivers, the Willamette River is a toilet. Cities continually dump their industrial waste and raw sewage into its waters. Herbicides, pesticides, and fertilizers, from cul-de-sacs to corporate mega-farms, merge with the effluent from the Portland Harbor Superfund site and the EPA's mixing zones to turn the river to poison. The Willamette joins the Columbia River, which is already burdened with upstream pollution and radioactive seepage from the Hanford Nuclear Reservation, still more cities join in the travesty, and finally at the Columbia's mouth (although this seems like the wrong body part), this mega-spill enters the Pacific Ocean. This dumping occurs continually, 24 hours a day, every day. In the Pacific, pollution from the Columbia and other rivers are thought to be contributing to massive dead zones just off the Oregon coast. As the name implies, they are lifeless. (A similar 7,000 square mile dead zone in the Gulf of Mexico originates at the mouth of the Mississippi.)

Ryan had taken his first professional job at DEQ. Given the title Environmental Engineer and flush with enthusiasm, he had intended to help clean up the Willamette. He quickly learned, however, that the DEQ was a permitting agency. Its purpose: to grant permits for polluters to keep polluting. And on this winter morning, Ryan was writing more permits. At the top of the heap was the application from Regal West, a paper mill. Ryan found that daily, Regal West was dumping thousands of gallons of untreated waste water into the river. A two-foot wide pipe, painted a cynical green, exited Regal's plant and ran straight into the water. Regal's expectation was to simply renew permits. But Ryan's proposal, nearly complete, would force Regal to install a million dollars worth of equipment to clean up their waste water. Ryan knew it would likely never fly; DEQ would veto it and Regal would never see it. He had done this before with other applications, challenging with technicalities and questioning DEQ's own proscribed limits. On two occasions, Gabe Riplinger had supported Ryan, and on these two, Ryan had won out. But Gabe was his only ally and Gabe was about to leave.

Monday morning, the offices filled quietly. Stu could be heard over the wall, sharing his stock market wisdom with a broker.

Ryan was consumed with Regal West, updating information and checking calculations. Karina caught him glued to his monitor.

"You're quiet this morning," she said.

"Hey. Busy."

"Did you like Friday's party?"

Ryan looked up and smiled. "It was great. Gabe enjoyed it."

"He seemed to. Evelyn had fun putting it together."

"You helped."

Karina nodded to the stacks of paper. "So when is the big day?"

"Friday." Ryan pushed away from the monitor. "Regal goes up for review Friday."

"And are you going to be bad?"

"Very."

Karina grinned broadly. "Sounds like you have an attitude, Mr. Evans. You get all the big ones. You got Justene. You got Wilkins-Simpson down in Albany. And Regal."

Ryan's head shook. "No. In fact, they've wised up. The next two projects are small. An old dry-cleaning place on the west side. A closed school out in Gresham with a buried heating tank."

"You think it's the penalty of doing the job too well?" Karina asked.

"I can only wonder. And of course, months have gone by and they still haven't rejected Justene."

Karina nodded. "I know."

"I mean, what the hell is the hold-up? They've taken forever. Gabe is leaving. I don't like it."

Karina flipped her red hair back and narrowed her eyes. "Maybe they're waiting for the protestors to tire out and leave town." Her face took a mischievous smile. "Or maybe, just maybe it's a conspiracy."

Ryan wasn't amused. "It doesn't smell right."

"I prefer conspiracy. You doing lunch with us at Benny's?"

The group—Karina, Tommy, Ryan, and whoever else joined—sometimes took lunch at Benny's Deli across the street.

Ryan's head shook. "I'm chained."

She turned away, smiling, but with her head shaking. "You're a sick puppy, Mr. Evans. Do you know you're compulsive?"

"Yes I do. It's a habit."

At 10:00, Ryan heard the whoosh of clothing. He knew the sound. It was Evelyn in her silk dress.

"Have you heard from Gabe?" she asked.

"Not since Friday. He didn't come in?"

"No." Her voice had a rare tinge of worry.

"Maybe he had an appointment," Ryan offered.

"No. He always calls if he's not going to be in."

"Did you call his house?"

"I saw him Saturday. We had dinner, but he didn't answer the phone all day Sunday and doesn't answer now."

Ryan thought. "Maybe he had one last vacation day?"

Evelyn red lips pursed together, her face skeptical. "I don't think so, but I'll check."

She turned and rushed down the aisle with her dress swooshing behind her.

Evelyn lived alone. With no family nearby, she filled much of her spare time singing in a Lutheran church choir and frequenting the Portland Opera with a small circle of single, middle-aged women.

She returned after a few minutes, out of breath. "Gabe is supposed to be here. He has appointments here, this afternoon. He always calls me if he's going to be late, but he doesn't answer his phone now and he didn't answer all day yesterday."

"Have you tried his cell?"

"He doesn't have one."

Ryan frowned.

She persisted. "Could you drive over there and check on him? That or we need to call the police."

Gabe's home was a 30-minute drive. He had no family nearby, only a sister in Minneapolis. "What does Mr. Lochner think?" Ryan asked.

"He's out of town."

Ryan eyed the stack of papers around him. "Okay, all right. I'll drive over. I'm sure he's fine."

"Thank you, Ryan! I'll go with you."

Ryan found the offer surprising. "That's all right, Evelyn. Don't worry. I'll be back after lunch."

The International truck banged and rattled through the parking garage. Outside, dark clouds were piling in from the coast. Ryan took Route 30 northwest through an industrial area populated with long-haul trucking, shipping transfer companies, and a rail line. Large trucks crowded the road.

After ten minutes, the route opened up to 50 miles per hour and businesses gave way to rolling fields and small dairy farms. Another mile and he passed the bridge to Sauvie Island. Home to farms, the island was an oasis close to the city that offered produce of all kinds in the summer and pumpkins in the fall. Pearson's Marina appeared on the right. The memories rolled by in glimpses. One distant summer when Ryan was ten years old, his father had traded an old broken-down truck for an older sailboat and moored it at Pearson's. For one season, the two had battled the Gorge winds and learned how to sail the 26-foot Catalina. A lack of money and frequent repairs had forced its sale.

Scappoose was a small rural community, with older homes spread out across rolling hills. There was no real downtown, only a gas station, BJ's restaurant, and a state police station. A new Safeway store nearby provided a landmark for the town. Ryan turned left at BJ's. He and Gabe had once eaten breakfast there, early on a Saturday morning before heading to the river to fish. Another mile and a series of turns delivered him to Forsythe Road, atop the hill. The white farmhouse appeared on the left.

A cedar rail fence bordered the front of the property. The house sat well back from the road and Ryan eased in and parked under the elm trees, next to Gabe's green Jeep. Two Oregonian newspapers lay in plastic bags in the driveway. He stepped out.

The house was dark. On the front porch, as if hiding from the rain, sat a large ceramic frog. A wooden swing hung from porch rafters and moved slightly in the breeze. Ryan climbed the steps and rapped the door with its brass knocker. Inside, Gabe's retriever, Shakespeare, began barking immediately. Through the bay window, yellow light shown dimly from the back. Ryan could see the outline of the interior he knew well. He tried the door again and the dog emitted a low howl.

He stepped off the porch and slogged through the wet grass and around the side of the home. Various massive bushes bordered the house, 30 years of plantings by a childless couple. Ryan ignored the stone path and wedged through the wet shrubs and up to the back porch, banging his head on a humming bird feeder. Water soaked his jeans. He pounded on the back door with his fists and called out.

The deep backyard extended down to a building on the right, which contained a garage and Gabe's shop. To the left, a white horse barn was set straight back from the yard. Apple trees bordered the fence and beyond that, pasture. Gabe's two quarter horses, large, dark animals, stood nervously at the fence in the rain. It was an odd thing. They should have been stabled.

Once more around the house, Ryan searched for a way in. There was no key under the mats, no key in the frog in front or the wooden raccoons in back. The wind picked up and rain began to fall in earnest. He returned hurriedly to the back yard. Gabe had offered more than once to give him a key and now, Ryan regretted having refused it. The horses stood in the increasing deluge. Their dark bodies twitched.

The black line of the garage door caught his eye. The side door was 15 yards away. He moved closer as a sharp gust pushed cold rain down his neck and back. The door was open, just a crack. He approached and pushed it. In the dim light was the blue Buick. He stepped inside the garage and strained to see. Someone was in the car, in the driver's seat. A figure. Silver hair. The head pushed back.

"Gabe?"

Nothing moved. Silver hair. A dark, gaping hole. Almost frozen, Ryan peered closer. "Gabe?!"

A thick spray of blood coated the head rest and seat.

"Oh, Jesus!" Ryan fled. Electricity surged and the explosion of thunder crackled overhead. "Gabe!"

He staggered across the yard and fell against the porch steps. He picked himself up and ran stumbling through the bushes to the front of the house. Inside the truck, he found the keys, started the engine, and charged out in reverse. The road was invisible, the wipers forgotten. He doubled over with nausea, but drove. The truck slowed in the street near BJ's. He opened the door and vomited. Against the red light, the International rolled across the highway and into the parking lot of the police station.

# Chapter 8

The state police station at Scappoose was in an old brick building. On a tall pole, the flag rapped violently in the storm.

Inside, a lady in her fifties sat behind a counter. The smile left her face when she saw him enter. "Can I help you?" she asked.

Ryan's voice was hoarse. "A friend. He's dead."

The lady gestured vaguely. "Uh, what? Come around here, what now? You say someone's dead? Captain Booth!"

Ryan slogged around the counter in a trance. He stood next to a folding chair while puddles formed at his shoes.

"Goodness. Sit down here," the woman commanded. "What happened?"

Ryan sat, held his head, and stared at the floor. His raspy voice was a whisper. "Gabe is dead. Gabe Riplinger."

"Captain Booth! Come here please!"

"He's in a car, in back. His head, shot. Oh my God."

The woman's jaw dropped. She yelled toward the back. "Captain Booth!"

Captain Booth charged through a back door, past a desk and filing cabinets to where Ryan sat. A tall man with glasses and a crew cut, he looked flustered. "What the hell's wrong?"

"This man says someone's been shot!"

"Where?" Booth demanded.

Ryan was still looking at the floor. His tears joined the rain water. His voice nearly vanished. "His house. Forsythe Road."

"Is this man alive?"

Ryan shook his head. "No."

Ryan accompanied Captain Booth, the county sheriff, and a deputy. They taped off Gabe's residence and posted the deputy overnight. A detective would visit the following morning and go through it all. After inspecting the external premises and garage, Booth and the officer had decided to enter the house. Ryan had waited with the deputy in his cruiser for an hour. Afterward, Booth and the sheriff had asked all the questions about Gabe's next of kin, his wife, her death, many questions. Gabe's sister in Minneapolis would be called. After hours of questions and snooping around the place, Captain Booth had concluded out loud that it looked like a suicide. There had been no break-in, no obvious theft. A gun had been discovered in Gabe's hand.

*Suicide?* Driving back to DEQ, Ryan's sight clouded over. He fought just to breath while he mouthed the word. Suicide?

He checked his watch. It was just after four. He dreaded the job that had fallen on him.

At work, Ryan went to Evelyn's cube. From there he could see Lochner's office. The door was open and the man was sitting and staring out the darkening window. Ryan put a hand on her shoulder. "Come on, Eve."

She looked up with moist eyes while clutching a white handkerchief. "Is he all right? What happened?"

Ryan gestured with his head. "Come on."

She stood quickly and followed Ryan into Lochner's office.

"Mr. Lochner, I need a minute with you," said Ryan.

Lochner turned in his chair. "Ryan, come in! Evelyn's been looking for you."

Ryan closed the door. "Eve, sit down." He turned a chair toward her.

She sat slowly.

Ryan spoke. "Evelyn asked me to drop by Gabe's home over lunch."

Lochner put down the nail file and nodded. "Yes, so what can you tell us? He decided to get sick for his last week? Evelyn's been beside herself, threatening to call in the feds."

A wrench wrapped around Ryan's throat. "I'm afraid Gabe has passed away."

Evelyn burst into sobs. Lochner's face blanched.

"He apparently died over the weekend," Ryan continued. He put his hand on Evelyn's shoulder while fighting off his own tears. "I'm sorry."

Lochner sat ashen with wide eyes. He stared at the far wall while Evelyn cried and Ryan tried to console her.

Lochner finally spoke, in a gasp. "Do they know what he died of?"

Ryan grimaced. "The police, the coroner. I'm sure they'll know soon enough."

Lochner ran a shaking hand across his scalp. His voice was faint and measured. "But they have no idea what killed him?"

Ryan eyed Evelyn. The question, the wording, seemed brutal. "I don't know. The authorities will know soon. I was thinking you could inform the group here."

Several excruciating minutes passed as Evelyn wept and Lochner stared at the wall.

Lochner finally rose and put his clammy hand on Ryan's shoulder. "I'll announce it tonight, before everyone leaves. This group is a family. We'll need to pull together."

Ryan entered the house through the back door with Gabe's dog, Shakespeare, in tow. In the kitchen, Meagan was busy at the sink. She turned and his face gave it away.

"What happened?"

Tuesday, Ryan hid at home. The night before, Meagan had taken the revelation hard. They had talked until late and spent the morning together, saying little and hugging a lot.

After she left for work, he fell into the couch with a wadded-up pillow and the television remote. There would be speculation at DEQ and he didn't want to be the one to tell them, especially Evelyn, that sweet old Gabe had put a gun in his mouth. Maybe it would never come out. An old man had quietly passed away.

Jerry Springer filled the room. The little white dog, Sophie, sat on the floor and faced Ryan with inquisitive eyes. After twenty minutes of Jerry, commercials, and the terrier's persistence, Ryan tossed the pillow and rolled off the couch. He ambled through the house and exited out the back door, with Sophie and Shakespeare following.

In the garage, he collected tools: an ancient electric saw of his dad's, a tape measure, hammer, and wrenches. The upstairs bathroom floor was rotted out. New flooring had already been bought on sale and waited in the garage.

Back inside, Ryan began removing the toilet. After disconnecting the plumbing, the porcelain water tank came off easy. The toilet bowl was heavy and he struggled to keep from gashing the bathroom door. He set the bowl and tank in the hallway, on cardboard, to protect the hardwood floor.

Next was the sink. Everything except the bathtub needed to be removed. By 11:30, the sink and the pedestal were lying in the hall and Ryan broke for lunch.

In the kitchen, he made a peanut butter and jelly sandwich and poured a glass of milk. The two dogs happily shared in the meal.

Ryan had just returned to his work when the phone rang. It had to be Meagan, checking up on him. He stepped around the fixtures and in the small den, checked the caller ID on the desk. It was Karina. He didn't answer.

The next step involved the electrical saw. The whine echoed loudly in the bathroom and Sophie fled downstairs. He cut the floor perimeter, made a few cross-cuts, and then set to work with a pry bar and hammer, tearing out the floor in pieces. Thoughts of Gabe invaded repeatedly. The man had offered to help put a new roof on the house. Ryan had politely refused; the thought of the old cowboy slipping off the moss-covered roof had worried him. But that was typical Gabe.

The work became tedious. Where the floor was out, Ryan sat down carefully on the open joists and pried up the last few pieces. Dark and rotted, the old wood splintered in his hands. The questions returned. There were no signs. Gabe woke up Sunday morning, after telling the world he had everything to live for, and blew his brains out? Ryan wiped the dust from his eyes.

The phone rang again. It was Meagan, to ask how he was doing. He was all right. She had grocery shopping to do and would be home by 5:30. He avoided mentioning the bathroom floor. Meagan's voice carried a melody, a rhythm that he treasured. She could make her feelings known in the most delicate way, and against that voice, Ryan was defenseless. After a few I love yous, he said goodbye.

The next morning, Ryan found the phone number for the state police in Scappoose. The same woman answered. He had not gotten her name.

"This is Ryan Evans. Is Captain Booth in? I'm calling about Gabe Riplinger."

"He is not. Do you have a specific question?"

"Well, Mr. Riplinger had no family nearby. Have you been able to contact his sister?"

"We have communicated with his sister, Mariam Steinhold."

"I see."

Ryan had met Mariam at one of Gabe's barbecues. She had flown out from Minnesota to visit. She was jovial, like her brother.

"Will there be an autopsy?" Ryan asked.

"No."

"Where is Gabe's body?"

"Are you next of kin?"

"No. I just want to be sure things are taken care of."

"That information is limited to next of kin."

"Could you give me Mariam Steinhold's telephone number?"

"I'm sorry, I cannot."

Ryan sighed. The notion of privacy was ridiculous. He had spent several exhausting hours with these people less than 48 hours before. "I'm the one who discovered him. You remember."

"Yes."

"So, is there a funeral home?" Ryan asked.

The woman sucked an indignant breath. "The body was picked up by Goodner's."

It sounded to Ryan like a trash pickup. "Goodner's?"

"Goodner's Mortuary."

After a search through the yellow pages and a quick call to Goodner's Funeral Home and Mortuary, Ryan learned the details. Mariam Steinhold had arranged a memorial service at the New Hope Baptist Church in Beaverton, for 1:00 Saturday. Good thing, Ryan thought. The ancient church in Scappoose was tiny. A private burial would be Sunday at the Green Hills Cemetery, for family only. Apparently, Mariam alone would bury her brother.

Ryan returned to DEQ at noon. A check of Tommy Campbell's cube found him reading the morning's paper.

Ryan hesitated at the entrance and Tommy jumped in his chair. "Crap! Don't do that!"

"Quiet in here."

"Tell me about it. It's been like a morgue. I mean…"

Tommy was tall and lanky, with orange stick hair and a boy's face. Thirty years old, he looked half that.

Karina arrived with a latte in her hand and stood at Ryan's side.

"There's a memorial on Saturday." said Ryan.

"It's in this morning's paper," Tommy offered. "They don't give a cause."

Ryan nodded and spoke slowly. "The burial is on Sunday. His sister is handling it. The Sunday gathering is family only, whatever that means."

Karina set her latte down. "You found him?"

Ryan nodded.

"Where was he?"

The inevitable questions, thought Ryan. "In the garage."

After a long pause, she spoke softly. "Do they know, I mean, do they have any idea of what happened?"

Ryan shrugged and began looking for a way out of the conversation.

Tommy's pencil tapped out a slow rhythm on the desk. "My sister knows a woman, she goes to Grace Community. It's Gabe's church in Scappoose. She said it was a suicide."

Karina's head shook. "What? Gossip!"

Ryan's shoulders sagged. He instantly became livid at the person who had decided to destroy the man's memory.

Karina caught him. "Ryan, what happened?"

Ryan's eyes rose from the carpet and danced over the cube walls. The floor was quiet. He sat down in the spare chair next to Tommy and pulled Karina in close. "Keep this to yourself. I mean it. I found him in the car." Ryan pulled a stuttering breath and whispered. "He had been shot in the head."

Karina's hand flew to her mouth. "My God!"

"He didn't suffer. I got the police and went back with them. They think it was suicide."

Karina's brown eyes were saucers. "Impossible!"

Ryan grabbed her arm. "Quiet!"

Tears welled in her eyes. She spoke through her fingers. "Oh my God! I thought it was a heart attack! He was so happy, at the party! He had plans."

A pause while they each acknowledged this fact. Tommy looked at Ryan. "You knew him better than we did. Does it make any sense to you?"

"No. It makes no sense to me."

# Chapter 9

The New Hope Baptist church was large and recently built, with a brown brick front and a tall, hopeful spire and cross. Sweeping lawns and flower gardens surrounded the building. On the approach up the wide sidewalk, granite stones birthed a waterfall that cascaded a distance over smooth river rock and emptied into a round green pool. On this Saturday morning, goldfish and koi retreated under lily pads as the sidewalk filled with mourners.

Under an opaque gray sky, the full flock from Grace Community Church, couples from bingo night, fishing buddies, and the group from DEQ made their way into the church. Even Rudy from Rudy's Fishing Supply attended. The rain held back in respect.

Meagan wore a dark dress and black wool coat, with a small black purse and heels. Over a white shirt and black tie, Ryan wore his only suit, a gray pinstripe, the same suit he had worn to his job interview at DEQ with Gabe.

Organ music drifted through the open doors and mourners filed slowly in. As Ryan and Meagan entered, Evelyn appeared at Ryan's side. She had been waiting for them. The three made their way to an open spot in the right, the sixth row back.

As they walked up, something happened that Ryan didn't expect. People turned. Whispers and raised eyebrows pointed them out and the hum of quiet conversation paused. Ryan was initially puzzled, but then understood. He had found Gabe. If the whispers were true, Ryan had seen Gabe at his worst. He took Meagan's hand and looked ahead to the altar and the cascade of flowers.

Finally, the pastor approached the altar. The organ music ended and the whispering subsided. Ryan turned to see that the balcony was half empty, but the main floor was completely filled.

The pastor introduced himself. A tall man with thick gray hair and black-rimmed glasses, Patrick Jolsen welcomed the crowd. He commented on the size of it, how this man they came to honor was obviously greatly loved. Jolsen's voice put the crowd at ease. He embarked on a sermon about the value of a life well-lived. He had known Gabe for decades. Gabe had given time to maintenance work at the church, painting, landscaping, and performing minor electrical work. Pastor Jolsen talked about Gabe's large circle of friends and how much he gave to each of them, at work, at church, to people in the community. The pastor went on to reveal something that few knew. Gabe and Mavis had met in Argentina while performing missionary work in isolated villages in the Pampas. They had helped build schools, dig wells, build shelters, and mid-wife mothers. And of course, the young couple had brought many to the saving grace of the Lord. And all for what, Jolsen wanted to know. For what? He paused.

The church was quiet except for the sniffling noses and an occasional crying child.

Jolsen stretched out his arms and answered himself. "The giving itself. That was their reward. Gabe and Mavis never sought recognition for their devotion, they rejected it. They never gave in order to receive. The joy they found in giving was their reward. Gabe was the man Christ wanted him to be. So I'll close with this. Count yourself blessed to have known them both. Honor Gabe by celebrating his life. And perhaps by looking at your own life and taking a lesson. Because it is the giving that matters. And keep *that* memory." Pastor Jolsen struggled for a moment; his own words nearly choked him. "Most of all, keep that memory."

The large gathering was moved. Meagan and Evelyn dabbed their tears.

After a minute, Jolsen invited anyone who felt so inclined to approach the altar and share a memory of Gabe. Initially, only handkerchiefs answered him. But first a Sunday school teacher, and then others that Ryan didn't know, walked up and offered their memories, stories of generosity and humor. The place was full of tears. Ryan briefly pondered getting up and saying something. He could have prepared a gentle lie. He could announce that Gabe had passed peacefully in his wicker chair on the back deck, while watching a thunderstorm race through the hills. Shakespeare had been at his side. Or he could tell them that Gabe's brains were spread all over the inside of his dead wife's car, that suicide was a horrific way to die, and that he, Ryan, craved more than anything to have never found him that way. The image had its own life. But neither story was true.

After escaping the traffic departing the church, Meagan punched the gas. The little tires chirped and the car quickly accelerated. "Let's pack for an overnighter and head for the coast."

Ryan fastened the seatbelt and turned to her. She continued. "We need to get out of town."

"Do you drive like this when I'm not with you?"

"We need a break."

"We can't afford it."

"Sure we can. We have the gift from Alex and Anne. We have the coupon book from the credit union. The rates are off-season."

"What about Sophie?" Ryan asked.

"We'll sneak her in with groceries."

"I need to finish the bathroom floor. You wanted to paint the kitchen."

"The house can wait."

Ryan exhaled a long breath. "Okay. Just keep the car on the road."

At the house, Meagan searched the coupon book and found what she was looking for. The Pelican's Nest was a hotel in Cannon Beach. Yes, they had a room. Yes, at the coupon rate.

Everything they needed for one night fit into a single soft suitcase. While Meagan locked the house up, Ryan put the suitcase in the trunk and tossed rain jackets and sweatshirts into the back seat. Sophie jumped in the car. Shakespeare had been taken in by Meagan's boss, John Kinsey, who owned a home with five acres and who already had a black Labrador that needed company.

The couple drove Sunset Highway west, past Beaverton and past the small high-tech corridor and into the country. The Sunset took them through rolling hills of fir trees, vineyards, and farms. Billowy dark clouds overhead barely contained themselves. He opened the sunroof and turned up the heat. She put a CD into the stereo and turned it up, Dire Straits. They drove up into the coast range and wound into the forest. The cold alpine air rushed in and clouds chased through the treetops. They spoke little.

The road wove through the mountains for a time and then joined Highway 101. Oregon's 101 follows an endless series of turns, climbing steep hills to reveal sweeping views of cliff and sea, and then descending as a roller coaster back down to the beach. Stunted pine trees all pointed eastward, deformed by the wind. In the spring, gray whales that have birthed their young in the Sea of Cortez are sometimes visible just off the shore, migrating north. Today the coast was cold, gray, and windswept.

The Cannon Beach exit dropped down off the highway, down into the trees and deposited them on the north side of town. The Saturday afternoon crowd was light. Couples in jeans and coats strolled the sidewalks. Restaurants and small shops were open for business, quaint book stores, art galleries and quirky little places that carried an assortment of items to attest to the trip. Except for a few eateries, it would all be buttoned up by 6:00.

They parked the Prius in front of a restaurant called Morris' Fireside. The place was a log structure, built of large timbers. The ceiling was open timbers up to the rafters. A generous stone fireplace was positioned in the center and they took a seat near it. They had eaten there before, even sat at the same table the previous August. Today, he ordered a burger and a pint of ale; she opted for a salmon filet sandwich and ice water with a lemon wedge.

She spoke between bites. "My mom called. They want to drive down for a visit."

"We just moved in," he protested. His muffled voice was void of enthusiasm.

"She left a message on the recorder."

He swallowed and mopped up the juice on his chin with a napkin that was falling apart. His face expressed complete disinterest. "We just moved in, Meggy. I want to get the bathroom floor done. We should paint the house and have the curtains up before they drive down to do their inspection."

"I told them to wait a while."

"Good. Say ten years?"

She gracefully ignored the comment. "They need to come down."

"We should take them to some ancient cattle barn in the country, tell them that's where we live."

She smiled at the image. "They're not that bad."

"They think I'm a bum."

She patted his hand. "But you're my bum."

Ryan's family had shallow roots. His younger sister, Julie, had died at age seven. She was chasing the family spaniel in front of their tiny rambler one Saturday and was hit by a passing truck. Their father, Jesse Evans, had worked as a dock worker at the Port of Portland. Jesse had perished in a climbing accident on Mount Hood when Ryan was twelve. Aside from Aunt Sirrey in Seattle (on his late father's side), Ryan's few known relatives were sprinkled across the country to invisible little towns in California and Nevada, as though hiding from each other.

In Ryan's youth, his mother had worked as a receptionist and nurse's aid at Emmanuel Hospital. But after the death of first her daughter and then her husband, Kimberly retreated to alcohol. As a teenager, Ryan worked nights at a Safeway store to help with bills. When he left for college on scholarships and loans, she was alone. After foreclosure forced her out, she moved to Alaska and married an alcoholic fisherman.

Meagan Evans came from a wealthy family near Seattle. Her father, Stanton Lewis, was a successful commercial real estate developer—malls and large office complexes. Her parents rejected Ryan from the start, never mind that he had graduated summa cum laude with a master's degree in microbiology.

The hotel was on the south end of town and perched on a bluff overlooking the beach. There were two wooden row houses, two stories each, painted beach-sand gray. Each unit had a patio or a second-floor balcony that faced the ocean. They registered, paid a small fee for the dog, and went to their first floor room. Meagan did a quick inspection: a large single room with a queen sized bed and a sleeper couch. A gas fireplace wrapped in stone. Along the wall opposite the beach was a fridge, stove, and cupboards. The place was clean.

Ryan stepped through the slider and called to her. Past the patio was a sand and wild strawberry lawn. Wooden steps led through tall brown grass down to the beach. The winter sun, brilliant orange, was resting just above the ocean and blanketed under thick overcast. Wind tossed the ocean about and threw spray up as far out as they could see. She zipped up her jacket and pulled him close and they watched the sun slowly succumb to the Pacific. The glow receded into the water, but then lit the bottom of the clouds on fire. The very last rays seemed to sear the gap between the earth and the sky. And then the color drained out, turning the air a cold, dark gray.

"Let's go in," she said.

A gust rattled the slider. The approaching nightfall was bringing another storm.

"Come inside," she repeated. Sophie whined, agreeing with her.

Ryan faced the sea. "I need to walk."

"Now?"

"I won't be long."

"It's getting dark fast. You could get lost."

"The hotel is lit up. I won't get lost."

Before she could counter again, he was into the sand and moving away. She watched as he disappeared down the steps. Frustrated, she turned inside with the dog.

The wooden steps were dark and slippery with the rain, but he made his way down the many turns and finally stepped into the sand. Above and behind him, the windows of the hotel glowed in the blowing mist. He turned into the wind. It pushed a steady spray into his face, but he trudged on over dunes and pieces of driftwood, and finally, flat packed sand. The howling wind cut through his jeans and dark waves crashed into the shore with a repeating roar. He sucked in the thick, salty current of air, took it deeply into his lungs. There was something here in the dark that he needed to feel, to understand. This ocean had been beating on this shore for an eternity. Timeless, it witnessed everything, the wants and the needs, the living and the dying. It crashed around him in the dark, drowning all else in the roar.

Far out, a single light pierced the darkness. It shone briefly on a wave crest and then vanished in the trough. Truth was in the sea. The cold Pacific surged around his ankles, sucking the sand from under his shows. Truth was here, about life and death, who stays and who goes, and why.

A second wave, numbing cold, crashed around his knees and pulled hard. Reluctantly, he withdrew and turned back to the hotel.

## Chapter 10

The color of his skin was a problem. He was dark, probably Mexican, and Darlene Lochner didn't really like Mexicans or whatever. They looked at her as they tended the flower beds, when Arland was at work. At 41, she was still trim, just like her younger sister, Ruthie, who lived in San Francisco. Pacific Heights.

The Lochner home was a beige brick two-story on the Westside, an "executive property" she had told Ruthie, with eight bedrooms, four garages, and a large lot. Out the library windows and between wooden blinds, she watched him rake up the last of the wasted winter leaves that had fallen across the emerald lawn. It was oddly warm out, much too warm for late January. And they were lucky today; it wasn't raining. But they came out even in the rain.

The day lilies would be planted there, bright yellow blooms to surround the 12 cherry trees that bordered the wall along the sides and back. She had insisted that they build the brick wall six feet high for security. But for godsake, what good was it, she wondered, when they were already inside the gates? Two more of them were blowing bark dust around the side of the home and they blew it everywhere. It wound up in the potted gardenias on the patio. And this was bad, but not as bad as the twins. When Scotty and Benjamin came home from college last summer and threw the party in the back? What a disaster! She had led the ladies from the Rotary through the back to show off the new pool and the Italian tile work, only to find that the twins had beat her to it! And with all their frat friends! Empty beer cans and marijuana butts were strewn about, even a condom! The ladies snubbed her for months!

Through the window, muscular arms raked the compost. Thick arms, no stomach. A perpetual tan against a white t-shirt. On a day covered in clouds, the brown shirt lay on the grass. She opened the blinds a bit more, the room needed light. He stopped working the soil and turned toward the house. To her. He was staring at her.

She had just finished talking with Ruthie about her new Louis Vuitton purse, and now the ringing phone jumped from her startled hands. She crouched below the window and grabbed it off the floor. "Hello?"

A man's voice. "This is Senator Phillips. Is Arland Lochner in?"

"Oh yes, yes! Just a minute."

Darlene, still crouching, covered the mouth piece and turned. "Arland! The phone! It's Senator Phillips!"

Arland Lochner was in the den at the opposite end of the house, busy in the final construction of an aircraft carrier, the *USS Coral Sea*. CVA-43. Lochner had never been in the military, but lately the notion of serving far out on the water for months, maybe years, seemed appealing. He was attempting to attach a delicate radar antenna with a drop of glue that glistened at the tip of a toothpick. But his hands wouldn't stop trembling.

"Arland?!" she called from the library.

Lochner relented with clenched teeth. "Shit." He picked up the portable phone and yelled. "I've got it!"

"It's Senator Phillips! Do you have it?"

Lochner's hand covered the mouth piece. "I've got it!"

He had never spoken with Senator Phillips and the man was calling his house? He spoke into the phone. "This is Arland Lochner."

The caller waited. Darlene lingered for several seconds, but the Senator was a private person. Finally, a noisy click.

"Hello, Arland."

Lochner's throat seized. The plastic antenna collapsed in his hand.

"Lochner."

"Wha, why are you calling me here?"

"Should I call you at work?"

"Jesus, no!"

"Approve it."

Lochner grabbed his forehead and whined ever so quietly. *"They killed him?"*

"Shut the fuck up. Approve it."

Lochner closed the door to the den and clutched his forehead. "It's too soon!"

"Approve it!"

"Wait until March, that's all! Let things die down!" Lochner was cowering in the corner of the room, now. "For God, how, how could—"

"Four weeks." The caller hung up.

# CHAPTER 11

Over the next few weeks, Ryan and Meagan were consumed with their house. The lady from Silvia's, an energetic woman named Rebecca, visited with books containing pictures of windows and samples for drapes, blinds, veils, and valances. They went through the home, taking measurements and comparing paint tabs and swatches. It took two visits to the house and three to the store to get everything decided. Meagan chose white laced-veils under lush drapes, warm mauve tones with dark brass rods and valances. When the bill was tallied, there was almost two thousand dollars left. Rebecca suggested new carpeting. The couple declined, for now at least. Carpeting would need to wait a little longer.

After submitting the order, they devoted evenings and weekends for two more weeks to cleaning and painting. At DEQ, the mood was somber; it seemed to Ryan that the air itself was mourning. He couldn't help but notice how little people spoke to each other, and everyone avoided poor Evelyn. He returned home from work each day, relieved that it was over. The marathon at the house was a welcome distraction.

The day before the installers came, Ryan arrived home with three more roller bushes, a new hand brush, and kung pao chicken from a Chinese takeout. They worked until late and by eleven, the smell of paint was so overpowering they were forced to open windows to the cold night.

The next day, Meagan stayed home to supervise as installers went through the house and Ryan worked finishing the bathroom floor. The crew's work was completed late in the day, all except for one missing valance. They would locate it and return the following week. Meagan was tired, but giddy. She toured the house repeatedly, checking each window, adjusting each veil. Her home had been reincarnated. It was fresh, clean, and warm. Her smile persisted until her cheeks became sore.

Friday morning, the coffee maker gurgled. Ryan sat in the squeaky green recliner and pulled on his socks. For some reason he always dressed upstairs, but came downstairs to put on socks.

He clicked on the television to the news and then returned to the kitchen to pour coffee. There, he stretched out nearly horizontal, eyes closed, legs straight, with his butt on the edge of the chair. Nearly a month had passed since the death, but going in to work was still difficult.

He nursed the coffee and waited for the caffeine to kick in. Voices from the television drifted in. The body count in Iraq. Trouble in the Middle East. Meagan was upstairs, probably adjusting curtains. Another sip of coffee. The word "Justene" filtered in.

Ryan got up and moved into the living room. The woman was talking, the word was out. DEQ had just approved permits to expand the Justene mine. The camera showed police chasing protestors as they heaved rocks through plate glass windows of shops downtown, a Starbucks, a Kinko's.

Ryan yelled upstairs. "Meagan!" He turned up the TV's volume.

"What's wrong?" She descended the stairs in her white terry robe and stood next to the couch while working her toothbrush.

The woman on screen gave a short history of the mine and the opening nearly four years previous. The picture showed the elegant lobby at the headquarters of Summit Resources, and then a shot from the ground level of a massive heap leach pad at the mine site, taken summers past. Finally, a close-up shot of one of the glittering gold pies the mine produced. The state had approved the expansion and new work would begin in May. A round, fleshy face shadowed by a white cowboy hat appeared. This was the Mayor of Fort Myers, Idaho, a Mr. Bobby Cody. He praised the mine for the 70 new jobs the expansion would provide to the area.

Then the camera went live to a few diehard protestors, who in a final fit of violence, set trash barrels on fire and shattered more glass. The police chased them down on horseback. The program moved on to other news.

Ryan gaped at the television. "I don't believe it!"

Meagan massaged his shoulder. "I'm sorry."

"How could they do it!?"

"I'll have a bagel with you."

He was still staring at the television. "I need to go in."

Shortly after eight, Lochner's office was empty. Evelyn was in her office nearby with a cup of tea.

Ryan caught her staring at hands. "Good morning, Eve. Is Arland in yet?"

She looked up. "Not until eleven."

"Did you catch the news?"

"About the mine? It was on the radio."

"I can't believe it."

"I didn't expect it." She frowned sympathetically. "I'm sorry. I know what it meant to you."

Ryan nodded, but said nothing.

"Try him at eleven. You might catch him then."

Ryan nodded again. They hadn't talked much since the memorial service. He fidgeted with a shirt button. "So, how are things?"

"Fine." The pinch in her voice wasn't convincing. She whispered, as though the news was sensitive. "I'm interviewing for a position in Salem, Department of Transportation. I need the change."

Ryan nodded. "I'll miss you. Don't just disappear, okay?"

Evelyn nodded.

For the next hour and a half, Ryan argued the merits of the decision with anyone and everyone nearby. Karina and Tommy agreed with him completely; there was no logic in the approval. Stu was happy. He owned stock in Summit Resources and Summit was up.

Five minutes past eleven, Ryan knocked on Lochner's closed door. His stomach churned. Lochner opened it, appearing tired.

"Do you have a few minutes?" Ryan asked.

"No."

"Tell me what happened."

Lochner scowled. "About?"

"Justene!"

"I don't have the time."

Lochner began to close the door, but Ryan stepped into the opening. He had trouble controlling the volume. "Why did I spend months researching and analyzing the site, just to have it approved, regardless of the results?"

Lochner frowned. He quickly motioned Ryan inside and closed the door. He moved across the room, sat on a credenza, swiveled his own chair around and motioned to Ryan. "Sit down."

Ryan sat.

A mechanical smile tugged at Lochner's mouth. The tone was fatherly. "Okay. Listen, son. The state examined everything in the applications, all of the accompanying documentation, the firm's construction and containment plans. We have no legal basis for denying it. This is the 1872 Mining Law we love to hate, that's how it works and you know that. And Ryan, the company is aggressive. A lawsuit to force us to approve would cost the state millions, and we would lose."

Ryan nearly choked on his reply. "What?? I have never seen a project that deserved rejection more than this! Did you read my work? My analysis and recommendations? I spent months!"

Lochner nodded. "Nice job, son."

"Arland, it gives all the legal and technical basis for rejecting the applications! With the mining history there? The acid drainage and existing tailings! The winter precipitation and the containment issues! It's the worst possible site for a heap leach mine! It's a disaster waiting to happen and they want to blow it up four-fold!"

Lochner wiped his face with a handkerchief. He leaned down toward Ryan. "Listen, son. Your job—and you're good at it—is to provide technical analysis of the issues and, where necessary, to propose solutions. I appreciate your sincerity, but the decision isn't yours. The big picture is about more than your conclusions. It's also about jobs. It's economic and political. Certainly you understand that?"

"No, I can't! Seven thousand acres? The containment ponds are overloaded every spring with rain and snowmelt, the whole area is a watershed for the Snake, and down river is the city of

Fort Myers. Fifty thousand people. You couldn't have read my work."

Lochner's thin eyebrows narrowed down sharply. "I did, as did others."

"But what about the elevated metals in the tributaries? These aren't background levels, the numbers are too high."

The Director stood. "I'm not arguing technicalities with you. This isn't a debating society. It's over. It's done."

Lochner moved to the door and opened it wide. "You did a nice job with it, Ryan. It'll be in your performance review."

"I could file an appeal."

"What?"

"To the permitting process. The rules allow it."

Lochner's head leaned back. One eyebrow lifted furiously. "Not if you want to keep your job. Drop it, Ryan."

Ryan landed in his chair and seethed. He had missed the deadline on the Regal permits. With Gabe's death, he had lost interest in work. Now, Justene consumed his thoughts.

Justene. Ryan's fingers drummed the desk. Why the hell did he spend months climbing all over the site, taking samples, running tests and coming to the only possible conclusion, just to have it ignored? Gabe had said it. "This one's different."

Using the computer, Ryan opened an online state directory and found the number he wanted. A man answered the phone. "DEQ Records."

"This is Ryan Evans at Portland DEQ. I want to get a copy of the permit applications filed by a mining company, Summit Resources."

A tired sigh. "Justene."

"Yeah. Is it popular?"

"We've had several calls today. Questions from the media, a few fruitcakes. I tell them we're just the state's filing cabinet. How much of it do you want?"

"Everything."

"Everything would take a small trailer."

"I need everything. All of the paperwork submitted by the company and everything prepared by the state."

"Jesus. You know, a lot of it's online."

"Yes, but I need copies of all the paper documents."

"Who is this again?"

"Ryan Evans. We talked before, a year back. I worked on the analysis for the expansion."

"Then you've seen it already."

"Not all of it. Besides, we need to be able to field questions here from the media. We need a complete set." Ryan exagerated. "How long will that take?"

The man cursed, not happy with the work he was getting. "A few days to copy, a few to mail. Like I have nothing better to do."

"I need it as soon as possible."

"Of course you do." The voice was sarcastic.

Ryan thanked him and hung up.

There was another call he needed to make. It had been eating away at him since that dark day. He dug up the state police phone number and found his way to the small office in Scappoose. Captain Booth was on duty.

"This is Ryan Evans. I went with you out to the Riplinger home?"

"I remember. How can I help you?" asked Booth.

"How is the investigation going?"

A quiet delay ensued. Then the man's firm voice, in control. "The investigation is closed. It was found to be a suicide."

The answer was expected and loathed at the same time. "I just can't believe that," Ryan said.

"Mr. Evans, there was absolutely no sign of a crime. Nothing stolen, nothing disturbed. Based on our investigation, the man was despondent over the death of his wife, his financial problems, and his pending retirement."

"What about the gun?" Ryan asked.

"Well, that was a small question. Based on the serial number, it was stolen from a gun store in Kentucky some 12 years ago. It was probably sold a few times privately and then purchased later by Mr. Riplinger. He did have several guns in the house."

"But with the guns he owned, the one gun he used was stolen? You can't trace its purchase?"

"He had two other pistols and two rifles. One pistol was a 22 caliber, a little small. The other was a collectable 45. This was a 9 millimeter, clean. In good shape and obviously cared for. He knew how to use guns. We don't believe it to be an issue."

"What do you mean? The gun that killed him was stolen? This could have been made to look like suicide. What about fingerprints?"

"We only found his."

Ryan closed his eyes. He shifted the phone to the other hand. "Captain Booth, I just can't buy this. I knew Gabe well and he was never that depressed. He had a lot of friends. He had plans. He had even started a new relationship with a lady here at work. No one who knew him well can accept that he killed himself."

"I don't think anyone ever expects this kind of thing. I'm sorry, Mr. Evans. The investigation is closed."

# Chapter 12

When Ryan began work at DEQ, he quickly became a workaholic. The first in his lineage with a degree and a profession, he wasn't going to blow it. Months passed before Meagan could talk sense into him and get him to leave by five. Or six.

But in the week following the Justene approval that consumed him so, he wasn't getting home until eight or nine each night, and she wondered if he was returning to his old habits. That Friday was a planned dinner date with Meagan's coworkers and their spouses. It was a quarterly event, paid for by the clinic owner, John Kinsey. Ryan assured Meagan that he would drive directly from work to the restaurant at 7:00. She left work at five and, from the house, called to remind him. His phone went to voice mail.

At the house, she collected fresh clothing from the bedroom. In the bathroom, she turned on the water and undressed. She pinned up her hair and knelt down to feel the temperature. A full minute passed before she stepped inside and closed the curtain.

When she finished showering, she slipped on a terry robe and opened the door wide. She dried herself and slipped on underwear. She wiped the moisture off the mirror and stood to examine herself. Her flat tummy seemed to be growing a tiny bulge. Her breasts were a little heavier. Close-up, she inspected the hint of a wrinkle under an eye.

She sat on the toilet seat and slipped on a pair of black jeans and a deep violet chenille sweater. She pulled a brush through her auburn hair, and then applied red lipstick and a touch of black eyeliner. A quick appraisal. A faint mist of perfume under the ear, jasmine. She liked what jasmine did to him.

Downstairs, she tried Ryan's phone again. He didn't pickup. She tried his cell phone with the same results. He rarely turned his own cell on, which she found incredibly irritating.

A little after six, the house phone rang. It was Alex. He wanted to know if they had gotten the curtains done. Yes, the last of the curtains were in and they were beautiful, she said. The new flooring in the hall bathroom and most of the painting was done. Upstairs carpeting was next, a few months out. The place was coming along. She again thanked Alex, who was waiting for Anne to return home from the medical center for her one day off. They had planned dinner and a movie out. Meagan said goodbye.

She checked the time again. 6:20. She grabbed the portable phone and slipped out the back door with Sophie. The rain had abated and the late winter air was frosty and still. The sun had set. Trees and homes blocked the horizon, but the sky was lit in a delicate twilight that gave the backyard, and even the air, a dark pink tint. She walked through the wet grass with the little white dog. The back yard was full of bushes, many bare and unknown, that ran along the fence and house and circled a fruit tree. They were naked now, but with spring not far off, the plants would soon reveal themselves.

The voices of children caught her. Through a stand of birch trees, she saw them playing on a deck, under a light. Concealed in the growing darkness and the trees, she watched two small girls and a boy chase after a large ball. Chubby in winter coats, they scurried about after the ball their own height, giggling and shrieking. The man laughed. He was tall and his low voice carried. They gathered around him, and that familiar longing washed over Meagan. It stirred low in her and then welled up into her stomach and deep in her chest. She was an only child, raised by a mother who was preoccupied with the image of wealth and a father who was consumed with achieving it.

The phone rang in her hand, a shrill, electronic announcement. The man looked toward the sound, to her hiding place in the trees. She turned and walked quickly to the house. It had to be Ryan, she thought. But it was a pushy sales person, wanting to "do a survey." She blurted a profanity and hung up.

Meagan put the dog inside, grabbed her coat, and left.

Reno's was a popular Italian restaurant in Northwest Portland, an old restored home with arches, columns, and prints of the Amalfi coast. Owned by a family from Tuscany, the food was authentic. The place was busy and the hostess led her to a round table in back. The others were already seated: Mary Lavoie, an associate veterinarian at the clinic, and her husband, Jack, a school teacher. Across the table sat Meagan's boss, John Kinsey, and his wife, Susan. The receptionist named Tawny and her newest boyfriend sat to the right. Greetings were exchanged as Meagan took off her coat and sat down.

After a minute, Susan asked. "Will Ryan be joining us?"

Meagan nodded. "He might be running a bit late, but he's on his way."

"Does he have a busy schedule?"

"This week has been tough. He has a deadline."

John laughed loudly. "I didn't know the state had deadlines."

They dipped bread in olive oil and sipped wine. After 20 minutes and two attempts by the waiter, they ordered dinner, ravioli in marinara sauce, spaghetti alle vongole. Meagan scanned the menu and decided to wait. At 7:30, she went to the lobby and called Ryan's office on her cell phone. There was no answer.

The insalata arrived, and then the main courses. The group ate and drank and laughed. Meagan nibbled on bread and began to worry. Had he been in an accident? Had the truck broken down? Outside, a cold drizzle was falling. Mary caught Meagan's worried eyes.

Then through the window, Meagan spotted his International. It swung into the parking lot and stopped near the window, belching a backfire that startled the group and ended conversation. The truck door slammed and 30 seconds later, Ryan arrived at the table with his hair tossed by the wind. He smiled weakly at her.

John stood up and shook hands across the table. "Ryan, you made it! Better late than never. Sit down."

Meagan's eyes were on fire.

When dinner ended, she left first and arrived home well ahead of him.

She confronted him as he entered the kitchen. "You promised me you'd be on time!"

"I'm so sorry. I completely lost track. You won't believe what I found."

She had picked at the food and consumed two glasses of wine. Her face was flushed. "I don't give a damn what you found! I work with these people! I called you all day. How could you forget?"

"I... I spaced it. I'm sorry."

He followed sheepishly as she flew upstairs into the bathroom and slammed the door. Her voice carried from it. "You're slipping off the deep end again!"

"I'm not, Meggy. I'll be done soon. You won't believe it, honey. The work is so shoddy. The original permits were never completed correctly. It looks like school children did the apps."

"You forgot to come home all week! You forgot dinner with my co-workers! How could you do this? And all over a damned hole in the ground that's four hundred miles from here?"

He spoke softly to the door. "I'm sorry, Meg. I'm nearly done. The documents I ordered came in. Two boxes Tuesday, one more today. I finished off two and brought the last one home."

The door flew open. Her eyes were fierce. "Here?"

"I'll finish it this weekend."

"You promised to put in the new front door tomorrow. Mom and Dad are visiting Sunday."

Ryan's jaw dropped.

"You forgot."

"I, I'll handle it. I will. I'm sorry."

Her auburn hair shook furiously. He pleaded with her. "This last box, this is the end of it. I promise."

"You're promises aren't worth much."

A pained look crossed his face.

Her chin dipped slightly to the left, the first tiny hint of softening. "Ryan. What exactly do you expect to accomplish with all of this? What? They're the government! They can do what the hell they want." She swept by him and into the bedroom.

He trailed. "Not if it's illegal."

"And you're going to stop them? You work for them."

She was standing next to the bed, half naked in her black bra, with her hands on her unzipped jeans. The light from the lamp accented her high cheekbone, her delicate shoulders, her breasts. He was completely distracted.

She shook her head. "Ryan? Sweety? Dream on."

❖

Saturday morning was cold and overcast. He returned from Home Depot with two new doors in the back of the International. On the front porch, he pressed the new button he'd installed the previous weekend. She didn't respond. He pressed twice more and she finally opened it.

Without speaking, they pulled a door from the truck and carried it into the garage. It would replace the old back door of the house. Back at the truck, they lifted out the new front door, carried it up the front steps, and leaned it against one of the porch pillars. Meagan stood back to look it over. Made of solid oak, it was heavy and sound, with two rows of three raised panels. At eye level, the four upper panels curved in to frame an oval window, a thick pane of beveled glass. The grained wood was finished in an auburn stain and smelled of linseed oil. She smiled.

"Let me get the deadbolt and handle." Ryan offered.

He trotted back to the truck and returned with the box containing the new hardware. He opened it and set the hardware on the porch, out of the way. The polished nickel handle, a foot long, carried a graceful curve. She picked it up.

"It's heavy duty." he offered.

She nodded.

"I took measurements twice before giving them the order. We may get lucky and have a perfect fit, but I doubt it. Can you get the tape measure?"

She returned a minute later with the tape measure and her University of Washington sweatshirt. She slipped it on while he took the measurements, first of the door opening, and then the new door. The door was oversized by a quarter-inch.

In the garage, they grabbed sawhorses, a saber saw, and a drill and carried it all to the front porch. Ryan measured and marked the cut and then carefully trimmed off the excess. They removed the old door, splitting and aged, and carried it out back. It would be cut up for fireplace kindling.

She went back inside while he installed the new hinges on the door and door casing. She returned carrying two cups of steaming coffee. They carefully slid the door into place and installed the hinge pins.

He closed the door and then stepped down into the yard. She grabbed both cups and joined him, just as a light mist began to fall.

This moment was different from the others, the weeks of cleaning and painting, the new bathroom floor, the curtains. The door was immaculate, almost too rich against the cracked paint on the siding. It changed the entrance completely. She imagined what the front porch would look like when the exterior was painted in the spring.

She hugged him with her free arm. "That's beautiful. Where on earth did you get all these skills?"

"My dad. You would have liked him."

"When can we install the back door?"

"Soon. I'll have the handle and lock installed here in an hour or two. Meggy, I'm sorry about last night."

# Chapter 13

Early Sunday morning while Meagan vacuumed, Ryan slipped outside with the dog to make the rounds of the house. He washed Meagan's blue Prius and then hid his International in the garage. The car had been a college graduation gift from her parents, indirectly. They had bought her a red Volvo, her father's choice, but she had traded it in for the Prius.

After a light lunch, she began preparing an early Sunday dinner of roast beef. He peeled potatoes. They spoke little. Afterward, Ryan changed into a pair of slacks and waited in the living room.

The black Mercedes pulled into the driveway at 3:00. He called into the kitchen, mimicking the voice from *Poltergeist*. "They're here."

The dark car was visible through the new curtains; they were obviously examining the old house and Ryan wished that he could have finished the exterior before the grand inspection. They had worked feverishly, for themselves yes, but also for this visit.

Meagan patted his shoulder and moved to the door. Before opening it, she turned to him. "Be nice, for me?"

He stuffed his hands into his pockets.

## THE MINE

She swung the door open and waved them in. Stanton Lewis locked the car and the couple approached the brick path. He paused to help his wife, as though navigating around some treacherous difficulty, and then clunked loudly up the wooden porch steps. Mr. Lewis was tall, with a head full of eternally dark hair that was graying perfectly in the temples. He wore beige slacks and a matching tweed sweater over a white shirt. He was still fit for his age and, Ryan noticed, rather tanned for Seattle in winter. And he hugged his daughter for too long, as if she had just returned from a year in Africa.

Rachel Lewis puckered up and kissed the air while giving her a daughter the perfunctory pat. Ryan extended his hand to Mr. Lewis, who obliged. They avoided eye contact.

There, thought Ryan, done. I've been nice.

For her parents, Meagan's marriage had been a nightmare. Their new son-in-law was a raving environmentalist, a throw back to the hippie years. Never mind that he had graduated summa cum laude with a Master's degree, environmentalists were idiots. They camped in trees and squatted like aboriginal Indians to block progress. He had worn long hair and a beard in college and they had secretly nicknamed him Sasquatch. Meagan had married him out of pity, they were certain of it. Growing up, she had always been afflicted with the guilt of wealth and a need to atone for it. She had often brought home stray pets, wretched little creatures that were quickly disposed of. To their horror, she became a veterinarian. And Sasquatch was just another stray she had found wandering. They prayed she would soon find her senses and file for divorce.

At the door, the couple did a quick survey. The worn furniture and the old woodstove caught them both. Mrs. Lewis managed a plastic smile. "So this is your new home."

Meagan replied hopefully. "Well, this is the living room."

Ryan waited out the grand tour in the kitchen as the procession moved from room to room, downstairs and up, wandering through the ancient house as though making a trip back in time, their voices growing dim, with Meagan apologizing and Mrs. Lewis proclaiming in awe, "That's nice, isn't it dear?"

Ryan waited.

In the living room, the parents sank into Aunt Sirrey's bottomless couch. Mrs. Lewis jumped up and glared down as though it were carnivorous. To Ryan's delight, a spring had apparently broken loose and he fought off a nearly irresistible smile.

She exclaimed as she wiped her pants, "Gracious, Meagan! You need furniture! I'll come down next weekend and we'll pick out a living room set. There must be furniture stores in Portland."

"The furniture is fine, Mom."

"Nonsense! It's ready for the bonfire!"

Rachel Lewis used this phrase to describe anything that needed replacing, last year's clothes, cars, useless friendships. The bonfire burned continuously.

Meagan was unflappable. "Mom, we just moved in. Besides, you've already given us the dining set."

"Don't you just love it?" Mrs. Lewis demanded to know.

"It's too nice, Mom. Thank you."

Under Mrs. Lewis' inquiring eyes, Ryan nodded in false agreement. Sure, the dining set was nice. Never mind that ornate French furniture was not what either of them would have chosen, and that they intended to return it soon for something more contemporary.

Meagan's father spoke. "When was the house built?"

Here it comes, thought Ryan. "The fifties."

"It shows it." The man's eyes inspected the woodstove. "I hope the furnace works?"

Ryan nodded with strained patience. "Yes."

"Did you have the house inspected thoroughly, the foundation, electrical?"

"Everything was inspected before we closed."

Meagan's eyes darted nervously to her husband. "Dad, Ryan put in the new bathroom floor upstairs. We've painted the house. We have new drapes, and we just put in the new front door. See?" She pointed proudly at the door.

Mrs. Lewis nodded. "It's very nice, Meagan."

Mr. Lewis continued. "What about the roof?"

'What the hell about it?' thought Ryan. "I'm putting up a new roof this summer."

"You're doing it?"

"Yes."

"Pay to have it done."

"I'll save doing it myself."

"Have you ever roofed a house?" Lewis' wide eyes were incredulous.

"It's not rocket science." Ryan was adamant about unnecessary expenses. He still owed $40,000 on college loans, something he'd never share with these people.

Mr. Lewis lifted an open hand. "Life insurance?"

Ryan blinked. "I'm sorry?"

"Do you have enough life insurance?"

Ryan looked to Meagan, who was watching her father closely. "I get it at work," Ryan answered.

"You need at least five million worth. You need to consider Meagan. You take a swan dive off the roof of this castle and land spread-eagled on that brick, she'll need to be provided for."

Meagan's eyes widened. "Dad! No one's going to die! Dinner's ready, let's eat."

They sat at the new dining table Meagan had set with a new linen cloth and French china. These were expensive wedding gifts from a severely conflicted mother. Such things unfortunately acknowledged the marriage, but it was her daughter, after all. The women brought in the pot roast, garlic mashed potatoes, asparagus, and salad. They sat across from each other, mother-to-daughter, man-to-man. Mrs. Lewis said short prayers of thanks to no particular deity.

Meagan passed the asparagus to her mother. "So how are things in Redmond?" she asked.

Her mother responded. "We're putting in double tennis courts in back."

"Tennis courts? Where?"

"Behind the pool. Right of the gazebo."

"Did you two take up tennis?" Meagan asked

The father's eyebrows arched. The voice was stern. "I've played tennis for years, Meagan."

Meagan laughed. "Sure Dad. But, behind the pool, that's where my maple tree is."

"We've taken down the maple tree," Mr. Lewis replied.

"You cut down my tree?"

Mrs. Lewis jumped in. "Oh, Meagan. It was old and rotted, ready for the bonfire."

"I used to climb that tree!"

"You did not. Besides, it was unsafe even then, and the leaves blew in everywhere."

Ryan smirked to himself. Cut it all down, every living thing. It all belongs in the bonfire. Be a good consumer and fill the skies with its smoke, the great fire of greed and status. They wouldn't use the tennis courts as much as they didn't use the swimming pool.

Mrs. Lewis went on. "Oh Meagan, I didn't tell you. We've been accepted to the Ridgemount Club. It's the most exclusive golf club in the country. They have associate clubs in Tahoe, Hawaii. Tell them how much it was, Stanton."

Stanton Lewis shrugged. "Too much."

Ryan smirked visibly; he couldn't suppress it. Mrs. Lewis prattled on with the names of club members, CEOs of major firms, NBA players, the host of a late night talk show.

Mr. Lewis turned his head now and shifted the topic. "So, how is the job, Ryan?"

Ryan's stomach flipped. "Good."

Under the table, Meagan's foot stroked the calf of Ryan's leg.

"Are you still working for the state?" Mr. Lewis asked.

Ryan nodded. Here it comes.

The tag team handed off again. "How is it paying?" Mrs. Lewis asked.

"Twice monthly, direct deposit," Ryan replied.

Silence. Meagan's eyes drilled her husband.

Ryan softened. "It pays well enough for now. Not as much as I might like, but my career…" He regretted his words immediately.

Mr. Lewis attacked. "You should consider real estate. Work as an agent or a broker. They're paid far more than you. And it doesn't require much training, most real estate agents are idiots. You could handle it."

Meagan's eyes opened wide as her foot feverishly massaged Ryan's leg.

The heat rolled off Ryan's face. "I have no desire to be a real estate agent."

"Why not?"

"It's personal. Some people are happy to cover the planet with shopping malls and office parks. I won't do that. You did call them idiots."

"Yes. But for idiots, they still make a lot more money than you."

The two men stared at each other. Meagan jumped up, nearly knocking over the chair. "Banana cream pie!"

Her father looked at her, annoyed.

"It's time for dessert, Dad! Banana cream pie! It's your favorite!"

With dessert, the conversation took a turn to Meagan's job. The topic of children never came up. The Lewis parents had promised themselves to avoid it. Kids would only complicate the coming divorce.

Meagan's parents departed at 5:30, not nearly soon enough for Ryan. The young couple escaped the house to get some badly needed air. The freeways loop the city and cross the river on bridges, providing a good view of Portland. They took the tour in the car and then dropped down onto Front Avenue for a slice of apple strudel alamode at one of the restaurants, Ryan's idea.

That evening, Meagan settled in the living room with a cup of herb tea. Ryan dragged the last carton from the mud room to the kitchen. The box contained engineering and topographical maps of Justene, the high mountain ridges to the south and east, and the Black Iron and Breitenbush streams that bracket the location. Over the previous year, Ryan had memorized it all. During three trips out, he had taken water and soil samples and numerous photographs.

During the previous hundred years, the area had been mined extensively. A few fortunes had already been made by the late 1800s, but when the gold veins finally gave out, the numerous mines that pockmarked the region were abandoned. Then came the cyanide. Now, entire mountains would be ground into toxic piles for the glittering yellow metal.

He was immersed in it around eleven, when Meagan appeared in a silk nightgown. She closed the kitchen blinds. She took the papers from his hand and laid them on the table, and slowly eased down into his lap. She kissed him on the lips.

"Thanks for today," she offered.

"Your parents don't like me much."

A corner of her mouth turned up. "It isn't you. No one would measure up. They'll get used to it when we have kids."

The silk nightgown followed the soft contours of her body. After a few passionate minutes, she pulled away. "How late?"

Ryan swallowed hard. "Not long."

She stood. "It's Sunday night."

"This will be the end of it."

She looked at him in a particular way, but he missed it. He turned back to his papers.

By 12:30, he had reviewed nearly all of it. Three stacks lay on the floor; the kitchen table was covered in piles. He rubbed his dry eyes. Maybe she was right. Maybe it was a lost cause. The Mickey Mouse clock on the kitchen wall told him to go to bed.

The last carton was nearly empty. He reached down, pulled out a thick document, and set it on the table. This was the original application from the company to expand the mine. Ryan thumbed the first few pages and sneered. Here were the signatures of the company's cronies, the chief geologist, the CEO, and the various contractors that had planned the expansion. He had met the site manager a few times, had seen a few suits during one visit.

He scanned the rest of the signatures, state officials approving the expansion. Lochner's signature was here. It was all neatly buttoned up. The application was the parent document and the fourth and fifth pages listed pointers to numbered documents that lay about the kitchen, including the EIS and the additional engineering and state required provisions. Ryan scanned the titles and found the pointer to his Environmental Impact Statement. Several month's worth of work, for what? His work was here somewhere. It was numbered ORDEQ-2004-1141.

He sat on the floor on his knees and rolled his fingers along the corner of each stack until he finally matched the number. Lifting the papers up, he pulled out the EIS and quickly saw that it wasn't his. This document was small, perhaps 100 pages. The author was a Robert Newberg. His signature, a long, elaborate flourish, was dated four years previous.

Ryan frowned. He checked the reference number again. He checked the number on the EIS. They matched. There were no other references to an EIS. His own work wasn't here.

"Are you all right?" Meagan was standing in the entrance to the kitchen.

Ryan's expression was dazed.

"Ryan?"

"They didn't use it."

"Use what?"

"My analysis. My work."

She covered a deep yawn and shook her head. "Come to bed."

He spoke as if in a trance. "They never used my work. They used this thing, written up years ago for the original permits."

Meagan closed her eyes and realized at this moment how much she hated his job. She honestly hated it. "So what does that mean, Ryan?"

"I'm not sure. I think it means I can appeal it."

"Why would they not use yours?"

The kitchen was quiet except for the hum of the fridge.

"Maybe an error."

"So they have you do all this research, write up an exhaustive document for this giant project, and then ignore it?"

He turned and their eyes met.

She entered the kitchen and dropped to her knees next to him. "Ryan, let it go. Let it go, please? It's not worth it. Even Gabe said this was different. Remember? He told you that… just before…"

A gust of wind rattled the windows.

"No." Ryan slowly shook his head. "No. It was a thief, maybe an accident, I don't know. He didn't die over this."

## Chapter 14

After a sleepless night, Ryan was at work by seven. The offices were empty. He wandered the floor nervously and wound up at Evelyn's cube, where he found himself looking absently at pictures that covered the wall. There were pictures of Evelyn's sister, Louise, and her family. Louise was married to a dentist, lived in Atlanta, and had two teenage girls with braces. There were pictures with friends at the beach, and still too many pictures of Gabe. Evelyn's move to Salem hadn't come in yet.

Gabe's office was open. After his death, the police had visited and asked a few questions of Lochner. They had dug around the office, but the visit was obligatory and pointless. Afterward, all of his personal office belongings had been shipped in a small box to his sister in Minneapolis, courtesy of Evelyn. The desk and an old padded gray chair were all that remained.

In the quiet of the early morning, Ryan sat and rested his hands on the worn arms. A faint smell, a woodsy, spicy smell caught his nose. Gabe's cologne. This was the only personal evidence that the man had worked there for so many years. Ryan gazed out the narrow window in the morning light and remembered his friend. The summer barbecues at his farmhouse with coworkers and their families. His happy, chubby wife with her hair in a bun, before the cancer. Fishing in a boat with a golden retriever, a dog that preferred swimming with ducks.

A voice barked. "Evans!"

Ryan nearly fell from the chair. Arland Lochner was standing in the doorway.

"What are you doing in here?" Lochner demanded. For a moment, he only stared. "You can be the first to meet your new manager. This is Marcos Lassiter."

Ryan partially recovered his wits and extended his hand. Did he say new manager? The man was tall and in his early forties, with pale white skin, a beak nose, and brown hair. He looked stone-faced at Ryan and offered a limp fish for a hand.

Ryan shook the fingertips and nodded. "I was just—"

Lassiter cut him off with a wry smirk. "The position is taken."

"Sorry?"

"You're sitting in my office, Mr. Evans. You work for me now."

Ryan nodded awkwardly while retreating toward the door, but he still mustered a share of courage. "Mr. Lochner, if you have a few minutes later. I wanted to talk with you about Justene."

Lochner and Lassiter traded quick glances.

Lochner turned to Ryan. "We talked already. Drop it."

Ryan couldn't drop it. He stopped in the doorway and faced Lochner directly. "You never used my EIS. The impact statement Nelson and I produced, over five hundred pages and eight months of research. I audited all the records, everything. DEQ used some rag created four years ago. What happened?"

Lochner's eyes were wide. He looked again at Lassiter and then huffed. His lips curled up. "What happened?! I run this organization, Mr. Evans! I am the Director of DEQ and you work for me! Do you get it? Now get out of here!"

The office cubes flew by. Ryan forgot his coat as he headed for the elevator. He needed air. On the main floor, Karina saw him just as she was entering. She hurried to catch him in the arriving crowd.

"Ryan. Ryan, what's wrong?"

He stopped and tilted his head back, debating.

"What is it?"

He motioned for her to follow and then headed past the deli bar to a table in the corner, near the windows. He kicked back a chair and sat down hard. She followed and took a seat.

She leaned forward. "You don't look very well. What happened?"

He flayed the air with a hand. "They never used my EIS! For Justene? They never used it! They substituted some irrelevant piece of shit written over four years ago, before the first mine was approved."

"How did you learn this?"

"I ordered copies of the permits, all the research, all state records on the site. I went through everything, finished up last night. My analysis isn't even there. Dammit, I read through all of it before I realized. The application references a study written by some idiot named Newberg. I confronted Lochner over it just now. He basically told me to go to hell."

Karina raced to catch up. "You confronted Lochner?"

"Who else?"

"You don't think it might have been a paperwork error?"

Ryan frowned. He had told Meagan exactly that the previous night. "No. When I questioned Lochner, he knew exactly what I was talking about and he blew me off. Listen, the permit applications and all referenced docs together form a binding document. The package as a whole dictates what the company, Summit Resources, must do to be in compliance with the state. This isn't some stupid oversight. It takes intention. Lochner pulled this crap so he could approve the permits."

# THE MINE

Karina's eyes were large. "What are you going to do?"

"I don't know. He can't do this, this can't be legitimate." Ryan pushed his fingers through his hair. "Dammit, I don't know what to do."

"If Lochner refuses to talk with you, I'd tell you to go over his head, but—"

"Over his head is the Governor's office."

The email message was clear enough. Back in his cube, Ryan typed and revised it for 20 minutes before closing out the window and deleting it. After a few minutes of staring at the monitor, he re-typed the message:

Mr. Lochner:

In my spare time, I've reviewed the Justene Mine application for the site expansion. I found that the cover form refers to an outdated EIS, one that was completed several years previous. It does not refer to the EIS and related analysis I completed for this application. The old EIS is not relevant to this application and may actually invalidate DEQ's approval. Please look into this. This is a legally binding document and it could present problems for DEQ.

Sincerely,

Ryan

The email message was on screen. It could have been a simple office error, which was wholly unlikely. Or it was intentional fraud, and if so, this email would at least start the electronic paper trail.

Ryan agonized for a few seconds more, finally replacing *Sincerely* with *Respectfully*. He then clicked *Send*.

119

Ryan was far behind schedule, still not finished with Regal West. He sat and stared at ugly Sammy. The mug smiled.

He scrolled through the online state directory, down to the Ns, Newbaum, Newbury, Newton. He found no Newberg. He called Human Resources.

"I'm looking for a Robert Newberg, but can't find him in the directory. Can you help?"

The woman in HR put him on hold for a few minutes and then returned. "We have no Robert Newberg working in DEQ."

"He apparently worked in DEQ about four years ago. Does your office keep records that far back?"

"Hold on."

A few minutes later, the woman responded. "The only Robert Newberg we have listed left state employment September 29, 2004."

"What office did he work out of?"

"Pendleton. They closed the Pendleton office two years back."

"Do you have a last known address or phone number?"

"That information is unavailable."

Ryan thanked her and hung up. He pushed the keyboard aside and propped his elbows on the desk. He buried his face in his hands. Newberg was likely fired. How could anyone write 100 pages of such crap? He didn't really have much to say. 'So Robert, where did you come up with that piece of garbage? Pendleton is a hundred miles from Justene. Did you actually ever go to the site and take a look?'

September 29. Ryan raised his head from his hands. He took Newberg's EIS in his hand. His signature was there. Next to it, the date he signed. September 28, 2004.

Ryan picked up the phone and called HR again. The same woman answered, slightly irritated now. She confirmed Newberg's last date of employment: September 29, 2004.

Email would be better, Ryan thought. He wrote up a quick note and shared the news.

"Karina, Mr. Robert Newberg doesn't work for DEQ. He finished his masterpiece EIS and signed it off one day before he left state employment. Coincidence?"

Her electronic reply was immediate. "Are sure? That looks weird! Tread softly!"

He wasn't interested in treading softly. There were too many questions, irritating little questions that needed answers. And no one in authority cared.

That evening, Ryan was sitting in the green corduroy recliner. It was comfortable, but prehistoric, and the slightest move evoked squeaks. Meagan was busy in the kitchen preparing dinner. Chicken breasts in marinara sauce. Diced eggplant in a little olive oil with brown rice and garlic. With a book on Mediterranean cuisine, she was becoming a great cook. Ryan would usually be nearby, pilfering samples as she worked, and they would be talking about the work-day or about the next phase in the house. This evening he was sitting quietly to the living room. The television was on low.

He had tried to push Robert Newberg out of his mind, without results. Over the Internet and from phone books in the DEQ's small library, he had copied down telephone numbers for all the Newbergs he could find in eastern Oregon. Three lived in Pendleton; six more resided within a hundred miles. There was one Raymond Newberg, two R. Newbergs. He sat with the television on and dialed while Meagan moved about the kitchen. The search seemed pointless; there were no Roberts. The more numbers he dialed, the worse it seemed.

Ryan dialed the eighth Newberg, in The Dalles, out in the desert. A man's voice answered. A recording, please leave a message. A quick glance to the kitchen: Meagan was occupied.

He cupped the mouthpiece. "My name is Ryan Evans. I'm looking for a Robert Newberg. He was employed some time back by Oregon DEQ in Pendleton. If you could help me locate him, I'd be grateful."

Ryan left his work number. He read the ninth number from the paper in his lap and dialed. A woman answered. He spoke low into the receiver. "I'm looking for a Robert Newberg."

Blue jeans appeared.

The woman spoke. "We don't have a Robert here. Just Marcus and Sissy, that's me."

Ryan's eyes traveled up the jeans to a wooden spatula, cupped in a paper towel. "Do you know of a Robert?"

"I don't. I'm sorry."

"All right, thanks."

Ryan hung up. He looked upward. "How's dinner?"

"It's ready." Meagan's voice was sweet, tentative. That voice. "Who was that?"

He put the phone in his lap and scratched his forehead. "Uh, I'm looking to see if I can find this guy, Newberg."

She blinked twice and pushed the hair from her eyes. "You're still chasing that?"

"Meggy, the whole thing, the original permits? The approval? I think it was all illegal."

Meagan stared, dumbfounded. Monday's 1:00 a.m. conversation on the kitchen floor was fresh in her mind. "Ryan, it's over. You said it yourself! They won! They have a multi-million dollar hole in the ground, and there is nothing you can do about it. You think you're going to shut it all down?"

He scratched his eyebrow. "It looks fraudulent."

She faced him directly, with the spatula clenched in both hands. His protests in high school and college, his unwavering principles, her parents' reaction to him, she found it all endearing. Not this obsessiveness.

"No, Ryan. It looks dangerous. At Gabe's party, he talked all about how he was going to get more involved, whatever that meant. He died that weekend!"

Ryan fell silent.

"Honey, this isn't some detective game."

"I know it's not a game."

"Then give it up! Now, for me! Let it go."

# Chapter 15

In a windowless office, a skinny, bald-headed man named Jordy sat at his computer and read email. A cigarette hung from his lips and smoke poured from his nostrils like water. He tugged at his blond goatee and occasionally emitted a dry snicker. Jordy and his partner, Don, sat and quietly scanned email. It was correspondence between DEQ biologists and their counterparts at Oregon's Department of Fish and Wildlife, between lab technicians and engineers. Email between various state agencies and the Governor's office.

The Information Technology office at Summit Resources was also its security office. The one-room facility was located down a quiet dog-leg hall, past the telephone equipment room. Far from traffic, a pushbutton lock provided entry through a gray steel door. Here, the term "information" had a very different meaning.

A third man sat and watched video tapes. The head of IT for Summit Resources, Joe Santini was barrel-chested, with black curly hair and a beard trimmed tight. The videos were of the countless protestors that had plagued the company for months, and had been taken from a brown van that was usually parked just down the street from the Wells Fargo building. They were videos of college kids, young professionals, dropouts, and out-of-staters. For many, faces had been matched with names, names with addresses. Some had young families and nice little homes in the suburbs.

Jordy and Don sifted through the emails each day, thanks to a software program timed to run on the state's computer servers in Salem. Coded by Jordy, a proficient hacker, the hidden program copied and forwarded all email sent or received by a long list of persons working for the state. The messages were forwarded daily to servers at Summit Resources and added to a large and growing database. And each day, all records of this illegal activity were deleted from the state's computers.

On Summit's own computers, another of Jordy's programs combed through the stolen emails and flagged those messages containing certain key words and names. The code provided an open view of the state's internal operations, its people and decision-making processes, and the status of Summit's applications. It also delivered utterly priceless gems of sensitive information. The haul included email about personal problems, illicit relationships, and occasional unhealthy addictions. Jordy was proud of his work. Compensated a mere thousand dollars (in cash), he would have done it for free. Sarinov called it "risk management." The only liabilities were Jordy and Don, and they would never talk. Silence was a badge, an earned credential. And they knew better.

Jordy relished his work. Occasionally, a particularly juicy piece came by and the best "juice" carried on for days, with explicit replies flying back and forth. This week, a new dialogue was underway. Tammy Finholm, a recent college hire, had been fired by her manager. She was claiming that he had groped her after asking her to work late, and that she had been fired for rejecting his numerous sexual advances. Married and with family, he was proclaiming innocence. Upper-level managers were quietly panicking; attorneys were getting involved. Jordy paged down with skinny yellow fingers and peered through the smoke.

Jordy was adept at spotting the most sensitive messages, and on this particular day, just before five p.m., he caught it. A person on the list, a certain Ryan Evans, had written an email that contained a key name: Robert Newberg.

Jordy snapped the cigarette from his thin lips. "Mr. Santini, take a look at 88349. And 88441."

Santini turned from the protestors and jabbed at his keyboard with sausage index fingers. The emails opened on screen. He read them quickly and then grabbed the phone.

Paddy's Tavern was a fragrant little hole on a main industrial drag in northeast Portland. North of Paddy's was a sheet metal manufacturer, south, a dilapidated strip joint named Sweet Cherries. For Paddy's, business had been barely enough until the strip joint opened. Then things went from slow to dead. Paddy's would be empty at seven on a dark Tuesday evening.

A man wearing a black trench coat with the collar turned up parked his white Lincoln Towncar at a gas mart two blocks over. He left the car under a flickering light, hoped it would be left alone, and walked quickly to the bar.

A cold easterly from the Gorge carried hard sleet that bit his face. One of Sarinov's nameless had called earlier in the day. Arland Lochner, his face bathed in crimson by the neon Budweiser sign, paused at the door and nervously checked the streets. Face-to-face meetings were rare, but he hated them. Certainly a parking lot in the suburbs would have sufficed.

It was darker inside than out. The smell of the bar hit him, years of smoke, alcohol, and body fluids. Under a feeble light, one tired patron sat permanently hunched at the bar. The bartender leaned back against the bar, stared into the shadows and smoked. A grossly stained apron girdled his vast gut. Seventies rock played on a scratchy sound system.

A row of booths lined the far right wall, empty except for the last. Lochner ventured across the sticky floor and slid in. Torn vinyl seats dragged at his trench coat.

"You're late," the man growled.

"What's wrong?"

"Evans is what's wrong."

Lochner sucked in the bar's stench and almost gagged. "What do you mean?"

"We know everything that goes on in that building. The kid is digging around, asking too many questions. He's challenging the permits. He's asking about Newberg."

Lochner's voice shuddered. "How do you know all this?"

"You don't ask the fucking questions. What the hell are you going to do about it?"

"He's nothing! What he's talking about can be explained, it's the bureaucracy. I'll keep an eye on him. This will go nowhere."

The man leaned forward from the shadows, his eyebrows and face contorted in anger. "You screwed up the date on the signature, you dumbass! He's yapping to co-workers. He knows too much and he's looking for more. If your damned little detective runs with this, the consequences will be severe, for everyone. Do you get it?"

The Allman Brothers howled. A frightening darkness closed around Lochner. "I'll handle it!"

"You'll handle it?" The man's barking words cut the darkness. "This is straight from Sarinov. You shut him down, or we will."

Lochner's head snapped back. "Another one will bring in the authorities! Please! I'll take care of him."

"Wise up! We know exactly what goes on at DEQ, HCD, and ten other state offices. We know when your little boy takes a piss. He's out of control. Fix it."

## CHAPTER 16

Miranda pushed an oak cart full of pastries and coffee into the conference room. She wore a snug blue skirt and white blouse that showed off her figure today. Her dark spike heels wobbled slightly on the carpet as she walked.

Greer pointed to the corner. "Over there is fine. I need a set of markers for the white board, there aren't any here. Plus an eraser. And over lunch, get a transparency projector."

Greer turned to the group of men seated at the long conference table. They were immersed in diagrams and specifications that described the construction of gold and furnace buildings at the Haystack Mine. The gold building was a large structure in which a stream of liquid, heavy with gold and silver, and toxic with arsenic, cyanide, and other poisons, would be continuously washed over beds of charcoal. The charcoal would later be burned away in a gas furnace, leaving the precious metals behind.

Three of the men were in ties. They were from a consulting firm, Reynolds and Strout Engineering. The other two were Greer's reports, Jim Leonard and Ron Schnell, young engineers who would work with the firm.

Greer addressed the group. "Do we need anything else?"

Leonard looked up. "I think we're good."

Miranda spoke. "You could use a pitcher of ice water, maybe some juice."

Greer addressed her. "I'll need someone to take minutes in here, decisions, conclusions. It'll be all week, through Friday."

"You wanted the Miner's Creek update printed out by noon."

"Get Rita to do that. I need you in here. She can cover for you the rest of the week. Use my laptop, it's on my desk. We'll get going in here in a few minutes."

Miranda nodded. "I'll be right back."

Greer turned to the group. "We have three days. We need to finalize the Haystack plans for state compliance with codes and we need to address all of the remaining issues raised by Utah's examiners. They're giving us grief over the size of the pad and the location of the ponds. Drainage from the area feeds four streams. On the far table there, we have a full set of their latest codes and complete topographical maps of the Wasatch Range."

Greer leaned on the end of the table. "Our deadline for resubmission is a week out. We need to wrap up Haystack by this Friday. Can we get it done?"

The suited consultants nodded politely while helping themselves to cinnamon twists. Hesitant nods from his two engineers offered a weak consensus.

The door opened partway and a young woman poked her head in, one of Sarinov's numerous female assistants. "Mr. Greer, Mr. Sarinov wants to see you," she announced.

Greer frowned. Sarinov didn't schedule many meetings; he ran everything on interrupts. "Now?"

"Yes. He says it's urgent."

Greer knocked as he entered Sarinov's office. A large bouquet of flowers sat on the cherry table. The man was standing at his glass wall and looking down at where the protestors had laid siege to the building two weeks previous.

"You wanted me?" Greer asked.

Sarinov turned. "Greer, fly up to Justene tomorrow morning, the chopper leaves at 8:30. The main leach pad has been filled with fresh ore. Yield is at 3.1. Get me another gram out of it."

Greer couldn't avoid scowling. Another gram of gold from a ton of Justene ore was delusional. "I'm working with Reynolds and Strout through Friday. They're here to finalize Haystack. I've got—"

Sarinov's head shook violently. "Delegate it! Delegate it and leave. Your guys can handle it. Pack for an overnighter."

"But Jacob, Harquail and his people did the permits to expand Justene. He knows that mine better than I do."

Wayne Harquail was VP of Development and Operations. He had worked for months on the applications for the expansion.

Sarinov's head shook again. "No. Harquail is busy, you can dial this in."

Greer slowly pushed the door close until it latched. He turned. "Jacob. Listen to me. I fully respect your opinion on this, but Justene is a sink hole. There isn't enough gold—"

Sarinov's eyes ignited. "We should be pulling out five grams! Dammit Greer, you're good at this! I've watched you! We're finally getting close to break-even, another half gram and we're there! You get up there up there and troubleshoot it. Do it! You break four grams and the VP slot is yours."

Greer stared at his boss. The sacred, elusive VP slot. If Greer's making VP hinged on success at Justene, it would never be. But often, the facts just didn't impact Sarinov. He simply ignored them.

Greer took a deep breath. "Jacob, I sited and planned Sugarloaf. I sited and planned Haystack, and Miner's Creek will follow. They'll all yield over six grams. It's not the solution, or how much cyanide, or the size of the leach pad. It's the ore quality. These mines have gold."

"No! I've told Westfall it's your show! Dammit, I want you to own this! Four grams!"

The next morning, Greer caught the helicopter on top of the high-rise. Not fond of freezing at 8,000 feet, he wore thick ski pants, insulated boots, a flannel shirt, and a gray winter parka. He was the lone passenger this time and attempted to relax. It wasn't easy. He had been forced to leave a warm office, jump into a freezing tin can, and produce a miracle from a three hundred million dollar fiasco.

After fighting the weather for an hour and a half, the chopper finally approached the mine. The arrival of so much harsh weather gave the site a different look. Snow had been plowed from the roads in the pit and around the buildings and deposited in massive piles. The cyanide ponds lay like giant, dark sores in the white world.

Greer noticed it as they passed the first pond. Below, a dark, ragged line ran like dried blood down the white berm. The meaning of it took a moment to register, and then Greer was up from his seat and at the pilot's side.

He tapped the pilot's shoulder and shouted over the engines. "Can you circle around again, around the ponds? Low and slow?"

The pilot obliged, dropped the chopper in low, and made a sweeping arc.

It was unmistakable. On the first pond, on the down hill side, a jagged line traced down the full berm, emptying in a dark swath that spread across the white perimeter road. A nearly identical breach was visible at the third pond.

The chopper touched down and as the jets unwound to a stop, the pilot turned. "Mr. Greer, the National Weather Service has a severe storm moving in. It was supposed to head north, but it's coming our way. We have three hours, max. Then we need to get out."

Greer nodded. "All right." He wasn't spending the night in this frozen hellhole, regardless of what Sarinov wanted.

Outside, the mine pit channeled the cold wind, driving ice pellets that stung Greer's face and ears. He trudged through the snow and up the steel steps of Westfall's trailer.

Inside, the metal box was dark and icy. Westfall was sitting in his chair like a black mummy, wrapped up in a parka with a hood over his head. A cigar glowed red in his face. A bottle of amber liquid sat on his desk.

"What the hell are you doing here?" Westfall's dry voice screeched.

Greer slammed the door against the stiff wind. "You've got major problems."

"No shit! We're freezing our asses off!"

"No power?"

"We lost power three hours ago! A generator is down and this place is hell without heat."

"You've got bigger problems. You've got breaches in the berms around ponds 2 and 3. You're spilling that crap into the water table, haven't you seen it?"

Westfall sneered. "Fuck, whatever! Millions of gallons of pressure, it's gonna leak."

Greer's mind stopped. Did this person have a clue?

"Get me a snowcat," Geer demanded. "I need to take a look."

"I don't have time for your shit! We've got other problems here."

"Get me a snowcat. You're coming with me."

"Like hell I am!"

Greer glared at Westfall. "You get me a snowcat and join me, or you'll be looking for another job."

Westfall jumped from his chair, with his red eyes popped wide. He stood and fumed, apparently considering the possibility of losing his blessed job in nirvana. He finally screeched a string of vulgarities and grabbed the black radio from his desk. "Thornton! Thornton! Get a cat over to my office, now!"

Westfall slammed down the phone and pounded the cigar into an ashtray. "I don't have time for this shit, Jenny! You're screwing with me and I don't have time for it!"

Greer zipped up the parka, pulled up the hood, and stepped outside to wait.

The machine pulled up after a bone-chilling 15 minutes. It was a large, noisy, four-door diesel truck outfitted with revolving tracks instead of tires. Greer banged on Westfall's trailer with his fist and then stepped down and climbed into the vehicle. Inside, the heater was on. A minute later, Westfall climbed down the steps and joined him.

Greer shouted above the engine to the driver, a bearded man in a parka. "Pond 3! Take the perimeter road!"

The driver put the vehicle in gear and the diesel clattered. Westfall lit up a new cigar while spouting fresh expletives. He puffed furiously, as though attempting to suffocate his guest. "These goddamned pencil-pushing office bitches think they can tell me what to do?!"

Greer cracked open the window and worked to ignore the provocation.

The trip to the ponds wound through a white network of roads, with snow piled many feet high on both sides. After ten minutes, the berm of the first pond came up on the right. Twice as wide as a football field, the snow-covered hill climbed 80 feet. Behind it lay a 12-acre pond of poison. The problem appeared dead ahead. A dark smear, 50 feet wide, covered the road. The driver approached within ten yards and stopped.

Greer stepped out, escaping certain asphyxiation. The wind whipped the sleet and the truck's diesel clattered. He cautiously approached the spill.

Ahead and to the right, a dark rivulet, three feet wide, drained from the side of the berm. Starting high above, it cut deeply through the snow and flowed all the way down to the road. There, it splayed out, black and viscous. On the opposite side of the road, the fluid collected into a long, dark ditch and then disappeared under the 12 foot wall of snow. For a moment, Greer only stared.

From his coat, he pulled a small digital camera and snapped off several pictures. He then turned back to the berm itself and looked for additional leaks. None were visible, but he caught something not apparent from the air. The slanted face of the berm wasn't flat. Down the face for at least two hundred feet, as far as he could see in the sleet, a giant bulge was unmistakable. He took more pictures and then pocketed the camera and began carefully climbing up the side of the berm.

The surface was crusted over with thick white-blue ice, but it cracked and he sank in past his knees. After several minutes, he had climbed half way up to the source. He breathed hard in the chilled wind. High above the truck, Greer anchored his feet into the snow and peered into the crevasse. The drainage was four or five feet wide and cut deep into the snow. Down inside, the stream was visible, but it was too opaque to judge the depth or rate of flow. Steam slowly wafted from it and disappeared in the wind. He could smell it, could taste in his throat. The thick, putrid taste of sulfur, and the odor of almonds. Cyanide. Greer took still more pictures. He then carefully inched away from the crevasse, turned onto his back, and slid slowly down to the road.

At the cat, Westfall was yelling. "What the hell are you taking pictures of?!"

"Sarinov and Harquail need to see what they have up here."

"We don't allow any cameras here! Sarinov's rules!"

"How long has this been here?"

"Who knows?"

"You have another breach on 3. Are there more?"

Westfall shrugged violently. "Fuck if I know!"

The response was nearly more than Greer could take. Westfall angrily chewed his cigar and spit it into the snow. Sleet pelted his leathery face, skin preserved like animal hide.

"Westfall, you have a train wreck here," Greer proclaimed. "You need to shut the mine down."

"Bullshit!"

Greer pointed a finger at Westfall. "You don't get it! The liner is broken! The side of this berm is expanded, you can see it there. This whole berm is in danger of giving way. And you have more just like it. I'm shutting it down."

"Like hell! We'll clear out the snow. Pack in 20 tons of fill!"

"No! Any heavy vehicles on this could cause the whole side to give way!"

"Twenty tons! That'll stop it! Hell, it's just ground water coming up."

They glared at each other in silence, as if lacking a common language.

Greer nodded. "Hell, yeah. Sure, that's what it is. It's fresh fucking mountain spring water. Why don't you get down on your knees and take a sip?"

"Screw you, jackass." Westfall leaned forward, his chest out. The bulge of the gun was visible under the coat.

Time to go, thought Greer. He moved toward the door of the snowcat. "I want you to kill operations here, now, until this is resolved."

"Like hell! You tell that to Sarinov!"

"I will. I will."

On the return flight, Greer was filled with anxiety, but also a cynical sense of satisfaction. Westfall and Sarinov had finally done it. They had overloaded the system for months, years probably, running too much cyanide, trying to suck out every last trace of gold. At now, two cyanide ponds were breached.

Darkness had already fallen when the chopper touched down on the Wells Fargo roof top.

At Sarinov's office door, Greer knocked. A muffled sound came from inside. Greer pushed the door open a few inches.

"Jacob?"

The dark office was lit only by the lights of adjacent buildings. Sarinov stood outlined against the windows. He turned. "Greer? What the hell are you doing here?"

Greer approached. The office was quiet and he spoke softly. "Jacob, we've got problems. We have breaches at the berms of two of the cyanide ponds. I'm estimating at least 300 gallons an hour. We need to build slews to recover what we can, and we need to stop leaching operations until—"

Sarinov laughed loudly. "What the hell are you talking about? We're about to make money there! We're not stopping now."

Greer took a breath. "We have a major problem on our hands, Jacob, and this is stateside. Maybe we can do this in Mexico or South America, but not here. This thing will only get worse. And downstream are people."

"So when the expansion gets going, we'll open up new ponds. We'll drain the leakers and fix them with the expansion."

"That's many months out. We're in danger of a major breach now. With all of the pressure, plus the spring rains and melt, the underside of the berms could burst. We need to act quickly."

"Don't get hysterical on me, Greer! I'll have Westfall's guys drop 40 tons of crushed rock on the berms. That'll stop it."

"But that won't fix it. It's deep in the liners. A serious breach and we could have dead fish floating in the Snake River." Greer turned square to his boss. "The state and the feds will crucify us."

Sarinov's hand landed on Greer's shoulder. "Greer, you worry too damned much. For chissake, I asked you to work on yield, not come back here with this. Shit happens. Justene's in the middle of nowhere. I operate a business! You're not some faggot working for Greenpeace, you work for me. And I want yield."

Sarinov turned Greer around and pushed him to the door. "Go home. Get some sleep. Screw your wife. When you come back tomorrow, make sure your priorities are straight."

Sarinov pushed Greer out the door and locked it.

A quiet voice floated out of the darkness. "He's a problem."

"Whatever. At least he's straight with me, not like the rest of you. He tells me everything."

"He's about to panic."

Sarinov snorted. "He's sited two mines for me and they'll both pay off big. And he's about to site two more. Greer has a nose for gold."

Joe Santini was invisible in the darkness. "He's a boy scout, with a conscience. He could cause a lot of problems."

"Never, and I'll tell you why. He and the wife love the money too much. No one will turn because the money is too good, and even if he did, he'd confess it in advance and ask for my forgiveness." Sarinov turned. "His mother raised him Catholic. You ever go to church, Santini?"

"Yeah, every Sunday. I confess everything, takes me hours." Santini stood from the sofa. "Your alter boy interrupted my last question. What do I do about Evans?"

"Watch him."

# Chapter 17

Greer awoke the next morning with a raging hangover. When he arrived home the night before, Barbara was out and didn't get back until after midnight. After a very short dinner with little Patricia and Bridgett, he spent the night in the den, in a panic, with a bottle of gin and another of soda water.

Arriving at work, he passed Miranda's desk with his eyes down, avoiding hers. Miranda followed Greer into his office with a double Americano, two lumps, and the Wall Street Journal. She had set up a personal espresso machine for him behind a divider near her desk. Greer rested his elbows on his desk and his forehead on his palms. The suit was gone; today it was open shirt, no tie.

She set the coffee on his desk. "Do you need anything?" she asked softly.

His dry voice rasped harshly. "Got any aspirin?"

She quickly retrieved the bottle from her desk. He shook out three and swallowed them dry. She handed him the coffee.

"How was the helicopter ride?" she asked.

He gulped the hot coffee and waived her off. Again the rasp. "Where's Leonard?"

"I'll get him."

She left and returned quickly with Jim Leonard. Miranda had briefed him about the state of their boss and now they stood quietly, several feet from his desk, as he held his head.

Leonard finally ventured a greeting. "Good morning, boss."

Greer lifted his head.

Leonard was less restrained than Miranda. "Oh jezze, you *do* look like hell."

Greer grabbed his head and winced. "Don't talk so loud. Does the conference room have coffee?"

Miranda replied in a near whisper. "I cleaned up and had the caterers bring in fresh coffee, juice, and pastries."

"How did it go here, yesterday?"

"Good," Leonard replied proudly. "On Haystack, we've completed the review of the pad. We're increasing elevation of the base by 50 feet—"

Greer's hand went up. "Leonard, *please!*"

Leonard was tall, blond, and always enthusiastic. He hesitated and then whispered. "Sorry. Uhh. We did good, hope to tie it up today. They have a flight out at seven tonight, so it'll be tight. We may need a final review. A few tweaks, nothing more. We can do that with overnight mail and should be able submit everything to the state March 7th."

Greer continued whispering. "We can't let this slide past the 7th or we'll miss schedule. I'm taking the 3rd week of March as vacation, starting the 14th. You're confident?"

Leonard nodded. "Yeah. Yes."

His boss exhaled a long sigh. "You don't need me after all. I can quit this damned place."

Leonard and Miranda traded looks.

Greer continued. "What about Ironwood?"

"We tried to get started on that, but the plans, the markups are missing. I had them. I was entering changes into the CAD system, but they're gone. I've looked everywhere."

Greer rubbed his temples. "Shit."

To Greer, the company often appeared to run on nothing but chaos. No management, no structure, just chaos. Sarinov knew little about site engineering, but he frequently injected unworkable ideas into the planning of the next mine, always to double, quadruple. Greer remembered seeing the Ironwood plans. "Sarinov."

Miranda spoke. "He and Mr. Warren left for New York. They won't be back until late Saturday."

Greer scowled. "Check his desk, Miranda. They should be lying out. A couple hundred pages." Greer looked at Leonard. "Diagrams too?"

Leonard nodded.

Greer scowled with obvious contempt. "Just grab everything on his desk. Leave it here, I want to check it over before we share it with Reynolds."

Miranda prepared another cup for her boss, Americano with two lumps, and then left with Leonard.

Greer held his head in his hands. How badly he needed the week off. For the last few years, he had made a point of getting the hell out of town in February, sometimes March, for a week by himself. Anywhere worked. This time it was a ski lodge in Idaho, away from the company. And away from Barbara, or perhaps just away from the anger over sex withheld and a wife who was never there to argue with anyway. This year, it was also week away from Bridgette. Beautiful, playful Bridgette.

Six doors down from Greer's office was the office of the Vice President of Development and Operations, Wayne Harquail.

All of the VPs viewed themselves to be Greer's boss; they all had opinions of what he should be doing and how quickly he should be doing it. But aside from Sarinov's frequent grilling, Harquail was his functional manager.

Greer knocked. Surprisingly, Harquail was in. Maybe, thought Greer, just maybe he could find a rational ally.

The man was on the phone. Harquail was tall, in his forties, and trim. He always wore a half smile, or it could've been a smirk—Greer was never sure.

Harquail pointed to the chair and then covered the mouthpiece. "Haystack?" he asked Greer.

"On schedule."

Harquail was always busy. His oversized, L-shaped desk was covered in paperwork, three large flat screens, and three telephones—including the one in his hand. Harquail turned away in his high-back chair and whispered into the phone, too low to be heard.

He swung around as he hung up. "What?" he demanded.

"We have a problem at Justene."

Harquail smirked. "Do we now?"

"Two of the four cyanide ponds are leaking. The berms are compromised, they're overfilled with excessive irrigation. I talked with Sarinov last night—"

"I know *all* about it." The tone was sarcastic.

Greer ignored the interruption. "We need to suspend operations there until we can mitigate the drainage."

Harquail's hand went to his chin. His eyes narrowed as though he was in serious thought. "Greer, you're earning a bad reputation here, as our corporate nanny. The area around Justene is permeated with old mine shafts. It's been leaking acid drainage for a hundred years, you can't tell how much is background and how much isn't."

"We're currently loosing 300 gallons of leach an hour. It's draining straight into the watershed."

Harquail rolled his gray eyes. "With the rainfall, there's ten times that much drainage occurring naturally. All of our mines leak Greer, get used to it. With the millions of gallons of that shit? The pressure on the berms and under the leach pads? Do you actually expect none of it to leak?" Harquail threw a hand up in disbelief. "Don't you have a week off coming up? Some winter trip to Nome?"

Greer wanted to reach out and slap the man. "Idaho."

"Take it. You need it."

"Did you know that Justene is running twice the limit of cyanide that our permits allow?"

Harquail's face went flat. "Shut up."

"Excuse me?"

Harquail tapped the desktop with his finger. "I don't want to hear it. All of our reports to the state are clean. We're clean. You tell me about Ironwood."

"But—"

"Ironwood! That's all I want to know about! You tell me about Ironwood!"

So this is how the game is played, thought Greer. "Ironwood is on schedule."

"Excellent! Now get out of here, I've got work to do." Wayne Harquail pointed to the door.

Lunch. Greer gave the group a full hour. He had planned to join them for a working lunch, but instead he retreated to his office and closed the door. At the small sink in back, he swallowed more aspirin, drank a full glass of water, and then splashed it on his face.

He staggered back to the desk. The conversation with Harquail left him angry. He eased down into the chair and thumbed through the stack of papers Miranda had left. They were the Ironwood mine specs and they were covered with questions, black marker questions from Sarinov about doubling the size of the pit and expanding the leach pads.

Greer snarled. "Stupid idiot."

The plans had already been through engineering for this site, with its specific terrain and topography. The mine was so colossal that the position of mountain ridges and valleys dictated its layout. But Sarinov couldn't accept limitations imposed by mountains. Just like Justene. Justene was too large for its location, yield was marginal at best, and he was quadrupling its size! And more bizarre, the state had approved it! What gathering of fools worked there?

Greer's gut began flipping cartwheels. He leaned over in the chair and held his stomach. His teeth were clenched so hard that his jaw hurt. Maybe he should run. He had already made a lot of money, maybe it was time to sell his millions in stock and quit the damned company, before Justene spilled its guts and the stock price crashed.

The idea was painful to consider, he was making half a million a year in salary and bonuses and another half a million in stock. Twenty thousand a week. Five hundred dollars an hour. He had done the math before, more than once. Fucking unbelievable money. When he made VP, if it ever happened, everything would at least triple.

If he quit, Barbara would leave him, probably that same day, and perhaps not a bad thing. The woman was never satisfied. She was greedy as hell and never, *never* satisfied. But beautiful. Such an evil combination.

Greer thumbed angrily through the plans and sneered at Sarinov's markups. The headache worsened.

Mixed in with the plans and diagrams were thick manila folders. He opened one. A man's name was at the top of the first sheet, Gabe Riplinger, his age, address, phone numbers. His employment history. Head of Water Quality at DEQ, widowed.

His hobbies. Also listed were the names of relatives and friends, their addresses. The fifth page was an eight-by-ten color photograph of the old guy with his dog, standing in front of a wooden boat. Following that were several more pages. These were email transcripts, with dates and names.

Greer briefly glanced up at the closed office door.

Here were copies of email about Justene. Riplinger was attacking DEQ's lax oversight of the mine. Many pages of email. Riplinger was very opinionated.

Greer pushed back from the desk and slid the papers onto his lap, below the desk top. At the bottom of the last page, someone had handwritten several notes. *Trouble. Plans to go public.* Below that: *$500K* Then a date. *January 13.*

Greer again checked the door.

Another folder was about a Ryan Evans, with the same information. Home address, phone numbers, place of work. Oregon DEQ. The second page listed the name of his wife, her occupation, in-laws in Seattle. And written in pen, *no kids, one small dog.* Two large photographs showed the couple leaving a Home Depot, obviously without their knowledge. Lots of email. Some sentences were highlighted in yellow, opinionated comments about the Justene expansion. The last page held similar scribbled notes in pen. *Trouble. Questioning Riplinger's situation. Asking about Newberg. Challenging approval. A candidate.*

Greer stared at the scribbled notes. *A candidate?*

He scanned a third folder. It was heavy and provided a similar bio on Arland Lochner, the Director of DEQ. Personal details of his wife, his two sons, a daughter. One son had been arrested at age 15 for auto theft, acquitted of rape charges. The wife was in and out of rehab. More photographs. Pages of emails. At the bottom of this backgrounder, the same person had again written *$500K*, and then one word: *Ours.*

The last folder. Senator Loren Phillips. A picture of the Senator and his wife, on a boat, smiling, drinks in hand. Miscellaneous background information.

Greer sat. His swollen brain refused to cooperate. *Where in the hell did this come from?* Miranda? She took it from Sarinov's office with the Ironwood plans?

He quickly shoveled the papers back into their folders. His watch read 12:20. Greer slid the folders into his briefcase, glided to the office door, and peered out.

The hallway was empty. The secretary pen was vacant; the ladies were at lunch.

He skirted down the hall to the copier room. Here, Greer opened each of the folders and without removing staples, photocopied most of their contents. The machine was never fast; right now, it crawled. Ten minutes later he left the copier room.

Greer slipped back down the hallway to "officer's row," where the company's VPs resided. Sarinov's office was unlocked and Greer entered quietly. He had been in here only the night before, arguing about Justene. At the man's desk, he opened the briefcase and set the folders down. He paused. The desktop was mostly empty. He pushed the folders casually off center. Greer then shut the briefcase, left the office, and quietly closed the door.

## Chapter 18

Twenty-four months previous, when the company began amassing stolen emails and profiling its friends and potential enemies, Sarinov had issued an edict. Not one video tape, illicit email or "red file" was to ever leave the confines of Santini's locked offices. The risks were too great.

The call came in the afternoon, as Sarinov and Warren were sipping whiskey in an airport lounge in Denver and the Citation was being refueled. The red files, the risk profiles on Evans, Lochner, Riplinger, and Phillips, were missing.

Santini, Sarinov's vaunted head of security, had broken a cardinal rule. He had brought the files into Sarinov's office the night before to review the Evans situation. While they were guzzling alcohol and reviewing strategy, Greer had dropped in unannounced. Santini had placed the red files on Sarinov's desk and, slightly drunk, forgotten them in the darkened office. The following morning, after discovering that he had not locked them away in his IT cave, he frantically searched every possible location—without results. Santini had to make the call.

The CEO was enraged. He stormed through Denver International while shouting profanities into his cell phone. Sarinov yearned to exact penalties for such a monumental mistake, but ultimately, there was little to be done. Santini was irreplaceable. He was the point man for the most critical tasks, from wiretaps to murder.

The second call was made as Sarinov de-boarded at La Guardia. Santini revealed the news: Greer had seen the red files.

So after returning to Portland late Saturday, at the end of the dogleg hall, Jacob Sarinov wrapped his right index finger in a white handkerchief and punched the security code on the keypad. It clicked loudly. He entered and closed the steel door. The deadbolt locked.

Santini motioned to a chair. "Have a seat Jacob. Coffee?"

The man had never offered coffee to anyone in his life.

Sarinov stood. The Armani suit was rumpled and his face was drawn. "What in the hell happened?" he demanded. "Are you sure it was Greer?"

Santini cleared his throat. "I sat in the conference room across from the copiers. I sat behind a plastic plant. From there I could see the copy room, but also keep an eye down the hall to your office. I figured that whoever had them would realize that they shouldn't and might bring them back. Over the lunch hour, I watched Greer leave the copy room with his briefcase in hand and head straight for your office."

"He made copies?"

"No other reason to be there."

"Did he have the folders in his hand?"

"In his briefcase. He entered your office and closed the door. After a few seconds, he came back out and returned to his office. I went in immediately afterward."

"You never saw them in his hand?"

"No, but—"

"How can you be sure he had them?"

*You can't be this fucking stupid*, Santini thought. "They were missing before he went in. They were on your desk after he left."

"Dammit! Are you certain he copied them?"

"I checked the counter on the copier. 322 copies were made from the morning at around nine, until he put the files back in your office. For a period of three and a half hours, that's too many copies. I know he had the files in his possession. He copied them."

Sarinov paced. "Why the hell didn't you just stop him?"

Santini's eyes narrowed. "Why does your perky little secretary have keys to your office? Greer's assistant got the keys from her! The only spare keys should be locked up in here."

Sarinov stopped pacing. His glare was lethal. "You brought those damned files into my office. I didn't ask for them, goddamn you! Your security files, in my office? I should fire your ass!"

A nasty little smile crossed Santini's broad face. Muted anger ranged. Fire me? Fire me? I know everything! You need me! Santini pulled a slow, deliberate breath and spoke with absolute serenity. "It won't happen again. We searched his office Friday night. He took the copies home."

Sarinov cursed under his breath and paced.

Santini breathed methodically, slowly. "So what's the damage, really? There isn't that much in those folders. We don't say 'Kill Riplinger.'"

Sarinov's eyes flew to the door. "Shut up!"

"The room is soundproof. It's Saturday night."

"I don't give a shit."

"The folders contain nothing more than background information. No explicit instructions to take action of any kind. Maybe we're over-reacting."

Sarinov turned. "They contain too much information! And your cute little code words aren't rocket science, anyone can figure it out! Greer wants to close Justene! Thanks to you, he has seen our files on the people at DEQ! The emails, Lochner, Riplinger and Evans, that rabid little Green Peace freak!"

Sarinov paced like an animal. One hand pinched his lower lip so hard that it looked as though it would burst. "I've got to know if Greer talks to Evans."

"Does Greer ever just pick up the phone and call DEQ?"

"Never! Where the hell have you been, Santini?" Sarinov stabbed the air. "All communications between the Summit and the permitting agencies, the regulators, it's all in writing and it all goes through Tucker and Harquail. Nobody just picks up the damned phone and calls the authorities!"

"We can tap his phones."

Sarinov stopped pacing. "Do it! Tap everyone, all of our officers. And legal, and accounting. Not me! I want twelve hours of backup per phone. I want monitoring on every call Greer makes. And while you're at it, do his home."

Santini leaned forward in the chair. "The company is easy. The house is another thing."

"You do it. Read your red files on Greer. Find a way, unless—does he have his own godamned file!?"

Santini leaned back. "No."

Sarinov's shoulders sagged visibly. He exhaled a long breath. "Bug his house phones. If Greer makes any calls to the state, especially Evans, I need to know immediately. It's time to bring him in."

"He's a boy scout."

"I don't give a shit, as long as he's our boy scout."

Sarinov moved to the door, the white handkerchief ready. His voice was ragged. "You track what he does with his free time, every minute. And don't you ever take any red files past this door."

Monday morning, Greer closed his office door, a door with no lock.

Back at the desk, his fingers shook as he flipped through the heavy phone book. The number would be listed in the blue pages. He was both exhausted and wired. Sleep had been impossible. With the record snow pack, the spring melt, and the breach underway, Justene would soon explode. He had a week or two, three at the most. If he was careful, Sarinov would never know who it was. It could easily be some environmentalist snowshoeing the back country and sneaking around the mine pit. They had done it before. Screwballs from Green War had dynamited the tracks of one the earth movers. They had once killed electric power to Justene for two days.

Greer dialed. The call went to a government operator. He asked for Ryan Evans. On the third ring, a man answered.

"Evans."

"Ryan Evans?" Greer spoke low.

"Speaking."

A pause. "Did you write up the state's environmental impact statement for the Justene mine?"

Ryan became puzzled; few people knew he was the principle author. "Yes I did, for the expansion anyway."

"So you know all about the site engineering and construction?"

"Who's calling?"

"Just listen. The containment ponds at Justene are on the verge of collapse. There are already two small breaches. The results will be catastrophic. You need to send a crew to the site and inspect everything."

Ryan paused. "Who is this?"

A metallic click sounded and Greer's office door swung wide open. Greer's eyes froze on Sarinov.

"Okay," Greer nodded. "All right. I'll bring it next week. Thanks." Greer put the phone in its cradle. "The Suburban needs a tune-up. What's up?"

Sarinov slowly closed the door behind himself. "How did Haystack go?" His words were measured.

Greer scrambled for his wits. "Good, good. We have some minor changes, editing work. We plan to submit to Utah March 7th."

Sarinov approached the desk. His usual rapid-fire energy was absent. But his eyes were busy.

"Did you find the specs on Ironwood?" Sarinov asked. "They were on my desk."

"Yes, Miranda found them."

The phone book, the blue government pages for Oregon State, lay wide open. Greer calmly closed the book as his left eyelid began to flutter.

"Miranda found them?" Sarinov queried.

"Right. She's good. Oh, Jacob. The leach pad revisions you asked for, to increase the size? I know we talked about it, but the site doesn't support an operation that large. Reynold's engineers agreed. They also advised against any changes. Actually the word they used was 'impossible.'"

Sarinov's eyes fell to the phone book. He then turned and left.

# Chapter 19

No sooner had Ryan hung up the phone when it rang again. He answered with apprehension. "This is Evans."

"Mr. Ryan Evans?" It was a woman's voice, timid.

No more surprises, please. Ryan's reply sounded more like a question. "It is."

"This is Mary Newberg. You called a few days ago. You're looking for Robert?"

"Umm. Yeah, yes." Ryan pulled a deep breath. "Where do you folks live?"

"I live in The Dalles."

"I work… I work at Oregon DEQ in Portland." Ryan dropped his voice. "The Robert I'm looking for worked for DEQ in Pendleton, four or five years ago?"

"Yes, he did."

"Is he available? I had a few simple questions about a study he developed."

The phone went silent for several seconds. Her voice was nearly inaudible. "He died four years ago."

The words delivered a cold chill.

"Are you there?"

"Yeah."

She continued. "He died in an accident. A fall from a helicopter."

Ryan stammered. "Would, would you mind telling me how?"

"How it happened? Mary Newberg's voice quivered badly. "He was working for the DEQ... was doing a survey with people from a mining company. Out past Pendleton."

"Justene?"

"Yes. He fell from their helicopter."

"The company helicopter? Summit Resources?"

"That's right."

Ryan's mind raced. He proceeded slowly. "Can I ask..."

"How does someone fall... over a thousand feet from a helicopter, in the rain?" Her unsteady voice rose and fell with her breathing. "Bobby wasn't stupid. He didn't take risks. In fact, he was afraid of heights. They said that while doing an aerial survey... he had opened the side door, stood at the edge. Was taking pictures. They said the helicopter dipped with a gust..."

The words suspended him. For Ryan, a moment of time slipped oddly, like a switch turning off and then on again. "I'm sorry. I'm very sorry." He was furiously gouging dents into a wooden pencil with his thumbnail. The next question screamed. It came as a whisper. "When did he die?"

"September 29. It was a Wednesday."

"September 29? 2004?"

"Yes. The day before Benjamin's birthday. Our son was just turning three."

The pencil snapped and fell. He leaned forward, dizzy, elbows on the desk. September 29! The man died the day after he signed the EIS?

"Are you there?" the woman asked.

"Was there an investigation? Who did the investigating?"

"The state police and the sheriff's department. They concluded that it was an accident. I've never been able to accept that."

Ryan could barely take it in. "I'm sorry. I'm sorry I bothered you."

"Why did you want to talk with him?"

"Uh, Summit is doing an expansion at Justene. I've been involved in the research."

"There was another man."

"I'm sorry, what?"

"Another man called from DEQ, six months ago. Gabe someone. He had a funny name."

"Gabe Riplinger? Gabe Riplinger called you?"

"Yes. He asked the same questions. I told him what I told you."

"Thanks."

Ryan hung up the phone.

After work on Monday, Greer called his wife's cell phone from the house. "Can you be home by eight? I picked up a few steaks. It's not raining. I'd thought I would light up the grill."

Her voice was indifferent. "What's the occasion?"

"We need to talk."

Barbara fussed with the phone; it crackled in his ear. They never talked, even by phone. They argued if they were both in the same room. She didn't answer his question.

"Where are Bridgette and Patty? Bridgett's car is here, but they're not."

"I think they're shopping."

"But her car is here."

"She said it wouldn't start. I said she could take your car."

"Bridgette has my Porsche?"

Barbara hissed loudly. "Yes!"

"Where are you?"

"I'm out!"

"No shit? When will you be here?"

"I'm out with the girls!"

He strained to catch voices. The background was indiscernible. His contempt simmered. "Out partying with the ladies from DARE?"

The phone was silent.

"Barbara!"

She had already hung up.

Sunset was coming a little later now. The orange ball had dipped below the coast mountains only 20 minutes earlier and it actually wasn't raining out. Below him, lights in the city came to life. Framed by the dark trunks of fir trees, distant streams of red and white light marked the traffic on Canyon road. Greer sat on the back deck under an awning and watched the western sky turn dark and the stars appear. Sheltered from the wind and wearing a jacket, he was comfortable.

Two raw, thick steaks were on a plate that rested on a glass patio table. He gulped down a beer, spouted a profanity, and threw the empty bottle. It sailed into the dark trees, making a hollow whoosh.

He had intended to wait for her, but she did her own thing. She liked to bar hop with "the girls," supposedly friends from her beauty salon days. She would frequently return to the house by two or three a.m. and crash on the davenport in the media room. He had debated hiring a detective. There had been fights. She had thrown things, expensive, breakable things. He had put his hand through the wall, and then he realized that he wasn't married, really. He was her race horse, Barbara's Bet. She did her thing, he did his. The house was big enough for a functional truce, but the marriage was all but dead. He had promised himself to cheat on her, and without really intending to, he had found Bridgette. With Barbara always missing, they had danced in the media room to the girl's playful music, had drank too much tequila more than once. They had started slow, kissed a couple times. A few weeks passed and they had touched each other, and then after a month, she had pulled him down onto a thick, white flokati rug and they had made love. Slow, intense love. She was spectacular, and he couldn't figure what the hell Barbara had been thinking in hiring the girl. Thinking about it all right now bothered him a lot. Life was far too complicated.

He spouted more profanity, grabbed another beer, and opened the gas grill.

Greer was asleep in the padded deck chair when the slider opened. Four empty beer bottles sat on the table, near the empty plate he had eaten dinner from. Two steaks, nothing else.

She kicked his chair. "Hey."

Nothing.

She kicked it again, harder.

He lifted his head from his folded arms.

"You wanted to talk?" she asked.

Greer looked up.

"You want a divorce?" she asked with a red-lipped smirk.

Greer rubbed his dry eyes. Barbara stood in her skin-tight jeans, with one hand on her hip and the other on the chair to steady herself.

He held his forehead. "What time is it?"

"I don't know."

"Are Patty and Bridgette back?"

She shrugged. "Yeah. What the hell did you want?" Her speech was slow and thick.

He drew in a breath of night air. "It's work."

"What did you do?"

"Nothing. They make a lot of money because of me."

Greer proceeded to tell her about Justene, the cyanide overloading, the acid breach. Somehow, she remained quiet long enough to listen.

"Sarinov insists on continuing. He needs to shut it down. I tell him, and he cuts me off. He says it's under control. But my name is all over this shit now, and when the state intervenes, and they will, my name is all over it."

Greer's head was spinning again, but it felt good to talk, even if she wasn't listening. His voice was calm, considering the words.

Her face contorted with impatience. "So what does all that mean?"

"Serious laws are being broken. I could go to prison."

She sat down across the table from him. This was the most talking they had done in months and she leaned in close, surprisingly attentive. "What are you planning to do?"

"I don't know."

"You wouldn't be talking to me unless you were planning something."

He looked at her and regretted that he was not completely sober. "Maybe I should go to the state about Justene."

Barbara pulled back, with her eyes wide under the flood light. "What?! And tell them that you're breaking the law?! Are you fucking insane?"

"To close it down, before it explodes. It's a disaster in the making, Barbara. And my name is all over it."

With a red mouth ajar, she stared at him. She leaned in again and took his hands. "Honey! Honey, look at us! We're rich! We're rich because of Jacob! You need to trust him, he knows what he's doing! If he says it's under control, you need to trust him."

Greer looked down at her hands, holding his. After so long, this contact felt repulsive.

She pushed on. "If you talk to the state about it, they will come down on you like SWAT! Yeah, you just might go to prison!" She shook her head. "No darling, no! It'll be all right. I need you. You need to trust Jacob."

'Darling?'

She stumbled around the table and fell into his lap. "You're a big worrier Jensen, you know that? You let things bother you too much. Promise me you'll trust him?"

He searched her eyes.

She unbuttoned her blouse under the broken clouds and intermittent stars. It was warm under the infrared glow. With a deft snap, she undid the blue bra and both cups fell to the side. Her smeared lips smiled. "You promise me? Promise? What would happen to me, with you in prison?"

His looked past her into the night and wondered why he had bothered. Nothing would happen to her. He would be convicted and sent away. She would marry whoever she was screwing. And she would keep everything. Millions, the house. Patricia.

# Chapter 20

Jensen worked hard the next couple of days, trying to distract himself from his troubles. There was plenty to keep him busy and if he worked hard enough the rest might go away, for just a little while.

At 3:00, one of Sarinov's slender, long-haired assistants knocked and opened the office door part way. "Mr. Sarinov wants to see you," she announced. "He's in the penthouse."

The penthouse? The penthouse was exclusive territory, a very large, plush apartment one floor up. Greer had visited the penthouse only once before, the month after he joined the company. It was a big dinner event, when Harquail had been appointed VP. From what he had could recall, the penthouse included an expansive lounge or boardroom with a view wall of windows, a dining room, a professional kitchen, and two master bedroom suites with sliders out to decks. The view was amazing. It had been loaded with fine furniture, a humidor, an expansive liquor selection and oversized high-def screens. And it was strictly the domain of the company's officers and their occasional guests.

Greer took the elevator and approached tentatively. The double cherry doors were wide open and all of the officers were there, Sarinov, Warren, Harquail, Tucker, even Otis and Widmere were present. Bruce Otis was VP of Human Resources; Scott Widmere was Lead General Counsel and was rarely seen in the building. All were in their immaculate, shiny suits.

Everyone except Warren was huddled near the windows. A minor conference was apparently underway. Warren was standing near the fireplace and as Greer approached, Warren cleared his throat. They all turned toward Geer and smiled.

Sarinov stepped across the room. He flashed white teeth. "Jensen, Jensen. Come in." He extended his hand to Greer's shoulder and guided him into the fold. "We have a little surprise for you."

Greer smiled cautiously.

Sarinov gestured to a group of richly padded leather chairs that surrounded a round cherry coffee table. "Have a seat, Jensen."

The group, all with broad smiles, sat down. Sarinov sat next to Greer. They unbuttoned jackets and crossed legs and looked entirely comfortable, all except Warren, who never looked comfortable. He sat with his lips pursed, his dark little eyes dancing. His jacket came off, revealing his tight, sticky shirt.

Sarinov spoke. "Jensen Greer, it's time to make formal what really has been informal for many months now. Your work for us, for Summit, has been outstanding. When we first hired you on, we had expectations, we had hopes of what you could do for us. You've exceeded them all. Yield at Sugarloaf is excellent, costs are controlled, margins are high. Haystack is on track. Miner's Creek and White Cloud are lined up to follow. All are excellent sight picks, plenty of gold, friendly regulators. And all are remote from prying eyes. Of course, you don't get credit for all of it. But we couldn't be more happy with your performance. So today, I want to announce a little promotion that I feel has been long overdue. I couldn't announce it before, I needed to be sure of the board. But the vote was unanimous. Effective immediately, Jensen Greer, you are the Vice President of North American Operations for Summit Resources."

The group of men stood up and applauded warmly. Jensen, still seated in his chair and feeling like a school child, smiled incredulously.

Sarinov continued. "Jensen, you will have responsibility for the day-to-day operations of each of our North American mines. You clearly have a gift for this. Harquail will move on to head up a new office, Vice President of Worldwide Exploration. He will handle planned expansion into Central and South America. And Jensen, I'm sure he'll be working closely with you and seeking your insight."

More warm applause. Harquail smiled and nodded his acknowledgement.

On the coffee table, seven short crystal glasses surrounded a tall bottle of 40-year old Macallan scotch. Next to that sat a silver box. Sarinov uncapped the bottle and half-filled each glass with the amber liquid. Sam Tucker rose and offered fat, brown cigars to each from the box. Harquail struck a long wooden match and they each lit up.

Sarinov handed a glass to Greer, who stood. With the group puffing and smiling, Sarinov ceremoniously lifted his glass. The rest joined in as he made it official.

"Congratulations, Jensen! Welcome to our little club."

They each tipped back the whiskey and took long drags off the Honduran cigars. Each in turn shook Greer's hand and Greer nodded and thanked them each of them.

Sarinov finally sat down and the rest followed. "So what does this mean?" the CEO asked, crossing his legs and smiling confidently. "What is it, to be a member of our little club?"

The "club" sipped and puffed and watched Greer's face as Sarinov spelled out the details. "Jensen, the perks are quite good. A million in salary, a minimum two million dollars in annual bonuses, and ten million in stock at today's closing price, to vest equally over the next five years. Each year will bring a nice raise and an additional five million in stock allocation, minimum. Jensen, you're about to become a very wealthy man. With appreciation, the sky is the limit. And you belong to a very exclusive club now. A very *private* club."

The others nodded solemnly.

Sarinov's expression grew stern. He pointed with his cigar. "Remember this Jensen Greer. Our club requires complete privacy. We're a closed community. We require loyalty, teamwork, and absolute commitment to the company, above all else. There is no other way."

The other VPs had all stopped puffing and were now fixated on Greer.

Sarinov continued. "There's a photograph in my office, you've seen it. *Success Takes All of You!* Don't you forget it. That little phrase embodies the heart and soul of this company, it's about commitment above all else. Don't any of you forget it. Congratulations, Jensen Greer. It's great to have you on board."

"Thank you, sir." Greer nodded stupidly. "Thank you."

"You're taking a week off in what, two weeks? Where to?"

Greer cleared his throat. "Idaho."

Sarinov lifted his cigar. "Where in Idaho?"

"Tamarack."

"Good. You deserve it. You've earned it. Flying or driving?"

"Flying."

"Good, driving it this time of year is dangerous. When you get back, we'll have a grand party to celebrate your promotion, hosted right here in the penthouse. And then we're going to update our five-year plan." Sarinov addressed the group. "Gentlemen, gold prices are skyrocketing. I want to bring a new mine on every year for five years straight. In five years, I want to have ten mines operating in the Western Hemisphere."

❖

Thursday afternoon, Greer sat in the kitchen nook and gulped down his third gin and tonic. All the females were out, the maids were done, and the massive stone and timber home was empty. From his perch high in the West Hills, he stared out at the storm clouds rolling over coast the range.

He had left work early and was trembling inside. They had set him up, and he knew it. Sarinov had made him Vice President of North American Operations. Yippee fucking hooray. Hooray for Barbara's Bet; it was nothing more than a con! He was their scapegoat, to take the fall when Justene, or any mine in North America, went south. The title didn't matter, he had no authority whatsoever. He was powerless! Yet he had all the liability in the world! And right now, Justene was leaking like a breached supertanker. If Justene went down, he would go down with it. Sons of bitches. He was their insurance policy. He was their lamb.

But maybe there was a way. If he could hang on for just a while. Pile up the money, rake in the bonuses and the stock for say, three years, and then retire young with 40 or 50 million. Then walk away. But first, first he needed to close Justene. Anonymously. The state could discover the leaks, suspend operations, and issue some little slap-on-the-wrist fines. He just needed to be very, very discrete. He could keep the money. And life could go on.

Greer read the number from a yellow sticky paper, grabbed the phone, and dialed. In the attic, a small transmitter turned on. It had been placed in a dark corner under a deep bed of pink insulation. Power had been spliced from an AC line and the only hint of the device's presence was a thin wire that disappeared behind wood framing.

At DEQ's offices, Ryan's phone rang. It had to be Meagan. She usually called mid-afternoon.

"Evans." He often answered that way, when she called.

"Ryan Evans?"

Not Meagan, but a man's voice. Familiar. "Yes?"

"Is this on speaker phone?"

"No."

Greer took a breath. "Listen. I need to meet with you. I want to give you information about the Justene mine. I have detailed knowledge of the mine, the site is in serious trouble. But this has to be confidential."

"Who is this?"

"Just listen. I have extensive evidence of illegal operations and I want you to act on it. Justene is about to rupture. If you want to close the mine down, this will let you do it. But my name, who I am, has to be kept strictly secret. My name cannot get out."

Ryan blinked a few times. He had taken a lot of crank calls, but this one was different. He leaned in over the desk and spoke low. "Why not go just go through regular channels?"

Greer stopped pacing the kitchen. He remembered the odd word in Arland Lochner's little bio. *Ours.*

"I'm not going through regular channels, they won't act fast enough. I want to work with you only, no one else."

Ryan sat motionless. Robert Newberg entered his mind. "Who are you? Tell me something to legitimize yourself."

"Only if you promise to tell no one, do you understand me? The only place that you can reveal my identity to anyone is in a court of law. If this ever goes to court, then I'll want you to stand up and tell them where you got this information, and that I tried to close it down. But only then. Only in court."

Ryan stood and scanned the tops of office dividers. The floor was quiet. "All right. If that ever happens, I'll tell the truth."

Greer ran a hand through his hair. The package lay on the kitchen island. It was packed with pictures of the mine, ground water reports on acids and cyanide, poisons and metal contamination. The emails transcripts, the bizarre folders on people with all the notation—these gems he would hold back in reserve, to use if things ever got extremely messy.

"Only in a court of law," Greer repeated. "Until then, you can never tell anyone how you got this. Do you understand?"

Meagan came to Ryan's mind, her pleading with him late on a Sunday night. His fingertips tapped the desktop. "I understand. When and where?"

"Tomorrow. Four pm. There's a place called Anthony's on route 224, on the south side of Estacada."

"Estacada?"

"We can't meet in Portland."

"How will I know you?"

"Just show up, tomorrow at four. Come alone. I know your face."

"What?"

A click and the dial tone blared in Ryan's ear. He dropped the phone back into its cradle and stared at it for a full minute, and then it rang again. Double rings. Three, four. It nearly went to voice mail.

"Yeah?"

"Whoa, you must be having a hard day."

It was Meagan. He apologized. She was at the grocery store. Would he mind pork chops tonight? Sure. Pork chops would be good. And baked baby red potatoes? Red potatoes, perfect. Good. I love you. I love you too. I love you so much.

A quarter-to-five brought another call. Double rings. Ryan stared at the phone and wondered who he had not talked with today.

"Hello?"

"Hey, looser."

Ryan sighed. "Alex."

"Hey, how are ya, buddy? You don't sound good."

"Not so much."

"I'm in Portland tomorrow, coming down to visit my dad for the afternoon, having dinner with him. I thought we might meet for lunch."

"That would be nice. I could use a long lunch."

"Pick a spot. Maybe the Scupper? Or that Irish place we went to a couple years back. What's it called?"

Ryan thought. "Kells. On Second. It's not far from here."

"That's it. I like that place. 11:30?"

"Good. It'll be good."

"Sonofabitch! I told you he was a godamned boy scout!" Rodney Warren's puffy eyes were opened wide.

"Shut up!" Sarinov demanded. "Get me a scotch."

Sarinov paced the penthouse. The doors were locked. Santini sat in a leather arm chair and watched Sarinov pace.

At 9:30 Friday morning, Jordy and Don had been evacuated from the IT cave and Santini had played back Greer's phone call to Ryan Evans. The signal from Greer's home had been picked up from an antenna on the roof of the building, one level up. Sarinov had just heard the recording for himself.

He clutched the glass of whiskey from Warren and downed it. "Give me the bottle," Sarinov demanded. "They're meeting today? Santini, we only bugged his house a few days ago! How much have we missed?"

Santini's voice was calm, as though having a casual chat. "Tapes of Greer's office phone are clean. The call we taped was obviously the first real conversation he's had with Evans."

Warren retrieved the whiskey bottle, poured another shot, and handed it to his boss. "What are we going to do about him?" asked Warren.

Sarinov took his position at the rain-streaked windows. "If he turns, it won't stop with Justene. The company will be investigated. Keep Greer away from your people, all of your sensitive data, sensitive computer files. I'm not sure what the hell he's up to, but we can't risk it. Keep your offices locked. No more flights to Justene. Santini, disable the copiers. They're down for repairs. If he starts pilfering cabinets, nail him. Confront him on the spot. Have guards search all briefcases leaving the building from here forward. Call it new security measures to thwart our competitors."

Sarinov turned from the windows and pointed at them with his shot glass. "No one is authorized to take company plans, test holes, or any site documents out this building! Search Greer thoroughly at the door tonight. Search everyone."

Santini, still in the recliner, gazed at the flickering gas fire. "What about today's little meeting?"

"You and your guys intercept him," said Sarinov. "If he tries to give anything to Evans, stop him. Don't let anything change hands. Intimidate him, scare the shit out of him! When he sees you, he'll pull back."

Santini snickered. "He'll know."

"I want him to know!" Sarinov pointed at Santini. "You have him covered completely. I want to know everything he does, his collection of shit goes nowhere."

The room grew silent as Sarinov turned back to face the window. "Goddamned kid."

Warren had begun hyperventilating and dropped into an armchair to rest. "But what about the next time he tries this? Can we intercept everything?"

CFO Rodney Warren had been in on nearly everything from the beginning, stock manipulation, doctored financial statements, risk profiles. Kickbacks to DEQ and a few strategic politicians. Not murder.

"We watch him," replied Sarinov.

In his round, pink face, Warren's eyes glowed. "But we can't let this go on! Whatever we do to stop him now, he could come back on us!"

Santini leaned forward with a wicked smile. His question dripped with sarcasm. "What do you suggest we do, Rodney?"

Rodney Warren's lips pursed tightly together. "We need to take care of him!"

"You mean like, murder? We off his ass?"

"Shut up!" Sarinov snapped. "We'll deal with him as we need to."

# Chapter 21

Kells was packed Friday at lunch time. Ryan found Alex sitting near the window. He tossed his jacket onto a chair and sat down. The place was finished in dark brown upholstery and generous woodwork, and offered a dry refuge from the rain. Flat screens suspended from the ceiling carried reviews of the previous night's NBA game. The Trailblazers had lost to L.A.

The server rushed over, a young blond woman in a black leather skirt and white blouse. Ryan ordered a corned beef sandwich with fries and an ale. Alex ordered the same, with a side of grilled onions, a shot of whiskey, and an ale. Alex winked at the woman, who hurried off.

"You're an alcoholic," Ryan said.

"I know, it's terrible. How are you, shithead?"

"I'm just great, dumbass. I thought I was a doctor."

"We're doctors when we're with the wives."

Ryan grinned. "I see. Well, happy Friday, dumbass. What are you doing here?"

"It's my dad's birthday. We had a lucid telephone conversation last week and he asked me to come down for his birthday."

Ryan nodded. "How is he?"

Alex's hands opened on the table. "Well, he was good then. God knows, today."

Ryan nodded. "How's Anne?"

"She's near dead, the internship is grueling. I don't know how she does it. You know, I hardly see her." Alex shrugged. "Anyway, I'm leaving for Beijing for six months."

"No kidding? For Microsoft?"

Alex nodded.

"When do you leave?"

"End of March. Back in September. I'm going crazy at home, I never see her. Did you know she lives at the hospital? It's inhumane. Doctors are crazy people."

"Six months is a while."

"It's worth it. The Chinese market is huge."

Ryan nodded. The drinks arrived.

Alex winked at the waitress again. "I'll need another beer!" he called as she hurried away.

Alex downed the shot and emptied half the beer before speaking again. "So doc, how's work? How's Meggy?"

Ryan took a sip of ale. "We finished painting the house and got the new curtains in. Thanks a lot for that. Meagan was giddy over it, still is. You didn't have to do that."

Alex's froth-covered moustache stretched wide with the smile. "I know. So let me see. Meggy gets home from work before you. She makes a sumptuous dinner and meets you at the door, naked, with a beer in hand?"

Ryan looked at his friend. "Are you having a hard time?"

Alex frowned and shrugged at the same time. He emptied the pint and his face flushed.

Ryan looked down at the table, the green napkin, his glass full of ale. Alex wiped the beer from his moustache. "What's up?"

Ryan drummed the table with his thumb. The Friday lunch crowd was becoming noisy. "I've just started my first beer and you've already downed a shot and finished off a pint."

"So catch up!"

"Alex, you drink like a fish."

"I can handle my damned alcohol! I have a couple with lunch on a Friday and you're giving me grief?"

Ryan frowned. "It's your liver."

"Things aren't easy, it takes the fucking edge off!" The noise suddenly required yelling.

"What's not easy?"

Alex's wet eyes fled to the ESPN highlights. "I didn't drive down here to get a damned lecture. I'm here to visit my sweet old dad, who doesn't recognize me anymore."

Ryan looked down at his beer and remembered the trips with the Palmer family. When his own father died, Dr. Nathan Palmer had made an obvious effort to pick up a little of the parental slack with Ryan, almost as if it was an obligation. Over the last year, Ryan had visited the man twice at the assisted living center, a few miles south of the city. Watching him fade was hard.

The moment became awkward. Alex's voice was resigned. "Let's drop it."

The server flew in, dropped their plates on the table, and kept going.

Alex yelled, "Donna, I'll have another pint!"

She nodded over her shoulder. He turned back. "How's your damned work?"

"Is that her name?"

"Whatever. How's the job?"

Ryan glanced outside. Across the street, in the rain, a man sat in a brown Ford Taurus. Ryan sipped his beer. "Works fine." He drummed the table top with a fork so that it bounced. "No. Actually, it's screwed up."

171

Alex raised a thick, blond eyebrow. "Spill it, doctor Ry."

Ryan leaned forward over the sandwich. "Remember Gabe Riplinger?"

"The old guy who shot himself?"

"Well, I don't think he shot himself."

"What do you mean?"

"Well first off, the gun they found in his hands was reported stolen back east, some 12 years ago. Too convenient."

"He could have bought it at a gun show."

"Whatever. Remember Justene? The pit mine east of the mountains?"

"Right. Crater Lake, only cyanide."

"That's it. DEQ approved the expansion a couple of weeks after Gabe died. He recommended rejecting the permits, he told me so. So he died, and a few weeks later they approved."

"Nice timing."

"Tell me about it. So the paperwork, the environmental study required to decide whether to approve the expansion? I wrote it up. Me and another guy who has since left, Miles Nelson. It took us eight months, great work. Got all kinds of compliments for it."

"You're a fucking genius."

"They never used it. They used a previous study, written four years ago. A completely, totally irrelevant piece of crap that was used to approve the original permits."

Alex snickered. He reached for his sandwich with both hands. "Your government, hard at work. So they pay you for your masterpiece and then toss it?"

"Exactly! And we're not even there yet, okay? The man who wrote this illustrious thing up? The original? A Mr. Newberg. He died the day after he completed it. His signature on the study is dated one day before his death."

Alex placed the sandwich back on his plate, un-sampled. "Honestly?"

Ryan finished his ale and set the glass down. It was tasting good and Alex was a great listener. "Yeah. Dead. And here's the topper, my friend. Take a fucking guess how Newberg died."

Alex searched the table for his beer. The only full glass held ice water and he eyed it with contempt. "The mining company popped him and threw him down the shaft?"

"More or less. You know, you have a way of killing the climax."

Alex leaned in. "Come again?"

"He fell out of their corporate helicopter. He fell a thousand feet to his death. I talked with his wife. Investigators ruled it an accident. She doesn't believe it."

"You're kidding me. Does she know about his signature?"

"I didn't get that far. She was having a hard time on the phone."

"I'll bet the investigation never got that far."

Ryan nodded. "A guy who is afraid of heights opens a helicopter door in the rain and falls to his death at Justene. A million miles from nowhere. It makes total sense."

"Does anyone else know this, about the signature?"

"I don't know. I've told no one."

"This is a little bizarre. I mean, the odds aren't in it. Both your boss and this guy are dead? And they're both connected to Justene? What are you going to do?"

Ryan's fingers bounced on the table. "I can't get a response from the head of DEQ about the substituted study. I don't think what they've done with the permits, the approval, is even legal. But he's ignoring me."

Alex sat silent, his eyes on Ryan.

"And one more thing." Ryan continued. "I got a call from a guy who seems to know a lot about Justene. Says he has a pile of evidence, violations, laws broken, that could close the whole thing down. He says a disaster is imminent. He's anxious to meet, he wants to hand it all over to me. And of course, he won't tell me his name."

Alex sat for a minute, taking it in. He glanced about the bar. Stock brokers, lawyers, and secretaries. Out for a liquid lunch.

"I need a beer to think," said Alex. "Do you often get calls like this?"

"They were heavy before the permits were approved, mostly just upset people and crackpots. But this guy. He's the most persistent, and he sounds rational, intelligent."

"You know, you might want to be careful with this."

Ryan frowned. He didn't like hearing his own fears. "He could be a total wacko. We've had more than our share."

"Does Meagan know about any of this?"

"A little. She doesn't know Newberg is dead. Or that I'm meeting anyone."

Alex leaned in now and his eyebrows jumped. "You're going to meet him?"

"This afternoon, a place out in Estacada."

"Today?"

"He says we can't meet in town."

"I should join you."

"You're spending the afternoon with your dad. I'll call you over the weekend and tell you about it."

"You could have problems with this. If this guy gives you hot evidence, incriminating evidence?"

"He's probably a nutcase."

"And this stuff incriminates the people who might have killed this guy, Newberg? And your boss?"

"I said he's a nutcase."

"Then why are you going?"

Ryan looked at his untouched sandwich. "I need to know. I just need to know."

Early in the afternoon, Ryan left DEQ. He headed east across the Burnside Bridge and then south on I-205 to Highway 224, past used car dealerships, fishing supply stores, and gun shops. In the falling rain, the route paralleled the gray Clackamas River. Stick-bare cottonwood and oak trees replaced buildings and the traffic thinned. After 50 minutes, through the town of Estacada, across another bridge and up on a rise, he found the place. Anthony's Hilltop Steakhouse sat in a clearing in the trees. Mounted high up, a large yellow sign had been damaged from a windstorm or gunshot. So now, the sign read *Ant Hilltop*.

He parked near the front in the muddy gravel lot and dropped the window an inch. One car sat to his left, an old Accord. Two more were parked off to the right. An older BMW, maybe Ant's car. The place was empty. Many years earlier, the white building had been someone's home. Under the heavy branches of old trees, green moss covered the shingled roof. An add-on had been stuck to the side of the building; its flat roof sagged. Overhead, clouds twisted in thick black coils, wringing out a cold drizzle.

Ryan sat in the truck with his hands on the wheel. He couldn't get killed buying a soda in broad daylight, he told himself. Buying a soda was harmless. Meagan might argue otherwise, and she had an unnerving habit of being right about some things that completely escaped him. At times, she could see the big picture that he missed. He could get lost in the details. He would never tell her about this meeting.

The loss of his sister and then his father had completely changed Ryan, and he knew it. He had become the responsible one. While his mother retreated to booze and pills, he became obsessed with details, with organization and preparation. Doing his own laundry (out of necessity), he kept his clothes immaculate. His grades were impeccable. For a time, after coming home from evening jobs, he had developed a tenacious habit of checking doors and window locks. Checking that the stove was turned off. Checking on his mother and her lit cigarettes. For a while, the obsessions controlled him. He thought he had banished them in college, but lately, there were moments when a particular fear would creep up on him.

Although it was cold, he felt a trickle of perspiration snake down his side, under his shirt. The steering wheel became moist in his hands and the question that had nipped at his mind all day, bit hard. Could the man on the phone actually know something, something that could undeniably close Justene? Thousands of protestors, letters to newspapers, and months of marches had failed to shut it down. A dubious approval process. A bizarre fall from a helicopter, a suicide that made no sense. Meagan had pleaded with him to let it go. He could drive away now. He could do what Gabe had told to him do. Forget about Justene.

He unbuckled the seatbelt and stepped into the drizzle.

Inside, the place was deep and dark with the bar on the left. Varnished wooden tables receded away from the window. Cedar planks covered the walls and wagon-wheel light fixtures hung from the ceiling. Anthony was a cowboy. A steel guitar moaned from the sound system.

At the bar, three girls, not 21, sat and sipped beers and smoked cigarettes. At the very back, a man with a ball cap was sipping a beer and consumed with a newspaper. Another was at the bar. Ryan took a seat in the corner by the window. The waiter came and he ordered a cola.

Outside, a diesel tractor with a load of lumber roared past, and then a Sheriff's car sailed through, its siren wailing. The newspaper extended fully in front of its reader and the girls sipped and whispered and giggled. The waiter delivered a red basket of fries to the ladies. Ryan's soda arrived. Another ten minutes passed and not one car pulled into the lot.

Ryan began to wonder, and then a yellow Porsche Carrera, a late model, entered the gravel lot and parked up close. A man wearing a trench coat emerged from it. He glanced around the lot and climbed the steps, a briefcase in hand, and entered. He scanned the room intently before his eyes rested on Ryan. He approached and sat down quickly, half out of the chair.

He leaned forward and whispered. "Ryan Evans?"

Ryan nodded. "Yes?"

Greer glanced around once more, and then put the briefcase on the table. He spoke softly. "Take it."

"The entire briefcase?"

"It's yours, all of it. The place is a wreck. Two of the four containment ponds are in serious trouble. They're running too much cyanide."

"If this is something I can use, they'll want to know where I got it."

Greer took a quick breath. "No. You listen to me. I work for the company, but you never saw me. You don't know me."

Ryan's hand rested cautiously on the case. "May I open it?"

"Not here! Listen. I need to know something. What happened to Gabe Riplinger?"

Ryan paused. The question threw him. "He died."

"How?"

"A gun shot, to the head. They said it was suicide."

"What day?"

"January 13. Why?"

From the back, the man at the table burst into loud laughter. Ryan turned to see the man with the ball cap set the newspaper down and smile broadly. Not at his paper, not toward the girls, but directly at Ryan. Twenty-five feet away, he smiled and nodded.

Ryan turned back to the man with the briefcase.

Greer's wide eyes were locked on the man across the bar. Unbelieving eyes. Greer jumped up from the chair, knocking it back, and bolted out the door. The briefcase was in his hands. The Porsche had been left unlocked and he was in it instantly. Tires sprayed gravel and the car was gone, just missing the parked Accord.

One of the girls gasped, "He hit my car!"

Ryan turned as the two men approached. They watched the Porsche disappear, and then the one with the ball cap reached down and righted the chair. He placed it directly in front of Ryan and rested his hands on its back. The juke box skipped and the music became gibberish.

"My goodness," Santini said, shaking his head in disgust. "People who drive like that are dangerous. Wouldn't you agree, Mr. Evans?"

Ryan's head snapped back.

Santini leaned closer, the bill of the hat nearly touching Ryan. He whispered. "You're almost newlyweds, you and Mrs. Evans. Let me tell you something. That fool who left here in such a hurry? He could be dangerous for you two. Lethal. Do you understand?"

The taller man moved in close. He cocked his head at Ryan and waited.

Ryan's voice crackled. The mention of Meagan brought a deep snarl. "Who the hell are you?"

Santini rose, touched the bill of his hat, and the two pushed through the door. A silver Mercedes, void of license plates, pulled into the lot. Santini nodded before getting in, and the car pulled away.

# Chapter 22

The white house was perched between the trees on a rise overlooking the wealthy suburb of Lake Oswego. It was set well back from the road, down a long stone driveway and behind steel security gates. In the falling light, Santini stood at the French doors under a wide stone archway. He pressed the button and bells chimed in the distance. A camera mounted above him kept watch. He flipped it the bird.

A man answered the door. He was thirtyish and fit, and wore a white cotton shirt, white slacks, and brown leather sandals. They had met before. The ice cream man, thought Santini. Two black Doberman pinschers flanked him in the doorway. Their dark eyes locked on the visitor.

The Good Humor man and the dogs escorted Santini down the long foyer, through rooms with unattended furniture, through more French doors and onto an elevated deck in the back. The doors closed behind him. In jeans and a Harvard sweatshirt, Sarinov was standing under a wide awning and staring out across the dark water. The lights of lakefront homes shimmered through the rain.

The Harvard man spoke without turning. "What happened?"

Santini watched the dogs as he spoke. "They met at the restaurant. Evans arrived first. Greer showed up and sat right down with him. He put his briefcase on the table. They talked for a few seconds. We couldn't hear much. Evans went to open it and we moved in."

Sarinov turned as Santini continued. "Greer, he panicked before I could even get close. He saw who I was, grabbed his briefcase and ran. I thought he would go cardiac."

"Greer gave nothing to Evans?"

"Not a thing. He ran like a deer."

"Who saw this?"

"No one but Evans and a couple of teenagers. The waiter was in the back. The place was empty."

"You got his attention?"

"I've never seen anyone move that fast."

Sarinov stood in silence with his jaw set hard. The black coats of the Dobermans twitched; their bright eyes were glued to the visitor. Santini didn't move.

Sarinov shook his head methodically, a slow gesture. He finally spoke. "Give me a plan for Greer. Make it an accident. Make it clean. Do the same for Evans, soon. And make them unique."

"Too many will attract attention."

The sun had already set. A wind rippled across the dark lake, blowing the rain in under the cover. Sarinov's knuckles were fused to the rail. "We don't have a choice. Track Evans. Put a wire on his home phone."

Saturday at 1:30 a.m. in a darkened room, Greer sat on the edge of a recliner and stared at a five-foot screen. Muted images flashed by as he pounded the remote: crying evangelists, porn, infomercials.

The surprise at the restaurant had jolted him. They were watching him! They knew! That neurotic bulldog, Santini, and someone he had never seen before, they were there before he arrived! They were watching! When? At work? Yes. At home? He had called Evans and set up the meeting on the house phone!

Greer pushed the smoke through his nostrils. There was a shooter at a MacDonald's in Texas. Another multi-billion dollar Ponzi scheme had collapsed; the manager had been found floating in New York Harbor.

Sarinov knew about the briefcase; he knew what was inside! He, Greer, wouldn't be meeting in a bar with a man from DEQ, with a briefcase full of bibles. And the date on the Riplinger papers. *January 13!*

Greer lit another cigarette and the flame danced in his shaking hands. After five years of going cigarette-free, he had broken. Now a glass bowl sat on the carpet, half-filled with butts. Next to that sat an empty cup of instant coffee. No alcohol. He needed his wits.

The briefcase was hiding in the trunk of the Porsche, which was hiding in the garage. He pondered losing its contents and running. But he had to do something about Justene. Christ, the place was on the verge of blowing! The more he knew, the more accountable he was. What evidence? Records of his trips to the mine. He was now VP of Operations. He had signed state reports on Justene operations every month for nearly three years.

Greer hammered the remote and the channels flew by, lighting up the room. How much time did he have? One week? Two? With the spring thaw and rains, no more that that. Even at that moment, Justene was spilling poisons like the Exxon Valdez.

Greer dropped the remote and massaged his temples. The plan had been to remain anonymous, but the bastards knew what he had in the briefcase. And they were dangerous.

Late Saturday evening, Greer passed his Summit Resources photo badge in front of a small scanner. The lock released with a click and he entered through the glass and steel doors. Inside, the lobby was quiet. Rain pelted the dark windows. Twenty minutes, he told himself. No more.

He walked toward officer's row with his full briefcase firmly in hand. They would never expect him to return with it.

"Sir!" a voice barked.

George, the weekend guard who used his job to catch up on sleep, was absent. A blond-haired man with a crew cut jumped from a chair behind the counter. He stood ramrod straight with a fresh khaki shirt stretched across a broad chest.

Greer nearly tripped. "Yes?"

"New regulations. After hours and weekends, everyone signs in and out."

Greer frowned, his best effort at serious indignation. "Whose regulations?"

The guard pushed the book towards him. A pen lay in the spine. "Mr. Santini's."

Greer set the briefcase next to his feet. He printed his name and signed. Two others had signed in, a man from finance, and Joe Santini. Santini had signed in at 7:10 p.m. and hadn't signed out. It was now 9:45.

The guard pulled the book back. "Identification?"

Greer fished his coat pockets and lifted out the elusive badge again. His noticed his fingers tremble.

"Wear it outside. It needs to be visible at all times," the guard demanded. "Mr. Greer, what's in the briefcase?"

"What?"

"The briefcase?"

"Oh. Work. I have a few things to finish."

"I won't search it going in, but everything gets searched going out. Company documents are not allowed to be taken off premises."

"Since when?"

"New rules, as of today."

"And what we looking for?"

"Any company proprietary information."

Greer nodded slowly and stepped away.

As he had done so many times before, he slipped through the glass doors and headed down officer's row, past doors adorned with gold plaques. Vice President and Chief Financial Officer Rodney Warren, Vice President of Worldwide Exploration Wayne Harquail, and the rest. Sarinov's office was deep in this wolf's den. Their half-truths and lies had been quoted at trade conventions, on television, and in the boiler rooms, pushing Summit stock. Summit's officers lived in opulence, feeding more off corporate fraud and investor greed than actual profits. Cherish it you bastards, thought Greer.

Several doors past Sarinov's office, Greer stepped inside his own office and closed the door. He set the briefcase on the desk and noticed his shirt bounce as his heart hammered away. What the hell was Santini doing here at 9:45 on a Saturday night?

Greer opened the credenza and pulled out a package of mailing labels. He turned on the computer and printer and waited; the machines took forever to start up. He fed a sheet of labels into the printer. From the briefcase, he retrieved Ryan's folder and entered his address into a file on the computer. He then printed the address on the mailing label.

From the credenza, he grabbed a large, white mailing envelope with the green and gold Summit Resources logo emblazoned across the top. He peeled Ryan's address label and pasted it carefully on the envelope. He paused to listen. The only sound was the printer fan.

From the briefcase, he pulled out several large color glossies of hemorrhaging cyanide ponds, illegal waste dumps, and black streams of poison flowing into the snow. Westfall had been hysterical; of course they didn't want pictures. Greer placed these in the envelope. He added the fraudulent declarations of cyanide use, close to three years' worth. Next to these numbers he had written his own estimates.

Next were the folders on Lochner, Riplinger, Evans, and Senator Phillips. They were crammed with emails and detailed personal information that no one legitimately needed. Words written here suggested things that, if true, would send people to prison. Included were pictures of Lochner and others, dancing with young nude women.

A click.

Greer's head jerked up. He heard it, a metallic snap. His eyes locked on the door knob across the room. He strained to hear above the printer fan and waited for ten seconds, but the knob didn't turn.

Greer quickly filled the white envelope. Mindless fingers fiddled with the backing on the flap until it finally came off and he sealed the envelope. He closed the file with the Evans address without saving it and turned off the computer and printer. He slipped the fat envelope into the briefcase, moved across the office, and quietly opened the office door.

The hallway was empty.

Greer floated down the carpeted hall, past offices, a large break area, and conference rooms. At the end, the hall opened up into a block of cubes, the Legal and Accounting departments. On the right, the mail room. He entered and quietly closed the door.

Up front were large counters. In the back were computers, copiers, and printers. The room was used by a very busy crew to prepare and send out truckloads of glitzy promotional material and copies of the company's quarterly financial reports. A new batch of PR packs was being prepped for mailing. One lay open. It brimmed with glossy spreads of Sarinov, Harquail, and young female employees. It shouted in bold about the success of Summit Resources, the phenomenal growth under the direction of its brilliant management team. A full page was given to Justene and its expected 'record-breaking yields.'

Several hundred white PR packs lay stacked in rows of plastic boxes. Boxes covered the counters and were stacked up against the walls. Monday morning, each envelope would be postmarked and delivered to the post office four blocks east.

Greer lifted his heavy white envelope from the briefcase. For a moment, he thought of Sarinov, hanging on the face of Half Dome. *Success Takes All of You!* Greer smirked. Maybe it's greed. Maybe the greed takes all of you. He thought of his own home, the mansion behind the security gates. Certainty about where all of this would end was impossible, but he wasn't going down for these people.

Greer slipped his envelope into a plastic box with 20 others, all identical in appearance, and it disappeared. He turned and opened the door. No one. He quietly closed the door, turned, and walked out the way he had come, past the conference rooms and down officer's row, past his own office. He slowed to a stroll and entered the marble lobby, carrying an empty briefcase.

## Chapter 23

Ryan was a wreck all weekend. He had phoned Alex twice from the upstairs den, but no one had picked up. Meagan had asked if he was all right. Yes, yes, he was fine. Just tired from work. He had agonized over telling her, but had promised her he would drop Justene. Telling her about Newberg's death and Friday's meeting just wasn't possible.

He arrived at work late on Monday. It was just another day. The floor was full. Everyone was quietly consumed. He ate lunch in his cube.

Karina noticed his seclusion, and after lunch, stood at the entrance to his cube. "Rough weekend?" she asked.

Ryan left his papers. Work wasn't getting his attention. He debated whether to confide in her. He needed to talk. He motioned her into his cube and in the lowest possible whisper, told her about Newberg's death and the interrupted meeting with the stranger at Anthony's.

"Karina, when he saw them, he ran. He bolted from there like his life depended on it."

Her eyes widened as her hand covered her mouth. She responded almost inaudibly. "Newberg is dead, too?"

Ryan nodded.

"What are you going to do?"

"The approval looks fraudulent. I don't think it's legal."

"But they threatened you? At the restaurant? Ryan, maybe you should leave this alone."

"But Lochner is doing nothing! I could get a judge to issue a injunction, to keep the expansion from going for—

Suddenly, Marcos Lassiter swept up behind Karina. A full foot taller, he barely avoided running her over. Ryan waved his hand low in a slicing motion. She turned.

Lassiter pointed a finger at Ryan. "You come with me."

Ryan looked at him, and then Karina. She was backed against the cube wall, her eyes wide.

"Evans, follow me." Lassiter turned and fired down the aisle in long strides and Ryan hurried to keep up.

At Lochner's office, Lassiter pointed Ryan inside and closed the door.

Arland Lochner was sitting, hunched over in the chair. He was in his usual white shirt and tie, but his armpits were soaked. He had apparently been on the phone; it sat square in the middle of the desk. Two building security guards, dressed in blue, stood next to him.

Lassiter pointed to a chair placed in the middle of the office. "Sit down."

Ryan sat, slowly.

Lassiter remained standing. "Mr. Evans, when you began employment with the state, you signed an agreement to refrain from removing state documents, applications, analysis, or legal findings, without explicit written approval of your direct manager."

Lochner paused and Ryan guessed where this was going.

Lochner's mouth curled up slyly. "Last week, you removed boxes full of such documents, state property, without my permission. Removal of state documents without approval is prohibited."

Ryan frowned. "Everyone takes documents out of here. I take work home all the time, it's how I get it done. Gabe knew all about it."

Lassiter's sneer was vicious. "Certainly you are aware that storing pornography on DEQ computers is illegal."

Ryan's head jerked. "What!?"

"Your system has over a hundred pornographic images on it. Over several occasions, you used state computers to visit pornographic websites."

Ryan jumped from the chair. "That is garbage!"

The taller security guard stepped up to Ryan with a growl. "Sit down."

"Bullshit!"

"Sit down!"

Ryan sat.

Lassiter spoke. "This isn't an argument. We aren't negotiating. The DEQ and the State of Oregon cannot permit these kinds of activities. Our systems cannot be used to store pornography. We're examining what legal obligations DEQ may have in reporting you to the authorities, but as of this moment, Mr. Evans, you're fired."

Again Ryan jumped from the chair, his eyes flashing to Lochner. "Arland! What the hell? If that crap is on my system, it was planted!"

The guard spoke again. "Sit down."

"This is garbage!" Ryan remained standing. His eyes implored Lochner, who was sitting with one hand holding the edge of the desk. Lochner's face was sheet-white.

"Arland!" Ryan shouted. Then realization. "This is about Justene. You didn't like my little meeting on Friday."

At the mention of Friday's appointment, Lochner shuddered.

Lassiter seethed, spitting the words. "The guards will escort you to your desk. You have one minute to get your personal belongings. You will talk with no one. You will be escorted to your vehicle and you will leave the building. Your employment with DEQ is ended."

Ryan spoke through clenched teeth. "This is about Justene! And Newberg! And Gabe! Arland, you tell me what happened to Gabe!"

Lassiter looked like he would attack. "Shall I call the police?"

Ryan turned. The yelling was done. "You call the police. You do that."

Lassiter opened the door wide. "Get him out of here."

Ryan stumbled forward. Behind her desk, Evelyn stared with a hand over her mouth. The guards escorted him, one in front and one behind, down the aisle. Heads popped up and coworkers stared. Karina stood in the aisle with her hands on her hips. "What's going on here?" she demanded.

Ryan placed a trembling finger over his lips. At his desk, he shoveled his belongings into a small box. A picture of Meagan. A calendar of sailboats. A bottle of aspirin, a box of tea, and Sammy, the mug.

Karina barged into the cube, pushing her way around the guards. She hugged him and placed a scrap of paper in his hand as she whispered. "Call me!"

He moved around her quickly, desperate for air, and marched down the aisle with his box in hand. The guards hurried to keep up.

The truck was parked across the garage and he walked to it without seeing. His heart hammered in his ears. As he reached the vehicle door and began to push in the key, a voice startled him.

"You got lucky today."

The man stepped from behind an adjacent van and stood at the front, to Ryan's left. Another man, tall and thick, boxed him in on the right.

Ryan fiddled with the key. "I'm sorry?"

"You got lucky, Mr. Evans. You only lost your job."

Ryan looked up. The voice, the faces. These were the two at the restaurant. He pulled out the key, closed his fist around it, and glanced about for an escape. "What do you want?"

The same one spoke. "Forget about Justene. Forget about the old guy, Riplinger. And Newberg. We want you go away Mr. Evans. Live happily and quietly ever after. Or you will wind up just like them. Just like them. Do you understand?"

Far away, a car horn echoed.

"Do you understand?" the shorter one repeated. The voice was casual, almost warm.

Ryan felt the muscles in his body twitch. His mind raced. The warning could not be more clear. He nodded. "Yeah."

The two turned and disappeared.

Ryan exited the parking garage and turned left as always, and a woman in a white Toyota locked tires with a screech to avoid him. She swerved and laid on the horn.

The truck wandered a hundred yards and he became suddenly lost. He weaved into the side lot of a gas station, between a white propane tank and a rusty Cadillac. He slipped it into park, got out, and leaned on the hood.

His hands shook. Nausea gripped him. Mary Newberg's voice filled his ears. Ryan became dizzy. He slipped down on a knee.

"You all right?" The gas station attendant stood a few feet away.

Ryan stood slowly and sucked in the cold air. Wind chilled the sweat on his face.

Meagan usually called him after lunch, but he wouldn't be at work to answer. At 2:00, he called her from the kitchen.

"Hi honey."

"Hi Ryan. What's up?"

"I'm at home."

"Are you all right?"

"Not feeling very well."

"Stomach or headache?"

"Both."

"Got a fever?"

"No. How are you?" Ryan asked.

"Umm, fine. Is everything all right?"

"Yeah." Ryan's voice quivered. "Just not feeling very well."

Meagan paused to evaluate the possible cause. "What did you eat this morning?"

"A cup of coffee, bagel."

"Hmmm. No pastries? None of those sticky buns?"

"No."

"Lunch?"

"Only what you packed."

"Well, take it easy. Lie down. Check your temperature. If you need to, you can call me. I'll be home by 5:30."

"Okay." He was hunched over in the chair, head on one hand. "Call me when you leave work?"

"Okay. You'll be all right?"

"Yeah. Love you, Meggy."

Ryan hung up the phone and began pacing the house. He checked the locks on the doors and windows and made a mental note to replace the back door soon. When pacing and checking became too much, he took the dog and drove the truck down to the river. He parked on a boat ramp and watched the swollen Willamette River roll by.

She came through the kitchen door at 5:30 and laid her purse and keys on the table. The wind had tossed her hair. He was sitting at the table with an empty bottle of beer.

She checked his forehead. "How are you feeling?"

He took a breath. "Okay."

She inspected him. No fever. Good color. Beer. "You don't exactly look sick."

With one foot, he pushed out a chair for her. "Sit down, Meggy."

"What happened?"

"You need to sit down."

She slipped into the chair.

He took another breath. He had never been fired for anything. "I got fired today."

Her head pulled back. "What?"

Ryan slid his hand across the table and rested it on hers. "They accused me of theft, of taking work home without permission."

Her eyes narrowed "What do you mean?"

"And downloading porn off the web."

She looked askance at him. "You're kidding me."

"No, honey. I'm not."

She stood up from the table. "That's just ridiculous!"

He nodded. "Yeah."

"You don't, you're not a porn guy. Like, hard core?"

"I don't know."

Her hand flew to her mouth. "Fired? Tell me exactly what happened."

"Lassiter came to my cube, just after lunch. He took me into Lochner's office and accused me of taking documents home without his permission and collecting porn on my computer. He gave me one minute to get my belongings and leave."

"Was Lochner there?"

"Yeah. He just sat there, sweating like a pig. He couldn't look at me. He just went along."

She shook her head. "No, no. And that's it?"

He couldn't tell her about the two in the garage. Not yet. She was pacing the kitchen now. He took another deep breath. "Sit down, sweetie."

"I don't want to sit down!"

"Please."

Meagan stopped pacing.

Ryan exhaled. "I accused them of planting it."

"No kidding!"

"I said it was over Justene."

Her eyes opened wide. She walked to the sink and then back to the chair. "They framed you over Justene? They can't do this! They're the DEQ! This is because of the calls you made? All the digging through records?"

Ryan's thumb tapped the table. "I believe so."

Meagan looked up at the ceiling. Tears rolled down her face. Ryan took a tissue and handed it to her. "Sit down, honey."

"This is insane! Gabe is dead! You've been fired, on ridiculous grounds! What the hell is going on?" She buried her face in her hands.

He stood and put an arm over her shoulders. She looked up again and drilled him with fierce eyes. "Ryan, this makes no sense!"

"I know."

193

"This, this isn't right! I want you to forget about Justene! I mean it! It's an obsession with you, Ryan. You know it's true! Get off this, this damned obsession!"

Ryan said nothing.

"I'm serious. You drop it, Ryan. Forget it. Forget DEQ, forget Justene! You promise me."

He nodded. "I promise."

There was so much he hadn't told her.

## Chapter 24

Monday afternoon, Greer took the elevator to the 38th floor of the US Bancorp Tower. Kennedy & Sorenson occupied the entire floor. The firm handled all stock transactions for the fine corporate officers of Summit Resources.

The woman at the counter greeted him. "Good afternoon, Mr. Greer. Lyle is expecting you. Would you like a cup of coffee?"

"No, thanks."

She smiled. "He'll be right out."

Greer stood in the lobby that over-looked downtown Portland and waited for only a minute. He had been here before, once to sell $1.2 million in stock to buy their home, then another million to invest in a retirement center in Bend, east of the mountains.

"Mr. Greer! What a pleasure!" Lyle Covington arrived with his hand thrust out.

Covington was a slender man with a pink V-shaped face, a pointed beak, and a bald head. He wore a light pink shirt with a cobalt tie. A wide smile joined his ears. The man grabbed Greer's hand and pumped with joy. The nose blared. "What a nice surprise! Come with me!"

Covington led Greer to his office, past the cubicles of lessers, the bullpen of younger brokers who handled the accounts of people with less than a quarter million dollars to loose. The bullpen was abuzz. The metals, oil, and commodity stocks were heading for the stratosphere and brokers were giddy with forecasts of riches. Buy! Buy! The market was blowing another bubble.

The door closed. Covington pointed to a padded leather chair, his arms outstretched as though guiding an airplane to a gate. "Have a seat, Jensen! How is the family!?" As though Greer's family was all this money manager really cared about.

"Fine. I need to liquidate a little stock."

"Oh?"

Women swarmed into the office carrying silver trays of cheese, fruit, salmon, a carafe of coffee, and a bottle of white wine. They set the trays on an oak table and hovered.

One turned and asked with a smile, "What would you like, Mr. Greer? Wine? Some lox and crackers?"

"I really don't have the time."

The woman gave a pouty frown.

Covington insisted. "We like to take extra care of our special clients, Mr. Greer."

On paper, Greer was worth 20 million. Fourteen million of this was still unvested, but six was available. He was a good-sized fish before and would become a whale soon with the new VP title. They would have arranged sex if he'd asked.

Greer's forehead creased in jagged lines. "I really don't have the time."

Covington's hand waved and the women scurried out of the room. The door closed.

"So you want to sell a little stock?" he queried.

"Five million dollars."

Lyle Covington's manicured fingers stifled a hard cough. "Five million dollars? Of Summit?"

Greer nodded and checked his watch. "I'm on a schedule today."

"But most of your holdings are unvested. And we'll need to file a form 144. The SEC requires it, you know. You want to sell five million dollars worth?"

Greer smirked. As if the SEC mattered to anyone. "Correct."

Covington erupted with something between a laugh and a choke. "But, Jensen, that stock of yours has a long way to go! What with the miracle at Justene, Summit is rated as a strong buy! We're projecting $130 per share. You'll be loosing millions! Are you sure that now is the time to sell?"

"Yes. And I don't have all day."

Covington's thin lips pursed together. "Of course. So, how are things over there at Summit?"

The question was blatantly obvious. Like, anything you might want to share with me? Like, why the hell you would want to dump five million, right now?

Greer shifted in the chair. "Things are fine." Things would definitely not be fine soon enough.

Convington opened a credenza and searched for those elusive SEC papers, which rattled under his nervous fingers. "Are you investing in other stocks or bonds? The FOREX? We trade in all of the markets."

"I'm making other investments."

The fingers stopped searching. Lyle turned. His wedge face was dead serious. "Such as?"

Greer sneered. "Commercial real estate."

The poor man began hyperventilating. The words induced a mild state of shock for most stock brokers. "Are you certain this is really what you want to do?"

"I am."

"The capital gains taxes are going to kill you."

Heat gathered around Greer's neck. He was half-angry and half-entertained. "This seems to be a problem for you, Lyle."

"My God, no! I would hope not." Lyle's fingers danced across the files. He suddenly found the required papers and scribbled on them for a minute. "All right, all right. Sign here. And here. This is your copy. The proceeds will be in your cash management account. You can write checks against it, if you need to, in five days."

Greer extracted the pen from Lyle's reluctant fingers and signed. He folded his copy of the order and the SEC papers and saved them in his jacket's breast pocket. He glared at Covington. "Five days?"

"The funds take time to clear." Covington pushed the glass of wine forward. "Jensen, it's late in the day. Please, have some wine. Suzanne and I are taking a week in Oahu. We'd love to have you and Barbara join us. My treat."

"Maybe another time. I'll find my way out."

Greer was up and gone. The door closed.

Covington whisked a napkin from the serving tray and mopped the sweat from his forehead. He grabbed Jensen's glass of wine, gulped it down, and then poured another. He drummed the desk and stared at his watch. After exactly 60 seconds, he got up and opened the door. Greer was gone.

He picked up the phone and dialed. "This is Lyle Covington. Get me Sarinov."

## Chapter 25

Greer took a long breakfast Tuesday morning. He coaxed his daughter into finishing her waffles and was poked only once with her fork. He hugged her more than once and appeared almost melancholy.

After breakfast, Bridgette left Patricia with Barney and met Greer outside. He was loading two suitcases into the Porsche. Barbara was asleep.

He opened the car door and Bridgette stepped toward him. In her snug blue jeans and a white sweater, she reached up and gave him a long, full kiss.

He pulled back from her and looked her in the eyes. "Keep an eye on Patricia for me. Things may get a little crazy around here."

She nodded. "Crazier than usual?"

Greer grimaced. "I'm not sure. I'll be calling in a few days, but I'll call your cell phone. You have my number. Call me only if you need to. But be sure you're alone when you do. And don't ever use the house phone to call me. Ever."

She nodded again. Her eyes were serious. "I understand. I'm worried."

"Don't be," he replied. "They're not interested in you."

"I don't mean me. I'm worried about you, Jensen. How dangerous are these people?"

The tone in her voice struck him, and how she spoke his name. Greer pushed the hair from her face. "Don't worry, baby. It'll blow up in a week, ten days, and then it should slowly blow over. When things calm down, I'll call you."

She nodded. Her eyes welled up. She pushed into him again and kissed him long and hard on the lips. He held her close, smelled her hair, her skin, and remembered how it was to feel this way. He finally pulled back.

Greer exhaled and stepped into the car. He started the Porsche and quietly drove out the stone driveway, past the pillars and up to the security gates. He paused and looked back at his home, at the neighboring stone and brick mansions scattered across the hilltop. Bridgette was standing in the driveway with her arms crossed. She waved.

Greer drove to Interstate 5 and then headed north, through Portland, and over the Columbia River. Traffic moved quickly through the city of Vancouver and for the next hour, the Interstate slipped by small communities, through forests and across rivers. Where the radar detector and traffic permitted, he pushed the Porsche to over 100 miles per hour. By 9:00, he was approaching Olympia. Traffic thickened and he dropped the speed to 50.

At the south end of the Puget Sound, the Interstate arced around the bay and the water glistened through the trees. At Evergreen Avenue, he exited and stopped into a mini mart for gas and a six pack of Heineken. It wasn't warm out, but he opened up the moon roof, jacked up the heat and let the crisp air blow in. He opened a bottle and drained it.

He hadn't thought to do this before, but he glanced in the mirror. How dangerous could they be, right now? Not in a week or so, after all hell broke loose, but now? For a week at least, he was free. But when the authorities came knocking and the stock price tumbled and their millions shrank, how dangerous would they be?

The freeway continued north into Tacoma, past Fort Lewis Army Base and McCord Air Force Base, where it presented the usual assortment of seedy hotels and bars. Tacoma sprawled for miles. He finally exited and bought a week's groceries at a Safeway store. Across the parking lot, he stopped at a fast-food joint for a quick lunch and to relieve himself.

Forty-five minutes later he passed by Renton and the Boeing plant. From the elevated freeway, he could see a row of planes parked along the runway below. The Space Needle appeared on the left, framed by Seattle and Elliot Bay. Downtown office towers loomed and the interstate swept underneath them. With the open roof, the traffic roared. The car emerged and Lake Union and the University of Washington appeared on the right. Another ten minutes, and Greer caught State Highway 104 West. This shot him straight down a hill into Edmonds. He turned onto Admiral Way, and after another half mile, arrived at Frasier Yachts.

Greer closed the moon roof and got out slowly, coaxing his legs back to life. The place was sprawling, with a main office building up front and more buildings on both sides. On the south side were acres of boats. The overnighters were parked under long roofs. Closer up, smaller boats were stacked three-high in covered structures.

Greer entered. Behind the counter, a young man stood up. "May I help you?"

"I'm Jensen Greer."

"Just a minute, Mr. Greer."

The man, his badge read *Lenny*, picked up the phone. Within 30 seconds, another man came bounding down the hall, his hand outstretched before he arrived. He was blond and stocky, in a red Frasier Yachts shirt.

"Mr. Greer, Jerry Frasier! How are you?" the man asked. A tanned arm shook Greer's hand.

Greer nodded. "How's the boat?"

Lenny had moved from behind the counter and handed a clipboard to his boss.

Frasier pulled a pen from his pocket. He looked stern. "Mr. Greer, you don't own a boat. You own a yacht." He leaned forward. "I have other clients with boats, 20-foot dinghies. They can't afford your fuel bill."

Greer nodded. "Fine. Is my yacht ready to go?"

Frasier pointed with the pen to the clipboard. "We de-winterized her and performed a complete tune-up on both drive systems. Fresh water tanks are full. We put in 200 gallons of diesel, she's three-quarter fueled. Propane tanks are full. We detailed her out. The total came to $2,240."

Greer had paid over five hundred thousand for the yacht; he didn't blink. But he didn't pay, either. Credit card transactions weren't wise, just now. "Put it on my statement. I'll catch it at the end of the month."

"All right. Do you have supplies or luggage?"

"In the car. Groceries in the seat, luggage in the trunk."

Down in front of the marina, two yachts were tied off. Greer, Lenny, and a third man lugged the suitcases and grocery bags out through the back of the building, down the brow and onto the docks. The tide was out, leaving riprap exposed above the water. Sea anemone and barnacles encrusted the rocks. The air was thick with the sea.

The *Golden Daze* was the largest vessel there, and Greer couldn't avoid smiling as he walked up. Two years old, the Carver's lines were sleek and aggressive. Entirely white except for a black stripe at the water line and dark glass windows, the vessel glistened. They stepped over the gunnel and onto the back deck, and then lifted the suitcases and supplies inside.

"Do you want the luggage in the forward or aft berth?" Lenny asked.

"Aft."

Greer climbed three steps to a half-deck and opened the slider. Inside, he walked through the salon and into the galley and set the groceries on a counter. The carpeting, marble counters, and cherry cabinets were spotless.

Forward of the salon, the galley was a full kitchen with a four-burner gas stove, oven, refrigerator, and sinks. Greer stowed the groceries in the cabinets and fridge. At the bottom of the fridge, someone had placed a black bottle of Dom Perignon champagne. A white card was tied to the bottle's neck. He carried the case of beer back outside and put it inside the fridge that was built into the wet bar.

Frasier strutted down the dock with his arms swinging wide. "A beaut', isn't she? San Juans?"

Greer nodded.

Frasier stepped aboard. "Two weeks?"

"More or less."

"Sounds like heaven. Let's blow out the motors and get them warmed up. The keys are up top."

The two climbed the steps up to the fly bridge. Frasier walked around the upholstered lounge and pilot's seat to the instrument panel and flipped a few switches. "How many times have you had her out?" he asked.

"Five or six. I used the boat more the first year."

"So you've got it down pretty well? Mooring and unmooring? Backing and pivoting?"

"Pretty much."

"Well the key is, go slow. When mooring, have your fenders out and your ropes and a pole ready. See these blowers? You should always blow out the engines for a few minutes before you turn them over, even though they're diesel."

Greer nodded.

Frasier stood with his hands on his hips. "Any guests? Wife?"

"No," Greer replied. Nothing else, just no.

"Well there's a bottle of very good champagne in the galley refer, a little gift. The season hasn't started yet, but maybe you'll find a little distraction. Where are you staying?"

"Wherever I tie off."

"Port Townsend?"

Greer's face was blank. "Haven't decided."

Frasier seemed puzzled but quickly nodded. "Full charts are in the chart box right there, for all of the Sound, San Juans, all the way to Alaska. There's a duplicate set at the helm below and binocs down there. There's a spare set of keys in the galley, far left drawer. We have some weather coming in tonight, so you'll want to get tied off before late. Do you know how to use the GPS?"

"Yes." Greer nodded impatiently.

"Well, let's do it. Go ahead and start up." He spoke like a Sears driving instructor.

Greer turned the two keys, in turn, and on the panel, tachometer needles sprang to life. A quiet rumble echoed from below decks.

Frasier continued. "I'll untie and push you off. We'll lock your car in the gated lot. The place has 24-hour guards. When you return, just show your driver's license."

On the pier, Frasier and Lenny untied the boat. Greer slowly backed the boat out of the slip and the dock slid away. Once well clear of the dock, he pushed the starboard throttle forward slightly and pulled the port throttle back the same. The boat rotated slowly in place. From high on the fly bridge, Greer could see down into the emerald water. Around the bow, it turned in white whirlpools. He checked the skies: a light breeze, high overcast. The temperature was in the low fifties.

When the bow had pivoted around to face northwest, he slipped the port throttle forward and slowly brought both engines up to a third. They rumbled quietly and the Carver lumbered up to ten knots. On the dock, Frasier waved. Greer found the switch on the panel, next to 20 others. He flicked it and the horns erupted with a harmonic blast.

A chore came to mind. Greer took the cell phone from his jacket pocket, turned it on, and dialed a number he had memorized. A woman's voice answered, a recording.

Tension pinched Greer's stomach as he spoke. "Mr. Evans, you know me. We met last week at Anthony's. Today is Tuesday. The package I wanted to give to you, I've mailed instead. You should get it today or Wednesday. It has everything you'll need to close Justene."

Greer thought of the folders. "There are other documents included. They come from the executive management at Summit Resources, regarding Gabe Riplinger, Arland Lochner, a senator, and you. I think the significance will be apparent. Good luck."

Greer turned the cell phone off.

Ahead, the bay was clear. He slowly pushed the throttles forward, bringing the diesels up full. The 14-ton yacht rose up and the sea parted in a wide, frothing V. He stood up from the seat, high on the fly bridge, and let the cool wind blow through his hair and jacket. He took in the salt air. He felt alive. It had never felt so good to get away.

Out on the water, a cold wind kicked up and Greer was forced to pilot the boat from the lower helm. He hadn't bothered to check the weather and now it put a chop and whitecaps on the sea.

He arrived in Port Townshend in the afternoon. He pulled up slowly and let the breeze nudge him broadside up to the dock. He then hopped onto the dock and tied off. The summer crowd of boaters was absent. The docks were mostly empty and rolling clouds promised more rain.

He stayed aboard all day. For dinner: a steak with a salad, tomatoes, a little French bread and a bottle of red wine. He closed the salon curtains partway and then sat in darkness, with the lights out, as a storm drenched the port. Far off, a blinking red traffic light bounced in the wind. He turned on the radio and found a jazz station out of Seattle. He finished the bottle of wine.

Around midnight he made the rounds, locking doors and hatches before turning in.

# Chapter 26

For Ryan, Monday night was sleepless.

Tuesday morning, after Meagan left for work, he spent the next couple of hours drinking coffee and pacing the house. His mind raced and when he finally couldn't take pacing any more, he grabbed his jacket and headed out the back door. After an hour of aimless driving, he pulled up in front of Gabe's house and stepped out of the truck. A *For Sale* sign leaned over. The wind had scattered small branches around the yard, had blown down a roof gutter along the front. The house looked abandoned.

He made his way around to the backyard. The horses were gone. He stood in the wet grass where, on Easters past, throngs of children of DEQ parents and from Gabe's church had searched for colored eggs. And then it was Shakespeare. He could still hear the dog's low howl.

The white door beckoned and he wondered why he was here. He pushed his hand to the tarnished brass knob. It turned. Inside, the cavernous garage was empty. The place was clean, right up to the dark corners, cleaned by people who pick up after death and then others who liquidate the estate: a lifetime of personal belongings, mostly little things that capture and speak of something ethereal. Some of it is retained by family, connections to the past. The rest of it is sold off, scattered to people looking for a bargain and who know and care absolutely nothing about the previous owner. Gabe had died here.

Ryan's breath shortened. Now that he knew everything about Gabe and Newberg, about the crooked management at DEQ and Summit, he was expected to just disappear. Vanish and remain silent about all of it for the rest of his life, and just maybe they would leave him and Meagan alone. He could never tell her, because telling her everything and doing nothing would drive her insane. He knew way too much, so why was he still alive? Because they had just murdered Gabe; another so soon would attract attention. But what about later? Would they be alive in one year? In five?

The doctor visit had taken only a few minutes, but the thought of returning to work was too much. Nauseated all morning, Meagan wanted to lie down. She would call the animal clinic from the house. Right now, she wanted to curl up in bed.

A brown van stopped at the top of the driveway and two men got out. The driver then moved the van ten yards down the road and parked. The two men wore fresh blue coveralls with labels that promised their virtuous nature. *Integrity Plumbing*.

They moved quickly up the drive, around the back, and onto the back porch. The ancient lock was pointless. The taller one slipped on latex gloves and deftly fished a thin, flexible bar into the jam. The door swung wide.

Sophie erupted. The little dog was grabbed and locked in the downstairs bathroom. On the kitchen counter, the electric cord for the answering machine was briefly pulled from the wall and the batteries were lifted out, deleting Greer's message.

They moved silently, touching little. A magazine bin in the kitchen held copies of National Geographic and Sunset magazine. The counters and table were clean. Closets were opened and closed. They checked behind doors, behind the couch. They had watched the house, had pilfered the mailbox at the end of the driveway. Clipped to the taller man's waist, a small black radio hissed. "Five minutes!"

They climbed the stairs two at a time and began checking bedrooms. In one were stacks of moving boxes, a set of barbells, a telescope. In another room, a desk and chair. The desk held nothing, bank statements and bills. In one drawer were pictures and greeting cards. *Happy Valentine's Day.* A metal filing cabinet contained college text books. Two large filing boxes crammed with papers lay in the opposite corner.

The shorter man charged into the master bedroom. The bedding was opened, the sheets and spread pulled down. Her tan nightgown lay folded over the back of the chair next to the dresser. With a neck like a bull and a black moustache, he smiled slyly. He had watched her move about with powerful binoculars, had already molested her in his mind. He lifted the gown up and pressed the glimmering silk to his nostrils.

Behind him, his partner snarled. "Knock it off! Check the closet! Hurry!"

The radio squawked. "Get out! Get out now! She came in from the other side! She's in the driveway!"

The tall one grabbed his radio. "Where is she?"

The driver eased the van into the driveway behind her car. "The back door!"

Between Sophie's relentless barking, door hinges let out a squeak. Then her voice. "Sophie?"

The tall one killed the walkie-talkie. They floated down the hall, their footsteps masked by the dog's hysterical barking.

Meagan set her purse on the kitchen table. She moved slowly into the dining room and stood. The bathroom where she heard the dog barking was across a short hall and opposite the stairs.

"Sophie?" Fear trembled in her voice.

The barking subsided to a whimpering whine. She placed her hand on the banister post and looked about. The front door was locked. There were no windows broken, nothing obviously wrong.

A breeze wafted down the stairs and the bathroom door rattled against the latch. The barking instantly resumed. Meagan smiled. She had left a window in the bedroom open an inch, for air. And in the bathroom, the small window was open just a crack. The wind had blown down the stairs and pushed the door closed behind the dog, which had a habit of drinking water out of the toilet. The little animal was now trapped. She laughed out loud.

She retrieved the still-whimpering animal, carried it through the kitchen, and put it outside. The barking continued.

Meagan left her coat and purse in the kitchen and headed for the stairs. The stomach cramps had worsened. A long, hot bath might help. In the living room, a newspaper covered the coffee table. Ryan's socks lay on the floor and the phone book was parked on the couch as though it belonged there. She sighed.

Her stomach protested, but she detoured into the living room to pick things up. Reaching down to fold up the paper, she saw it. A black hair. Like a bristle, it was short and thick against the white paper. She knelt low. No one in the house had black hair. Outside, the dog was possessed.

From above, a creak sounded. Familiar, it sprouted from the spot in the upstairs hall when she stepped out of the bathroom. She strained to hear it again but heard everything else instead: the dog, the furnace turning on. Meagan shivered. Her eyes flashed across the room for something to swing. The black fireplace poker leaned against the brick. Not breathing, she moved to it and grabbed it by the handle.

Another creak.

She slipped closer to the stairs. She labored to hear the tiniest of sounds until the silence made it own noise. Nothing. Listen.

Something? A breath?

The front door with its new deadbolt lock was 20 feet away. The lock was missing the key. Didn't it need a key!? A mile separated her from the back door.

Against debilitating fear, she raised the poker high and peered into the stairwell. To her absolute shock, a man looked down from the top of the stairs. He flew down the stairs in a second and her poker came down hard, the iron tip of it slamming against his head. He staggered and she turned to run, but he tackled her. Half under the dining room table, he grabbed fists of auburn hair. She rolled under him and threw her right palm toward his larynx, but missed and hit his massive chin. He grabbed her hair with both hands and slammed her head into the dining table pedestal. With a moan, her hands fell to the floor. He swung two hard blows to her head. She was unconscious after the first.

Ryan parked the International, unlocked the back door, and entered the house. He laid his coat on a kitchen chair and called out. "Sophie?"

The little dog never missed greeting him. He did a quick tour in search of the animal. In the master bedroom, he picked up Meagan's nightgown from the floor and draped it over the chair. He closed a window and then returned down the stairs and stopped at the landing. It was the runner rug, an eight-foot, brown and white Berber. She was precise about where it went, positioned in front of the dining room table. But now it was off at an odd angle, pushed under the table. He knelt down and straightened it.

She must have come home for something and let the dog out, and it had run off. Stepping through the mud room and the back door, Ryan stood at the edge of the porch and called for the animal. The phone rang. It was probably Meagan, he thought. He went back inside and answered it.

"Hello?"

"Hi Ryan."

"Karina."

"How are things?" she asked.

"Terrible. Where are you?"

"Home. I called in sick. What happened?"

"Of course, they fired me. They fabricated a pile of lies to get rid of me. They said I took state documents home without permission. They said I surfed porn sites, that I had porn on my computer."

Karina became quiet, absorbing the significance. "The place is rotten to the core. I'm quitting."

"Listen, Karina, it's worse than that. As I was leaving yesterday, I was met in the parking garage. Two guys came up to me. They said I needed to go away, forget about Justene and Gabe, and Newberg, or that I would end up like them."

"What? What happened?"

"Right after I was fired, I was confronted by two guys in the parking garage. Karina, they admitted to everything. They killed Gabe. And Newberg. They told me to disappear."

"Jesus!"

"They killed Gabe. Karina, they killed him. They shoved Newberg out of a helicopter. He was dead the day after he supposedly signed off on the original study on Justene. They falsified his report."

"What, what about Arland? And Lassiter?"

"Lochner and Lassiter are corrupt. Both of them fired me, and seconds later I was threatened by those animals."

"They kill people?!"

"Not Lochner, not DEQ. People from Summit."

Her voice shuddered. "They could have killed you!"

"Not yet. There's too many."

Karina was crying.

"When are you quitting?" Ryan asked.

"Now! I'm not going back!"

"You need to wait."

"What?! And go to work freaked out of my mind?" Karina spoke between shudders.

Ryan tried to calm her. "Listen to me. You need to act as normal as possible, like you know absolutely nothing. I'm going to the media with all of it. I'm telling Meagan everything today and I'm sending her out of town in the morning. Then I'm going to talk to the media and blow this wide open. Gabe, Newberg, the fraudulent documentation, the dates. The more people who know, the safer we are. And I'm calling an attorney. I'm going to get an injunction issued against the expansion."

She whispered. "Ryan, I need to see you."

"No! Stay away from me! When you leave DEQ, do it quietly. When this hits the media, then leave. And Tommy, tell Tommy I'll call him in a few days. Tell no one else. Keep this quiet. You both need to be dead quiet about this. Don't do anything until after this hits the news. I'm going to make as much noise as possible."

"You think they're watching?"

"We can't take any chances."

She was still crying.

"Listen, Karina, we'll be all right. This'll work out. Just don't move too quickly. Act like everything is fine. After this hits the news and everyone knows, then leave."

"Call me."

"I will. I'll call you in two days. Be careful, Karina."

Ryan hung up the phone. He held his head in his hands. He had just told Karina information that could easily get her killed, but information she needed. And he had told his wife nothing.

In the kitchen, Ryan checked the Mickey Mouse clock. It was a little after four. She would be home in just over an hour. He made more coffee. He grabbed a yellow notepad from the drawer beneath the telephone and sat down at the kitchen table. He needed to make plans.

A few minutes after five, Ryan put down the pen, moved to the back door and checked for the dog. Sophie never roamed, but the porch was empty.

Thirty minutes later, he called her office at the clinic. "Hi honey, it's me. If you had to work late or had a late meeting or something, you didn't mention it. So call me or come home?"

He then dialed her cell. The phone rang, not only in his ear, but in the kitchen. On the counter, behind the napkin holder—her cell phone was plugged into the wall charger.

Ryan checked the answering machine for messages. The display glowed a green "0". He took in a breath. Shopping?

By 6:00, daylight was fading. The crimson red of the sunset was fierce, but an army of dark clouds filled the sky and were quickly squelching the light down to a bright band. Ryan watched rain drops streak the window.

A corkboard was hung at the end of the cabinets. It was half-covered with rows of yellow paper squares containing telephone numbers of friends, Aunt Sirrey, her parents, and others, printed in Meagan's hand. One of the squares said simply, *I love you, Ryan!*

There were times, although he could never admit it to her, when he didn't want the chocolate kisses and spontaneous love notes stuffed randomly into his life. They felt great, but somehow unsettling, as though guaranteeing a future where loss and anguish would arrive on some terrible day.

He found Mary Lavoie's home phone number on a paper square and dialed it. Mary was an associate veterinarian at the clinic.

"Mary, this is Ryan, Meagan's husband. I'm sorry to bother you. I'm looking for Meagan. Have you seen her?" A pause.

"She what? Eleven o'clock? This morning?" Ryan pulled out the chair but didn't sit. "Did she say where she was going? No. No, she's still out. I haven't seen her. I don't know, I thought she was at work. Call me if you see her? Yes, I will. Thanks."

He paced into the living room and then pivoted back into the kitchen. Meagan had left work just before 11:00 for a doctor's appointment and never returned. Seven hours?!

From outside, a dog's bark sounded. Across the kitchen and through the mudroom, Ryan opened the back door. The wind poured in. "Sophie?"

He flicked on the floodlight and moved down the steps into the wet yard. He called again, and then turned and saw the little dog in the driveway, sitting like a statue. "Sophie!"

The sound of tearing paper rolled overhead and the deluge began, but the dog sat motionless.

Ryan approached it, across the grass and onto the gravel. "Where have you been?"

He reached down for the animal, and then noticed it. A red glint. A small patch on the gravel, glossy red in the floodlight. He pushed the dog back. Another patch lay nearby. He found a twig and touched the color. It clung to the twig, red, sticky. Ryan carried the dog up to the floodlight and searched the fur for any wound. He ran back to the blood and knelt down close, inches from it. Two glistening patches the size of golf balls draped the gravel in red.

## Chapter 27

The officer rolled down the window and was met by a wild-eyed man, soaked with rain.

Ryan shouted into the wind. "What took you?! My wife, she left work this morning! She had a doctor's appointment at eleven, she's missing!"

"Calm down." The dashboard lights and computer screen lit the officer's face. The name plate on his khaki shirt read Sergeant Don Bolton. "What's your name?"

Ryan scowled. He had already told the 911 operator everything. "Ryan Evans! Look, come here! There's blood, on the driveway, up here!" He turned and ran up the driveway, shouting over his shoulder. "But the rain!"

The downpour had formed large puddles and rivulets that collected to create a stream. It swept across in front of the cruiser's headlights and then ran down the driveway. Behind Ryan's truck, under the floodlight, four rocks sat in a large muddy puddle. He had intended them to hold down the plastic garbage bag, to protect the blood from the rain, but now the entire bag was submerged.

Ryan dropped to his knees. "There was blood here! What the hell took you so long?"

Bolton walked up behind Ryan; the partner followed with a black flashlight. The two officers looked at the puddle, the rocks. Bolton grunted. "You're sure it was blood?"

"Yes!"

"How much?"

Ryan looked up, shaking his head. "Two big spots." He approximated with his index finger and thumb, and then dropped his hand. "But now…"

All three looked at the muddy water. The junior officer, a kid with acne, shrugged. "Not anymore."

Ryan shot the kid a lethal glare.

Silver-haired Bolton spoke. "Is there anything else? Any other signs out here?"

Ryan eyes returned to the growing puddle. "I don't know! What took you?"

Bolton took the kid's flashlight and quickly scanned the top of the driveway, the brick walkup to the back porch steps, and then around the truck and down the driveway. "You're sure she's not inside?" Bolton asked.

Ryan was floored. Like, maybe she was lost in a closet? "What?!"

"Let's go inside," said Bolton. "You can tell us everything."

Inside, within 15 minutes, the officers conducted their interview. Bolton spoke. "So there was nothing out of place, nothing missing?"

"In here." Ryan walked into the living room. "Here, this runner was moved. It was off center, pushed off toward the table like this."

The officers looked at Ryan. Bolton spoke. "How unusual is that?"

"It's never like that! It wasn't that way when I left. And like I said, the dog was out for hours, and I didn't put the dog out. It was out when I got home. It sat down in front of the blood."

"So maybe your wife came home and let the dog out."

"No! She came home! But something happened here!"

"Where's her car?"

"I don't know!" Ryan's hands went up.

Bolton's face was expressionless. "How long have you been married?"

"Three years."

"And your wife never comes home late?"

"Not without telling me!"

"Does she have a cell phone?"

"She left it here at the house."

"Hmm." Sergeant Bolton took a look breath. "Mr. Evans, maybe you're jumping to conclusions. Do you mind if we take a look through the house?"

It felt pointless to have these two wet men poking through the house, as though Ryan might have misplaced his wife. "Help yourself."

Downstairs, Ryan huddled over the woodstove while the water from his shirt splattered onto the black metal. Wet boots stomped around the house. Upstairs and down again, they ended their short investigation.

Bolton rubbed his chin. "Well, seeing as her car isn't here, and as I said, there are no reports of a Meagan Evans at any local hospital, no Jane Does. You're sure she isn't out shopping?"

Ryan expelled a frustrated sigh. "Listen to me. She always calls or leaves a note if she's going out. It's 9:20 now. She's been missing since 11:00 this morning! She never goes out without letting me know, ever."

"Family nearby? Friends or relatives? Call them."

"We don't have family in Oregon."

The two officers headed for the door. Bolton spoke. "Try to calm down, Mr. Evans. She's probably out shopping with friends. If she doesn't turn up by tomorrow, we can talk."

"Tomorrow?"

Bolton turned, with his hands up. "What can I do? There is no evidence of a crime here. You say there was a little blood on the driveway, but with all the rain, we can't follow that up. It was dark when you saw it, it could have been anything. Maybe your cat killed a bird."

"We don't have a cat."

"Maybe your dog killed a cat," the kid offered. He smiled, happy with his contribution.

Bolton continued. "Listen. Your wife came home, she let the dog out. And now she's out shopping."

Ryan shook his head. "At least put out an APB!"

Bolton offered a patronizing smile. "We do that for missing children." He opened the door. "Call me tomorrow. You can tell me how late she got in. I'll bet you $20 she's at the mall."

The kid nodded. An easy $20.

Ryan palmed his forehead. "Sergeant Bolton. Don. Please!"

The two moved down the front steps to the cruiser. Ryan followed. Bolton talked as he walked. "It'll be all right. Call me tomorrow."

Ryan stood in the rain and watched the cruiser drive away.

Ryan closed the front door and locked it. Aside from the storm, the house was quiet. It was the oddest thought, that somehow he could head upstairs, walk into the master bath, and find her soaking in the giant old tub with her hair pinned up.

In the kitchen, he dialed every number on the corkboard except her parents. He apologized to Mary for the hour. Yes, Meagan was still out. Yes, he had called the police. He asked which doctor she had visited, the name? A gynecologist. Mary didn't know who. Meagan had left the animal clinic at 10:30 and not returned. Mary knew nothing else. The woman made him promise to call as soon he learned anything.

No one answered at Anne and Alex's in Seattle. He left a message and made more calls. Her parents were last. Seattle was a four-hour drive, five in the storm. Meagan didn't drive to see her parents, not unless their marriage had suddenly crashed without warning. Still, he hoped for any reason. Just be there. It rang four times and the recorder picked up, the voice of her mother. He left the basic details and asked them to call immediately.

In checking the house for a lost woman, the police had not bothered with evidence. Ryan retrieved a flashlight from the kitchen and turned off the downstairs lights. On his hands and knees, he turned on the flashlight and placed it flat on the floor. He scanned the floor under the path of light for anything usual. Under the kitchen table, under the chairs and in the corners, he looked for the tiniest oddity. He inspected the chair seats and counter tops. The dining room, living room, and upstairs all received the same scrutiny.

In the dark, he sank down on the last step in the stairwell. The search had yielded a paperclip and a button from one of his shirts.

His stomach twisted. He had telephoned everyone; the world was unavailable. Sitting would drive him insane. He slipped on his jacket, grabbed the flashlight, and left the house.

The rain had eased, but not the wind. Under the light, broken tree branches lay scattered around the yard and driveway. His sacred plastic trash bag that had covered the blood had blown away.

He backed the International out of the driveway.

At the West Side Animal Clinic, he killed the engine and stared at the darkened structure. The building was single-story, spread out, and dimly lit by street lights. It was past midnight. She was due back here in less than eight hours.

He stepped out and walked to where she usually parked the Prius. Under the flashlight, he found a cap from a beverage bottle and a cigarette butt. Pine needles and small branches from fir trees littered the ground

Ten minutes later, Ryan pulled into a strip mall. The grocery store had a coffee house and a small outdoor garden center. They often bought coffee here, Americano for him, a latte for her. Meagan loved to sip coffee and smell the hyacinth or jasmine or whatever was in. They always parked two or three rows back, on the right. A few cars belonging to janitors and guards were clustered up front. No blue Prius.

A Border's bookstore and a Home Depot received the same treatment. As a last resort, he drove to a large shopping mall. He circled the empty complex twice.

At 3:15 a.m., Ryan dropped his jacket on the kitchen chair. There were no phone messages.

# Chapter 28

Wednesday morning, Jensen Greer was up early. The sky was gray and a ceiling of clouds hung low. He had little appetite and ate a slow breakfast, a bagel with a glass of orange juice.

Just before 11:00, a family pulled up in an older 40-foot Chris Craft. Greer helped them tie off. He made a pot of strong coffee for the three of them, the husband, his wife, and himself. They stood outside, talked, and drank it under the clouds. The couple complimented his coffee and his yacht while the kids and their black lab ogled the purple starfish and white sea anemones that encrusted the pilings.

By afternoon, Greer became antsy. He started the motors and the man helped him untie. The kids waved from the dock as he pulled the boat away. He avoided the horns.

He headed north by northwest, into more open water. An hour out of port, he killed both engines. Their quiet rumbling and the soft whoosh of rushing water ended as the boat eased to a stop. The morning mist had burned off and patches of blue sky appeared. The cool air was still. He climbed the stairway to the fly bridge with a bottle of beer and took it in.

To the north, islands were covered in evergreen and red-skinned madrona trees. Their shores were not gradual but fell in steep cliffs to the beach. The Olympic Mountains, capped with snow, broke through clouds to the southwest. Northwest lay the San Juan Islands and Vancouver Island, British Columbia. There was not another boat within miles.

He drifted with the current as the water turned and rolled in gentle whirlpools. Black sea birds raced silently by, inches off the glassy water. A memory flashed, of driving in to work, week after week, and facing the army of protestors. The insanity of it all. And then it hit him: they would win! The bastards would win! Not because of their own crusade, but because of the actions of an insider.

He laughed at the thought, tipped the beer bottle back, and then threw it into the sea. He sucked in the fresh air and yelled to no one in particular. "Fuck'em! Fuck'em all!"

Greer stood and smiled, enjoying the moment as the drone of a plane sounded. A blue plane with pontoons, it came in low from the south, circled in a wide arc, and headed east.

Later that afternoon he brought the *Golden Daze* into Friday Harbor, on the eastern side of San Juan Island. He had been here before: Front Street with its rustic little B&B hotels, restaurants, the ferry terminal. The marina had over a hundred slips and the docks were arranged in an arc, following the curvature of the bay. Beyond the port, the green island rose up quickly.

Summer finds Friday Harbor filled, but on this cool day in mid-March, it too was mostly vacant. He moored at the end of a finger. The nearest neighbors, a small cabin cruiser and an old tugboat, were 20 yards away. This would do for now, thought Geer. If needed, he could head into Canadian waters. The San Juans and Gulf Islands go for miles. He could cruise the Inland Passage all the way to Alaska. He could hide for a long time. They would start looking at Tamarack.

He had the urge to call Bridgette, but resisted.

After locking up the boat, Greer went for a walk. But the wind came up and brought in another drenching rain. He ducked into a deli and ate a late lunch with the newspaper.

When the rain finally eased, he retreated to the boat, closed the curtains, and kept an eye on the TV.

Greer awoke the next morning to light permeating the boat. Still in his underwear, he slipped open the curtains and discovered that the sky was more blue than gray. The sun's appearance changed the mood of the port. He showered and shaved. He made coffee and a cheese omelet in the galley and enjoyed breakfast on the back deck.

Inside, he washed dishes and even made up the bed. While pulling into port the previous day, he had noticed a string of white buoys marking the locations of crab pots. Perhaps he would try a little crabbing in a day or two.

He turned on the television and scanned stations for half an hour, but the news had nothing about Justene.

A few minutes later, Greer emerged from the boat wearing running shoes, shorts and a sweatshirt. He walked up the docks, past empty slips, sailboats, and cruisers. At the entrance to the marina was a self-serve kiosk. He filled out the envelope with a fictitious name and address and the true name of his boat. He deposited the $50 in an envelope into the steel slot: moorage for two nights.

Greer turned left under a giant maple tree and onto the sidewalk. Traffic was light as he jogged past small coffee shops and B & Bs, with steeply pitched roofs and narrow, gated entries. Yellow and blue pansies grew from cedar boxes. He ran past the landing for the Washington State Ferries and turned right, up Spring Street. A beer pub appeared, Mahoney's. It looked like a good place to sit and drink a pint or two.

Back at the entrance to the marina, under the maple tree, a man sat on a wooden bench. He wore sun glasses and spoke into a cell phone. Greer had walked right by him.

Another man crossed the street and entered the marina. This man carried a small tool chest in his right hand and made his way quickly down the docks, past the kids and the boats. He approached the *Golden Daze*, discretely glanced around, and stepped aboard.

Late in the day, neighbors from the cabin cruiser found their way down to Greer's yacht. From Redmond, John was a mechanical engineer and his wife, Marie, was a physical therapist. Marie's younger sister, Alexandra, was an assistant manager at a bank in Snohomish.

A few stars emerged overhead and the four grilled steak and prawns on the aft deck. Out of the wind and under the warm glow of a propane heater, they drank Coronas and laughed. They munched on vermouth prawns, and Greer couldn't help but notice Alexandra's long legs. The evening sky turned steel-blue and a half moon appeared in the east. The temperature dropped and they huddled closer together.

After telling all about herself, her husband, her sister, and their pets, Marie asked Greer, "What about you?"

He hesitated. Alexandra, in her white shorts and Gonzaga sweatshirt, pulled her knees up and wrapped her arms around them.

"I have a young daughter, Patricia. My wife and I are divorced," Greer finally said.

Marie continued. "What do you do for a living?"

Greer mumbled the words in his mind. Cyanide heap leach mining. None of them sounded good. "I'm a VP for a small software company. We create software for doing chemical analysis, molecular modeling."

It was a lie he had used before. He could be one of those type-A Einsteins who created vast fortunes out of little ones and zeroes. They smiled.

The white moon climbed higher and a breeze swept in from across the water. They laughed and drew still closer. Marie, who was verbally bottomless, sat on one side and Alexandra sat on the other. John's eyes were closed.

Just after midnight, the heater flickered and died. The deck was in darkness, lit only by the partial moon, high in the sky. Light from a distant floodlight was blocked by the boat itself. In the darkness, Alexandra's hand reached out and found his. Marie prattled on a few more minutes while Greer pretended to listen, and then John finally suggested that they turn in. Greer watched as Alexandra's silhouetted legs walked the 20 yards back to the cabin cruiser.

Inside the yacht, he stumbled down to the aft stateroom and collapsed on the bed.

Nausea. His head throbbed viciously. The smell. Putrid, rotten. He was drowning in the stench. In the dark, Greer staggered into the bathroom and fumbled for the light switch. His head was throbbing. In the mirror, sweat dripped from his red face.

The faintest click sounded and a deafening explosion reverberated across Friday Harbor. Entire sections of the *Golden Daze* jumped into the air. Screams could be heard as people awoke to the roaring, red flames. The fireball was fierce, igniting a second blast that blew out a generator gas tank. Burning fuel and debris showered the dark water as men scrambled onto the docks. John from Redmond grabbed a hose and, from a distance, began spraying the dock. There was no hope of battling the blaze on the yacht itself, and within 20 minutes, the entire craft had burned to the waterline. The remaining hull, breached and weighted by the engines, suddenly filled with sea water and sank. Black smoke filled the violet pre-dawn sky. Small debris and fuel fires littered the water's surface, but little else remained of the *Golden Daze*.

# CHAPTER 29

Ryan slept the night in fits, dozing for ten minutes and then waking with a start, only to confirm each time that it wasn't a horrible dream. He finally dozed off for 30 minutes but was up just after 6:30.

He turned on the television and, in the kitchen, searched Meagan's corkboard. Finding the name he wanted, he was forced to wait until 8:00 to make the call to a Doctor Rachel Barnett. The doctor was not in. Yes, Meagan had been in the day before at 11:00 and left by 11:40. Ryan informed the receptionist of Meagan's disappearance. The lady was busy and terse. Ryan asked to have the doctor call him.

Upstairs, Ryan washed up; there was no time for a shower. He grabbed a photograph from the bedroom dresser. It was a close-up of her, sitting on a driftwood log at the beach. The sun was out bright and her long, auburn hair framed her face. Back downstairs, he grabbed his coat. It was damp from the previous night.

Where the blood had been in the driveway, there was only mud.

At the clinic, John Kinsey, Mary, and Tawny, were all greatly concerned. Ryan queried them for several minutes, but they had seen nothing out of the ordinary. They made him promise to keep them informed.

The cop peered down from his perch from behind a thick pane of glass. "Your wife's name?"

"Meagan Evans."

Sergeant Delaney worked the computer with index fingers. He was in his fifties and heavy, with a gray moustache. "The report was filed just last night. You got more to add?"

"My wife is still missing. I want to speak with a detective."

"Detective Mathius is on duty. Let me see if he's available."

The conference room was down a short hall. No windows. Detective Mathius, gray-haired and with a paunch, sat across a large oak table with a short stack of papers. Officer Schaffer, younger and obviously a weight-lifter, sat at the end with a recorder.

Mathius placed a filterless Lucky Strike cigarette between his lips. "Give me a few minutes to read this. You want any coffee?"

Ryan declined and waited while Mathius read and played with his cigarette.

After a minute, Mathius spoke. "All right. I take it that Meagan Evans hasn't been located?"

"Uh, right."

"There is no chance you two argued and she decided to spend a couple of nights with a girl friend? Or her parents?"

Ryan's head shook. "No. And I've called them all. I couldn't reach her parents, but they live in Seattle. She wouldn't drive to Seattle without telling me."

"We require 72 hours before we can file a missing person's report, but we can at least put out a BOLO, a be on the lookout.

The BOLO will alert police agencies statewide. And we can get missing person paperwork started now, so we'll have it filed."

Ryan nodded.

Mathius played with the cigarette with one hand and took notes with the other. "Okay. I need you to tell me exactly what happened yesterday, to be sure we didn't miss anything."

Ryan slid the photograph of Meagan across the table. He took a deep breath and again described in detail the events of the previous day. Detective Mathius wrote while the younger cop watched his recorder.

Mathius asked the questions. "Have you contacted this doctor, Doctor Barnett?"

"An hour ago. She's in Southwest, off Hall Boulevard. Her office said Meagan showed up at eleven and left by eleven-forty."

"Anything odd at the house? Any sign of a struggle?"

"There was the blood on the driveway. By the time the officers got there, the storm had washed it away. There's a carpet runner downstairs, in the dining room. It was way off at an angle, as though someone had slipped on it."

"And where were you all day?"

"I spent the morning out, returned around 1:00."

"I see." Mathius scribbled.

Unconsciously, Ryan drummed the table. "This is going to sound insane, but a lot of bizarre things have happened over the past few months. I think they're related to my wife's disappearance."

Mathius glanced up. "Really? You tell me about that in a minute. Occupation?"

"I'm a biologist. Up until this week, I worked for Oregon DEQ, for three years."

"You lost your job this week? What day?"

"Monday."

The eyebrows went up. "Monday? Fired or quit?"

Ryan shook his head. "I was fired."

Ryan proceeded to tell them about Gabe's death, about the Justene mine, his investigation of the permitting process, about Robert Newberg's death and the signature date on the EIS. Mathius interrupted twice to ask how these things were related to his wife. Ryan revealed the interrupted meeting at Anthony's, his surprise firing, and then the warning he received from the same two in the garage. Near the end, it poured out like a flood.

Mathius struggled to follow it all, and at the mention of porn, the corner of his mouth curled up. He pulled the unlit cigarette from his lips. "So you downloaded porn onto government computers, and they fired you? Child porn?"

Mathius looked to Schaffer, who feigned a look of surprise.

Ryan jabbed the air with a finger. "No! No way! I never downloaded porn of any kind. I challenged the approval of the mine permits and they set it all up to force me out!"

Mathius lifted a hand up. He shook his head and made no effort to hide his incredulity. "How is all of this related to your wife?"

"I've been against the mine from the start. The briefcase had something they didn't want me to have. They warned me twice. They told me to back off, or I'd end up dead, like Riplinger and Newberg. They came to the house looking for me and ran into Meagan."

Mathius and Shaffer looked at each other. Mathius blinked repeatedly. "They who?"

Ryan's hand slapped the table top. "People from the mining company!"

"Uh huh. This Newberg, tell me more about him?"

"A DEQ employee out of Pendleton, he died four years ago, the day after he supposedly signed off on the state's paperwork."

"Fell out of a helicopter?"

"Yes."

The two eyed each other again. Mathius spoke. "Give us a few minutes."

They stood and left the room. Thirty minutes passed and Ryan was about to start looking for them when they finally returned.

Mathius sat down. "Mr. Evans, are you taking any medications?"

The question signaled a serious detour. Ryan's feet were bouncing on his toes. He furiously shook his head. "No, I am not."

"Not on any drugs, not under the care of a doctor or a psychiatrist?"

"No! You're not hearing me! You can talk to my co-workers. Gabe Riplinger was murdered! Suicide is just not believable! The mine approval was completely unexpected. I'd been digging into it, I found major problems with it. DEQ fired me to get rid of me." Ryan hammered the table with an index finger. "Her disappearance is connected to this!"

Mathius cocked his head to one side. His tone softened. "You believe that people at the Oregon Department of Environmental Quality murdered your boss and kidnapped your wife?"

Ryan could barely contain himself. "No! The company! They're in bed with Summit! People at the top are involved! My new boss, even Director Lochner! It sounds ridiculous, I know. But the company, Summit Resources? They cut us off at the restaurant, at Anthony's. This guy showed up in a suit and an expensive Porsche. He's not some nutcase. He had this briefcase full of papers. These guys knew him. They scared the hell out of him, and they knew my name. The same two threatened me in the parking garage." Ryan's hand slammed the table again. "My wife is missing!"

Mathius' eyes narrowed down onto his cigarette. He slid it under his nose and inhaled deeply enough to suck the tobacco from it. He rolled it in his fingers, seemingly obsessed.

"So these people from the mining company. They were really looking for you, but grabbed your wife instead."

"Yes! Listen, they hurt her! There was blood!"

Mathius' face was blank, his voice was monotone. "The officer's report says there was no evidence of a break-in or struggle. None. You claim there was blood. We have nothing on any blood."

Ryan was screaming at them before he knew it. "We had a damned flood! The rain washed it away! Godammit, I'm telling you what I know! My wife is missing! I don't know what else to do!"

"Mr. Evans, Ryan, you need to calm down."

The door opened. Another officer entered and stood with his arms crossed. Now there were three.

Mathius continued. "So where is this company, Summit Resources?"

"Downtown, on Jefferson Street."

"And where is this mine you're talking about?"

"Jesus, it was in the news for months! Past Pendleton, south of the Snake River."

A huff issued from Schaffer. "That's over 400 miles."

Mathius fiddled with his crooked cigarette. "Ryan, where do you think your wife is? Where would you have us look?"

"You're the detectives! Talk to the people at the DEQ, and Summit! You do it or I will."

Mathius shook his head. "No. No, you won't. We handle it. You work with us. Do you understand?" He pushed a clipboard at Ryan. "I need names and telephone numbers of all of your wife's friends, co-workers, and relatives. All recent acquaintances. I need the schedule of her typical week, where she goes, Sunday through Saturday. And then her activities yesterday, from the moment she got out of bed. I want contact information for your employer, your boss. Would you be willing to take a polygraph?"

"Me?"

"Mr. Evans, over 90 percent of the violent crimes committed against women are committed by their boyfriends or husbands. It's standard department procedure. We need to exclude you."

Ryan's hands opened wide. "When?"

"Tomorrow, the next day. It's early."

Schaffer nodded in agreement. "She'll probably turn up before then."

Ryan stared in amazement at Schaffer.

"And one more thing," Mathius continued. "We need to do a quick physical. Nothing personal. Just a look at your arms and legs, your back. Scrapings from your fingernails."

Ryan shrugged. "Fine. When?"

"Now."

"Great. But I want you to send people to my house. The police stomped all around last night, but they didn't search for anything. There must be evidence."

"We'll send someone out to look around."

"No! I don't want just a cop. I want forensics people, experts."

"We'll send someone out."

Ryan checked his watch. "It's 9:30 now. When?"

Mathius huffed. "We'll try for today."

"When do you start talking to Summit and DEQ?"

"Mr. Evans, we're still trying to determine if a crime has been committed. And one more thing. It's important. If you go to the media, don't tell them anything other than her personal description, the car, and the license plate. That's it. Give them a picture. But don't tell them anything whatsoever about DEQ or the company. And nothing about blood. You only talk to us, even things you remember later. Do you understand? This way, if someone knows more than they should, it'll raise a flag."

Ryan nodded. Mathius pushed a business card and looked Ryan directly in the eyes. "If you can think of anything more we need to know, something you've forgotten, or maybe you just need to talk. You call me."

Outside, Ryan sat in the truck and tried to think. He had already visited every store, every shop, every place she might have stopped after the doctor visit. There was a view spot, Council Crest Park, that overlooks the city all the way to the airport and south past Beaverton. They sometimes visited the park when the weather was nice. It was 20 minutes away.

A few cars were parked at the top of Council Crest, tourists from California who weren't hostage to the eight-to-five schedule. Five teenagers were crammed into a parked Honda Civic. There was no blue Prius.

He spent the rest of the day pacing the house and searching the yard and driveway. He called Alex and Anne's number again and left another message. He called her parents again, with the same results. As daylight retreated, he flipped on the television and paced some more. He could call Aunt Sirrey. He could call his mother, if he had the number.

Mary Lavoie called just after eight and Ryan brought her up to date with the little information he had. The end of the day approached and he realized he had not seen her dog all day, not since it sat down in front of the blood the previous night. Out the back door, in the dark, he called for Sophie.

He wanted to drive some more, but there was no place left and he wanted to be by the phone. He caught the local news at 10:00. At 2:30 a.m., he was back outside, standing in the driveway, in the rain.

# CHAPTER 30

The phone on the coffee table jarred him awake. He grabbed it before the second ring.

"Hello?"

"It's Alex. I got in late last night, just played your message. What happened?"

Ryan sat up on the couch and rubbed his face. It was morning. The television was on. His watch read 7:30. The nightmare returned.

"Meagan is gone." Ryan nearly broke down. "She's been kidnapped."

"What?"

Ryan unfolded the details. Alex listened and then spoke. "I'll be there in four hours. Anne is at the hospital. She can't come down. But I'll be there before noon."

Ryan's voice cracked. "Thanks."

In the kitchen, he drank a small glass of milk. He reached for the phone again and dialed the police station. Mathius was hard to find and Ryan paced for several minutes before the man spoke.

"Detective Mathius."

"Where are your people?" Ryan demanded. "I asked for a forensics team to check out this house and that was yesterday morning. Where are they?"

Mathius sounded irritated. "Evans, I was just about to call you. They'll be there this morning. Be at the house to let them in."

Mathius didn't wait for a reply and hung up.

Ryan tossed the phone on the couch and started pacing the again. On a pass through the kitchen, he stepped into the mud room, opened the back door and whistled for Sophie. The yard was empty.

He needed to do something, anything. Look for her in the truck, ask the neighbors what they might have seen, call more people. But he had to wait, at the house. And be off the phone. So he made more coffee and paced.

A car rolled up outside. The police, thought Ryan. He checked out the front window. A red Miata was in the driveway. He opened the front door as Karina climbed the steps.

"How are you?" she asked.

Ryan's voice wouldn't work. He stood in the doorway.

She continued. "I quit DEQ yesterday, I couldn't wait."

He nodded absently.

She assessed him with inquisitive eyes. "What happened?"

The ache tore at his throat. "Meagan's been kidnapped."

"What?!"

"Day before yesterday. She went to a doctor's appointment and then vanished." Ryan stepped past her onto the porch and pointed. "There was blood up there, blood. But the rain…" His hand made a sweep.

"My God! You called the police?!"

He nodded, his glistening eyes fixed on the driveway. "They think I did it."

"What!? Are you sure? I mean, have you called everyone? Friends?"

He nodded.

She stepped forward and threw her arms around him. He leaned into her and broke down.

Inside, at the kitchen table, he told again the events of the past 48 hours, ending with the visit with Mathius.

Karina's eyes welled. She took his hands across the table. "Let me go to the police with you. They'll believe us."

He shook his head. "No. They suspect me. They'll think we're lovers, that you and I..."

"Did you tell them everything? About Gabe? DEQ?"

He nodded. "They asked me to take a polygraph test." A deep, broken breath escaped him. "Karina, you shouldn't be here."

"No! My God, I can't believe this!" Karina's eyes grew large.

"You need to leave."

Her voice was shrill. "Who *are* these people?"

"They're dangerous. You should go."

"No, Ryan! No. We'll go to the media. Get on the phone and call a TV station."

"Karina, the police are coming to look around. You should go."

"You need help!"

He stared at Meagan's blue daffodil vase, resting on the table. "Am I crazy?"

"What?"

"Gabe. Newberg. This. Am I nuts?" Listing off the evidence, he answered his own question.

She looked at him. "We need people. The house needs more people, or we can't stay here."

Ryan hadn't considered this, that he should be afraid for himself. "I need to be by the phone, in case she calls."

"Then get more people over here."

"I called a friend in Seattle, Alex. He'll be here soon."

"Do you have a gun?"

"An old 12-gauge. My dad's."

"Get it."

A sharp knock at the door came at noon. Through the living room window, Ryan could see the police cruiser parked beside Karina's Miata. He opened the door and introductions were made. Officer Barnes and Detective Wilson entered and stood just inside the closed door.

Wilson spoke. "Mr. Evans, we're here to take a look inside your house. How many people are in the house now?"

Ryan gestured. "Just the two of us."

The detective addressed Karina. "Are you a family member?"

"I'm a friend."

"You'll need to wait outside."

Karina grabbed her coat and stepped outside.

Wilson continued. "All right. It says here that you suspect a possible break-in and kidnapping here, Tuesday? When did you determine your wife to be missing?"

Ryan's head fell to the side. He wondered, didn't the police share notes?

"She had a doctor's appointment at eleven Tuesday morning, but never returned to work. The last person to see her was her doctor."

"So she never returned to the house?"

"I'm sure she did. When I came home, the dog had been let out. We never put the dog out when we're gone. I found blood outside on the driveway. The rain washed it away, but it was there. I can show you where it was."

"It says here that you left the house and returned in the afternoon. What time was that?"

"A little after 1:00."

"And did you notice anything missing or disturbed? Any signs of forced entry?"

"Yes. The doors were locked, but a carpet was moved off at an angle, over there. I installed a new door and lock on the front, so I think they came in through the back."

"Is there anything missing?" Wilson asked.

Ryan shook his head. "No."

"All right. There's no one else in the house now? No pets?"

"No."

"Okay. I'll need both of you to leave the house. You can wait outside or take a drive, whatever you want. But you can't be in the house."

"Why not?"

"Police procedures. When we're doing a forensics examination of a residence, we require that the occupant is not in the home."

"I need to be by the phone."

"We'll be here."

This requirement irritated Ryan. "How long?"

Detective Wilson shrugged. "Three hours, at least. I suggest that you go run some errands or visit friends. Check back here in three hours."

"Let me get my jacket."

Outside, Karina was sitting on the porch steps. Overcast coated the sky with a uniform gray, but the rain had stopped. The police carried three metal suitcases of equipment into the house and closed the door.

Ryan sat down next to her. "I need some coffee. There's a Starbucks at the bottom of the hill."

They sat at a small table and ignored the jumpy reggae music. Ryan sipped an Americano and stared out the window across the parking lot. He and Meagan had been here only the previous weekend. He had been here ten hours earlier, in the dark. His mind revisited everything he had done, searching for whatever he might have missed, people, places. Karina sat quietly.

He finally turned to her. "How did you leave? How did you quit?"

"I wrote a letter and handed it to Lochner. I told him I needed to spend some time with my sick mother in Seattle, I might move there to be near her. I told him that was my last day."

"Your mother doesn't live in Seattle."

"He doesn't know that."

"Did he say anything about giving two weeks' notice?"

"Not a word. He said he understood. That was it."

"I bet he does. Where was Lassiter?"

"He was out, thank God. He scares me." Karina looked Ryan in the eyes. He was drained. "What are you going to do?"

"Find Meagan."

"I can help."

❖

The police were still inside the house when they returned, and a third cruiser now sat in the driveway. Ryan got out of the Miata. He alternately leaned against the car and paced, waiting restlessly for someone to emerge. After another hour, the front door finally opened. Detective Wilson came out with a metal suitcase in each hand.

Ryan approached as Wilson placed the cases in the trunk of the cruiser. "Did you find anything?" Ryan asked.

The man shrugged. "Hard to say. Mr. Evans, you have a gun in the house."

"The shotgun? It's mine. Did you find anything?"

"At this point we've simply gathered samples."

"But it's been over three hours, and you called for more help. You must have found something."

"We collect samples, that's all. The state lab will process this and then we'll know if we have anything."

The cop, Barnes, emerged from the house with a small white vacuum and the third suitcase. Behind him, a third man in plain clothes exited the house and moved to the car.

Ryan tried to quell his rising anger. "So when will you people know something?"

Wilson answered. "It's hard to say. Check with Detective Mathius."

"Can you at least tell me if there was a struggle? Did someone break in?"

Wilson closed the trunk and grimaced. "You'll have to talk to Detective Mathius."

Ryan watched as the three got into their cruisers and drove away.

"They found something!" Ryan growled. "They found something and they're not saying!"

He was pacing again. Through the kitchen and into the mudroom, he pulled open the back door and inspected the lock for signs of tampering. The old assembly was loose and marred from age; it was impossible to tell anything. The new front door and lock were nearly impenetrable, but the back door lock was useless.

Back through the kitchen and into the living room, he sat down on the edge of the couch and cradled his head in both hands. "I can't do this. I can't just wait!"

Karina sat down with him. "We need to go to the media. We'll get her face on TV. Where's the phone book?"

"In the nook, below the phone."

She left and returned with the book. "Did you get any sleep last night?"

"I don't know."

"Have you eaten?"

Ryan had to stop and think. "No."

"Here, look up the local TV stations. And radio."

She went back into the kitchen and returned shortly after, with a ham and cheese sandwich and a glass of water. Ryan was sitting on the couch with his head in his hands, the phone book in his lap.

She set the sandwich and glass on the coffee table. She sat down next to him and rubbed his shoulder. "Have a bite to eat."

The television droned low. From next to the couch, she picked up the ancient pump shotgun he had brought downstairs. She opened up the chamber and inspected it. "Do you know how to use this?" she asked.

His red eyes looked askance at her. "Be careful."

She opened the box of cartridges, methodically loaded the gun, and then sighted down the barrel. He watched. "Where did you learn guns?" he asked.

"My dad. He died in a hunting accident. Someone thought he was a deer in plaid."

"I'm sorry. You never told me that."

Karina nodded. "Nine years ago. I don't talk about it much. Four rounds in, one chambered. I'll leave the safety on." She slid the gun along the side of the couch. "It's here on the floor, next to the couch."

He looked at her. Karina was unlike any girl he had ever met. Quite female, but very much a tomboy.

She picked up the phone book and opened it as he watched the news. "We'll get photos of her on television, a description of the car, the plates," said Karina. "We'll get everyone in the state looking for her. Have you talked with the neighbors?"

"No. I should have done it while the police were here."

"I'll go with you. With volunteers, we—"

"Wait!" Ryan's hand flew up.

The newscaster's voice was faint. In the upper-left corner, a face. Ryan lunged to the screen and cranked the volume until it roared, upending the small table, the water, the shotgun shells. On the screen, a man's face was inset next to a large white boat. There had been an explosion in the San Juans. A half-million dollar yacht had exploded and burned. The owner was dead, Jensen Greer of Portland. A close-up of Greer filled half the screen. Ryan sat inches away, with eyes wide, mouth agape. A middle-aged couple described the fire. A propane explosion was suspected, authorities were investigating. His face again. Jensen Greer, an executive at Summit Resources.

Someone was knocking at the front door. Ryan yelled at the television. "The man with the briefcase! That's the guy with the Porsche!"

Another man's face appeared. He looked sad. His white shirt and tie were loosened and a young woman stood solemnly next to him. Text beneath read *Jacob Sarinov, CEO of Summit Resources.*

Sarinov looked upward several times. The morose face said tears were imminent. "The, the company is completely shocked," he said. "We are all grieving at this terrible loss. Jensen Greer is, was…a wonderful human being, a family man. A great man to have on our team. This is a terrible day. We offer our deepest condolences to his family."

Ryan gripped the corner of the television. "They killed him!"

The banging on the door grew louder. Karina grabbed the shotgun and aimed it at the door. "Who is it?" she yelled.

"Alex!"

Karina lowered the gun and cautiously opened the door.

Ryan was still glued to the television, his right hand pulling a fist of his hair. "They killed him! Jesus, they killed him!"

"Who?" Alex asked.

"The guy with the briefcase! He wanted to close Justene and they killed him!"

Karina turned down the television. Ryan was on his knees, his head in his hands. "They have her!"

Alex spoke. "Who has her?"

"The mining company! Summit Resources."

"You've spoken with the police?"

"They don't believe me! They think I did something!"

"What did they say?"

At this moment, Ryan jumped up, grabbed the shotgun, and stepped toward the door. Alex was directly in his path and his hands flew up. "Where are you going?"

"Get out of the way!"

"Ryan." Alex's hands grabbed the gun.

"Move!"

"No, no! Not a good idea, buddy."

"I know who has her!"

"No, listen." Alex shook his head furiously, with his hands gripping the shotgun. "This won't work! You'll wind up dead and Meagan won't have a husband. We'll find her. Ryan, listen to me. You can't charge into an office building with a shotgun! We'll find her."

Ryan's knuckles gripped the gun. His teeth were clenched. His hoarse voice whispered. "They have her!"

"We'll get her back. I promise. Let go."

Karina's hand landed ever so lightly on his shoulder. Ryan's grip slowly loosened, and then his hands dropped to his sides.

"We'll go to the media," she said softly. "We'll get her face on the television. We'll camp on the police, push them to make sure they're doing all they can. We'll put up flyers, everywhere. Your neighbors, someone saw something. We just push, Ryan. We keep pushing."

# Chapter 31

Alex unloaded the shotgun and hid it in a closet while Ryan paced the house. Outside, the light was fading. Another day was slipping by. Dazed, but very wired, Ryan checked the windows for nothing in particular, checked the television news. He was hostage to the news, the dreaded story of the car, a body.

Seven calls came in from friends to ask about her and Ryan lunged to the phone. Keys to the vehicles disappeared. Alex became his shadow to keep him from grabbing a butcher knife and charging out the back door.

Ryan quizzed the neighbors on foot with Karina. The few who were home had seen nothing, but it was better than sitting in the house. They would do it again in the evening.

Karina made the announcement from the living room. "They're here."

Out the front window, a large white van had pulled into the driveway. It was adorned, Mt. Rushmore-style, with the three photogenic faces of the CHANNEL 5 NEWS TEAM. Big hair, square jaws, and white smiles. Karina had made the calls while Ryan paced.

Ryan opened the door as a woman climbed the steps with three men in tow. She was in a dark blue business suit, with brilliant red lips and blond hair. One man wore a jacket and tie, the other two wore jeans. They were not one of the faces on the truck.

"Mr. Evans?" the woman asked.

"Yes."

She extended her hand and announced, "I'm Sandra Mills-Hopinger of Channel 5 News."

Introductions were completed and the two in suits sank into the bottomless couch. The two in jeans waited by the door.

Mills-Hopinger began. "So tell us, Mr. Evans. What happened?"

Pacing back and forth on the squeaky hardwood, Ryan told for the tenth time the story of Meagan's disappearance.

Donald Lawton, the one with the tie, spoke. "There's no chance she's with relatives or friends?"

"None."

Sandra Mills-Hopinger leaned forward on the edge of the couch, her note pad on her white-nylon knees. "Was there any evidence of a struggle?"

Ryan glanced to Karina. "Yes."

"What?"

"The police have asked me to avoid specifics."

"You have to give us something here. How serious was it?"

"Undeniable."

The woman pondered this. "Do you have any idea who could have taken her?"

Ryan's eyes floated from Karina to Alex, and then back to the woman. He wanted to scream the details, every last one. "I can't say."

The woman huffed. "So your story is that your wife's been missing for over two days, the car is gone, and that's it? You must know more."

"There were undeniable signs of a struggle. I just can't say anything else."

"I see. Well, Ryan. The story of how you came home, how you made the phone calls and went looking for her, how you talked with the police, their examination of the house, that's how the interview will go. We can get Meagan's name and face in front of over half a million viewers. We'll try to run it on tonight's 10:00 news, and we'll likely repeat it tomorrow. Does this sound like a good idea to you?"

Ryan finally sat down. He wondered, wasn't this an incredibly stupid question? He nodded. "Yes."

Don Lawton, the man in the suit, spoke. "Then we need for you to sign a small agreement with Channel 5. This is basically just a Waiver of Liability and Content Rights Agreement."

A scowl burst from Karina. Lawton continued, "We all want more than anything to see Meagan returned safely, but we can't make any promises. Of course, any events that may occur after the broadcast of this interview are beyond our control. Do you understand?"

Ryan was leaning forward, hanging on each word. His eyes were bloodshot. He nodded while kneading his hands. "How soon will you broadcast it?"

"Hopefully tonight, definitely tomorrow. The Program Manager decides what gets broadcast and what doesn't. We only conduct the interview."

Karina spoke up. "Who is he? We'll call him."

Mills-Hopinger slid forward and took Ryan's busy hands. "Ryan, don't worry. We'll carry it. All right?"

Ryan's head bobbed. "Okay."

Lawton slid the contract across the coffee table. "Initial here, and here. Sign here." He pointed to Alex. "You can witness."

Ryan quickly initialed and scribbled his name. Alex knelt down, perused the contract, and signed.

The crew lugged in lights, cameras, and tripods, while Sandra Mills-Hopinger checked her face in the bathroom. Ryan had showered earlier at Karina's suggestion. She gave him a quick once-over now and combed his hair with her purse brush. Dark rings circled his eyes. He sat on Aunt Sirrey's old recliner, as instructed. A chair was brought in from the kitchen for Mills-Hopinger. Microphones were clipped to collars and the cameras were set up, one on Ryan and one on the interviewer. Alex and Karina retreated out of view.

Mills-Hopinger raised her left hand. Her right patted Ryan's knee. "All right. Ryan, take a deep breath for me. Relax. Here we go. Ready? On me. Three, two, one."

"This is Sandra Mills-Hopinger of Channel 5 News. I'm with Ryan Evans of Portland. Ryan's wife, Meagan Evans, is missing and may be the victim of a kidnapping. Ryan, when did you first suspect that something was wrong?"

Ryan again told the story, the short version. In his lap, he aimed two photos at the camera lens. In one taken only weeks previous, Meagan was wearing his old plaid shirt, loosely buttoned, laughing, and holding a wet paint brush. Her hair was pinned up, but a wisp had fallen down across her cheek. A second photo taken the previous summer showed her in front of her car, an Oregon coast bluff in the background. Ryan hated showing the photos. They were private moments. But they were the most recent of her and the car.

"So the last information you have on her is that she left her doctor's appointment and then vanished. Is that right?" Mills-Hopinger asked.

"Yes."

"What leads you to believe that she met with foul play?"

"There was a struggle."

"What kind of struggle?"

Ryan looked at her with his dry, burning eyes. His voice quivered. "A struggle."

"Have you contacted everyone, called her family and friends?"

"Yes. Well, almost. It takes time to track everyone down."

Mills-Hopinger nodded with a deeply sympathetic face. "So tell us about yourselves. Meagan is a veterinarian. What is your occupation?"

Ryan took another breath. He glanced into the kitchen, where he could see Lawton whispering into a cell phone. "I'm a biologist."

"How long have you been married?"

She didn't ask this in the dry run. He cleared his tight throat. "Three years."

"Were you planning a family?"

Ryan's jaw dropped.

"I'm sorry, *are you, are you* planning a family?"

Ryan nodded.

For the opposite camera, Mills-Hopinger pursed her red lips together. She canted her head to the side, appearing to be deep in thought. "Mr. Evans, tell me. What's your gut feeling here? Do you feel she is alive?"

An audible gasp burst from Karina. The camera lens remained, its blinking red light demanding an answer.

"Yes, of course," Ryan replied.

Mills-Hopinger looked into the camera. "You see her picture. Meagan Evans, 27 years old. Five-feet, five-inches tall. Auburn hair, brown eyes. Driving a blue Prius. The plate is Oregon, BMK 6201. Ryan, if you could talk to her right now, what would you say to her?"

Ryan adjusted the photos toward the camera. He found it greatly unnerving to speak to the machine as though it was his wife. "Meggy. Meggy, we're doing everything we can to find you. Everything." He turned away.

"There she is, Meagan Evans on your screen. If you've seen her or the car, we urge you to call the Oregon State Police. The number is there at the bottom."

Mills-Hopinger stood.

Donald Lawton suddenly stepped around the assembly and lights, leaned forward, and whispered into her ear. She turned and paused, her eyes dancing from Karina, to Alex, and finally Ryan. "Just one more question."

The lights flashed back on and the camera was again glaring at Ryan. Mills-Hopinger sat back down. Her voice was tentative.

"Mr. Evans, I don't want to alarm you. A woman's body has been found under the Burnside Bridge. Do you have any comment?"

At this, Alex bolted forward and covered the camera lens with his hands. "You're done."

Karina pushed the television crew out the front door. Alex deposited the last of their gear on the porch, slammed the door and locked it.

Karina turned. "Bitch."

In the kitchen, Ryan was on his cell phone. "Mathius! This is Ryan Evans. What's this about a woman's body?"

"What are you talking about?"

"Under the Burnside Bridge!"

"Where did you hear this?"

"Is it Meagan?"

"I have nothing on it yet. We just got this."

"When will you know?"

"Tomorrow, maybe the next day. Don't get too worked up over this, Evans. Chances are some addict was killed over a little meth. Don't jump to conclusions."

Ryan was quiet.

"How did you get this?" Mathius asked. "Are you listening to scanners? Don't do that, it'll drive you nuts. Any developments, I'll call you."

"So what happened today? Did you talk with anyone?"

Mathius sighed audibly. "Mr. Evans, your wife isn't officially missing yet. I know you see it differently, but the law doesn't consider her missing for 72 hours. That's tomorrow."

"The hell! Did you get my message about the guy in the San Juans? Greer? They killed him! Did you get that?"

"I got it. We haven't looked into it yet."

"What?"

"It all takes time, Evans."

"Mathius, this is the same guy! The guy with the briefcase! They killed him!"

"We're looking into it."

"I'm telling you, these guys have my wife!"

"We'll check it out!"

Ryan paced, with his right hand pulling on his hair. "So what the hell did you do today? Who did you talk to?"

"Evans, settle down. Today, I called and left a message with the doctor, your wife's doctor. We're trying to locate him."

"It's a woman!"

"Whatever. We're trying to find your wife's parents in Seattle. She may be with them. Have you considered that?"

"You didn't talk with Summit Resources, did you? Or Lochner at DEQ?"

"Evans, this investigation has just begun. We don't just go barging into corporate offices and interrogating CEOs. They're on a list, but right now, we're looking for your wife and her car. And actually, we need to talk with you again. I need you in my office tomorrow morning, around ten? We have a few more questions."

"Fine."

"Tomorrow then. We've only started."

Outside, the wind kicked hard against the windows, making a snapping sound. Streaks pelted the glass. Ryan took a bottle of Jack Daniels from the cupboard under the sink and half-filled a glass. He took a gulp, grimaced, and eased into the chair. He took a long, weary breath. The ceiling spun around him slowly. It can't be her, dear God, it can't. They wouldn't kill her and dump her under a downtown bridge. More likely somewhere in Forest Park, or the Columbia, where her body would float for miles and get snagged in the reeds somewhere. To be found one summer day by kids out fishing.

He took another full gulp and let it burn. Above him, the ceiling was yellow. A few weeks earlier, he and Meagan had removed the old wallpaper and painted the kitchen walls a light tan, but the ceiling still needed paint. He closed his eyes and saw her, wearing his shirt. Her long hair, the perfect smile.

He thought of his mother. Years previous, after completing the marathon of applications for scholarships and loans, Ryan was ready to leave for college. Opportunity had opened a door, but he could barely bring himself to leave. When he finally did, it shook her to the core. She truly was alone. She eventually left for Alaska and married someone, a fisherman, an alcoholic. Never a call, Ryan received a short scrawled note two years previous announcing the marriage. It was a civil union, maybe ten minutes. The note had been forwarded from his old college address. He had tried to reply, but her return address wasn't any good. She wasn't listed in any phone books; he got no hits from Google. Meagan had pushed him to hire a detective.

Ryan rested his head on his crossed arms. His dad would've been here in a heartbeat, if he were alive. Ryan remembered the bearded face, the bright eyes and the booming laugh. His dad and a climbing partner had been ascending the Cooper Spur route on Mount Hood's northeast face and been blown off a 900 foot ledge by a surprise spring whiteout. Their desiccated bodies weren't recovered for another two years.

A hand landed on his shoulder, tearing him from his thoughts. Ryan wiped the streaks from his face. Karina sat down next to him. "What did Mathius say?" she asked.

"I'm going in tomorrow."

Alex slid Meagan's blue pitcher of wilted daffodils to the side and took a seat across the table. He poured an inch of whiskey into a glass and took a gulp. "You might think about getting an attorney," he said.

Ryan shook his head. "They aren't listening. They're wasting time. Every minute that goes by…"

"It's what they think automatically, you know that," said Alex. "It's always the husband, the boyfriend. You might want to talk to an attorney."

"I get an attorney and it'll look like I'm hiding something. They haven't talked to anyone! They spent hours here today, and what do they have?"

Karina massaged Ryan's shoulder. Alex continued, gently. "What it looks like doesn't matter."

"But I don't have time. Every second that passes. All I have are the police, who suspect me, and that bimbo from Channel 5. They'll run the story once or twice, and then everyone will forget."

Karina offered quiet encouragement. "We can do flyers tomorrow. I'll get them made up, first thing. They'll have her picture, her car. The license plate and where to call."

Ryan's voice was drained. "I need someone by the phone."

Alex replied, "I'll be here. I'll use my cell and start calling her friends to post fliers."

Ryan's eyes were locked on the far wall. He spoke as if in a trance. *"Where is she?"*

"We'll find her," Karina continued. "How many fliers? Two thousand? I'll make them in the morning and we'll spend the day posting them."

Ryan rose from the table and shuffled to the sink. Behind the curtains, another day was turning dark. He spoke, more to himself. "Tomorrow fliers. Then what?"

His right hand, still holding the whiskey, slammed down on the counter top with a sharp crash. The glass shattered in all directions and Karina jumped from the chair.

He turned to them, unaware of the blood dripping from his hand. His jaw shook. "Can you stay, a few more days? I don't know…"

Karina answered him. "You don't have to ask."

She took a clean dish towel and wrapped his hand. He pulled away and headed for the back door. Alex signaled her to let him go. He didn't have keys.

Outside, Ryan's broken voice called in the darkness. "Sophie! Sophie!"

# Chapter 32

At 8:15, Alex was on his cell phone, quietly updating Anne. Ryan and Karina were watching the news. It was an unspoken rule, now. The house phone was to be left free. The television was to be left on the local news.

Ryan stood. "People are home from work. I want to check again with the neighbors."

Karina inspected him. He looked miserable, with dark eyes and a bloodied towel wrapped around his hand. His breath smelled of whiskey.

"Your neighbors won't answer the door," she said. "Did you stop the bleeding?" She unwrapped his hand. An inch-long cut just below his thumb oozed blood. "You need stitches."

"I'm fine."

"Wait."

In the bathroom, Karina found three elastic bandages. She returned and carefully wrapped them around the wound.

They made the rounds in the Miata. On Palantine Road, several homes were within a half-mile in either direction. His immediate neighbors recognized Ryan and although no one knew him by name, they were all concerned. Ryan could have continued for miles, knocking on doors, showing her photo and asking if anyone had seen his wife. It was therapeutic.

He saw it on the return leg to the house. A car was parked on the shoulder, under the trees. A brown Taurus. He grabbed the long, metal flashlight he had taken along. "Stop the car, here," he ordered.

She slowed. "It could be any—"

"Stop! It was here yesterday!"

"Ryan."

"Stop the car! Leave it running, with the lights on!"

She stopped the Miata ten yards from the car. He got out and began walking. A Ford Taurus, brown or gray, it faced toward his house. The street light silhouetted two, a man in the driver's seat, slouched down, and perhaps a woman next to him. Ryan clicked on and pointed the flashlight toward the car. The driver's head was canted just so. He was watching Ryan in the mirror. The passenger knelt forward as if to reach for something. The engine started. Maybe 20 more steps, armed with only a flashlight. Ten more steps, five. Ryan was beside the car now, just behind the driver. The passenger turned. Ryan hesitated.

Suddenly the engine roared and the tires sprayed gravel. The car began slipping down into the wet shoulder, but found traction and left with the wail of tires. The plates! Ryan searched for the license plates, but they were dark.

Karina's Miata rolled up next to him. He opened the door and jumped inside. "Go!"

"What?"

"Go! Go now!"

She floored the gas pedal. The red tail lights had already vanished around the corner.

"Hurry! Did you see the plates?"

"No!"

The Miata came around the corner and stopped at the intersection at Palantine and Multnomah. The car had vanished.

To the left, the road took a curvy run down the hill to the freeway. To the right, it crested and led down to the mall, Starbucks, and the nursery.

Ryan jumped in the seat. "Turn right! Floor it!"

Karina did as asked and wound the little car through the gears. They crested the hill doing 60. A long, gradual downhill slope lay before them and the road was empty, except for what was obviously a large truck in the distance.

"Dammit!" Ryan slammed the flashlight into his good hand.

Karina slowed the car down and turned into a driveway. He shook his head. "The plate was dark! The light was out!"

"Who do you think it was?"

"Who the hell would be parked on the road and watching my house, at this time of night? And why did they leave in such a hurry?"

At the house, Ryan told Alex about the Taurus. His reaction was immediate; his finger jabbed Ryan's face. "You don't do that without me! You decide to confront someone, I need to be there."

"There wasn't time."

"Ryan, if something happened, I could have helped."

The sound of the doorbell startled them.

Ryan's eyes darted around the living room "Give me the shotgun!"

Alex headed for the front door. "Calm down! Christ, I ordered pizza while you two were out."

Alex unlocked the deadbolt. A young man stood at the door, under the light. His eyes were wide; he wasn't quite sure of what he had just heard. Alex gave him two twenties, took the box and locked the door.

Ryan turned out all of the lights except for the bathroom light off the hall. In a darkened kitchen, they ate pizza and drank soda and waited for the news. They talked about who could have been in the Taurus. Karina wasn't sure. Ryan was certain.

The news came on at eleven and carried several stories about everything else. This was interrupted constantly by long chains of commercials. Finally, the story of a young woman under the bridge. A Portland teen, homeless, a known meth addict. It struck Ryan that she was someone's daughter. A short, sad life, capped by a 60-second news story.

The interview with Miles-Hopinger had taken 15 minutes and was hacked down to just over 90 seconds. They showed the picture of Meagan at the beach with Sophie in her arms. And then, the close-up. Her face filled the screen. Her eyes, her elegant cheekbones, her dark hair. The smile meant only for him. She floated on screen for a few priceless seconds and held the three of them breathless. Karina wiped tears. Alex stared at the floor.

The story of Greer's death was rerun and Ryan memorized the face of Jacob Sarinov.

Then a man began screaming the praises of a new stain remover.

At midnight, Karina was put up in the spare bedroom. Alex slept downstairs on the couch.

In the master bedroom, Ryan turned on the light. To hell with them, he thought. Let them see it. He had avoided the bedroom for two nights. The beige gown still lie draped over the chair. Everything in the room was her, the color of the sheets, the comforter, the new curtains. On the dresser, a glass held flowers she had clipped from outside. February flowers, they were small, pink, and star-shaped with slender green leaves. Intensely fragrant. She knew the name. They were wilted.

He sat slowly down on the edge of the bed and pulled off his jeans and shirt. He lay down gradually, pulled the cold sheets up, and turned out the light.

The memory of their first date came to mind, high in the Spruce tree. She must have thought he was crazy. Football at the U of W in Seattle. Take-out Chinese food in his studio apartment. All-night cramming for tests. Moonlight skinny dipping at Lake Crescent.

He saw her in the lingerie he had bought at Victoria's Secret. At first, she was timid to wear it, but she enjoyed what it did to him. It was a dark blue, two-piece, with just enough to cover the essentials. They stayed up half the night with the lights on low. In the morning, an empty wine bottle and underwear lay on the floor.

A gust of wind battered the window. The questions devoured him. Was she alive? Did they hurt her, here? His throat felt like it was wrapped in a vice. He turned on the lamp. From the nightstand drawer, he retrieved a bible given to him by his mother when his father died. Ryan never prayed. He opened the book randomly and began repeating her name over and over again.

In the early morning, he stumbled out of the bed and resumed pacing the house.

A call Ryan had been dreading came early Friday morning.

"Ryan? This is Stanton Lewis! I've got messages from you and some detective in Portland! What the hell is going on down there?"

Ryan sat down and tried to steel himself. "Meagan is missing."

"What the hell happened?"

"I came home Tuesday afternoon. She wasn't here. I called her friends from work, from the church, everyone I could think of. I spoke with the clinic. They said she left for a doctor's appointment at eleven that morning and never returned."

"She never returned home?! What?!"

Ryan could hear Rachel Lewis shrieking in the background. "No. I called the police. They came out, but—"

"What are you telling me?"

"The police thought she was out with friends. I filed a missing-persons report."

"This is Friday! You haven't seen her since Tuesday morning?"

"That's right."

"It's been three days!"

Ryan fought to keep from breaking down. "I know. I know. The police put out an APB, for Oregon and Washington."

"Did you two have a fight?"

"No. Nothing like that. She was expected back at work. I called Channel 5 news, they came by, did an interview—"

"You called the news media?"

"Yes! They carried the story on the news last night. And this morning."

Stanton's questions brought a waterfall of cries from Ms. Lewis. His muffled voice could be heard attempting to calm her, without success. He returned to the phone. "What about the car?"

"It's gone."

"What, what happened?! Were you two fighting?! Did she leave you?"

"No, we weren't fighting."

The phone went quiet; he had covered the mouthpiece again. A moment later, he returned. "Godammit Ryan! How could… how the hell! For chissake, she's your wife, our Meagan! How could you let this happen?"

"I, I…"

Lewis continued yelling. "What are the police doing? Are they investigating?"

"Yes."

"What do they have?"

"I'm seeing them again this morning."

Rachel Lewis was sobbing. Then his voice, a muffled yelling at her. He returned to the phone. "How the hell could you do this? You couldn't take care of my daughter?"

Ryan's voice left him. Mercifully, Lewis hung up.

# Chapter 33

Detective Mathius entered the lobby with a tight-jawed smile. "Good morning, Ryan."

They shook hands.

"Come on back."

Mathius led him through the locking door and down the hall, past the large conference room they had used two days earlier. They took another leg past steel doors and gray cinder-block walls and entered a small room with a steel table and chairs. No windows. The wall to the right was covered in mirrored glass.

"Have a seat." Mathius pointed to the chair opposite the mirror.

Ryan sat and noticed that the chairs and table were bolted to the floor. Another man entered. He was in his forties, trim, with dark crew-cut hair.

Mathius sat and gestured. "Ryan, this is Detective Carson Williams. He's helping me with this case. Carson knows as much as I do."

Williams remained standing. "How are you this morning, Ryan? May I call you Ryan? Get any sleep last night?"

Ryan shook his head. "No."

Mathius poured coffee from a carafe into a foam cup. "Coffee?"

Ryan nodded. "Thanks. What have you found?"

Mathius answered. "The woman found under the Burnside Bridge was a street kid, a meth head. She was strangled."

Ryan closed his eyes. "It was in the news."

"I saw *you* on the news," said Mathius. "We've had over 20 calls come in, people thinking they've seen someone resembling your wife or the car. Of course, they're from all over the map, four in the metro area, one up off I-5, towards Ridgefield. A couple out on the south coast. You broadcast a message out to half a million people asking if anyone has seen a pink elephant and you will get 50 eye witnesses."

"I only need one. Are you following up on each call?"

"Of course."

Ryan eyed Mathius. It sounded a lot like sarcasm. "So what did you find in my house yesterday?" Ryan asked. "Three people spent hours inside my house. What did they find?"

"We'll get to it. Have you or your wife had any serious arguments lately?"

"No. Why?"

"Have you had any accidents inside the home, in the last few weeks? Falls or cuts?"

"No! Dammit, Mathius! What did they find?"

Mathius pulled out a fresh Lucky Strike, slowly, deliberately. "Based on the evidence in the home, we think there may have been a struggle, some altercation."

Ryan's eyes widened. "What did you find?!"

"We found a small amount of blood, type A, same as your wife's. And a very small sample of O positive."

"Where?"

"I can't say."

"How much?"

"Not much. Enough."

"But you can't tell me where you found it?"

"No, I'm sorry. O positive is relatively common. What blood type are you, Ryan?"

Ryan was certain the man already knew the answer. "O positive. What about fingerprints?"

"Every house has plenty of fingerprints. We're processing them. We need to get your prints to exclude them, plus a blood sample."

"Fine. What else?"

"Aside from that, the house is clean. I have to say, we haven't seen that much fresh paint in very long time."

"We've been remodeling."

Mathius nodded. "We noticed. You know, it doesn't really look like an intruder. You're sure your wife wasn't injured recently, accidentally?"

"Jesus Christ, Mathius! No, she wasn't! That's it? That's all of it?"

"It is for now."

Mathius was sitting with his elbows on the table. He pointed with his unlit cigarette to the bandages wrapped around Ryan's thumb. "What happened to your hand?"

"I dropped a glass in the sink. It was an accident."

"Are you prone to accidents?"

"No, I'm not!"

"Maybe a bit temperamental?"

"Do you believe I killed my wife?"

"Whoa. Ryan. Who says she's dead? All we are doing at this time is gathering information."

"Well, while gathering your information, have you bothered talking to the people I named? Specifically, the CEO at Summit Resources? Or DEQ? Lochner or Lassiter?"

"We'll get to that."

Ryan jabbed his finger in Mathius' face. "Did you see the story on Greer? The boat explosion up north? They killed him! Did you see that?"

"I did."

"And?"

"The local authorities are looking into it."

Ryan's hand flew up. "What the hell is there to look into? He was a bigwig at Summit! It was a gas explosion and the boat sank! He turned on them! He tried to give me a suitcase full of evidence and they wasted him!"

Mathius stopped playing with his cigarette. "Get a grip, Ryan. Put your hands down. So, if his company is up to no good, why didn't Greer just go to the police?"

"He was afraid of the company."

Mathius blew out an elaborate sigh.

Ryan shook his head. "You're just not picking this up. The man is blown to hell in a million-dollar yacht and you think, golly fucking gee, another accident! These danged boats blow up every day!"

"Watch your language. It's under investigation."

"That will take months." Ryan slapped Newberg's EIS on the table. "Mathius, this is a state document, a formal DEQ document evaluating the consequences that the Justene mine will have on the environment in eastern Oregon. This is required by DEQ for new or expanding industrial operations." Ryan pointed at the papers. "As you can see, there are signatures approving the statement. This one here is Robert Newberg's. He worked at DEQ's Pendleton office when Summit Resources first applied to open the mine. He signed it September 28, 2004. Pay close attention here, Mathius. Newberg fell to his death from a helicopter on September 29! He died the day after he signed! It makes no sense! The helicopter was operated by Summit Resources. You can call Newberg's widow. This is her phone number." Ryan pointed to the number he had scribbled on the top sheet. "Are you following me?"

"Where did you get this?" asked Mathius.

"As I've already told you, I was assigned to do the analysis for the mine expansion, for this same mine. I worked on it for eight months. When it was done, the state ignored my work. Instead, they reused this piece of shit." Ryan pounded the stack of papers with his fist.

At this, Mathius leaned over the table and smiled so slightly. "You're really into this conspiracy thing, aren't you?"

Seconds passed while both men stared at each other. Williams stood and watched.

For Ryan, the disconnect was incomprehensible. He yelled the words. "Damn you! God damn you! Why don't you believe me?"

"Because it's not believable, Ryan. The state isn't involved in fraud. They don't engage in kidnapping or murder. Why would these people abduct your wife?"

"We've been through this! The company was looking for me, or whatever documentation they think Greer gave me. My wife walked in on them."

Mathius returned to his cigarette. "I did speak with Mr. Lassiter today. That was a revelation. He informed me that you were fired for theft of state property, that you liked to surf hard core porn sites on the web. That you downloaded over a hundred nasty images."

The days of fear, no sleep, and little food left Ryan a wreck. His fist slammed the table as his voice exploded in the small room. "Bullshit! They planted that crap in my computer to justify firing me! I was challenging the legality of the approval and Lassiter needed to get rid of me!"

Mathius leaned in again. "Some of these sites may have been child porn. If that's true, it's a federal offense."

"That is pure garbage! I'm going to the media with all of it, including your goddamned incompetence!"

Mathius seemed unruffled, but the contorted cigarette finally snapped between his fingers. He flicked the fragments across the room and glanced at the one-way mirror.

"Let me tell you what I think happened," said Mathius. "You were fired. You got home from work in a very bad mood. Meagan learned what happened and why it happened, and she confronted you. This was probably no big surprise to her. The big blowout, one of many I suspect. And in a rage, well…"

Ryan's shoulder's dropped. Williams and Mathius traded looks. The detective's voice softened to a whisper. "I have it about right, don't I?"

Ryan's head shook slowly back and forth. "No."

Ever so slightly, Williams nodded. Mathius continued calmly. "If you have nothing to hide, prove it. Take a polygraph so you can prove your innocence."

Ryan threw his hands up. "Great! When? Now? Unlike you, I'm busy!"

"Monday."

"My wife has been missing for three days, and you're closed on the weekends?"

"My examiner isn't available until then." Mathius cocked his head to the side. "I spoke with Stanton and Rachel Lewis today. Your in-laws? Seems there's been some strife in your marriage."

Ryan stood slowly against uncooperative legs. Rachel and Stanton Lewis, never without their opinions. Ryan combed his fingers through his hair and noticed his hands were shaking badly. Then his knees. Williams noticed as well.

Mathius pushed his shoulders back in the anchored metal chair. He put both hands on the table, palms up. It was his very best voice. Calm, relaxed. "Talk to me, Ryan. I'm not saying you intentionally hurt anyone."

Nausea swept across Ryan, in the hot little room. He stepped to the door and opened it wide.

"Where are you going?" Mathius asked.

"I'm done with both of you. I am done."

"Stay in the city, Ryan. It would look very bad if you suddenly took a trip."

The truck door weighed a ton and Ryan fought rubber legs climbing in. At the police station, he sat in the vehicle and tried to collect himself. He took the cell phone and punched in Karina's cell number.

At Kinko's, they loaded three boxes into the International, just over two thousand color images of Meagan, her car, her description, and a plea. At Karina's insistence they met again, at Elmer's, a pancake house. The hostess tried to steer them to a small table near the fireplace, but Ryan ignored her and sat down in a booth next to the window. Karina draped her jacket on a chair and slid in across from him.

Ryan gestured with a nod. "Meagan and I sit over there."

She reached out and took his hand. "How did it go with the police?"

Ryan shook his head. His eyes glistened. "They tried to get me to admit that I killed her."

She tried to think of something to say. He looked demolished. "We'll find her, Ryan. There are volunteers due at the house at 2:00, all her friends. After you eat something, we'll head back and organize them."

Ryan was looking at her, but he was somewhere else entirely.

Karina continued. "We can start on the west side today. We'll pick the main streets and hit all of the businesses, door to door. Tomorrow, we'll get more help and go all the way down to the river."

Ryan's tired eyes had locked on a family, a couple sitting down with two children. One was a girl with long auburn hair. His voice was barely audible. "I appreciate everything, but…" His hands opened up.

"What?"

He looked at Karina. "I know who did this. Not exactly who, some pathetic piece of garbage they paid. But I know who."

She bit her upper lip.

"The police aren't following up. They think I'm a killer. I've lost 80 hours since it happened. I'm running out of time."

She wanted to reach across the table and hug him. "If we put a couple thousand fliers out there, someone will come forward," she said calmly. "Someone saw something."

"It's been over three days, three nights! I can't go on like this."

The desperation in his face frightened her. She began pleading. "We'll do the fliers! We have them printed, you have volunteers at the house right now! Let's do the flyers."

A tall, heavy waitress with thick, rubbery arms appeared. Her look demanded cooperation. "What'll it be?"

Karina pushed the plastic menu at him. "Eat something, Ryan. Please."

The driveway was filled with five cars and three more were parked along the road. Inside, Karina counted nine women and four men. On such short notice, it wasn't bad. They were Meagan's friends, Mary Lavoie, Tawny, and friends from church. Some had seen the news. The rest, Alex had contacted via Meagan's corkboard.

Ryan mumbled his thanks to the group. Half of them were in tears and women he didn't know hugged him. Karina herded them into the living room, spread out a map on the coffee table, and immediately began giving the orders. Volunteers were paired up and each pair was assigned a street and a starting intersection. It was just past 3:00. Work the main streets until 7:00, starting at the north and east sides of town and working west. Work the right side of the street to avoid crossing traffic. Go for two hours, and then stop and write down the address. Reverse direction and do the opposite side. Post the flyer at eye-level, on or near the front door. Hit every place, fast food stores, mini-marts, stores of every kind. If the business is closed, tape it to the door. For large businesses, there isn't time to find a manager, just tape the flyer on the glass. If interrupted, then ask. Cover as much ground as possible. Quit at 7:00 and meet back here at 9:00 in the morning. And bring more help.

Each pair was equipped with four rolls of tape and two hundred flyers and sent out. Karina stayed behind with Tommy to answer the phone. Ryan and Alex left in Alex's car.

They drove to Canyon Road in the West Slope and began working west. Alex drove and Ryan walked from business to business, posting as he went. Alex would pull ahead a block or two, park in front and wait. Every twenty minutes or so, Ryan would sit in the car for a minute to warm up.

A few people asked questions, but most ignored him. The lady at a real estate office seemed very sympathetic and happy to have it posted in a window, but then Ryan watched her remove it a few seconds after he walked out the door.

The most difficult stop was Lolita's Flowers. Ryan had ordered flowers there several times. The owner knew Meagan, had seen the news story, and burst into tears when he entered.

After two hours, Alex put the car in park. "Okay, my turn. You drive."

Finally at 7:00, they picked up burgers at a fast-food place before heading back to the house.

In the car, Alex spoke. "We made good progress. Tomorrow we'll go all the way out to Farmington."

"Do me a favor?" Ryan asked. "Drop by Home Depot for me? I need a few things."

Fifteen minutes later, Ryan got into the BMW with a small bag in his hand.

Alex started the car. "What'd you get?"

Ryan set the bag between his feet. "A couple things."

At the house, Alex set the burgers on the kitchen table. Karina set a carton of orange juice and three glasses on the table. "How did it go?" she asked.

Alex pulled out a chair and sat. "We covered Canyon Road all the way out to Hall." He pushed a chair out with his foot while he unwrapped a burger. "Sit down, doctor Ry. We've got gourmet burgers and greasy fries waiting for you."

Ryan slid down into the seat and questioned Karina. "They ran it on the news again?"

She nodded. "They did. You need to eat."

Ryan looked absently at the hamburger and then pushed it back. He rubbed his face, with the three-day beard, and then folded his arms on the table and rested his head.

Alex whispered. "Is it in the papers?"

She pointed into the living room. Alex took his food and got up quietly to find the paper.

Karina remained with Ryan. His hair lay in a tangle. The green cotton shirt was damp and ruffled up around his shoulders. Every breath was a long, laborious draw for air, broken by shudders. She lifted her hand and gently touched his hair. The previous night, he had paced the house until four in the morning. He had entered her room and stood for half an hour, staring out the window. He had called Meagan's name from his sleep. Never had she seen anyone so torn. She leaned forward and kissed his head.

After some time, he stirred.

"How long was I out?" he asked.

"A little while."

Alex spoke. "You've been snoring it up."

The whiskey bottle had disappeared; Karina had put it away more than once. Alex took it from the cabinet now and poured a double shot in a glass. He eased into the chair and downed it.

"I'm not going with you tomorrow," Ryan announced.

Alex looked up, first at Karina, and then at Ryan. "Where are you going?" he asked.

Ryan looked at Karina. She stood and walked into the living room. He continued quietly. "The CEO, Sarinov, did this. He knows where she is."

Alex's head fell to the side. He studied his empty whiskey glass. A tiny air bubble had been trapped in the glass and was magnified by the curve, making it appear distorted. He finally spoke. "How?"

"I'll catch him in the parking garage. It may take a day, but I'll get him."

"Ryan, tomorrow is Saturday."

"They work Saturdays."

"The company? The CEO? How do you know this?"

"I know."

Alex sat and studied the bubble, not at all sure what he was hearing. "You're serious."

"Yes."

Alex closed his eyes. It was temporary refuge from the approaching insanity. After a minute, he opened them again and opened the plastic bag that was sitting on the table. It contained a roll of duct tape and plastic ties.

"How?" Alex asked.

"We park in the garage of his building, the Wells Fargo building. We wait for him to arrive and take him as he is getting out of the car. We throw him in the truck, tape his mouth. We bind his arms and legs. It might take 20, 30 seconds at most. I hold him with the shotgun, you drive."

Alex breathed hard. "Jesus, Ryan, that's crazy. I'm telling you, it's crazy."

"You drive."

"Where?"

"There's an old road up towards Scappoose, off highway 30. It heads into the woods. We used to bicycle up there as kids. A couple of abandoned houses, half a mile back. You remember."

"A long time ago. How far do we go with this, Ryan?"

"As far as I have to."

"So what do we do with him after he tells us? Or doesn't? If you're serious, then we've kidnapped and tortured him. What happens then?"

Ryan grabbed a cold French fry and squeezed it until the grease oozed. "He shows us where she is."

"Ryan, he doesn't know. He's the CEO of a company. You think he ordered this?"

"He knows. I'd bet my life on it."

"You will. So let's pretend he tells us, then what? What happens to him afterward?"

Ryan's expression was flat. He didn't care in the least. Kill him and leave him in the woods.

The expression frightened Alex. "Dammit! Figure it out, Ryan! You beat the hell out of him, maybe he tells you something, probably not. Then what?"

"He'll tell me."

"*But then what?!*" Alex was shouting now. "What do we do with him? He's half-dead! He doesn't just get up, straighten his tie, and go home!"

Ryan was silent.

"You're certain?" Alex asked.

"I'd stake my life on it."

"*You will indeed! And mine!* And when they charge us with kidnapping, torture, maybe murder, then what?"

"I was insane. Out of my mind."

"*But what the hell was I?* What was I, Ryan?"

The question hung in the air.

"I cannot go on like this," Ryan finally said. "The flyers, the interviews, they won't get her back. It's been over 90 hours."

Karina had been standing at the entrance to the kitchen with her arms crossed. She sat down now, in tears, and grabbed Ryan's hands. "We can talk with the police! We'll get all your friends, everyone at work! We can vouch for you!"

"I don't have the time to convince anyone! I don't have the time! They won't hold her a week because they like keeping her around! She's a witness, she can send them all to prison! They've killed three people, she's nothing to them!"

Alex tried to speak as calmly as possible. "So to hell with sanity."

"Don't you get it? The police are certain I killed her, I'll be locked up soon. What can I do from jail?"

The only sounds were the television in the living room and the tapping of sleet against the window. The headache had returned to Alex's brain. He turned the glass with the air bubble and dreaded the next question. "When?"

Ryan pushed his fingers through his hair. "Tomorrow morning, early. I need someone to drive." He looked at Karina. "You can't be involved in this. You don't know a thing, not a thing. Keep doing what you're doing."

Alex's shoulder's sagged. This was so out of control, so far from reality. He pushed the cold hamburger at Ryan. "Eat something, you're loosing your mind. And try to get some sleep tonight."

Ryan took the whiskey bottle and drank it straight. He coughed once and wiped his mouth on his hand.

Alex rose from the table and escaped to the living room.

## Chapter 34

He had never noticed how quiet the house was. How silent. After midnight, he dropped his jeans and shirt on the floor and stepped into the shower. The water popped out in starts and fits. He barely noticed how cold it was. He let it run down his head and face, felt it run over his closed eyes, his nose and lips, down his back and between his legs. If it could rinse everything away. In the light, it fragmented into tiny, glistening spheres, each another world. The sound echoed strangely, as though he was submerged in it, a distant hissing and gurgling. He didn't think to lather. He just stood for a while, immobile, and then turned it off. Showering was wrong. He put on his under shorts, forgetting to dry off. Eating and sleeping were wrong. Living was wrong.

In the bedroom, the blanket and pillow were strewn on the floor. Lying in her bed was wrong. His depth perception was off; the doorknob, 15 feet away, seemed pressed to his face. He turned out the light and looked out the window into the rain-soaked night. A streetlight flickered through moving tree branches. His mind approached a path he had struggled to avoid. What if? He imagined her face, her still eyes, pelted by the rain. He thought of his father's remains lying in a grave on a hillside. It had lingered nearby since Tuesday evening, a fear he had fought continuously. Now it screamed at him. What if? Meagan had been a dream, a life that he had neglected to protect. What did it mean to live if she were no longer alive?

Tears fell, but they weren't only for her. They were for himself, his dreams of a family. Dreams of a daughter and a son from her. Audrey and Rudy. They had already chosen names. It gathered around him, swept over him, thick and suffocating, a fear he had fought desperately to ignore.

From under the door, a dim light flickered. He slowly moved to the door, opened it, and made his way down the hall and then the stairs, hanging on the banister. Karina was sitting on the couch with blankets, a cup on her lap. The TV glowed.

She turned to look up at him. "I couldn't sleep," she whispered.

He stood, wobbly in his underwear, hands on the banister.

"Are you all right?" she asked.

Ryan was hyperventilating. His eyes were ablaze. He stood, all but naked and still wet from the shower, and began to sob.

"Ryan!" She went to him and threw the blanket over his convulsing shoulders. She felt his cold hair. "Ryan, please don't do this!"

He sank down on the stairs. The cries were guttural, heaving sobs, pushed out from deep inside.

"Ryan, please! Baby, it's okay! Please!" With the blanket, she held him as close as she could. "It'll be okay! No no, please!" She held his head, kissed his hair, and cried with him.

Ringing. The phone was ringing. By the second ring, he stumbled into the kitchen alcove and turned on the light.

"Hello?"

No answer.

"Hello?"

Nothing. The phone was dead. He hung up and looked at the caller ID. An unfamiliar number.

He returned to the living room and peered outside between the curtains. The night was black. In the room, the fire in the woodstove had died down to a few red embers. He turned off the television and, in the dark, crawled back under the bedspread.

Ringing. He was up and in the kitchen quickly. The same number glowed green. Area code 541. He picked it up. "Hello?"

Silence.

He strained to listen. Dead silence. And then a tone, a series of tones. Slow, deliberate. Then again, the same four tones.

Ryan stared at the receiver, and then screamed. "MEAGAN! MEAGAN!"

The pattern repeated one more time, agonizingly slow and oblivious to his voice.

MEAGAN!"

The dial tone answered him.

He fell to his knees in the dark, yelling into the phone. "Meggy!"

The lights turned on. Alex was in the alcove in jeans. "What happened?"

"It was her! She called!" Ryan yelled at the phone. "She—four notes! It was her! A game we played in college! Four notes! I left it on her recorder for her to guess the song. *Say You, Say Me!*"

Alex stared at him, utterly confused.

"What happened?" Karina asked.

"It's a song! The buttons, 1595. *Say You, Say Me*! Lionel Richie!"

"Did anyone speak?" asked Karina.

"No! But no one else knows this game we played! She liked that song, it's her!"

Alex was still lost. "So you answered the phone and Meagan pushed keys?"

"Yes!"

Karina understood. "Hang it up! Hang it up. She might call again."

Ryan hung up and looked again at the caller ID. He thrust his hand at Alex. "Give me your cell phone."

Alex dug the phone out of his pocket. Ryan took it and dialed the operator. It rang nine times before anyone picked up. He yelled into the phone as he paced the kitchen. "For an area code and prefix, can you tell me where a call is coming from?" A pause. "Right!" Ryan read off the number on the caller ID. "Yes!" He motioned frantically for a pen and paper. "Enterprise? Enterprise in Oregon? Can you give me a street address? Why not? Can you tell me who it's registered to? No no, listen! This is a matter of life and death! I have to know, please, my—"

The phone dropped. Ryan fell back against the kitchen counter. He jumped up and, with his good fist, slammed a cabinet door, splitting it cleanly in half. A snarling growl exploded through his teeth. "She's at the mine!!"

Karina shook her head. "What?"

"They have her at Justene! It's coming from their phones, Summit Resources! The only phones they have near Enterprise are at the mine!"

"No, wait," said Alex. "Jesus Christ, Ryan! Have you lost it?"

Still in underwear, Ryan flew into the living room and grabbed the shotgun he knew was hidden in the closet. He probed behind the television and grabbed the box of cartridges Karina had stashed there.

Alex put up his hands. "Just a second!"

Ryan's hand fished the bowl on the counter top. "My keys!"

"Stop!" Alex said.

"Where are my keys?"

Alex looked at Karina.

"Ryan, are you sure it's her?" Karina asked.

"Who else is going to punch in the notes to a love song at four in the morning? From Enterprise, on their phones! On Summit's phones!"

Ryan's friends looked at each other. Alex began talking with his hands. "Doc, you received a phone call."

"Two calls!"

"Okay, and no one talks, no one says a thing. But someone punches in buttons, four, five buttons?"

"It was a game. No one else knows this!"

"And, the call, the call is coming from Enterprise? Way the hell out east? Maybe it's a wrong number! It could be a cell."

"Give me my keys!"

Alex's incredulous eyes searched Karina's face first, then Ryan's. "How well do you know this place?" he asked.

"I studied it for months! My keys!"

Resigned, Alex opened a cabinet door and retrieved the keys from behind a stack of plates. Ryan ripped them from his hands.

Karina spoke. "Get dressed. And eat something. You haven't slept in days, you need to eat. You'll need food and water. Clothes for her. She was in office clothes?"

Ryan ran upstairs. Alex searched the cupboards and dug up a package of fig bars and two one-pound chocolate bars. Karina pulled a two-liter bottle of cola from under the sink. Ryan returned, now dressed, with his arms full. On the table, he shoved Meagan's hiking boots, ski clothing, a pair of jeans, and a sweatshirt into a large backpack. He packed the small pockets with shotgun cartridges and a hunting knife. Karina put the food into a grocery bag while Ryan grabbed his boots from the mud room, sat down, and began lacing them.

With one boot laced, he stopped and looked up at her. She was standing in the corner with her arms crossed and tears streaking down her face.

He went to her and held her shoulders. "Can you stay, please? In case she calls again?"

She bit her quivering lip and nodded. "Not alone."

"Get her friends? Tommy?"

"I'll get someone."

He embraced her fully for several seconds. "Thank you, Karina. Thank you."

She pulled away and took her brown purse from the counter top. From it, she pulled out a black revolver. "It's a 38, loaded with six rounds. The safety is here." She dried her eyes with one hand and flicked a small switch with her thumb. "Here it's on. Here it's off, you can fire it. Leave the safety on unless you need to use it."

Alex shook his head. "What else do you have in there, Karina?"

"Be careful." She hugged Ryan and then Alex. With the backpack, two guns, and two parkas, they slipped out into the night. The rain had stopped, but not the wind.

Alex yelled over his shoulder. "If you don't hear from us by tomorrow night, call the state police."

"Be careful!"

"My car?" Alex asked.

"No! We'll need four-wheel drive."

Alex eyed the International with suspicion. "This will get us there and back?"

"Get in!"

Ryan backed out of the driveway and slammed the truck into gear. It roared off into the dark.

At 4:30 on a Saturday morning, Portland was still asleep and they were able to make it into the city and onto the 405 freeway in minutes. They passed over the city on ribbons of concrete and picked up Highway 84 to begin the long drive east. The road was a lighted channel through a forest of darkened office buildings. In another hour, it would begin to come to life.

Fifteen minutes passed and the city had all but vanished before anything was said. Ryan stared ahead into the night, with his hands locked on the wheel.

Alex cracked the window half an inch. He almost had to shout to get above the rain and the howl of the tires. "So are you really sure?"

Ryan's glance was incredulous.

A tentative pause. "You know you're exhausted," said Alex. "You're obliterated, doc. You're not thinking straight, you know that. Someone pushes a few buttons. It could have been a wrong number. A prank. How—"

"No one else knows the game we played! The phone uses tones! I left notes on her recorder. We did that back and forth, it was a game. Don't you get it?"

Alex avoided the obvious question: Why couldn't she talk? "You're certain it's the mine site? Could they have another site nearby?"

Ryan shook his head. "No! The operator said the call was from Summit Resources, in Enterprise. Enterprise is the nearest town, but it's small. Summit has nothing there. It has to be the mine!"

Alex nodded slowly.

Ryan could see his uncertainty. "You don't have to do this. You have Anne. Call a cab on the cell and I'll let you out."

Alex's eyes fell from the faint eastern horizon to his hands, barely visible in the truck. "No."

The pause was drowned out by the rain.

"When did you last call her?" Ryan asked.

"I'll call her tomorrow."

"Call her now."

The truck roared on. Alex ignored the advice and, instead, pointed to the shotgun propped against the torn bench seat. "You don't want to get pulled over."

Ryan glanced at the illuminated needle. The limit was sixty-five. He lifted his foot slightly, and the truck banged a few times and slowed to 70. Within seconds, the needle was back up to 80.

Portland was replaced by a grass- and tree-covered floodplain that spread out in the dim morning light. To the east, under a black overcast, a feeble glow silhouetted the dark cascades in pink.

The steep confines of the Columbia Gorge grew quickly around them. The rock arched up in ragged columns that climbed into the low clouds. In places, snow coated the rock and icy waterfalls tumbled down. The downpour grew and the wipers groaned.

Ryan yelled above the noise. "We'll eat in The Dalles."

They flew past Bonneville Dam and the Bridge of the Gods, past Hood River, ignoring speed limits and probability. They spoke little. After another hour, they emerged east of the Cascades into the Columbia Basin. Here, the air grew colder and the rain becamed mixed. Light snow covered the rolling hills.

At The Dalles, they dropped off the highway. Across an intersection was Ronnie's Truck Stop. Ryan preferred a Burger King to save time, but the needle was on E and this was the exit.

Inside Ronnie's, the smell of fried eggs and bacon filled the air. A row of truckers was perched at the counter. They smoked and drank coffee and talked about the weather and the price of diesel. The place was smeared with years of fried food and gritty air. Country music wailed.

Ryan and Alex found a vinyl booth along the windows, a distance from the others. A wiry woman with a pink blouse and flaming-red hair appeared. She tossed two plastic menus on the table and poured coffee from two feet up, splashing liberally. Peering through the coffee and ketchup stains, the two ordered the Trucker's Special Number One. Three eggs, bacon, hash browns, toast and coffee.

She yelled the order. "Two ones, easy!"

Ryan swallowed three aspirin from a small bottle and rinsed them down with the coffee. The headache was permanent. He was wired tight. He offered the bottle to Alex, who took two.

Alex dumped an ice cube into his coffee and downed the cup. He lowered his head and eyed the patrons behind Ryan. "So how do we do this?" he asked. "How well do you know the place?"

Ryan grabbed the butter knife and began playing with it. His voice was hoarse under the country music. "The whole camp lives in trailers. They have trailers for housing, a cafeteria, a few offices. There are ore crushers called grizzlies, other buildings, processing buildings. All of that is to the north. The trailers are on the southeast side. She called from one of those trailers. The bastards have her in one of those trailers."

Outside, a wind gust slammed the windows. Alex swallowed the rest of his coffee and rubbed his face. "How many people?"

"Maybe sixty. Ten or so guards patrol the place, watch operations. They're basically there to scare off trespassers and guard the gold."

"Sixty? Guns?"

"I'm not sure. Pistols. Maybe a few AK-47s. But they're not fully automatic."

"Oh. Good. Not fully automatic."

"No one's expecting visitors up there, especially in this weather. And they're worried about the gold, they won't be standing around guarding Meagan. We can get her and be gone before they know it."

"How much gold?"

"I'd guess five thousand ounces per month."

Alex leaned forward and whispered. "Three hundred pounds of gold a month? Two tons a year?"

"We'll hide the truck. We'll watch and pick the likely buildings. You take the shotgun, I'll have Karina's 38. We need to get in and get out."

"How many rounds in the shotgun?"

"Four. I brought the box."

Alex rubbed his temples. Mixed rain lashed the windows. Near the table, water drained off the wooden sill and joined a puddle on the floor.

Ryan spoke. "This isn't going to be easy."

The puddle grew larger. To Alex, the insanity of it all was like a runaway train, unstoppable. "Maybe we should talk to the police," he offered quietly.

Ryan's eyes lit up. "Are you fucking crazy? They'll see us coming like some damned Mardi Gras parade! She would disappear before we got close." Ryan began stabbing the wooden table top with the knife. "Listen. I think that if we have to shoot, we shoot to kill. I'm not screwing around. If it happens that we hurt or kill some—"

"Jesus!"

"Don't hesitate, Alex! Anyone interferes, we shoot! Don't choke!"

Alex spit the words between his teeth. "Shut up!"

The trucker on the end, an older guy with rain-soaked jeans and a cowboy hat, turned toward them. But then the red-haired waitress demanded something and he turned back.

Alex ducked behind Ryan and whispered. "For chrissake, shut up! Look, they don't all carry weapons up there. If someone sees us, especially from a distance, they won't even know we don't belong there. We can run, depending—"

Ryan's eyes narrowed. "We run like hell and we stay tight. Someone gets in the way, we shoot! I'm not fucking around!"

Alex wanted to reach over and shake him. "Ryan! Chill out! We won't even get there if you don't relax. Take it easy. We'll have cover in the dark."

"We're not waiting till dark!"

"You want to go charging in there in broad daylight?"

"They'll be spread all over the damned site! It's big, 1800 acres. I don't want her to suffer the end of another day, do you understand me? I want her out before dark."

Alex shook his head. "You said they had helicopters. We'll be sitting ducks in daylight."

Ryan's head fell down into his hands. Chet Atkins cried.

Alex spoke. "Calm down. Calm down, doc. Relax. We need supplies, we need things."

"I saw a hunting store when we pulled in."

The red-haired waitress appeared with two plates in her hands. "Make room, boys!"

Ryan lifted his head just as both plates landed on the table with a loud crack.

"Hard night, cowboy?" She turned and left.

Alex ate his breakfast, Ryan picked at his, and the bill was paid. In the icy, gray rain, Ryan spotted the billboard. Danny's Sporting Goods. He swung a hard right and a few minutes later, they were sprinting through the store. Ryan arrived at the counter with his arms full: a map of the Wallowa Mountains, boxes of ammunition, three small bottles of water, four energy bars, a small pair of small snow gloves, and bolt cutters.

Alex joined him with a bag of hand warmers, a box of waterproof matches, two small flashlights, and binoculars. The clerk eyed the unusual assortment of merchandise but said nothing.

Back in the truck, Ryan unfolded the map and began pointing. "La Grande is another two hours. The mine is about 20 miles northwest of Eagle Cap, right here. We'll curl around east on Highway 82 for 30 miles, and then go north on 3 at Enterprise. The access road is right about here. They have a gate and a chain link fence that runs out on both sides for a ways. We'll get around the fence and drive in behind this ridge. Right in here. We'll hide the truck and hike over the ridge."

Ryan rotated the map. "I'm not sure, but I think there's a second fence. It runs from the base of this ridge around to the southern side. The south side, here, is backed up against the mountain. There shouldn't be a fence. We'll get in here."

"Where do you think she is?" Alex asked.

Ryan studied the map. "All of the trailers are on the southeast side. She's got to be in here somewhere."

"This hike. Is it below the tree line?"

"Part of it. A couple hundred feet of elevation. We can hug the trees until we cross the ridge."

"It'll be snow-covered."

"Yeah." Ryan jabbed the map. "There may be another fence down inside. If so, we can cut it."

"Is it electrified?"

"I'm pretty sure nothing is electrified."

Alex palmed his forehead. "You're pretty sure? How much gold?"

"It won't be hot. People go up there in the summer, activists, environmentalists. They'd love to, but the company can't have people frying on high voltage."

Ryan folded up the map, started up the truck, and pulled into the gas station across the street.

Ten miles east of The Dalles, traffic came to a halt. After a few seconds of standing still, Ryan opened the door and ran up the road to a semi truck. Oncoming traffic flew by, throwing water over the divider. The truck driver rolled down the window and Ryan yelled in the rain. "What's the problem?"

The driver called down. "There's a slide over the highway, one lane is closed."

Ryan sprinted back to the International. They inched along for another 30 minutes and slowly approached the jam. A mountain of mud and rocks covered most of the roadway, but police cruisers were letting a single line of traffic through.

A few miles farther up they crossed over the Deschutes River. In July, it ran clear and sparkling, 20 feet below the bridge. Now inundated by snow melt and rain, it was a wide churn of muddy water all the way up to the overpass. A hundred yards out it smashed violently into the Columbia.

They continued into the eastern basin in silence, with Ryan's fists locked on the wheel and Alex wondering how the next twelve hours would end.

They stopped in Pendleton, a ranching town, to top off the gas tank. As they were getting back in the truck, Alex offered to drive. The thought occurred to him to just drive to a police station, or take the keys and throw them some place irretrievable, a gulley, the roof of the mini mart. He wasn't sure he could do it, but Ryan refused his offer.

Before driving away, they paused at the stop sign. Across the brown and white plateau, their destination was visible in the eastern sky: the snowcapped Wallowas. Always inviting before, they were foreboding now.

"You think I've lost it," Ryan stated calmly. "You don't have to do this."

Alex eyed him. He couldn't remember a time before Ryan. "I know."

"Then call Anne," said Ryan. He was still gazing at the mountains.

"I can't do that. If I told her the truth, she would go crazy."

They finally hit La Grande five hours out of Portland. After the turn onto State Road 82, they began the climb. The increasing elevation brought forests of Ponderosa Pine. The truck passed quickly and unnoticed through the mountain towns of Elgin and Wallowa. At Enterprise, they turned north on 3. Here, the snow had accumulated all winter and the road was a channel through the white forest. They ascended higher until finally a wide road appeared on the right. A ten-foot high steel gate blocked the entrance. On it, a yellow and black sign, eight feet wide, was perched up high.

PRIVATE PROPERTY
NO TRESPASSING
AREA PATROLLED BY ARMED GUARDS
VIOLATORS WILL BE PROSECUTED

## CHAPTER 35

Ryan pulled the truck well off the road and killed the engine. The road was empty in both directions. The sky was overcast and dark. Heavy snow blanketed the evergreen trees and their sloping white branches hung heavy.

Ryan lowered the window. There was only the wind, but he still whispered. "This access road loops around east and south. The mine is still a good ten miles in."

Alex looked into the trees. "That fence is over ten feet high."

Ryan started the truck and crept forward, looking into the trees for where the fence might end. A wide, ice-filled ditch paralleled the road. After creeping forward a hundred yards, he stopped at a place where the trees were thin and the ditch had caved in. The chain link fence, itself covered in snow, disappeared into the forest.

Alex spoke. "You're going over?"

"There's no other way."

"Those posts are steel, probably sunk in concrete."

"It'll give between the posts."

"Don't get stuck. There's a small opening." Alex pointed slightly ahead.

Ryan crept forward and stopped. He moved a lever on the floor, putting the truck in four-wheel drive. Up and down the roadway, not a single car was visible. He turned the truck to face the fence directly and then backed as far up as possible into the bank on the other side. He picked a path between two large trees and floored it.

The truck sailed across the road and slammed into the ditch, throwing up snow and mud. The motor bellowed and the tires howled, and the truck climbed up out of the ditch and then careened through the trees. But the track was off. Alex ducked as trees ripped off a side mirror. The steel fence appeared and the front of the truck slammed into it and lifted. For a brief second it seemed they would climb up over, but the vehicle stopped and the tires spun.

Ryan let up on the gas and backed down off the fence. He backed up 20 feet, angled left to avoid a post, and floored it again. The fence held the truck suspended, but only briefly. This time it collapsed and they drove over.

They maneuvered through the last 50 feet of forest, burst into the open, and shot down an embankment onto another road. Ryan turned hard right and slid to a stop. He killed the hammering motor. Silence. Fresh tire tracks led off in both directions. This was a service and patrol road.

Ryan's heart was pounding. "We lost the muffler."

Alex's eyes were wide. "No kidding."

"This goes straight back to the access road."

"They'll see our tracks."

Ryan started up and the engine hammered away, bellowing their presence. The access road came up immediately. He approached slowly and, seeing no vehicles, turned left and began driving.

Alex yelled over the engine. "How far?"

Ryan checked the odometer. "This goes east for about eight miles and then turns south to follow the ridge. We need to get off after the turn, before the ridge takes off."

"What about oncoming traffic?"

"We'll have to be quick."

Alex stared ahead. "Where's the next gate?"

"It's a mile or so after the turn south. Just before the mine."

"We have to get off well before then."

"We will."

"I have a better idea," said Alex. "We stop before the turn. We get off the road and hide the truck. We'll hike up a mile or so and see what's ahead."

Ryan was adamant. "No! It'll take too long! And I don't want to hide twice. I want to get in and get out!"

Alex's hand clutched the grip in the headliner. "What's our story if we get caught?"

Ryan's eyebrows narrowed down as he looked ahead. He ignored the question.

The wind picked up and it began to snow. In the deep pack, the road was safe at 30 miles per hour; Ryan was doing fifty. Snow-covered shoulders, 20-yards wide, stretched up into the forest on the right and dropped off steeply into the valleys to the left. The broad road offered both visibility and exposure. As they climbed higher, Douglas fir and Ponderosas were replaced by sparse, spindly pine. These were deformed by the wind, their short, white branches all pointing east.

To the south, in between the trees, it was visible now and again: The sheer, gray walls of the pit. Stretching a mile across, it was a giant cavity cut into the mountain. Ryan pointed and it took Alex's breath away. The white peak rose behind the pit, covered in snow that would serve no protection. It would soon fall to explosives and machines.

The road swept broadly to the right, a turn Ryan didn't remember. A ravine opened so that even with the falling snow, any vehicles would be visible for half a mile.

Alex took it in. "We're too exposed!"

Ryan pressed the pedal down. Finally, the road straightened out. Up ahead, the path appeared to be blocked by a wall of white.

"This is the turn south!" Ryan yelled. He pulled Karina's pistol from the back pack and set it on the seat. As they approached, he slowed the truck to a crawl; they were blind to what might be around the turn. Ever so slowly, they made the turn, and the empty white road climbed still higher.

Ryan hit the gas again. "It's a straight shot up from here, maybe a mile and a half. That ridge." He pointed to his left. "We'll drive in as far as we can, get in on the other side."

Alex's voice was tense. "I don't like this! Let's get off now, hide the truck. We'll walk up through those trees. We can survey the place."

"Another half mile, a few more seconds!"

Alex whipped around and checked behind for vehicles. A half-mile rolled by, surely there would be a gate and guards any moment. Ryan searched the shoulder and trees for a place to hide. Alex yelled over the engine. "Get off, Ryan!"

Dead ahead, the back wall of the pit filled the roadway. Something else was there. Above the road, a rising plume of blue.

"Diesel! Get off now! Get off! Get off!"

The International jerked hard to the left and shot across the shoulder and up into the trees. They flew for 50 yards, slamming and careening hard over snow, rocks, and small trees. Another 30 yards and Ryan killed the engine.

Ten seconds of near silence passed, and then came the sound. The roar closed in and reverberated through the trees for half a minute before draining away to a muted rumble.

Ryan whispered. "Gold. Probably escort trucks and the gold truck."

A minute passed. There was only a low growl in the distance, the noise of heavy equipment from the mine itself. Behind them, their path through broken tree branches was evident.

"I don't think they even slowed," said Alex.

Ryan opened his door. "Let's see what we left." He stepped out and began running back to the road.

They crouched low and approached cautiously. The signs of their presence were all over the bank, deep tire gashes in the snow, a trail of broken branches. Alex turned. "Let's go."

At the truck, they started up again. Alex fastened his belt. "Behind the ridge?"

"Right."

"Don't get stuck. How far?"

"Half a mile."

"Through these trees?"

"You see a road?"

"I can't believe I offered my damned beemer."

"Neither can I."

The last half mile took 30 minutes and climbed several hundred feet. Small boulders and short pine trees repeatedly blocked their progress. Alex kept an eye on the ridge as they slipped behind and then moved parallel to it. In several places, deep snow nearly stopped them. Ryan finally shut down the hammering engine and they sat in blessed silence.

The truck was barely concealed by the pines. Perhaps a hundred yards away, the trees ended and the ridge took off at a steep angle across a white slope, climbing still higher. Dark clouds rolled and twisted overhead. Close up and alive, they were shedding snow.

Ryan's eyes were on the ridge. "At least the truck is the right color."

"Unless we need to be found."

Ryan pointed to a small notch in the white wall. "There's a cut, a low spot. I think we can get over there."

"We didn't bring any climbing gear."

"I'd guess it's a couple of hours up. The snow is good for this. It doesn't look slick."

Alex looked at his hiking boots. "We need snow shoes."

"It's not that far," Ryan tried to reassure.

"What's your plan? We can't just go storming in there."

"We hike up to that cut and get a look. All of the buildings are on the other side of that ridge. They'll quit most of the work at five or so, return to the buildings by five-thirty or six. We're out before then, heading back over the top."

"Out by five-thirty? Ryan, what are you smoking?" Alex's tone was angry. "It's 2:15 now. That's a hard climb up, it'll be 5:00 before we even get up there. And we can't go barging in there in daylight! No. We wait until four, right here. We hike up, survey the place and pick out target buildings. Then we hike down in twilight. We arrive in the dark, find her and get out. And we've got to get out before morning, past the gate and gone. I'm not driving out in broad daylight."

Ryan looked at his friend. He didn't trust his own judgment, but the push to keep going was overwhelming.

Alex read his mind. "Take a damned nap, doc. At least try. You need the rest. We'll leave at four."

"I'm setting my watch for 3:30. I won't sleep."

"Just try."

Alex opened the truck door and stepped out. He trudged around the back through the snow and relieved himself. Then he opened the back door, climbed in, and tried to get comfortable.

Ryan followed suit. Outside, the faint drumming of heavy equipment echoed in the distance. Back inside the cab, he set the alarm on his watch. He set the shotgun down on the cab floor and lay down on the torn bench seat. He closed his eyes, but his mind raced. He would need the bolt cutters, and the knife, don't forget the knife. Is she hurt? Can she walk? Remember her coat, boots. An endless train of thoughts fought heavy eyelids.

A crash rippled across the valleys and Ryan's head jerked up hard. A fierce blue sky filled the windshield. He sat up and checked his watch. A quarter to five!

He reached back and slapped Alex's shoulder. "Wake up!"

It came again, a staccato of popping bursts.

"What's that?"

"Dynamite. Let's go."

They stuffed the pockets of their nylon parkas with the flashlights, water bottles, and chocolate bars. In the backpack, Ryan put the hunting knife, binoculars, and more food. It was nearly over-filled with her clothing and boots. He took the revolver and a box of 20 rounds. Alex stuffed the hand warmers and shotgun rounds into his zip pockets. They left the bottle of cola on the front seat and stepped into the snow.

Ryan slipped on the backpack. "Give me the bolt cutters, in back."

Alex reached inside and passed out the cutters. He then lifted up the shotgun. "Do we really need this?"

"Yes, we do."

"They'll kill us?"

# THE MINE

Ryan nodded emphatically. "Yes, they will. And dump us out here. They killed one of their own, you saw it on the news. They've killed three that I know of." Ryan looked up to the ridge. "Are you ready?"

Alex looked at his friend. Ryan was mentally fried and physically exhausted. They were both unprepared for what lie ahead. A very strange phone call had brought them here and the caller had not even spoken.

"I hope you know what you're doing," said Alex. "And remember where we parked."

Ryan pointed to the cut in the ridge. "We're at around 6,000 feet. And we're about eleven o'clock from the cut, maybe a half-mile away."

## Chapter 36

For the first few hundred feet, the going was manageable. Several feet of snow covered the ground, but it was firm enough and Ryan found he only sank in up to the middle of his knees. There was always a drift and a shadow, where the snow had piled up on the windward side of boulders and trees and left a shadow on the leeward side, a cup in the snow.

The sound was foreign and it came up fast. A helicopter. They quickly crouched between trees as it swept in from the north, following the ridgeline. Dark and menacing, it flew in low and turned toward them. The two climbers dove under the nearest pine. The machine, with its engines shrieking, hovered nearby and blew dense clouds of white crystals into the air. After several long seconds, it continued up the ridgeline.

Alex yelled. "Did they see us?"

"Wait!" The whine and pop faded. Ryan crawled out from the under the branches, but crouched behind the tree.

"They found the tracks," said Alex.

"They were here for only a second. If they spotted us, they would have waited, maybe dropped smoke markers or something. Come on."

Alex emerged from under the tree. "There are miles of mountains out here. They wouldn't fly up our ass by chance!"

"Come on!"

They continued and the angle increased with each step. The rumble from the mine grew muted, blocked by the ridge, and soon the only sound was their heavy breathing and their crunching boots in the cold snow.

The sickly pines gave up here, strangled by the extremes. Ahead, the flawless white slope was barren of hiding places. Ryan stopped behind the last small tree. He punched his boots into the ice and sat.

Alex knelt in the ice and surveyed the climb. A cold wind blew over the crest, catching loose snow that rolled down in a curl. He spoke between breaths. "We'll be wide open."

"We'll rest here and then be quick."

"There's no cover."

"We can't go in the front door!"

"They know we're here! They've already made us!" Alex gasped for air while shaking his head. "Dammit! One wrong number at four in the morning, and we're here on the side of this mountain?"

Ryan turned. He heard the words. "Then get out of here! I know who was on the phone!"

"What's on the other side of this ridge?"

"What do you mean?"

"Is it sheer? Can we get down?"

Ryan was up and moving now. He yelled over his shoulder. "Head back to the truck!"

The air was thinner this high and Ryan cursed himself for not being in better shape. For the last 45 minutes, they climbed bent over, leaning into the ridge face and punching each step into the ice. It was less than a thousand feet up, but it felt like a mile.

Ryan turned to catch his breath and saw it. Even in the shadow of the ridge, the trail of their foot prints glared on the white mountainside. "Hurry!"

They finally reached the cut. It was a narrow, deep channel in the ridge, the sides of which were covered in ice. They stumbled in and leaned against the ice to catch their breath. The biting wind poured through the channel and sliced through their parkas. Ryan trotted ahead.

The passage opened into a shallow bowl and a crevasse off to the right. Thick blue ice encased the walls and ground, and they pushed along, slipping repeatedly. Light from the setting sun glared off the walls. At the end, the passage was nearly choked off. Towering 20 feet overhead, twisting columns of ice wrapped the rock on both sides. It had been sculpted by the wind and was laced with myriads of deep blue rivulets.

Crouching, they peered down the western slope. Three hundred yards distant and perhaps 750 feet lower was the edge of the mine. Trailers were collected in groupings and they were closer than Ryan had thought. Due west almost a mile, the heap leach pyramids rose up. Near the pyramids, Ryan could make out two dark spots that he recognized immediately. These were the fragile cyanide ponds; the others were hidden behind the pyramids. To the south, the yawning, terraced pit was backed up against the peak.

Alex's jaw dropped open. He yelled into the wind. "How big?"

"Over a mile across."

"I can't believe they can do this."

"It's all public land," Ryan yelled sarcastically and waved his hand. "Made for fucking you and me! Thanks to the 1872 Mining Law and no oversight, any son-of-a-bitch who wants to can turn it into a toxic waste dump!"

With the wind tearing at his breath, Ryan gaped into the colossal hole in the ground, at the missing mountain side and the ancient peak that would soon fall. A public treasure, millions of years in the making, reduced to giant piles of toxic rubble, traded away for lakes of poison, and gold. Precious gold. He had worked diligently, obsessively, but in ignorance. After Gabe's murder, he was in the way. Oblivious, he had run headlong into blind greed. Now it had all come to this: Animals had Meggy. It had occurred to him before that they might have wanted her as a hostage, but panicked idiots take hostages. Sarinov was no idiot. Meagan had simply returned home at the wrong time, and now she was their problem, a problem they wouldn't keep.

Ryan leaned into the ice and said a short, fervent prayer. He then rolled over a small ledge, carefully slid down 30 feet, and took cover behind an icy outcropping. The snow pack was deep and the drop was intimidating. Alex followed, keeping an eye out for the chopper.

In the biting wind, Ryan rested his arms on the outcropping. He peered down through the binoculars. "There are three groups of trailers. In the foreground, the largest group of eight or nine is for housing. Beyond that and on the right, two doublewides. I think that's the cafeteria. To the left, farther back, another group of maybe five."

Ryan knew everything about the geology of this place, but nothing of the people. Did they know there was a prisoner, a woman held here? Could anyone be trusted? He continued. "Beyond the trailers are the helicopter pad and a small hanger. Down toward the pyramids are four larger buildings, light blue and white. Those are processing buildings, chemical and pump houses. To the north I can see the incinerator and gold buildings. Plenty of guards there."

Alex spoke. "At least you know the place."

Ryan glanced at Alex. He was sitting in the snow with his head in his arms, shivering. Ryan crouched to flex his stiffening knees and tapped him with the binoculars. "Take a look. The cafeteria is on the right, you can see people lined up. Farther back on the left, five or so trailers. Back by themselves. They may be offices. Whoever brought her up here, I think they're keeping her close. He needs to keep her a secret."

"From the crew."

"Yeah. Sixty people. Not everyone down there is a criminal. He's kept her his little secret. She's got to be in one of those trailers on the left."

Alex adjusted the focus. "A lot of people."

"Anything going on with the trailers on the left, in back?"

"Two guys have just left those trailers, looks like number two or three from the left. They're walking toward a doublewide. Everyone is gathered around the big trailers. Dinner time."

Ryan checked the sky. The sun was a few degrees, perhaps 30 minutes from the horizon. "It's almost six. It'll be dark before seven."

"Check this," Alex said. "In the group on the left, number two from the left. That trailer has no windows. But in the center group, all the others have windows."

Ryan was hovering. "Let me see." He grabbed the binoculars.

The setting sun glared in the lenses and his pounding heart shook the image. "You're right. I can't tell if it was made that way or if it's boarded up. I see another like that, behind. They're close. Maybe the windows are on the other side."

"But two sides are visible and for both, I saw no windows."

"Maybe they have a jail, a place to lock up a troublemaker or a drunk."

"Or maybe it's just storage."

For the next twenty minutes, while fighting his freezing hands and feet, Ryan watched as men entered the cafeteria, ate, and left. The first group had converged at the café around 6:00 and at 6:40, a second group formed as the first exited. All those in the first group returned to the main trailers. No one entered the trailers on the far left. He again searched the processing buildings for a clue, without result. The red sun slipped below the Cascade Range, killing the direct light and bathing the area in a red glow. Visibility was falling fast. Ryan stomped his feet and searched frantically. Close to an hour had passed. Traffic had died down. Nothing gave a hint. And then he saw something.

In the dying light, Ryan's pulse jarred the binoculars. "I have a guy. He, I think he's carrying food. He's climbing the steps to a trailer, one with no windows. He's stopped at the door. Taking a while. I can't see! Wait! He turned on the light. He turned on the light and went inside! He had food! He unlocked the door and carried in food!"

Alex rubbed his gloved hands together. "Maybe he's working late."

"But no one left that trailer! It was locked! He screwed around at the door! He already ate, no one else went inside the cafeteria in the last 20 minutes!"

"He could be the cook."

"A cook would eat in the cafeteria! He took food to someone!" Ryan grabbed the backpack and stowed the binoculars. He slipped the pack over his shoulders and picked up the bolt cutters.

"So what do we tell them when they catch us?" Alex asked.

No answer. Ryan was heading down the darkening slope.

Alex grabbed the shotgun as a cold gust whipped up the ridge.

The sun and its meager warmth vanished as though a switch had been thrown. Under broken clouds, the quarter moon came to life, but it provided little light.

The step descent into the mine slowed the climb down and in the darkness and stiff wind, each step needed to be tested. After well over an hour, the terrain finally flattened out and they neared the compound perimeter. There was no fence, just mountains of snow deposited by the plows. They crouched behind berms.

The cafeteria trailer was lit up. Directly ahead were the dorm trailers; the lights were on in all but one. No one was outside. The grinders and trucks were silent and except for the cold wind, the night was, too.

Ryan whispered. "Come on."

He scurried ahead in a crouch with the cutters in hand. Alex followed close behind. They slid down a six-foot snow bank and moved past the dorms. With the ice crunching under their steps, they ran 75 yards near the trailers in question. These structures were the size of mobile homes, elevated five feet to get above the snow. Flat roofs were covered with snow and ringed with long blades of ice. Frozen slush coated the ground.

Aside from a single light near the dorms, darkness engulfed the area. At least three of these trailers were without windows. They moved to the closest one and climbed the steel porch. Under Alex's small flashlight, Ryan found the door locked, a simple keyed lock. He pondered calling her name, but thought better of it.

Alex searched for something to pry with; the blade of the hunting knife would snap. On the ground under the deck porch, he found a flat metal bar left over from the porch construction.

He kicked it a few times and broke it loose from the ice. Back on the porch, he positioned the bar up with one hand and held the light with the other. Ryan hammered down with the bolt cutters and the clang of metal-on-metal rang out. With a hard thrust down, the frame gave and the door popped open. Their small lights illuminated a room full of cabinets, boxes of canned foods, office supplies. Behind an interior door, more of the same.

They exited and quietly pulled the door shut. Kneeling low on the deck, they studied nearby trailers. Ryan spoke low. "The guy with the tray went into one of these."

Light snow began to fall. They flew down the steps and ran to the next unit. This one had a window in front. Ryan wrapped the bolt cutters with his coat and slammed them down on Alex's pry bar. The coat muffled the noise but ruined his aim. It took three hits before Alex could pry open the door. This trailer was obviously an office, with desks and cabinets. The smell of cigar smoke permeated. More supplies filled the back room.

Ryan attacked the first desk in a search of keys. The top drawer opened, but the side drawers were locked. They popped the drawers with the bar and under the flashlight, found a case of whiskey, boxes of bullets and packs of cigars. No keys. Alex searched the second desk. It was unlocked, but yielded nothing. Ryan scowled. "Come on!"

Outside, the dark silhouette of the last trailer, farthest from the dorms, was barely visible. The snow hadn't been cleared here and they waded through it. This trailer was missing the steel porch and a small wooden porch had been shoved up to the door. In the shaking circle of the flashlight, Ryan climbed the steps.

A heavy steel clasp and fresh industrial lock secured this door. Something of value was inside. He opened the cutters wide and closed down on the bail. It resisted. He wrapped his arms around the handles and squeezed hard. The lock gave a cracking pop and fell.

But the door knob was still locked. Ryan pounded the door with his shoulder, but on the tiny porch, he couldn't get it to budge.

With barely enough room to stand, Alex held the bar with one hand and held the flashlight in his teeth. Ryan swung the cutters down hard. The ringing smash was impossibly loud, and the pry bar slipped and disappeared into the snow.

Ryan cursed. "Dammit!"

Alex jumped from the porch and disappeared. Thirty seconds passed. Ryan called in desperation. "Alex!"

"Got it." Alex climbed back onto the porch and again positioned the bar against the jam. Ryan arched back and slammed the cutters down. Again, the resonating clang, but the bar dug in. He pulled back hard on the bar and steel door popped open.

Under the light, the long, dark box was empty except for a cot at the far end. A thin mattress lay on the floor. Ryan stepped inside. "Meggy?"

A muffled cry startled him. He turned and peered behind the door. A figure cowered in the corner. Auburn hair. A swollen, black eye. Tape wrapped her head and covered her mouth. Her white blouse was ripped; her jeans were half on. She shook her head in a muffled plea.

Alex whispered in the dark. "Oh God. Oh God."

"Meggy, it's me! It's Ryan!" He turned the light into his face. "Meggy!"

She leaned forward, but her arms were held back. He pulled at the tape and slowly removed it from her mouth. She pushed into him, shivering violently, and convulsed in sobs. He held her for a brief moment and then took her by the shoulders. Alex held the light and Ryan shuddered. A monstrous bruise engulfed her left eye and cheekbone. A long cut ran down her face.

Ryan slowly turned her. "Her hands!"

Steel handcuffs bound her raw wrists together and blood ran down her fingers. A length of chain weighed heavily on the cuffs. She blurted the word between choking sobs. "Hurry!"

While Alex held a flashlight, Ryan carefully maneuvered the cutters and broke off the cuffs. Her arms fell free and she turned and embraced him. Her body shook.

Ryan pulled off his backpack and ripped out the parka and clothing. He grabbed the sweatshirt and pulled it over her.

She spoke in shudders. "Damned… chains."

# THE MINE

Ryan pulled out the ski pants. He gently laid her down, and with the flashlight in his teeth, zipped up her jeans and slipped on the ski pants over them. They put on her boots and parka. Ryan unwrapped a chocolate bar. "Can you eat? Eat some of this."

She sat and nibbled the chocolate while he wrapped his arms around her, trying to warm her body.

After 30 seconds, he pulled the water bottle from his parka. "Drink," he said. "Good. Okay. Can you walk?"

A nod. Her voice was faint. "I called."

"You did!"

She looked into the dark. "Hurry."

Ryan's voice choked. "Let's go."

He saved the water and chocolate. He stood and slipped on the backpack, and then helped her up. The cutters were left on the floor. Alex was guarding the door, peering through an inch opening. "Ready?"

"Yes."

# CHAPTER 37

The two men stepped into the dark and helped her down. Snow blew, and the cold wind carried a warning: the smell of cigar smoke.

The dark figure rounded the trailer with a red glow in his mouth. The flashlight bobbed as he approached. They froze. Meagan's hand pulled hard on Ryan as she gave out a whimper. The figure stopped and lifted up his light. Reflected by the white snow and trailer walls, it illuminated everything. The cigar fell. A glass bottle dropped from his hand and he went for something in his jacket. Glinting metal came up.

A flash and a blast exploded. Meagan cried out. The shotgun slug threw him back and down; his light flew over his head.

Alex stepped forward. The hole in his chest was large and the snow around him was sprayed with flesh and blood. With a trembling hand, Alex pried the gun from the man's hand and flung it hard into the darkness.

Under the small light, Ryan peered into the face, the frozen look of surprise. Deep scars, yellow teeth, a black moustache. His last breath escaped his body; it reeked of whiskey. The desire to cave in the man's skull was over-powering.

She pulled frantically on his hand. "Please!"

They fled around the trailer and encountered another flashlight. Another had followed. They were a tag team. This one turned and ran. A warbling sound filled the night. Across the compound, flood lights lit up the site all the way down to the gold house.

The way out led directly past the dorm trailers, but the area would be crawling. They spotted it: a path to the right led in a zigzag to a mountain of snow two hundred yards away. Beyond that, darkness. They tore across the ice. The mountain of white seemed to retreat rather than draw near, and then suddenly they were upon it, around it. Ryan slowed, she continued past him. Alex's voice. "Stay close!"

They ran over and around obstacles of ice and snow, across a perimeter road and down into a shallow gully. Here, the ground suddenly collapsed and they crashed into feet of ice water. After fighting through the ditch, they clawed up the incline and slogged on until darkness swallowed them.

Ryan bent over to catch his breath. His voice was a whisper. "Meagan!" He turned on the light against his chest where it made a small blue glow. "Meagan!"

She came to him, sobbing between breaths. He held her for a several minutes while ice water dripped from their clothes.

Alex was nearby, barely visible. "We can't stop!"

Ryan could feel that water had flooded his boots and he shivered violently. "Damned water! Meggy, we have a long run, a long hike."

"How far?"

"A ways along the base of this ridge. And then over the top."

Meagan's voice was shrill. "I'm not going back!"

They ran into the wind and their soaked clothing froze immediately. Off to the left, the mine complex glowed. The lights of vehicles were visible, racing between buildings.

Ryan yelled in the night. "Hurry!"

The trek was an obstacle course in the dark, over and around mountains of ice and drifts from avalanches that had fallen from above. They began to slow with the numbing cold. The wind stole Ryan's cap. Ice stung exposed skin.

The roar of a snowcat swept up. Ryan pulled Meagan and yelled, "Down!"

Search lights panned the ridge base. The shafts probed the night, but falling snow smothered their reach. The vehicle passed by.

They journeyed on. Ryan stuck next to her, encouraging her. Alex led with a dim flashlight.

"How far?" she pleaded.

"Not far."

They slowed to a walk, stumbling in the howling darkness. Ryan stopped. "Wait! It's here somewhere. The cut in the ridge."

The warbling finally stopped and except for the blowing wind, the night was silent. Light from the complex glowed, but against the rising ridge, it vanished. They searched the dark for a few minutes. Not even the ridgeline was visible. And then a sliver of moonlight broke through.

Ryan spotted the cut. "There, on the right! Come on!"

They began the climb. Feeble moonlight broke through intermittently and they stayed close together. Halfway up, Ryan knelt over, fighting to get his breath in the bitter cold. His arm was around hers and she sank down in the snow and shivered violently.

"How far?" she asked again.

He answered between gasps. "Almost there."

Time passed, ten minutes or an hour. The howling wind sucked the heat from their freezing bodies and Ryan wondered if they had made progress at all. But then it changed. The flow of ice, the hissing sound. Rather than rushing up the slope, it funneled past them with a shriek. They stumbled into the channel and groped along.

Ryan's knees wanted to fold. He felt an irresistible desire to rest. He groped for her. "Meggy." The blowing ice felt like hot sand. His voice was smothered by the wind. "Meggy."

An arm hit his head. Yelling. Alex pulled them. He was yelling and pushing them down a bending path. "Get in!" A wall of ice was before them. "Get in!" Under the feeble light, a crack in the ice, inches high. "Get in!"

Ryan obeyed. He crawled into the dark cave on his stomach. His arms and legs moved like wood. On his side, he turned to pull her close and wrapped his clumsy arms around her.

The voice was insistent. "Take them!"

He fumbled in the dark. The hand warmers. He shoved them inside her coat.

The breeze caught her hair. A path of light rose into the summer sky and burst, filling the night with a waterfall of green and red streamers. She turned and laughed.

He tried to move, but his right leg was pinned. Pain fired down his back and side. He raised his head and collided with something hard.

The cave was ice-cold and dank. He rolled toward her, but the rock clutched his shoulder. Muscles ached. His feet and hands throbbed. Dim light penetrated. He could see the dark rock folded tightly around him.

He turned his head and felt her hair. Under the strands that crisscrossed her face, a black swath covered an eye and cheekbone. Her shallow breaths, barely visible, rose and fell. Except for this, she seemed a corpse.

He pulled his wrist up to his face and pulled back the sleeve with his teeth. The watch dial glowed 11:30.

"Meggy," Ryan whispered. "Meggy."

She stirred. Her cracked voice responded. "Where am I?"

"With me. Don't lift your head up, there's no room."

A tired sigh.

"How are you?" he asked.

"You found me." Her voice melted into quiet sobbing. "I didn't know… if you'd make it. If you were safe."

"Your phone call. How did you call?"

"I was chained to the bed. It was screwed to the floor. I broke it loose."

"How did you call me?"

"A phone. The, the man, he thought he broke it. The numbers, they were hanging off. I couldn't talk or hear, but I pushed the buttons, hit the numbers. I couldn't tell. My hands were behind me. I pushed the four numbers. The song. I did it over and over. Until he came back."

"Meggy. We started driving right after you called."

Out of the silence, a muffled sound like the popping of fireworks echoed faintly. The helicopter. It came in close. Hidden in the rock and snowdrift, they lay still until it faded.

Meagan whispered. "They've found us?"

Alex answered. "Wait."

For 15 minutes they lay in dead silence and listened for any sound: voices, footsteps in snow. There was only the muffled wind.

Ryan spoke. "They're gone."

Alex replied. "Wait. They could have dropped someone."

Solid granite lay an inch from Meagan's face. It seemed to be crushing her and she struggled to fight the rising panic.

Ryan finally spoke. "Let's take a look."

With an arm, Alex pushed a hole through the drift that had piled up over the entrance. The thick pack fell and he slowly cleared an opening with his feet and arms. Bright light and cold air poured in. Alex cautiously crawled out. After a minute, he quietly announced, "It looks clear."

They crawled out of the cave one at a time, squinting hard in bright daylight and a blue sky. The storm had dumped the white powder and piled it up high around the cave, but the wind had made a large V-shaped funnel around the opening.

Ryan looked at the deep drift. "We wouldn't have made it."

Meagan noticed the silence. "They've stopped working. Listen."

The mountains were intensely still.

Alex spoke. "They never shut down?"

Ryan shook his head. "Not during the day and only partially at night. They're probably listening for us, the sound of the truck. They probably have everyone in the camp looking for us."

"I doubt they'll call the police."

Alex pulled his cell phone from his parka. It turned on with a familiar chirp and Meagan's eyes lit up.

He turned the display toward her. It read NO SERVICE.

"Sorry, I had to try." Alex scanned the top of the bowl. "I want to climb up and look around. If that chopper comes…" He gestured to the cave.

"Be careful," Meagan replied. "Come back soon."

Alex turned and they watched him climb slowly out of the bowl.

The couple sat in the snow. Ryan gazed at his wife and she smiled at him in spite of the pain. He could see her face fully now, the long cut, the massive purple bruise that started above her left eyebrow and ended at the corner of her mouth. Her face was swollen. Dark red covered her nose and lips.

"I look pretty bad?" she asked, lightly touching her cheek.

"You look fine." He didn't know how to ask the next question. "Are you okay?"

She understood and tears quickly flooded her eyes. "I'm okay. I am."

He put his arms around her. "I'm sorry. When did they take you?"

"I came home early, last... Tuesday? They were inside when I got home." She reached up and touched the back of her head. Her lips quivered. "I came to in the back of a van. I was blindfolded, gagged. Tied up for hours. What did they want?"

"I think papers from the mine."

She looked at him. "My God. What day is today?"

"I think Sunday. How are you? Your hands and feet?"

Her feet were on fire. Her toes felt wooden. She lied. "Okay. A little sore."

"We have a hike down to the truck."

"I can do it," she said quickly. "What about you?"

"I'm good." Ryan slipped Karina's gun from his coat pocket and unlocked the safety.

Meagan whispered. "Where did you get that?"

"Karina. She helped at the house, with flyers, everything."

"Flyers?"

"We put up a thousand fliers. We had your friends from the clinic and some of mine help. We got the TV news to run your story."

Above them, an object moved and Ryan jerked up the pistol.

Alex stood at the top of the drift, up to his waist. He took careful strides down to them, hugging the wall. "We're alone, but there's room to land. If they wanted to get up here, they could do it."

Ryan addressed his friend. "How are you? Fingers and toes?"

"My feet are frozen. Damned water."

Alex sat down in the snow and grew quiet. He looked up at the blue sky for a moment and then to his friend. "Ryan. All the way out here, I didn't believe you. All the way."

"You saved us last night," Ryan replied. "Twice."

Alex simply shrugged. "I've never been so cold. I stumbled down this hole, fell really. Tried to find my way out with my flashlight and noticed that crack in the rock, right in front of my face. Pure chance."

"Your cave saved us," Meagan said.

A long moment passed before Alex spoke again. "Who was he?"

Meagan took a breath. "My keeper."

Ryan's jaw clenched. Ice crystals swirled around them. Alex lowered his head and he seemed to be searching the snow.

She put a hand on his shoulder. "You did the right thing, Alex."

Ryan nodded. "You did."

Alex looked at his gloved hands. "I saw the gun, it scared the hell out me. I didn't really think."

She took a long breath. "I'm sorry, Alex. I'm sorry. But you did the right thing."

Ryan reached down and pulled the backpack out of the cave. He emptied the food from it onto the snow. "We have plenty of food. Energy bars, chocolate, fig bars. I think we should make this last two more days. We'll be on the road in less than 12 hours, but there's no point in pushing our luck."

Alex agreed. "Four more meals. One this morning, one tonight."

They sat in the snow and ate breakfast. "How far is the truck?" Meagan asked.

"Maybe half a mile. A little climb down." Ryan answered.

She looked up at the high snow bank encircling them. "I want out of here."

"We can't go down in daylight," Ryan said.

Meagan faced her husband. "We're stuck up here another day?"

Alex raised his right arm, covered in blue nylon. "We stick out like neon."

"What if they come for us?" she asked.

Ryan tried to sound confident. "They won't find us, not if we stay put. On the slope, we'll be wide open. We'll get out tonight."

Meagan looked at her black boots. Her toes were numb; her feet throbbed. She dreaded what they might look like. "I can't take another storm."

"It should be clear tonight. We'll have a good chance." Ryan's arm went around her. "We'll be okay."

Meagan pulled her knees up. "My feet."

"What about them?"

"They're not good."

"Both?"

"The right is worse than the left."

Ryan knelt down, pulled up the pant, and unlaced her right boot. He slowly pulled it off and pink water drained from it. Bits of red ice and blood stained her cotton sock. He carefully peeled off the sock and revealed five black and blue toes. The smallest toe was split open and oozing blood. Her foot was red and swollen. Ryan gently touched her toes.

"I don't feel the little ones," she said.

Ryan pulled off the other boot and sock. The two smallest toes were dark blue and the foot, bright red, but no cuts, no blood. He spoke. "Here, lie down in the cave, at the entrance. Standing or sitting up puts pressure on your feet. Come on."

The two of them picked her up, keeping her feet out of the snow. She sat down on the lip of the cave and slid in partway. Ryan slipped the backpack under her head as a pillow. He squeezed the water and blood out of her socks and laid them on the edge, hoping they might dry. He then removed his parka, opened it, and gently laid it over her legs.

Lying on her back, she looked up at the tall sides of the drift. "How many bullets do we have?" she asked.

Ryan sat next to her. "Ten or so shotgun rounds. The pistol is loaded. There's a box of bullets in that backpack."

## Chapter 38

The rest of the day was spent in or near the cave. The urge to climb out was strong, but their tracks would be visible from the sky. Rest was robbed by the distant beating of the helicopter.

Late in the afternoon, the beating grew suddenly. It swept over them and the three quickly wedged themselves and the backpack inside the cave. It hovered overhead as if daring them to show. After several petrifying minutes, it finally drifted off. But now they wondered if killers hadn't been delivered to hunt them down. They hid in the rock and waited.

Finally, the sky began to turn. Soft pink painted high tendrils against the blue. The color deepened and reflected in the mountains so that the air itself glowed. Finally, in the twilight, they emerged.

She carefully pulled on her socks and boots. Alex replaced the round that had been fired in the shotgun and Ryan slipped on the backpack.

"If you hear anything, shout a warning and get down," said Alex. "Dig into the snow and try to hide."

Meagan stood and tested her feet. They were stiff and burned, but she could walk.

They climbed single-file out of the bowl and struggled through the drift-covered channel. The sun had formed a thin layer of ice on the deep snow that broke into segments as they trudged on. Their breath hung in the cold air.

After pushing for 20 minutes to the end of the passage, the ridge finally opened up and the eastern slope stretched out before them: a sweeping drop covered in flawless, pink snow. At the bottom of the slope, the short pine trees were tiny spikes.

Meagan's eyes shifted to her husband. "You climbed this?"

Ryan nodded and pointed. "The truck should be straight out from here, and a little to the left."

Meagan looked down.

Ryan turned to her. "You can do it. It'll take some time."

The sound. Reflexively, they ducked.

The whine and beating of the chopper echoed in the darkening mountains as the machine flew in from the south. Two searchlights shot out bright beams. It flew in low and passed along the base of the ridge below them, before slipping behind another ridge.

They stared at the slope. In the falling light, it looked like a mile drop.

"We'll be on it all night," Alex said.

They studied the darkening terrain another minute. Finally, Meagan spoke. "We can slide."

Ryan was emphatic. "No."

Alex nodded. "I've seen people do this. It's called glissading. With the powder, we should be able to slide down."

Ryan's eyes darted to Alex. "There's ice on it, glaze. We'll crash into those trees at the bottom."

Meagan pulled in the drawstring at the bottom of the parka. "It looks like mostly powder."

"Meagan, it's too steep!" Ryan reached for her sleeve.

Alex responded. "I've seen this. You sit down and lean back, go feet first. They usually have a hammer, a small pick to slow them down."

She agreed. "It'll work."

To Ryan, her voice seemed more vulnerable than ever. "Meggy, please!"

She turned to him. "I can't hike down like this. My feet aren't good, I'll fall and slide whether I want to or not."

She pulled from her husband and slipped carefully over the edge, anchoring her feet in the snow. They followed. She searched the trees. "Where's the truck?"

Alex pointed. "Straight out, over to the left a bit. I'll go first. Watch me, see how it goes. See where I end up so we can find each other. And watch for the chopper."

Before they could speak, Alex rolled onto the snow. The slope was immediate. He turned onto his back, sank in a few inches, and gained speed instantly. The powder flew up in a wake, and for a few seconds, it was orderly. But then it suddenly kicked up in bursts. He was tumbling. Then the cloud blew off. Half way down, his body lay still on the mountainside. He remained there a few seconds, and then launched himself again. The cloud returned. A few more seconds passed.

Something moved at the bottom. In the falling light, Ryan strained to see. The object melted into the trees. "My God!"

"He made it."

"He's injured! He must have broken ribs! You tumble like that, you'll get hurt!"

"We don't have a choice."

Ryan's eyes searched the sky. The improved weather would let the chopper fly all night. "Meggy."

"We can't spend the night on this mountain. I saw him, Ryan. He made it."

After half a minute, Ryan finally conceded. "Go slow. Here, flash this light for me once when you get down." He pushed the flashlight into one of her pockets and zipped it up. "If you get into trouble, hit it three or four times and I'll hike down. Go slow, don't roll! Feet first! I can't believe what I'm saying!"

He pulled her hood up tightly around her head, closed a strap, and tucked in her hair. "Meggy."

She hugged him tightly. "I'll be okay. Follow your own advice coming down. Don't tumble."

They hugged again for several seconds. She kissed him, lightly for her sore lips, and then pushed away. "I love you, Sasquatch. I love you. See you at the bottom."

Ryan couldn't reply.

In what seemed like one motion, she climbed out on top of the ice and was gone. The slide began so fast that Ryan's heart jumped as his wife's form seemed to disappear into the darkness. Her lighter body made no initial disturbance, but then she flipped or rolled; a brief cloud marked it, like a small explosion. Nothing else.

Seconds passed. He screamed her name in dark. "Meagan!"

He stared at the tree line. A black sky and a few stars had replaced the twilight and the trees were all but invisible. And then he saw it. A light, very dim. It moved up and down, and then it vanished. Did he imagine it?

The second the light went out, a roar engulfed him from behind. The chopper had flown up the inside of the ridge, made soundless by the inside wall. Searing lights blinded him and he fell back, tumbling and falling down the slope. He slammed into the snow, was up again with arms and legs flailing, and then tumbled back onto the ice.

"Ryan!"

Pain. He tried to move. He rolled and slowly brought up one knee. His body throbbed. Alex took him under his arms. The whine of the chopper could be heard. Up the slope, they had caught a glimpse of his blue parka, but they were moving too fast and Ryan had disappeared. Now, bright lights scoured the mountainside.

They hobbled 50 feet and into the short pine trees as Ryan called, "Meagan!"

"Here!"

Ryan stood and winced. Sharp stabs fired across his chest. The whine of jets and shafts of light penetrated the trees.

Alex's voice. "Come on!"

Ryan found her sleeve and they pushed deeper.

Meagan spoke. "I can't see anything!"

Ryan answered. "The truck is here, somewhere." He fished the small compass out of his pocket and felt the broken glass. "You made it down all right?" he asked her.

"I lost my gloves. I didn't break anything."

Alex kept going. "Come on."

They trekked another hundred feet through the snow, around rocks and trees, blindly tripping and falling as they went. Alex finally stopped. "It's got to be here."

Ryan suddenly realized it. "I lost the backpack, on the way down. It had the food."

They became quiet. They huddled together in the dark while the chopper blades echoed off the mountains. Ice hissed through the trees, blown off branches by the wind. In the distance, a new sound rumbled through the mountains. It went on for several seconds.

Ryan spoke. "I've never heard anything like that."

Alex's voice. "Avalanche?"

"I don't know. Where the hell is the truck?"

Exhausted and injured, they sat in the dark forest. The fall down the slope had battered them. Meagan searched the woods, a random smear of black and dark gray. "What's that?" She pointed uselessly in the dark.

The two men peered about them. The object, a dark blob, was not far away. Alex answered. "A boulder."

She stood up slowly and hobbled to the object. She scraped off the snow with her sleeve and then banged it with her hand. It gave a hollow thump. She moved back, found the door handle and gave it a hard tug. The snow encasement cracked and the truck's dome light burst on like a floodlight.

Alex lunged forward and closed the door. "God, Meagan! Ryan! When I open it, reach in and kill the dome light."

The truck wasn't warm, but it provided shelter. Alex spoke in the dark. "What's the best way out, Ryan? East?"

"We can't go east, Hell's Canyon is east. And they'll be waiting for us at the gate. The access road heads north for half a mile. Just past the turn, the trees thin out. We can turn off and head cross-country. Find a state road."

"We can't take the access road," Alex replied. "They'll be all over it."

"But we'll burn too much gas running cross-country in low gear. Too many trees and boulders—it'll take hours. On the road it's two or three minutes." Ryan rolled down the window a few inches and listened. There was only the wind. "I don't hear them. Maybe they think we're dead."

Alex spoke. "We don't have the shotgun. Do you still have the pistol?"

Ryan nodded invisibly. His mind was tired and it hurt to think. "Yeah. Beat the heck out of me coming down."

Meagan spoke. "There's no other way out?"

Ryan replied. "No. We're 30, 40 minutes from the road through these trees. We get on the road and drive for a few minutes. Then we'll head cross-country until we find a state or logging road."

Ryan reached into his coat pocket and pulled out the pistol. He reached across and bumped Alex with it. "Take the gun." He pulled a crushed box from another pocket. "A few bullets here. My pocket is torn, most of them fell out."

Ryan opened the door and stepped outside. He pulled a lug wrench from the back and smashed the truck's rear brake lights. Back inside, he took Meagan's hand in the dark. "We'll make it."

The truck started with a roar that shattered the silence. Ryan slipped it into gear and for the next 30 minutes, the vehicle slid and bounced violently, causing the three to wince against the pain. Alex rolled down the window, and every few seconds, flicked on the flashlight for an instant, just enough time to form a mental image of the obstacles ahead.

The noisy truck finally emerged from the trees. Without headlights the night was pitch-black, but the wide, snow-covered road was still barely visible. Ryan idled the truck down the long bank, turned onto the road, and stepped on the gas. The engine bellowed. The dashboard was dark and he guessed they were doing 40. He drove as Meagan quietly prayed.

After three or four very long minutes, the gray V that marked the road ahead disappeared.

"This is the turn!" Ryan called out. "We get around this, go a little ways! Look for an open spot on the right! A break in the trees!"

The truck crept around the corner and twice they nearly veered off. Meagan's voice trembled. "How can you see? I can't see!"

Ryan fought the urge to flick on the headlights. "Look right, the trees thin out! It'll come up quick!"

Alex flicked on the flashlight, but the beam was feeble. An area without trees could be a 500-foot drop. "I don't see anything!"

Ryan slowed, and this was providential. Something massive and dark blocked road. He locked the brakes and the truck swerved wildly to the right and then slammed into and onto it.

They slid to a stop as the engine choked and died. Ryan turned on the headlights.

The road was gone. For the full reach of the lights, black water and mud churned like a writhing animal, and the truck was sliding quickly with it. Not far away, the black river rolled over the shoulder and vanished.

Ryan frantically turned the keys. The engine belched, but it started. He threw it into reverse. The motor bellowed and tires howled, but the truck continued its sickening slide. Then the tires caught and the vehicle bounced violently backward, turning and spinning around. It came to rest facing uphill, half-submerged in a ditch full of black ice water. Ryan punched the gas. The truck turned and slid lengthwise into the ditch, and then climbed out and back down the road, back way they had come.

Alex's voice boomed. "What is that!?"

"The cyanide ponds! The berms have breached!"

They were trapped. Alex yelled it. "Get off! Get off the road!"

Ryan jerked the wheel hard left, and the truck charged down a slope and into the trees.

# Chapter 39

The International bounced savagely. The headlights revealed a long ridge ahead and they made for it and raced along its back. This was a logging road that ran for several miles. Deep ravines appeared as the ridge began a long descent.

A bright light suddenly flooded the truck and glistening chards of glass exploded into the cab. Alex's head lurched forward. He reached up to his face and blood ran down his fingers.

The chopper's shaking lights swallowed them as rounds from a high-powered rifle slammed into the cab ceiling and dashboard. The front windshield blew out in a silver sheet and the cold night rushed in.

Ryan stood on the brakes and jerked the wheel hard right with both hands. Suddenly overtaking the truck, the chopper's landing gear collided with the roof. The craft lurched downward and left, its blades nearly catching the ground.

The truck flew into the ravine, careening over granite and sage. Darkness made steering pointless, but the truck wanted to roll. The International nearly tipped forward and then slammed into the bottom of the ravine.

# THE MINE

Nausea engulfed Ryan. Awareness drifted. The floor was gone. He found and pulled the door handle; it wouldn't budge. He remembered the windshield and slowly climbed out the front of the cab and rolled onto the cold ground. Against wrenching pain, he reached in and found Meagan. He opened the seat buckle and she fell to the ceiling. He dragged her out through the windshield.

The helicopter's light hovered near the top of the ridge. Ryan called to his friend. He reached in, felt Alex's coat, and pulled hard. It took several minutes to drag Alex out.

"Meggy." Ryan called.

She was sitting on the ground. Ryan found Alex's hair and felt the blood on his fingers. "Wakeup."

Nothing.

"Get up."

In the faintest moonlight, Alex staggered to his feet.

Ryan tugged on his wife. "Meggy, come on."

In a stupor, they hobbled down a rocky path that grew steeper by the step. Meagan limped and clung to Ryan for balance. Alex shuffled nearby.

Behind them, the merciless beat of the chopper. Its red light blinked and one remaining searchlight probed the dark. The truck had been found.

She collapsed to the ground. He pulled at her. "Come on."

The trail flattened out and a dark clearing opened up. She fell to the ground again and Alex sat down with her, as if joining a picnic. They heard the soft roar of water and watched the dark body of a river float by. The Snake.

Ryan looked back at the chopper's lights and spoke, more to himself. "Shotgun."

There was no reply.

"Shotgun."

The blinking red light held Ryan. A warm trickle ran down his face. It would be better to drown, he thought. Better than execution. He turned back to the river, but noticed a shape off to the right. It was barely visible in the moonlight.

"Over there," said Ryan. "Help me carry her."

They carried her near the dwelling and left her under a juniper. Ryan touched her shoulder. "Don't move."

With one hand over his eye, Alex held the flashlight and Ryan opened the cabin door. In the dim light, an old stove sat in one corner, near a rotted wooden bunk. The remains of table lay strewn about. The whine of the chopper grew louder.

"Run," said Ryan.

The reply was a mumble.

"Alex. Run."

Alex's black form floated in the dark. He then turned and vanished.

Ryan returned to his wife. He slowly lay down next to her and put his arms around her. He felt her body jerk. Wind kicked up debris. He kissed her hair as the howl of the helicopter grew louder. He held her and wished he had the revolver.

"A boat!" Alex's voice came from the darkness. "A boat."

Ryan repeated the words to himself. "Where?"

He stood up and followed Alex around the cabin. The long, dark object lay on the ground. "Check it," said Ryan.

Frantic, but stuck in slow motion, they felt the length of the bow and across the transom. It was wooden and with no apparent breaches.

With his good arm, Ryan grabbed a side and lifted. He could feel Alex help and the boat rolled onto its side.

Alex found both oars lying along the cabin wall. He dropped them into the boat and without speaking, they each grabbed a side of the bow. They stumbled like drunks in the dark, but managed to drag the boat to the river's edge.

The chopper had followed the gully and the light was revealing the cabin now. She lay motionless at the edge of the quivering circle. They ran to her in a wide arc, grabbed her under the arms, and dragged her to the river. They lay her in the boat, pushed it into the water, and climbed in.

Ryan started talking again. "Sit there, in the middle."

They pulled the oars through the water. Injuries made the work excruciating, but the boat moved. They both turned to look, still paddling with what was left.

The chopper had landed. Men were visible with rifles and lights. Although in severe pain, they kept paddling.

Several minutes passed before Alex pulled the oar out of the water. "Listen."

The chopper had not gotten airborne yet. Ryan reached down for her. "Meggy." Ryan strained to see her face. "Meggy," he repeated.

She moaned.

He turned. "How are you, Alex?"

"Bad."

"How's the eye?"

"Fucked up." Alex gasped for air. "My face. Chest. I'm busted up."

Ryan heaved a painful sigh against his own broken ribs. "We hit a boulder."

"You don't drive… for shit."

Meagan was curled up in the bottom of the boat. Ryan took off his parka, folded it once, and placed it under her head.

"Meggy?"

She didn't answer. They sat in the boat and drifted with the current.

Alex's questions came slow. "Where to?"

"Fort Myers."

"How far?"

"Don't know. Forty miles."

"Nothing before?"

Ryan pushed his mind, but it hurt to think. "I don't know."

Alex's voice was pinched. "I'm not good."

"Hang on."

Alex tried to lie down at the end opposite Meagan. Ryan sat up straight; the stabbing in his ribs required it. His brain wanted sleep, but the river was high and running fast. He wondered about the rapids Hell's Canyon was known for. He checked his watch. The glowing dial read 2:40, but the crystal was cracked.

He slid the oars into the locks and in the dim moonlight, tried keeping the boat straight. When the bow turned against the pathway of starlight, he pushed or pulled one oar or the other to compensate. His hands were ice cold and his shoulder was seizing up. The burn in his ribcage brought tears.

After a while, he stopped to rest. The boat turned and dipped, and the water slapped the wooden bottom. The darkness and the river's soft roar cloaked them like a blanket. A crescent moon and scattered stars lit the crooked path ahead. He reached over with a cupped hand and drank the cold water. He breathed the icy night air, slowly against the pain. They were alive. They had died at the cabin. Now on this river, they were being carried away, from death to life. For just a moment, he let himself rest.

At first a nuisance, the sound quickly grew to a reverberating staccato roar that tore him from a deep sleep. In the weak glow of dawn, the blinking red light surged down the river. The howling beast turned in a fast arc above the canyon walls. They had found the boat's drag marks though the snow and sand. Downstream was the only place left.

Hide! Ryan pulled hard on the oars, but his arms were useless. His chest and shoulders burned and the boat bounced out of control.

The roaring river took the boat and spun it wildly. Ryan heaved on the oars, in futility. It bounced and shot over and through the white water. They clung to the small wooden craft as it careened off a violent roll, disappeared into a foaming trough, emerged, and smashed into the next wave.

When the battle finally ended, they were drenched. The oars were gone. Filled with ice water, the boat moved like a submerged log. Ryan searched for the machine's lights in the dawn sky. They were gone, but a new sound came. An airplane. It flew in a hundred feet off the water and passed over them.

Ryan's body shook against the cold. His legs were numb. He tried to warm his fingers in his mouth. Meagan sat motionless in the bottom of the boat with water up to her chest. Her lips were blue; her eyes were closed. Her blue hands clung to the gunnel.

Alex was slouched awkwardly over the rear seat with his legs wedged between boards.

Morning came, filtered through still eyes. In the icy breeze, the water in the boat took on a bright red glow. Sparkling waves followed him along, glittering saucers, dipping and turning. They moved with him. Ryan peered down into the water. Fish. Sparkling silver and gold, they followed him.

In the morning light, a boy and his father stood on a bridge and gawked. They stared down at the countless fish and at the three bodies that slipped beneath. Trucks and cars were parked on the bank. There was a commotion, over what, Ryan wondered. He raised his head and squinted in the sunlight. Another bridge. A police car. Flashing lights. People pointed.

A man threw down a yellow rope. He ran along the bank while recoiling it and then flung it out again. The rope landed across Ryan's lap. They yelled, "Get it! Get it!"

Ryan's body slumped forward.

"Hold on!" The man ran along the water's edge. "Hold on!" He pulled and ran to keep up.

## Chapter 40

Warm sheets. Across a room, white drapes allowed in a streak of sunlight. He turned his head; it throbbed. He tried to move, but found that his chest was wrapped in a contraption, with straps around his shoulders. A large bouquet of flowers consumed a table in the corner.

Auburn hair caught his eye, visible between beige curtains.

Against the throbbing head, he slowly swung his bare feet around and noticed the IV line taped to his hand. A catheter was draining off urine. He pulled a little slack and tried to stand, slowly, but was immediately wobbly. Every muscle and joint throbbed. He leaned toward her while pulling the IV. Her face was turned toward him and he shuddered.

Her left eye was still patched with blue and red. A white bandage covered the right side of her face, hiding that eye. Her face was swollen round. Her nose and lips were dark. A bandage encircled her head and where skin was exposed, it was bruised, cut, or frost-bit. He stood, lightly holding the bed rail, and watched her breathe.

Someone whispered behind him. "You're up."

Startled, Ryan wiped his tears.

She was a middle-aged woman. Short cropped hair was dark and streaked with gray. She moved quietly, checking IV bags while he closed up the back of his gown.

She spoke low. "I'm Brenda Kass. I'm the charge nurse. How are you feeling?"

"Tired."

"I want you to lie down."

"How long have we been here?"

"Three days."

"How is she?"

The nurse looked at Meagan and whispered. "Coming along. She has cuts and bruises on the front and back of her head, a concussion. The cut to the face. Some frostbite to her nose and lips. A fractured left ankle, a cast has been applied. Frostbite to toes on her right foot."

Ryan fought off tears. "Dear God. Will she lose any toes?"

"A doctor is going to look at it. Other than all that, she's doing pretty well. We moved you both out of ICU just this morning. Do you want to know about yourself?"

Ryan grimaced.

"You have two fractured ribs on the left, a concussion, ten stitches on your forehead. But you're improving steadily. I want you to lie down."

He looked at his wrist. "What's the IV for?"

"You both ingested toxins on the river, arsenic, heavy metals. The IVs have binding agents to clean you out."

A long sigh escaped Ryan. He leaned back against his bed. "Tell me about the river."

The woman looked him in the eyes. "The Snake River is poisoned. It's dead, for miles. The Fort Myers water supply is shutdown. We're trucking water in."

Ryan remembered the breached ponds. He closed his eyes.

"Why were you on the river?" she asked. "People don't drift the Snake this time of year."

He looked at her and recalled the hell of the previous few weeks. "It's a long story."

"People want to talk with you about it. The police, state officials."

"Why me?"

Her face showed surprise. "The city has no fresh water supply, they're afraid the wells are contaminated. They're asking people to evacuate. We have hundreds of people sick from poisoning, possibly two deaths. The governor has declared it a disaster area. You were picked up on the river, in the middle of it all."

Ryan took a moment to absorb the news before asking the next question. "Where is my friend, Alex?"

The woman's eyes flew. She pulled Meagan's curtain closed and turned to Ryan. "He didn't make it. I'm very sorry."

"What?! That can't be!! He was with me, in the boat! He was there!"

She put a light hand on Ryan's good shoulder and looked him in the eyes. "I'm sorry. I'm truly sorry."

Ryan's eyes flooded. "How?"

"I'm not sure I can say. The police are involved."

"But he was alive!"

"Mr. Evans, you're lucky to be here. Be thankful you two made it. We're you related?"

"Like brothers."

"I am so sorry. If you need anything, page me, hit the green button there. If you want to talk with a priest, a counselor, we can arrange it. And Mr. Evans, the authorities want to talk with you. I told them maybe tomorrow."

Brenda Kass left the room.

Ryan sat on the bed and wept.

In the early afternoon, she moaned.

The sound stirred him from dozing and brought him to his feet. He pulled the tubing around and grasped the rail. She smiled weakly. She lifted an arm and they hugged.

He whispered in her ear. "We made it."

A quiet moan.

Ryan pulled the curtain around them. "How do you feel?" he asked.

"Fine," she whispered.

"You're always fine."

"You?"

Ryan nodded. "I'm okay."

She began to weep. "You found me."

"We did."

"How long?"

"Here? I think three days." Ryan pointed to the flowers. "You've had visitors."

She looked toward the table. "Mom and Dad?"

Ryan nodded. "I saw them this morning. I thought I had dreamed it."

Ryan remembered the last phone call with Mr. Lewis. He held Meagan's hand as she feel back to sleep.

He woke late in the day with the commotion of dinner being served. Ryan slid out of bed and found her gazing out at the blue sky. He pulled the tray cart around to help her with the meal: a cup of some kind of bullion, crackers, gelatin with sliced bananas, and apple juice.

She smiled. "You were sleeping."

"I'm a little tired."

"How are you feeling?" she asked, her voice still weak.

"Stiff. Sore. How about you?"

"Tired. Sore everywhere. My feet hurt."

"They're having a doctor take a look at your feet."

She looked at him with sleepy eyes and smiled.

"Feel like eating anything?" he asked.

She shook her head slowly.

"Me neither. Honey, I can't believe you called me. You found a way," said Ryan.

She reached for him and they hugged again. "We made it," she whispered. She then pulled back. "Alex?"

Ryan's eyes fell.

"What's wrong?"

For a second, he debated not telling her just yet. "I don't know what happened, honey. I don't know. He didn't make it."

"What? What happened?" She began to weep.

"I don't know." Ryan couldn't keep himself from tearing up. "He didn't make it."

"Did he drown?"

"I don't know. I don't know, Meggy. He's gone."

At eight the following morning, Doctor Bauer examined Meagan's right foot and gave them the good news. She would keep her toes. Bauer was short and bald, and his demeanor was warm and confident. Meagan was fully awake now and she was relieved. The left ankle was fractured and was already wrapped in a cast.

After Bauer left, Ryan took her hand. The cut across her cheekbone would need surgery later to reduce the scar line. But the bruise was shrinking and her natural color was returning. The bandage around her head had been removed. Aside from the missing hair in back where they had stitched a wound and her dark blue lips, she was starting to look more like her self.

Meagan looked at him and knew his thoughts. "Am I ugly now?"

Ryan's chin dipped. "You're beautiful."

She pointed to the girdle under his white bathrobe.

"They've got me cinched up. Two cracked ribs. And a side of coleslaw."

There would never be a good time for the next question, and Ryan struggled to ask it. He checked that they were alone, and then spoke softly. "Honey, were you violated?"

She bit her lip. Her chin quivered furiously and her fierce eyes brimmed with tears. "No! He tried, twice. He was drunk. I screamed my head off, and I kicked him hard, in the crotch, in the stomach."

Ryan stared. He wrapped his arms around her. "My God, Meagan. You are amazing. All of this was my fault. I'm sorry. You asked me to stop. I couldn't walk away."

Later in the morning, Rachel Lewis came through the door. She carried a profuse bouquet of mixed flowers, so many that they concealed most of her face. Stanton followed her in, carrying a large red suitcase. They swept in, not saying a word, and only briefly eyed Ryan.

She set the vase on the table near the window, a table overrun with flowers, and pulled the drapes closed around their daughter.

Sitting in bed, Ryan wondered if perhaps he should take a walk and leave them alone, if he could just get down hall a ways. But at this moment, Nurse Kass entered and stood at the foot of the bed.

"Mr. Evans, are you up to a visit?" she asked.

"Who?" The question irritated him, that he needed to ask it. He didn't have family.

"You have official visitors. I've got them parked in a room down the hall. I gave them 30 minutes, if you're up to it."

"Give me a few minutes."

In the small bathroom, Ryan found the vanity kit provided by the hospital and freshened up. He had planned to take a shower and shave off the week-plus beard, but that would have to wait.

An orderly waited with a wheelchair. Nurse Kass pointed to it. "My rules."

Ryan pulled open the curtains and kissed his wife on the top of the head. "I'll be back."

They wheeled him down a long hall and through a door marked "Staff." No fewer than six people filled the room, five men and a woman. One man was a cop. Three others were in suits. A rotund man wore a plaid shirt and a white cowboy hat.

The large room was furnished with padded chairs, a couch, and a coffee table. They set the chairs around the table and each took a seat, surrounding Ryan. He closed the bathrobe around his legs and realized how much he hated foam slippers.

A slender, dark-haired man with a skinny black tie spoke as he pointed at each in turn.

"Mr. Evans, I'm Detective Charlie Kunz with the City of Fort Myers Police Department. This here is Idaho Lieutenant Governor Stan Cummings. That's Judy Montrose with the

Federal EPA. That there is Douglas Remy with the Idaho DEQ. And Sheriff of Nez Perce County, Elliot Parks." Kunz now pointed to the cowboy with the hat, who paced behind the others. "And that's the mayor of Fort Myers, Bobby Cody."

Ryan nodded at the six of them.

Mayor Cody stopped pacing and stood with his arms folded across his plaid gut. A knock sounded at the door; the orderly opened it and two other men entered, men in white. Hospital security, perhaps to even things up a little.

Detective Kunz resumed. "How are you feeling, Mr. Evans?"

Ryan nodded. "Okay."

Kunz placed a tape recorder on the table in front of Ryan and pushed a button. "All right. Mr. Evans, as you must be aware, there has been a disaster on the Snake River. The river is dead from the area northeast of the Justene mine, all the way past Fort Myers, some 50 miles and growing. The main water supplies for Fort Myers have been shut down. You were pulled off the river in the middle of this. What you were doing on the river?"

Ryan sighed. "It's a long story."

The group stared. The detective responded. "We have time."

Ryan pulled a painful breath and started at the beginning. He told him who he was, a biologist, a former employee of Oregon DEQ. He told them about Justene, the application to expand the mine and the original environmental impact statement, about the death of Robert Newberg and his signature on the original study.

The mayor stopped pacing for a moment and asked "what the hell" this had to do with his river. Ryan pushed on. He talked about his own EIS and the fraudulent approval. He told them about Gabe, and about the meeting with Greer and Greer's death. Behind the group, the mayor paced noisily. The others listened.

Ryan told them about Meagan's kidnapping and the trip up to the mine to rescue her. When he was finally done, the mayor stopped pacing. They stared.

The anger welled, but Ryan's voice was remarkably calm. "They kidnapped her, shackled her, terrorized her. They tried for days to kill us. They shot at us from the helicopter. We nearly froze to death. My truck is wrecked in the mountains, it's full of bullet holes. And they murdered Alex Palmer." When he was finished, Ryan bent forward and closed his eyes.

Stan Cummings leaned in. He was tall, in a brown suit. "Mr. Evans, you and your wife have been through a lot. I need to ask you, with all your suspicions about DEQ, why didn't you take it up the chain of command? Or go to the police?"

"I did! I took it to the head of Oregon DEQ and I got fired. The next day people broke into my house, looking for documents I think. Instead, they kidnapped my wife."

Mayor Cody crowded in between the chairs. His red face shook and he spit when he yelled. "So what in the hell happened to my river?!"

Ryan addressed the mayor. "The berms around the containments ponds gave way. I don't know how many ponds, probably all of them. Millions of gallons of poison, drainage, have flushed into the watershed, into the Snake. It's full of sulfuric acid, cyanide, arsenic. Heavy metals like chromium and mercury. It's a menu of poisons. I warned them."

"Godammit!" the mayor bellowed. "My city gets its water from that river! We drink it, we irrigate with it! How long will this go on?"

Ryan shook his head. "I don't know. Several months at least. Years."

The room became quiet.

Remy, the head of Idaho DEQ, finally spoke up. "Lieutenant Governor Cummings, Mrs. Montrose, and I flew over the area yesterday. All of the containment structures have washed out. We're using heavy equipment to try and shore up what's left."

Mayor Cody looked like he would attack something with his hat. "Good godammit! I've got hundreds of people sick from this, we're evacuating the whole place! I want to know how in hell this happened!"

Ryan replied. "How did this happen? I'll tell you how! Gross fraud. Corruption. Illegal permits. Open pit mines, heap leach mines, they're flawed, they're prone to disasters like this. What happened was inevitable. You talk to Arland Lochner, he can tell you all about it."

Douglas Remy pulled a short breath and frowned. "I'm afraid we can't do that, Ryan. Mr. Lochner committed suicide this morning."

The words blew Ryan away. He sat with his mouth open, his hands gripping the wheelchair.

Sheriff Parks spoke. "Everything you've told us, about the deaths, about the fraudulent impact statements, it can all be verified?"

Ryan nodded. "The deaths are all on record. I have copies of all documentation, including Newberg's signature, dated the day before he died. I seriously doubt that the signature is his."

Parks continued. "Your wife. Instead of calling you, why didn't she call the police?"

Ryan eyed the group. He was certain they wouldn't believe him. "The telephone? Her captor had broken it. The mouth and earpiece were gone. There was no way for her to talk or listen, it was just wires. But the buttons, the keys were there. The buttons use tones. She used the buttons to punch in… to punch in a song, a sequence. Something I would recognize. I used the caller ID to locate her."

The mayor's large head shook in disgust; this made no sense to him. The others were nearly as perplexed.

Judy Montrose of the Federal EPA asked the next question. "What was the song?"

Ryan waved his hand. "Something… just something we knew."

She persisted. "What?"

Ryan could feel his throat tighten. "It was just a game we played in college."

"So what was the song?"

Ryan frowned and turned away. Something very personal was being lost. "*Say You, Say Me*."

Kunz frowned. The mayor huffed.

A smile appeared on the woman's face, as she quickly dabbed an eye. "Lionel Richie? And you used caller ID to locate her? Your wife is extremely resourceful."

Ryan nodded. "She's incredible."

Again, the sheriff spoke. He looked at his notes. "The person that Alex Palmer shot. Where is the gun?"

"Up there, somewhere."

"We haven't found a body. The only death was that of Mr. Palmer."

"I would guess that they hoped to kill us and cover it up. Tell me what happened to Alex."

Sheriff Parks examined his hands. "Alex Palmer suffered a gun shot wound through his shoulder and chest. A single bullet from overhead. He bled to death. He was dead when we found you on the river."

Ryan fought tears. Alex had bled to death right in front of him. It was in the water, in the boat. He had thought it was the sunrise. "They shot him from the helicopter," he said.

"It's under investigation."

Ryan exploded. He pointed angrily at the sheriff. "I want charges filed! These animals left a trail of crimes! They invaded my home, imprisoned and brutalized my wife! They had her chained up in a trailer, she was freezing to death when we found her! They tried to kill all of us! They killed Alex! I want prosecutions!"

The sheriff nodded. "It's all under investigation, son. Trust me. I'll be contacting you."

Leaving the conference room, Ryan dismissed the orderly. He shot the wheelchair down the hall, passed elevators, and along a row of windows that ended at the corner. He stopped there, at the last window, and looked out at the Wallowas.

## Chapter 41

Back in their room, he found Meagan sitting up. Her parents had left and he slipped down into the chair next to her bed. She had brushed her hair and freshened up. Her eyes were moist.

"You've been up," he said.

She nodded.

"You're looking better. The swelling is going down, your color is better. Your parents are gone?"

"They said they had chores, will be back later."

Ryan nodded.

"The nurse came by, said they want to run some tests on me, my kidneys."

Ryan eyes became alarmed.

She smiled. "They say it's nothing too serious. You're just improving a little faster than me."

"When?"

"Later today." She took Ryan's hand. Her eyes welled up. "Tell me what happened to Alex."

Meagan was rolled out of the room for her tests just before noon.

Lunch for Ryan consisted of a sandwich of turkey, limp lettuce, and cheese, along with a plastic tub of orange juice and a very dense slice of apple pie. He took the sandwich to the window. He had been on IVs for days and had somehow missed breakfast. This was the first real food in days, but his appetite was missing.

Out the window, the city's streets were nearly empty. In the parking lot below, two television vans were parked among the cars. Their white satellite dishes were pointed south and looked like spilled chalices of holy water. Beyond the lot and buildings of downtown, the Snake River weaved through the city. Police cars and barricades were positioned along its banks.

Ryan found the television remote and flipped through the channels. Soap operas and game shows. CNN was covering another story of insider trading.

Abruptly, the program was interrupted. Text scrolled large across the screen. A voice read out loud.

"This is an announcement from the Federal Emergency Management Administration. To all persons living in Fort Myers, Idaho, or near the Snake River. The Snake River has been poisoned. The water contains high concentrations of arsenic, sulfuric acid, and heavy metals. Do not drink water from the Snake River or from wells that are within five miles of the river. Do not shower or bathe in this water. Do not swim in the Snake River. Do not consume fish or other animals from the Snake River. The water cannot be made safe. If you have consumed water or fish from the Snake River within the last seven days, seek medical attention immediately. You are asked to leave the city until authorities can determine that the water is safe. If you must stay in the area, drink only bottled water from known sources. Water is being trucked in and is available at local area schools. This water is being rationed, use it for consumption only. Please remain calm. This message will be updated hourly."

A message from Governor Lowry followed. The man was sitting at his desk, with his sleeves pushed up and his tie loosened. The state seal and flag framed him. In the most fatherly tone possible, he smiled and asked for calm. His office and state officials were working closely with FEMA. The source of the problem had been identified and everything possible was being done to return the situation to normal. He asked all those who could leave the city, to do so for at least two weeks.

After several minutes, CNN returned. At the top of the hour, the story was about Fort Myers and the Snake. Video footage shot from a helicopter showed the river, covered with the carcasses of fish and small animals. As far as the helicopter flew, as far as was visible, fish covered the banks. The announcer eventually ran out of words, and for more than a minute, the broadcast was simply silent video of the catastrophe.

In a short clip, the Mayor of Fort Myers was outraged. His white hat flew violently and his red face spit into the camera. "I was never told about the risk at that mine, so help me God! I will get to the bottom of this! The people of Fort Myers can trust their mayor! The guilty will be punished! Justice will be served!"

A related story. The two people pulled from the river the morning of the disaster were the missing couple from Portland, Ryan and Meagan Evans. Both were being treated at a local hospital for poisoning and various injuries. As reported previously, a third man had died at the scene, but his name was still not being released. Although there was no apparent connection between the three and the Snake River disaster, the matter was under investigation by state and federal authorities.

Ryan suddenly felt a strong desire to take Meagan and leave town. Instead, he picked up the phone and dialed Alex and Anne's telephone number. The recorder answered, for which he felt great relief, and then guilt. Ryan left a short message with a voice that barely cooperated. "We're at St. Joseph's Hospital in Fort Myers. Call us as soon as possible."

A new nurse entered, a young man, pushing a cart.

"Mr. Evans? My name is Dan. I need another blood sample. We're still checking to see if you're radioactive. You glow in the dark, you know." He smiled, enjoying his humor. "Which arm?"

Ryan knew the drill. "The left is worn out. Try the right."

A brown rubber band was wrapped around Ryan's upper arm. The man probed Ryan's arm with his fingers. "Make a fist. The news says you're a biologist, right? Do you know how long it'll be this way?"

"The river? A very long time."

"All because of a gold mine? Unbelievable. Doesn't the government regulate this crap?"

"Apparently not."

Nurse Dan unwrapped a syringe and gingerly slid the long needle into Ryan's vein. "Okay, open your hand. When we're done here, I need you to drink down that bottle of fluid. We're still flushing you both out. You two are like the river, except of course you're alive."

"How is the city handling this?"

"About half the people have left town. It's not like we can all fly away. Some folks drive to other towns and fill their cars up with water jugs, plastic milk cartons. They're hawking water for five bucks a gallon."

Ryan shook his head. "Speaking of water, I need a shower and a shave."

Dan nodded. "You sure do. The city is rationing it, but the hospital has its own supply. We've got two tankers outside, full of fresh water. There's soap and shampoo in there, a razor. But go easy, don't stretch. That girdle comes off with these four straps. When you're all done, push the call button, I'll give you a fresh one and help you put it on."

After showering, shaving, and putting on the new girdle, Ryan sat down to rest. He was still sore and his ribs hurt.

In the latest running of CNN, they had revealed the name of the third person, the deceased. Alex Palmer. Ryan turned off the television and tried Anne's number again. There was no answer. He left another message.

A short time later, the phone rang. It was first time had heard the phone in days and the sound was odd.

"Hello?"

"Ryan?"

"Hi Karina." He had forgotten all about her.

"Ryan, I saw it on the news! Everyone's been worried sick about you! Are you all right? How is Meagan?"

"I'm okay. Meagan is coming along. We'll be coming home soon."

"Thank God. They're not letting anyone through. I had to talk the hospital operator into letting me speak with you."

There was a long gap before she continued. "I saw the news about Alex."

Karina began crying softly. Ryan tried to think of something to day. Her voice broke. "I'm so glad. I'm so glad you two made it."

"So am I."

More silence. "They broke into your house."

"What?"

"I left the morning you left. I couldn't stay. I forwarded your calls to my cell phone. You had work boxes upstairs, papers about Justene in boxes. I took it all, took your dog, and locked the house up. They broke in that night. They turned your place upside down."

"Dammit."

"I called the police. They took notes, pictures. I told them what it was all about, Summit Resources. I told them about you and Alex, about Meagan. I'm pretty sure they thought I was crazy, but they did check for fingerprints, took photographs."

"What day was that?"

"Saturday night."

"What day is today?"

"Thursday."

"Unbelievable. Where is Lassiter?"

"Tommy says he's missing. He hasn't been in to work."

"Yeah, no kidding," Ryan replied.

"Did you hear about Lochner?"

"Yeah."

"It's so sad," said Karina. "First Gabe, then Lochner."

"It explains a lot about Lochner, the corrupt bastard. He was in way over his head."

"I still can't believe it."

Ryan had little to say to this.

After a moment, Karina continued. "Tommy and I and Mary, we cleaned up your place. We picked everything up and vacuumed. Did your laundry."

Ryan took a deep breath. "Karina, you've been priceless through all of this. I don't know… you and Alex."

A long pause followed. "It's okay," she finally said.

"You said you have Meagan's dog?"

"I have Sophie."

Ryan palmed his forehead. "Karina."

He could hear the smile in her voice, even as she cried. "It's all right."

The day's second call came half an hour later.

It was the hospital operator. "Mr. Evans, we're screening your calls. This one is a Detective Mathius, with the Portland Police. He wants to talk with you."

Ryan closed his eyes. Damned Mathius. "Okay."

The voice crackled. "Ryan, you've been in the news! I thought I told you not to leave town."

Ryan couldn't think of a suitable reply. "Whatever."

"I'm kidding. I'm kidding, Ryan. I'm never wrong about these things, never. I can read who is being straight with me, I can feel it. But I was wrong about you."

Ryan pulled a deep breath. "No shit."

"Look, I'm sorry. But you made it. You and your wife are safe."

"We lost Alex Palmer."

Mathius said nothing. Ryan could hear him breathe.

"I'm sorry, Ryan," he finally said. "You have my deepest condolences."

"Fuck you."

The phone went silent and Ryan nearly hung up.

"When will you be back in town?" Mathius finally asked.

"Why do you need to know?"

"Portland Police and Oregon State are opening investigations into the deaths of Gabe Riplinger, Robert Newberg, and Mr. Palmer. They want to talk."

"I also want full charges brought against these people for the kidnapping, imprisonment, and attempted murder of my wife. Against the CEO, Sarinov."

"I have no doubt that will happen, Ryan. We'll be talking with you."

Twenty minutes later Ryan tried again to reach Anne. It rang repeatedly and he thought it would go to voice mail, but she finally picked up.

"Hello." Her voice was weak.

"Hi Anne."

She began to cry.

"Anne."

She struggled to regain her voice. She finally spoke. "Sheriff Parks called me. He told me about Alex."

"Did he tell you how it happened?"

"He told me how he died."

Ryan took a hard breath. "He went up there with me to find Meagan. She had been taken, kidnapped. The police didn't believe me. Alex and I, we went into the Wallowas to find her, to the mine. She was being held prisoner there."

"Is she all right?"

"She's okay. We're okay. Anne, he saved our lives."

"I watched it on the news. I still can't believe it all. Why did they take her?"

"The operation, the permits for the mine were illegal. I had met with a whistleblower from the company. DEQ had fired me over this and I was about to go to the media, get an injunction filed. The company wanted to stop me."

"It's so bizarre. I can't believe it, I can't…" Anne's voice broke. She began to cry again.

"He saved us, Anne."

Silence filled several seconds before she spoke again.

"I'm having his body brought back to Portland," she finally said.

"Anne. I didn't think it would end this way. I can't tell you…" Ryan couldn't finish the sentence.

There was no response. She had hung up.

In the early afternoon, Meagan was returned to the room. She smiled and gave a thumbs-up as they wheeled her in. Her parents seemed to be psychic, because they followed her in only a minute later with shopping bags full of clothes from the nearest mall.

Rachel Lewis began to pull the privacy curtains around Meagan's bed, but Meagan protested. "Mom, no."

Ryan stood from his chair. "Honey, that's okay. It's all right."

He retreated to a patient lounge. Here, a father was reading a hunting magazine while his young son played with toys. Cartoons bounced across a television screen. Ryan sat on a padded bench in his bathrobe and foam slippers. He picked up the newspaper, the Oregonian. It was all Fort Myers and the Snake River. The EPA effort to clean up the mine site would take years and several hundred million. Summit Resources had declared bankruptcy; their tiny three-million dollar bond was already exhausted. According to the CFO Rodney Warren, the company was broke.

Ryan tossed the paper in disgust. He reached for a magazine, Newsweek. The graphic cover, in red letters, read *Death of the Snake*.

Stanton Lewis entered the lounge. He walked across the room and sat down slowly on the short padded bench, next to Ryan, who felt the urge to run. The man's glistening eyes rested on the child. He rubbed his hands together and cleared his throat.

He whispered without taking his eyes off the child. "Thank you, Ryan. Thank you."

Ryan didn't know what to say. But Lewis didn't wait for a reply. He stood and left the room.

The second interview occurred on the sixth day in the hospital, in the afternoon. Though he could walk, Nurse Cass still insisted on a wheel chair and they steered him into the same room. This time, a police officer was posted at the door. No hospital security.

Inside the room, there was only Detective Kunz, wearing the same black tie, and Mayor Cody.

Ryan shook hands and they sat down around the small coffee table.

Kunz cleared his throat. "How are you today, Mr. Evans?"

Ryan nodded. "Better."

"Mr. Evans, we have a few more questions. But let me say first, you need to be honest with me. What were you really doing in the Wallowas?"

"Chasing fireflies. Do I need an attorney?"

"You tell me."

"I was there to get my wife."

"You expect us to buy that story about her playing out love songs on the telephone? I did a little background on you son. You're one of them goddamned tree huggers, a protestor. You're an extremist. And you were obsessed with shutting down that mine."

"Is protesting a crime?"

"You had been all over that mine, writing letters to the press. You worked for the DEQ, and you raised hell about that mine. You were obsessed. So the big expansion got approved and they fired you. It was more than you could handle. You decided to take things into your own hands. You and your wife and Palmer, you went in there with explosives. You blew open the cyanide ponds and presto, your catastrophe happened, just like you warned. You covered yourselves with this story of a kidnapping."

A long moment of silence unfolded. A snide smile crossed the detective's face. Mayor Cody leaned in close with his white hat in hand. He was nearly drooling.

"You have nothing to say?" asked Kunz.

Ryan slowly shook his head. "Do you have any idea of the environmental catastrophe this is? Do you? I am an ecologist. I'm not a terrorist. What makes you think I would want to cause such a disaster?"

"Do you expect us to believe that the whole thing blew open on the very night that you went up there to get your wife? Your friend, Palmer? We found explosives residue on Palmer's fingers from the dynamite you people planted."

Ryan thought for a moment, and then understood. "It's from the shotgun! He fired the shotgun! I know you really want to nail someone. Go nail Sarinov. I was fired because he wanted me gone. Greer wanted to shut it down and they killed him. They took my wife, imprisoned her, terrorized her. She would have died. They murdered Alex. They killed my boss, Riplinger, they killed Newberg. And the director of DEQ, Lochner."

"Lochner committed suicide."

"He may have, but dead people are everywhere and none of this adds up for you?"

"We'll be interrogating your wife."

Ryan stood up. "No you will not! You will not be interrogating my wife! You can find us in Portland after we hire an attorney."

Ryan stormed from the room.

One interview with the media was arranged. On the morning of the last day, one camera crew from CNN set-up in the same conference room that Ryan has visited before. Ryan and Meagan's interview lasted an hour and covered everything from Gabe's death to their rescue on the river. Although the interviewer tried to get Ryan to assign blame, he took pains not to accuse any person of anything for which he didn't have proof. But all the facts were told and the conclusions were inescapable.

Later that morning, news crews with cameras were waiting at the hospital's main entrance. To avoid them, hospital security and Nurse Cass escorted Ryan and Meagan out a service entrance on the opposite side of the hospital. A rental car was waiting just outside the door. Meagan's parents and Karina had both offered to drive, but Ryan politely refused. He needed to make this drive home with Meagan.

Outside, the smell of it rode the wind.

"The river?" she asked.

Ryan stood at the car door, with Meagan in the wheelchair. "Yeah."

The river had died and everything in it had died and had collected on its banks for miles, where it now rotted. Flocks of seagulls, hundreds of miles from the Pacific, cawed overhead. Crews were still removing fish carcasses and the stench filled the city.

Nurse Kass and several hospital staff hugged them both goodbye. The orderly waited behind Meagan.

At the car door, Ryan paused. In the distance, the white Wallowas loomed large against the blue sky. The longest winter he could recall had finally ended. It had started months previous, it seemed now, with the intention of taking out Justene.

He looked to her. "Ready?"

She nodded. He helped her into the car.

Traffic was sparse. The road home was the same route taken in, many days earlier. It passed by the same towns in reverse, Pendleton, The Dalles. It was punishment for them to be on this road, returning home without their friend.

There had been three holes in the boat, which helped explain the water. Luckily, it had been made of wood. A metal boat would have sunk in minutes. The notion of a trade devoured Meagan, her life for Alex's. They pulled the car off at Hood River for a late lunch and wept.

# Chapter 42

They arrived home late in the day and parked the rental car in the spot normally reserved for the Prius. Her car had still not been located. Alex's BMW sat where he had left it, under the maple tree which was now laced with green. Daffodils and crocuses had sprouted in thick bunches around the front porch. The yard was verdant. In the late afternoon sun, blue jays darted through the air.

He stepped out of the car and pulled out the crutches. He opened her door and helped her out. He found the key Karina had left in the barrel planter at the far end of the porch and slipped it into the deadbolt lock. Upon opening the heavy door, the fragrance hit them both. The coffee table was covered in pink and white lilies.

She eased down on the green recliner, her body still sore. He moved the flowers and rested her casted foot on a pillow, on the coffee table. Did she want any herb tea? Or hot chocolate? Yes. Tea would be nice.

In the kitchen, he filled a brass pot with water. He turned on the burner and felt a deep wave of peace wash through him.

While the water heated, he methodically checked the entire house, opening every door. They were alone. The bedding linens had been changed, the laundry done, the dishes washed, and the floors vacuumed and mopped. He promised himself to have the back door and locks replaced the next day. And to get an alarm system, and a big, loud dog.

Returning to the living room with the tea, Ryan found her asleep. He quietly set the cup on the table.

On the front porch, he picked up the accumulated newspapers, and beneath one, noticed a white envelope. Full-sized and fat with its contents, the sender's name screamed: *Summit Resources*.

It fell from his hands. Ryan stared at it for several seconds, and then, very carefully, picked it up again. It had been postmarked twice, once for $3.10 and again four days later for an additional $1.36.

Realization. This was the evidence from Greer. Dead Greer. The man had dropped it in the mail, and while the company's thugs were terrorizing Meagan and ripping their house apart, this package they were searching for had been returned to Summit Resources for postage due. There, a mailroom employee had dutifully weighed, stamped, and re-mailed it.

Ryan had the urge to light a fire in the woodstove and burn it all. Instead, he quietly closed the front door, leaving it unlatched. He glanced around the yard and then out to the street. The neighborhood was silent. He sat down on the front steps and carefully opened the seal.

The first thing to come out was a manila folder with a tab labeled *Riplinger*. Ryan opened it and looked at an eight-by-ten glossy of an old man. He was standing, with a golden retriever, in front of a wooden drift boat.

# Author's note

**Did you enjoy this book?**

THE MINE is my first novel and is self-published. This means that a standard publishing house was not involved in production, and that sales are limited to select independent bookstores in the Northwest. If you enjoyed reading THE MINE and would like to see it more widely available, I invite you to *offer your review at Amazon.com*, and to ask your bookstore to carry it. Many thanks.

**Now, a little background**

The Justene Mine is a fictional creation. However...

In 1990, the Summitville Mine in Colorado released a flood of cyanide, heavy metals, and sulfuric acid into the Alamosa River. The spill killed all aquatic life over 17 miles of the river and contaminated downstream farmland. The Canadian company, Galactic Resources, quickly filed for bankruptcy and abandoned the site. The mine is now an EPA Superfund site and to date, the EPA has spent over 200 million dollars for ongoing clean-up and recovery. Toxic drainage from the area will continue into perpetuity.[1,2,3]

Robert Friedland, the former CEO of Galactic Resources, then formed Golden Star Resources, and with another company, opened the Omai Gold Mine in Guyana. In 1995, the Omai Gold Mine released a major spill of cyanide and heavy metals into the Essequibo River, Guyana's main river. The disaster killed countless fish, the main food supply for people living along the river. President Cheddi Jagan of Guyana declared a 50-mile stretch of the river an Environmental Disaster Zone.[4,5,6]

Repeated toxic releases from the Zortman-Landusky gold mine in Montana culminated with a release of 20 million gallons of cyanide solution onto 17 acres of land. Cyanide appeared in local tap water. Citizens and environmental groups eventually sued Pegasus, the operator, under the Clean Water Act and

Pegasus later filed for bankruptcy. Acid mine drainage now contaminates almost every stream that emanates from the mine site, and federal cleanup costs will likely exceed $100 million. In 1998, Montana voters passed a law banning all open pit cyanide leach mines. The law was upheld in both the Montana and Federal Supreme Courts.[7,8]

The Brewer Gold Mine, located one mile west of Jefferson, South Carolina, is sited along a ridge that divides Little Fork Creek and the Lynches River. In 1990, a dam burst, flooding the Little Fork Creek with over ten million gallons of solution containing cyanide and a long list of heavy metals. The spill killed 11,000 fish and decimated 50 miles of the Lynches River. In 1999, the Brewer Company abandoned the site and the mine is now a Federal Superfund Site, placed on the EPA's National Priorities List. Taxpayers will be paying many millions of dollars for cleanup into perpetuity.[9,10]

How bad can it get? In January of 2000 in Eastern Europe, at an operation run by the Romanian-Australian firm Aurul, a mammoth spill of mining effluent poisoned the Szamos, Tisza, and Danube Rivers. The result was a major extermination of aquatic life in over 150 miles of river systems and the poisoning of water supplies for river communities in Romania, Hungary, Serbia, and Bulgaria. Hungary removed well over 300 tons of dead fish from its rivers and Hungarian officials declared it the worst disaster since Chernobyl. Over two million people were affected.[11,12]

## The 1872 Mining Law

The above disasters are only a few of the most serious. For the past 137 years, mining companies have been operating under the 1872 Mining Law. This law was signed into force by President Grant to promote development of the Western U.S. The law allows companies and individuals to buy public lands rich in minerals for $5 per acre (1872 prices), mine the land to exhaustion, and pay zero royalties to taxpayers. The law provides for no environmental protection. The U.S. EPA asserts that mining operations have contaminated the headwaters of more than 40 percent of the watersheds in the West and that remediation of the half-million abandoned mines in 32 states may cost more than $35 billion.[13] The Clinton Administration instituted some minimal reforms, but these were overturned by the following Bush Administration.

### Disasters in the making

In Minnesota, the Bureau of Land Management and the U.S. Forest Service are considering opening up the Superior National Forest to large-scale mining. Over 32 permit applications from major companies have been filed to date. If allowed to operate, these mines will create large open-pit scars, generate countless tons of toxic mining waste, and continually create drainage thick with sulfuric acid and heavy metals. All of this, in a wilderness that is rich in wildlife, is adjacent to Minnesota's famous Boundary Waters, and is just northwest of Lake Superior.

And at possibly the most productive salmon fisheries in the world, Alaska's pristine Bristol Bay will soon be host to the largest open-pit, cyanide leach mine in North America: The Pebble Mine. This mammoth 20-square-mile gold mining complex will be located just upstream from Bristol Bay. A breach at Minnesota's Boundary Waters or at the Pebble Mine could easily cause large-scale, long-term disaster.

### Resources

This summary is a tiny fraction of the story. From mountaintop-removal coal mining in the Appalachians, to open-pit cyanide leach mining in Alaska, the mining industry is in dire need of reform. You can learn more at these sites:

- The Pew Campaign for Responsible Mining www.pewminingreform.org/
- The Sierra Club: www.sierraclub.org/
- Earth Works: www.earthworksaction.org/home.cfm/
- Natural Resources Defense Council: www.nrdc.org/

- Friends of the Boundary Waters: www.friends-bwca.org/
- Ohio Valley Environmental Coalition www.ohvec.org/index.html
- Save Our Cumberland Mountains www.socm.org/
- Western Organization of Resource Councils www.worc.org/

---

[1] The Summitville Mine and Its Downstream Effects, USGS http://pubs.usgs.gov/of/1995/ofr-95-0023/summit.htm
[2] Colorado Dept of Public Health and Environment, Hazardous Materials and Waste Management Division, Summitville Mine http://www.cdphe.state.co.us/hm/summitville.htm
[3] Who Owns the West? Environmental Working Group http://www.ewg.org/mining/report/index.php?stab=CO&chapter=5
[4] Cyanide Spill Has Disastrous Effect on Guyana's Economy: Knight Ridder/Tribune News Service, August 25, 1995.
[5] Statement by Ambassador Odeen Ishmael, Permanent Representative of Guyana to the OAS, to the Permanent Council of the OAS. Washington DC, August 30, 1995 http://www.guyana.org/Speeches/cyanide_oi.htm
[6] Omai Gold Mine, Halifax Initiative http://www.halifaxinitiative.org/index.php/miningmap/914
[7] Environmental Impacts at Fort Belknap from Gold Mining, Carleton College http://serc.carleton.edu/research_education/nativelands/ftbelknap/environmental.html
[8] Babbitt Issues Parting Shots: New Rules Aimed at Curbing Hardrock Mining in the West: *The Washington Post*. 15 January 2001
[9] U.S. Environmental Protection Agency, National Priorities List http://www.epa.gov/superfund/sites/npl/nar1725.htm
[10] U.S. Environmental Protection Agency, Brewer Gold Mine http://www.epa.gov/Region4/waste/npl/nplsc/brwgldsc.htm
[11] U.N. Starts Sampling Danube After Romanian Cyanide Spill, *New York Times*, February 16, 2000 http://www.nytimes.com/2000/02/16/world/un-starts-sampling-danube-after-romanian-cyanide-spill.html
[12] Romanian Cautious on Cyanide Risk, BBC News http://news.bbc.co.uk/2/hi/europe/642258.stm
[13] Liquid Assets 2000: America's Water Resources at a Turning Point http://www.epa.gov/ow/liquidassets/

**Author bio**

I am a husband, a father of three grown sons, and a career writer for the science and technology industries. With real work consuming 50-plus hours a week, I began writing THE MINE in earnest in 2003 and completed it in the fall of 2009. Countless early mornings and cups of black coffee were surrendered to writing this novel.

My hobbies, which I have given little time to lately, include reading, traveling, boating, and hiking. I live in Oregon with my family.

I sincerely hope you enjoyed reading THE MINE and would like to get your thoughts on the story. Feel free to contact me via email. Simply visit the website:

www.themine-thebook.com

Warm regards,
Daniel Cobb

**Purchasing**

You can purchase copies of THE MINE at Amazon's CreateSpace URL for the book:

www.createspace.com/3372515.com

or at www.amazon.com.

**Wholesale**

Retail booksellers and environmental organizations can purchase copies of THE MINE at wholesale. Information is available at:

www.themine-thebook.com

**Representation**

This author seeks agent representation. Agents should be members of AAR. Contact information is available at:

www.themine-thebook.com

Made in the USA
Charleston, SC
26 January 2010